JOIN THE AUTHORS

ENOUGH OF JAN

'A compelling and delic...
murder and secrets'
Claire Douglas, *The House at Number 9*

'Jane never ceases to surprise me'
Emma Curtis, *Keep Her Quiet*

'Jane is so very good at creating characters who get right
under your skin'
Teresa Driscoll, *I Am Watching You*

'Jane Corry is the new queen of the psychological'
Kate Furnivall, *The Guardian of Lies*

'Grips with menace and dread, yet touches the heart'
Nicci French, *The Favour*

'Few writers can match Jane Corry'
Cara Hunter, *Hope to Die*

'Yet another twisty, exciting book that I couldn't put down'
Heidi Perks, *The Other Guest*

'Jane Corry writes consistently enthralling stories about the
dark side of family life'
Peter James, *Picture You Dead*

'Jane Corry's psychological novels have sold more than
a million copies so far'
Sunday Express

'Fans of psychological thrillers will be hooked after
the first page'
Closer

ABOUT THE AUTHOR

Jane Corry is a former magazine journalist who spent three years as the writer-in-residence at a high-security prison. This often hair-raising experience helped inspire her *Sunday Times*-bestselling psychological dramas, which have been translated into sixteen languages and sold over a million copies worldwide. This is her ninth novel.

www.janecorryauthor.com

I DIED ON A TUESDAY

JANE CORRY

PENGUIN BOOKS

PENGUIN BOOKS

UK | USA | Canada | Ireland | Australia
India | New Zealand | South Africa

Penguin Books is part of the Penguin Random House group of companies
whose addresses can be found at global.penguinrandomhouse.com.

First published 2024
001

Set in 12.5/14.75pt Garamond MT Std
Typeset by Jouve (UK), Milton Keynes
Printed and bound in Great Britain by Clays Ltd, Elcograf S.p.A.

The authorized representative in the EEA is Penguin Random House Ireland,
Morrison Chambers, 32 Nassau Street, Dublin D02 YH68

A CIP catalogue record for this book is available from the British Library

ISBN: 978-0-241-99612-6

www.greenpenguin.co.uk

MIX
Paper | Supporting
responsible forestry
FSC® C018179

Penguin Random House is committed to a
sustainable future for our business, our readers
and our planet. This book is made from Forest
Stewardship Council® certified paper.

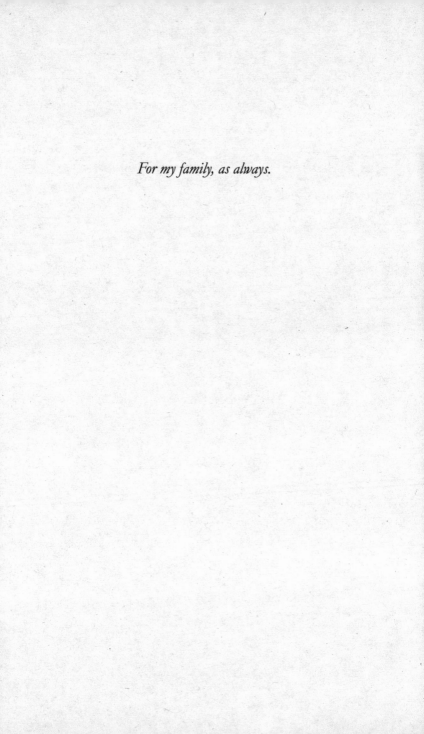

For my family, as always.

PART ONE

I

Twenty Years Ago
The Day of the Accident

Janie

On the day that I died, the sea was exceptionally flat. There was nothing to indicate that anything was amiss or that, in forty minutes, I would be out of this world.

Looking back, I can be quite precise about the time because it generally takes me thirty-five minutes to swim across the bay and back. If the sea is rough, it can take a little longer because you have to fight your way through the waves and pretend not to be frightened.

I'm good at pretending. Besides, the sea doesn't like cowards. It can smell blood.

I prop my bike against the railings opposite the Seaside Hotel, the only one open on the front now. In summer, it's quite busy but autumn is setting in. Business will perk up a bit when it gets to half-term. But right now, I savour the peace. It's 6.30 in the morning. No one is around. Not even a dog walker. It's as if the world has slept in. But the sun — the sun! — that's awake all right! It's rising now before me, like the tip of a giant beach ball, bathed in apricot and gold.

For a moment, I just stand there, drinking it in. If someone had made something like this in a factory and then put it in an art exhibition or the window of some fancy shop, it would sell for millions.

3

But people take the sunrise for granted. I'm ashamed to say that I used to do that too. Until everything changed.

I make my way down to the beach. It's the stony variety. If you want sand, you have to go further along the coastline. The water comes up to greet me and I flinch when it hits my skin. I can't describe the shock of the cold. It's amazing. 'You're one of those all-the-year-round swimmers?' people will sometimes ask me.

It's an addiction. It makes you feel alive! Yes, there are times when my fingers go numb, even though I wear swimming gloves. But then I think of the hot shower I'm going to have when I get in, providing Dad's not got there first. Although it will be hard to leave him, I can't wait to have my own bathroom when I get to London!

There's a point after you wade in, when it's time to immerse your shoulders and actually start swimming. I've reached that point now. Sometimes I'm scared. I know that the sea can turn on you, just like that. But I also get a sort of primeval need to feel the cold. To be part of the water. So I take a deep breath and launch myself in. I don't go far out because I don't like being out of my depth. Never have done.

Once, I met a seal. At first I thought it was a whiskery old lady in a grey cap. Our eyes locked. Then she went under as if she was sliding down an invisible underwater fireman's pole. Just like that.

My throat almost closed with panic. Where had she gone? Although I don't like diving, I forced myself to go under to try and find her. But I wasn't wearing goggles and the salt blinded my eyes so I couldn't see.

I felt terrible when I got out, but then someone on the beach asked if I'd seen the seal and I almost slumped down on the pebbles in relief. I hadn't let an old lady drown after all.

Back across the bay now. Swimming gives you thinking time. I'm going to miss all this when I leave. 'You'll be fine, Janie,' Dad says to me when I have the odd wobble. 'It's your dream job. I'll still be here if you have time to come and visit.'

'Of course, I will,' I tell him.

He's right. It IS my dream job. It's only a junior position but they said it was 'the first rung on the editorial ladder'. Books are my passion, along with the sea. I've made my choice. And it's the right one. I know it.

Mum would have told me to go. 'She'd be proud of you,' Dad's always saying. 'Besides, you can't stay here for ever, can you? Not if you're going to work for a hot-shot London publisher!'

The rocks are coming up. You have to be careful not to go too near when the sea is rough or it can throw you against them. One year, a tourist was cut really badly. Locals get caught out too. You can become over-sure of yourself or become too wrapped up in your own thoughts and forget to avoid that bit further out between the rocks where there's a rip tide. Someone drowned there a few years ago. I can't think about that though; not now.

Three more days before I get the train to London. I'm packed already. 'Are you sure you don't want me to drive you?' Dad keeps asking.

'Thanks,' I tell him, 'but we both know that's not a good idea.' Neither of us can cope with goodbyes at the best of times – too many memories of the one farewell we were never able to say.

I make my way out of the water and then do what I always do when the sun is rising: turn back to breathe in the early morning light casting a path of gold on the water. 'How am I going to manage without you?' I ask myself.

Walking up the stone steps to my bike, I remove the padlock. The truth is that I never lock it properly anyway. I just push the two ends together, so it looks secure. When your fingers are cold from swimming, it takes too long to turn it round to my code number: 1115.

I throw on my fleece but still I'm shivering as I cycle back along the promenade. It's colder than I'd thought. Perhaps it's time to start wearing a wetsuit.

Mind you, I won't be here much longer, will I?

A seagull is flying overhead. It's screaming as if trying to tell me something. I wobble a bit and then straighten up. A few years ago, I fell off my bike because the shoelace on my right trainer came undone and got trapped in the spokes. I broke a small bone in my elbow. 'You were lucky it wasn't worse,' Mum said.

I'm turning down a side lane now towards home as a short-cut. It's still quiet. No traffic. No bikes. No walkers. Then again, I'm earlier than usual. I'm not sleeping that well, to be honest. I'm both scared and excited about my new life. I'm hoping – and this is a dream I keep to myself in case it doesn't happen – that a job in publishing might help me become a real writer myself.

That's when I hear it. When the noise punctures my thoughts. When I hear the screech. Not a seagull. More the kind of ear-piercing sound a car makes as it brakes suddenly.

But this time it's a large white van with horizontal chrome bars across the front in a sinister grin.

It's coming straight towards me.

There isn't time to gasp with horror. There isn't time for the stomach-churning fear you read about. There is no time at all to brace myself for the body-ripping agony of impact.

Yet strangely as the massive wheels crunch over my bones like a fierce punch of a wave, and the smell of burning rubber hits me, there's time for one more thought.

I'll never find Mum now.

2

Twenty Years Later

Robbie

He knows when his wife calls out to him that this is it. There's something in her voice that has never been there before. A mixture of fear and disbelief. An unspoken plea that says, '*Please tell me this isn't happening. What is going on?*'

Irena doesn't know. How could he have told her? Only three others are in on it and they've all disappeared. He's Googled their names enough times and can say, hand on heart, that they could be anywhere on earth – or in hell, for that matter. Of course, there is a fourth. But there's no way that person would want this to come to light.

In a way, it doesn't matter who it is – the result will be the same in any case.

The van. The bike. The crunch.

'I'm coming,' he calls back. He's on the top floor, where Irena has hung the gold and platinum disc music awards he's accumulated over the years. There's also a gallery of photographs showing Robbie with the world's rich and famous.

Sometimes when he looks at himself in the pictures, it's as though he's seeing someone else.

7

His wife has framed some magazine and newspaper cuttings too. 'The nation's favourite "family man musician"' is one of many. Next month, he's due to be on *Desert Island Discs*. One magazine wanted to feature their 'stunning Grade-II listed Surrey mansion' but he turned it down because he wanted to preserve his family's privacy.

'Robbie!' Irena calls out again, the fear in her voice rising this time.

But his feet won't move. He needs to breathe in this favourite part of the house, which he loves, not because of the awards but because of the view over the gravel drive below (where one police car is already parked) and the acres around them. It's all so different from the cramped council house in Devon where he'd grown up. Yet right now, he'd give anything to be back there. To be eighteen years old. Before the accident.

He looks out at his daughter, riding her pony around the paddock. At his son practising his bowling technique. He's just been selected for the county's under-12s cricket team. How will Robbie break this to them?

Both children are stopping now. Turning to look at a second police car arriving, its tyres crunching on the stones. He'll have to explain to them. Have to explain to everyone.

Yet as he takes the first step down the circular mahogany Regency staircase, Robbie can't help feeling a strange relief. After all, hasn't he been waiting every day of the last twenty years for this to happen?

When he finally reaches the bottom of the stairs, he finds two policemen waiting for him. Irena looks terrified. His whole body feels frozen.

'Mr Manning?' asks the taller one.

He nods.

Their eyes are hard. He notices one of them glancing briefly towards the home-cinema room – the door is open – and then back to him. No doubt they saw the indoor pool through the glass on their way in.

'Robert Manning, you are under arrest on suspicion of . . .'

The words wash over as they caution him. It's as though this is happening to someone else. His ears start to ring with shock. His skin becomes clammy. His mouth dries up.

Irena's face looms in and out as though he's about to faint. 'Robbie, tell me this isn't real,' she gasps. 'You couldn't have done that . . .'

His body is numb. His lips can't – or won't – form a reply.

The police officers handcuff him and lead him quickly towards the door.

His wife's face is white as she hurries alongside him. She puts a hand on his arm.

'It's all right,' Robbie manages to whisper.

But it's not. It's about as far from all right as you can get.

'Where are you taking him?' demands Irena.

'To the station for questioning,' says the younger police-man grimly. 'Then he'll probably be charged.'

He's about my age, thinks Robbie. In his forties or per-haps early fifties. He might have been to one of my concerts. Listened to my music. Been taken in by all that 'good family man' stuff.

Irena is still gripping his arm. 'Wait! I have seen the films. You must not be questioned unless you have a lawyer present. We need to call Paul.'

This was the man who had been handling his contracts ever since he'd made it big, telling him when they were safe to sign.

But the word 'safe' had now taken on a different meaning.

'Paul's an entertainment lawyer,' Robbie hears himself saying, although the fear ringing in his ears makes it sound as if someone else is talking. 'He won't know anything about . . . this sort of thing. We need a criminal lawyer.'

As he speaks, Daisy comes running in, her riding hat tucked under her arm. Simon follows, cricket ball in hand. His children look confused. Dazed. As if the sky has fallen out of their world.

Which it has.

'*Criminal lawyer?*' repeats Daisy. 'Dad! What's going on?'

'Why are you wearing handcuffs?' asks Simon.

Robbie tries to speak again. To reassure his daughter. His son. His wife.

But he knows he can't say anything that will make it better. Because the past has finally caught up with him.

3

Vanessa

'I'm shit-scared, Vanessa.'

How many times had she heard witnesses say this (although usually more politely)? More than she could count.

And it wasn't surprising.

Vanessa looked around the court lobby. It was enough to unnerve anyone, let alone the thirteen-year-old boy sitting next to her, waiting to give evidence. Just look at these lawyers swaggering by! Why couldn't they wear normal clothes like everyone else instead of dressing up like black crows with wrinkly grey wigs? It was bloody daft.

Mind you, it was clear that some of the stuffier people around here disapproved of the clothes *she* wore! Vanessa went to a great deal of trouble to make sure that she flaunted the brightest, happiest outfits she could find.

'You look very colourful this morning,' Judge had said the other day.

'I'll take that as a compliment, M'lud,' she'd replied, touching her forehead in a mock deferential style. Vanessa had found, rather to her amusement, that she'd reached the stage in life where she didn't care what others thought. It was wonderfully liberating!

'Seriously,' he said, 'I like it. You do a good job of cheering everyone up.'

'You're not so bad yourself,' she replied.

His compliment had warmed her, although she wasn't sure that Jack would approve. *'Touch on the flirty side, don't you think, love?'* he might have said.

Vanessa was used to people flirting. She might just have had her sixty-ninth birthday (spent quietly in front of the telly watching *Strictly Come Dancing*) but the other day, to her delight, the bus driver had queried her senior bus pass!

Of course, she and Judge (as she teasingly called him, even though his first name was Richard) operated on a purely professional level, despite the fact that she'd had a soft spot for him since her first case three years ago. She'd been so shy then. So nervous about starting something new . . .

Vanessa's mind went back to when she'd left her job as a store detective. She and Jack, who'd just retired from the police force, had started leafing through some travel brochures to book their very first cruise. Then her mother, who'd long-since moved to Tenerife, wrote to say that she wasn't very well and maybe Vanessa wouldn't mind coming over.

Wouldn't mind? Vanessa had been suggesting it for ages but her mum was always 'too busy'. When Vanessa flew out the following week, she found her mother had breast cancer. 'Didn't want to tell you before, love. No point in making a fuss.'

She died the following week.

Not long after that, Jack was diagnosed with prostate cancer. The end was so fast that she could scarcely believe it had happened. Perhaps that's why she still heard his voice every now and then.

Common sense told her that it was wishful thinking, or maybe habit from living with Jack for so long that she always knew what he would say – whether it was commenting on a new outfit or deciding what she should buy for tea. But whatever the reason for Jack's voice in her head, Vanessa found it comforting.

In fact, she might not have survived the gaping hole he'd left behind if it weren't for the job ad in the local paper. It was Jack who'd pointed it out – the invisible, still-there Jack, who never left her.

'A witness service volunteer?' she'd asked. 'What's that?'

'*Read the bit below*,' he'd said. '*It's someone who looks after witnesses in court who are scared or vulnerable. You'd be good at that. 'Sides, it would keep you busy. Stop you hankering after me. It says you don't get paid but you don't need the money, not with my pension. You just need something to do.*'

Vanessa wasn't sure at first. But Jack nagged and nagged in her head as if he was standing right next to her. When he did that, there was no stopping him. 'Why would I want to spend my time in a boring court?' she'd demanded.

'*You could add a bit of colour*,' he'd shot back. '*Dress up. Give them something to look at.*'

Jack had always loved it when she'd glammed up. 'No one's got a body like yours, Nessie,' he'd say, running his hand over her curves. No one else called her that. Only Jack, and that was just for special occasions.

So in the end, she'd given in. It had proved to be the right decision – the last few years had been some of the most interesting in her life. She'd supported girls who were terrified to face their rapists, comforted a man who'd been abused by his female partner, and now, today, she was going to sit by a teenager whose evidence was crucial in bringing down a violent local gang leader.

'*I'm proud of you, love*,' Jack had said this morning, as she walked to the court in Exeter. Vanessa had been nervous until then, especially with the seagulls screaming overhead with a sense of foreboding. But Jack's words gave her a warm feeling. She'd lost count of the number of times her detective husband had come back from court where one of the suspects he'd known had 'darn well been guilty' had gone free because the witness was too scared to give evidence for fear they, or someone they knew, would get hurt afterwards.

'Retaliation' and 'respect' were two big words in the city's underworld. Each was as dangerous as the other. Come the evening and parts of Exeter changed from being a shopping hub for law-abiding citizens to a city where gangs hung around on certain street corners, hands in pockets, eyeballing other gangs.

A witness service volunteer was meant to be a 'helpful companion' to a witness who was due to give evidence. This person would explain what was going to happen during an archaic process. At least, it was in her mind. What they needed, Vanessa had often thought, was to hold a trial in a bright room with normal-looking folk. Maybe some relaxing music to calm everyone down.

'I'm shit-scared, Vanessa,' repeated the boy again, bringing her back to the present.

'You don't have to testify,' she said. She'd have liked to have given him a hug but you weren't meant to show affection like that. Besides, although Tyler was only thirteen, he was taller than her. At five foot one herself, she'd have needed a stepladder to give him a motherly peck on the forehead.

The boy looked down at his trainers – bright white with Gucci's 'GG' branding on the sides. They were a stark contrast to his worn jeans, but Vanessa had been in the game long enough to know designer trainers were a status symbol amongst criminals of all levels.

'Zac might get me if I *do* tell,' he mumbled.

'He might,' said Vanessa. This was often a witness's biggest fear. If they shopped someone – especially a gang member – the others might take revenge. She wanted to reassure him, as she usually would, yet this time she had a nagging feeling that he might be right.

'But if I don't say what he did, he'll just do it again, won't he?'

'It's possible,' admits Vanessa.

As she spoke, a tall, painfully thin youth swaggered by, his eyes fixed on Tyler. He said nothing but he didn't need to.

'That's one of Zac's mates,' whispered Tyler after the youth had gone past. 'He's trying to scare me.' Then his voice hardened. 'Well he's not. That cocky bastard isn't going to get away with it.'

Suddenly her young charge had changed from being a terrified witness into an 'I'm going to get you' witness. Vanessa had seen them all.

Then one of the officials nodded at her.

Vanessa felt as nervous as if she were about to give evidence herself. 'They're ready for you, love,' she said.

The 'love' just slipped out. She couldn't help it – Tyler

was young enough to be her grandson, if she'd had one. Every now and then Vanessa still felt an emptiness in her chest for the babies she and Jack had never been able to have. Perhaps if they'd had the medical tricks they have nowadays . . .

'We've got each other,' Jack would tell her. If only that were still true.

The memories almost distracted her from her job. 'I'll be close to the witness box if you need me,' she said as they went into the courtroom. But Tyler's eyes were on the defendant. The poor kid was shaking, despite his earlier words, and it wasn't surprising.

This Zac, with his bald head and narrow eyes, did not seem like a nice man. The black-and-yellow tattoo (that went down both sides of his neck before disappearing below the collar of the cheap, shiny maroon suit he'd clearly been advised to wear) did not signal peace. Nor did the clenched fists by his side, or the scowl as Tyler swore his witness oath.

Perhaps sensing that Vanessa was looking at him too, Zac turned his face to her. His top lip curled as if suppressing a smile. Ugh! That man sent shivers down her spine.

Up in the witness box, Tyler looked even younger than he'd seemed when sitting next to her. The stuff he was saying should never have happened to anyone, let alone a child.

'Can you tell the court about your relationship to the deceased?' asked the lawyer.

'Kieran was my cousin, wasn't he? Like a brother to me, he was. It's why I told the police everything I knew.'

'And what did you know?'

'Well he did some work for Zac. In fact, he took me with him on a job once. I was interested. Thought I might earn a bit myself. But Zac said he had to test me to make sure I was fully committed, like. So he . . .'

Why, Vanessa wondered as he went on to say things that made some jurors visibly shudder, had someone not suggested that Tyler gave his evidence on video? Was it because he'd been encouraged by the prosecution to do it in person? Some jurors might be more convinced that way.

Just as she'd expected, the jury delivered a guilty verdict. 'A life sentence is too good for him,' she muttered. Everyone knew that 'life' could be as little as twelve years. Jack had still believed in the death penalty, which Vanessa felt was going too far – what if the person was innocent? 'They never are,' Jack would say firmly.

As they left the courtroom, Vanessa spotted a detective who had worked with her husband. She tried to catch his eye, but he didn't seem to notice. Shame. Vanessa found comfort in chatting to her husband's colleagues and sharing memories. She also rather liked the idea that, in a way, she was working in her husband's field. 'Catching a criminal is just the first stage,' he would say when he was still alive. 'The job isn't done until the culprit is punished.' In fact, Jack would get into a foul mood if some 'bastard defence lawyer' got the suspect off.

'Would you like me to take you home?' she asked.

'Nah. You're all right.'

I'm all right, thought Vanessa. But would he be? What if one of the gang tried to get him in retaliation?

Uneasily, she made her way back to the shared witness support office, which was housed inside the court. It was quite cosy, with its old wooden desks, a coat stand by the door and a kettle in the corner next to the biscuit tin. There were also stacks of pamphlets with titles like 'How Witness Support Can Help You'. The reassuring pictures inside didn't show what she could see from the window now: police cars coming and going, and prisoner vans with slits for windows.

'Well done,' said Carol, her supervisor, before Vanessa had even taken off her jacket, a rather nice pre-loved Ralph Lauren design that she'd found in a charity shop. 'Nice result.'

Her supervisor praised Vanessa as if she'd been the prosecution barrister, but Vanessa never felt great after a case, even if they won. The trauma that witnesses had to go through was far worse than the public realized.

'I don't like that Zac,' she said.

'Nor do any of us. Thank goodness he's going down. Talking of which, have you heard the news?'

Gossip was rife amongst the court staff. People prattled: who was sleeping with whom; which witness wasn't reliable. There was even a lawyer who had broken the law himself. (Luckily, he'd been disbarred now. It had been before her time but people still talked about it.) Sometimes they heard about cases before they were common knowledge.

'What news?' asked Vanessa.

Carol looked as if she was about to bite into a juicy peach. 'It just broke out online. The police have arrested a man for the Janie White case. I've had it on good authority that a suspected drug dealer on remand grassed him up to reduce his own charge.'

Vanessa felt goosebumps run through her. Janie White? One of Jack's old cases! He'd been one of the first at the scene. In fact, he'd made it his 'bloody mission' to find the mystery hit-and-run driver who had mowed down the beautiful eighteen-year-old girl two decades earlier.

The poor child had had so much to look forward to before the accident. It was amazing she'd survived although Jack, in his own blunt way, had declared that 'the lass is no more than a blooming cabbage'.

'Apparently,' continued her supervisor, 'this witness was there at the time and knows exactly who was driving.' Her eyes were gleaming. 'You won't believe who it is.'

Vanessa's mouth was dry. 'Who?'

'Robbie Manning!'

She delivered this final sentence like a waiter bringing a sumptuous dish to the table.

'*The* Robbie Manning?' gasped Vanessa. Robbie Manning was a national treasure. A family man. A good guy who did a lot for charity. Everyone knew that. 'Are you sure?'

'One and the same.' Carol's eyes glittered. 'He was a teenager when it happened. What's more, the evidence against him is pretty incriminating. Not only have they got this bloke who says he was there at the time but Janie is going to testify.'

Vanessa was trying to take all this in. She usually prided herself on being quick on the uptake, but this had been Jack's really big case all those years ago. The one he'd never been able to solve. The one that had upset him to his dying day.

'I thought Janie White couldn't speak after the accident. How can she give evidence?'

Carol leaned forward conspiratorially. 'It's not common knowledge, but I was told that after her last stroke, she got some new kind of speech therapy and suddenly started singing.'

'*What?* How's that possible if she can't talk?' asked Vanessa.

'I didn't understand either until I Googled it. Look!'

She passed over her phone.

After a left-sided stroke, read Vanessa, *many individuals suffer from serious speech disorders but are often able to sing.*

'Blimey!' said Vanessa. 'I've never heard that before.'

'Don't go spreading this,' said Carol. 'I was told in strict confidence.'

'Of course I won't,' replied Vanessa, reminding herself – not for the first time – not to trust any of her secrets to her supervisor. Carol was always blabbing. Frankly, Vanessa didn't know how she got away with it.

'If Janie wants support in court . . .' Vanessa began.

'You don't need to ask, love. You're the first name on my list. You're so good with people. Mind you, it depends on Robbie Manning's plea. My bet is he'll say he's innocent.'

If someone pleaded guilty, of course, a case wouldn't go to trial. The accused was simply sentenced. But a not guilty plea meant there'd be a jury to decide the verdict and witnesses to give evidence, and maybe one of them would need a supporter.

'Thanks,' said Vanessa, imagining how much it would have meant to Jack if she were asked to look after Janie.

'*You bet it bloody would,*' said her husband in her head. '*I wasn't able to catch the bastard who did this. But you can be there to help, Vanessa.*'

They'd always been a team. Hadn't they said that to each other again and again? It was why she still heard him. Maybe it was wishful thinking. Maybe it wasn't. Either way, it was comforting.

'Surely he wouldn't plead not guilty?' Vanessa said. 'Not if all the evidence is against him?'

'You'd think so, wouldn't you?' Carol replied. 'But you know what some people can be like. They make excuses until the bitter end.'

Poor Janie White. Vanessa's heart went out to her.

Then she thought of Robbie Manning, whose music she'd always liked. Not anymore. Instead, she wanted to vomit. After all, what kind of person would leave a young girl dying in the road?

Only someone very wicked, she decided. Someone who deserved to go down for years and years.

From the *Daily Mail*:

ROBBIE – HOW COULD YOU?

In September 2004 Janie White had her whole future before her. The stunning auburn-haired 18-year-old, who'd been much loved by locals for her sunny smile, was due to leave her family home in Devon to start her first job in London when she was knocked off her bike in a hit-and-run accident and callously left for dead. Miraculously, she survived, but Janie – who hasn't been able to speak since that day – will never be the same again.

Janie loved to write stories and swim in the sea, but the life-changing injuries she suffered, and the resulting multiple strokes, have confined her to a wheelchair and inflicted permanent physical damage besides partial facial paralysis.

For years, the police have been hunting for the monster who ran down this innocent girl in cold blood. But lack of evidence meant the case remained unsolved without any firm leads.

Until today, when one of our most famous and best-loved celebrities was arrested for this evil crime.

Robbie Manning has not yet been charged, but his arrest has shocked the nation to the core.

We pray you didn't do it, Robbie. You're a family man; a role model for so many of us. You are proof that fame doesn't ruin the real, traditional values of a modest upbringing. Your kids go to the local comp. You do the school run. You don't have a chauffeur. You don't go on lavish holidays. You do so much for charity.

We hope from the bottom of our hearts that you didn't commit this terrible crime. Because if you did, you will have betrayed the nation's trust.

One thing is certain: if you are guilty, all the fame in the world won't save you now.

4

Seconds After the Accident (Precise Number Unknown)

Janie

The white light is like a pinprick at first. Far away. But then it gets nearer.

So close that it's like a cloak. I can almost put it on. If I do, it will give me total peace. Don't ask me how I know that. I just do.

Then it whispers.

'Come to me.'

It's Mum. That's her voice.

Every bone in my body – even those that are shattered – aches for her.

She's wrapping her arms around me. And that's when I know Mum is dead after all – so I must be dead too. But at least she's come to find me.

Then I hear another voice. It's a man's. Not a Dad-sounding man. Someone younger. He's crying. Sobbing.

'No. Oh God, no. Please tell me you're alive.'

If I am really dead, how can I hear him?

'Help me,' I try to scream. 'Help me.'

But the words won't come out.

5

Robbie

The cell in the police station is smaller than any of the toilets at home. (Six altogether, or is it seven? He can never quite remember.)

Shaking, Robbie takes in the blue plastic mattress on the floor as well as the basement window, which has a thin crack down one pane as though someone has tried to break it. The grey paint on the wall is peeling off and there's a name written in ballpoint: *John Williams, 24/12/2022.* Another, which looks as though it's been scratched into the surface, says, *Get me out of this f . . . place.* No name. No date.

In the corner is a small beige washing-up bowl with a sign next to it saying 'In case of sickness.'

Robbie feels a wetness between his legs. A slow trickle of urine runs down his thighs and onto the ground. Christ. He hasn't wet himself since he was a child. His Armani jeans (a recent birthday present from Irena) are soaked through.

He puts his head in his hands and sinks to the floor, rocking back and forth. In a minute, he tells himself, he will wake up and find that none of this is true.

The door opens. Robbie doesn't want to look because that would mean it *is* real. But something inside compels him.

A policeman comes in. He's bulky; sturdily built. When he speaks, his lower lip protrudes as if he's trying to suck air.

He looks at the vomit on the floor, which has missed the bowl. He looks at Robbie's stained trousers.

He makes no comment.

'Your lawyer has arrived,' he says, as if Robbie doesn't deserve the privilege of having the legal representation that he is entitled to by law.

That's when he sees the woman behind. Surely, she's too young to get him out of this.

'Are you –'

'I'm a solicitor experienced in criminal law, Mr Manning,' she interrupts, as if reading his mind. 'My name is Yasmine Smith. Your entertainment lawyer contacted me.'

Then she looks around, her eyes narrowing. 'Mr Manning shouldn't be in here,' she says to the policeman. 'He should be in the interview room.'

'It's busy,' he retorts curtly.

'I see. Then we'll take a seat, shall we? Bring us two chairs, will you, and a change of clothes for Mr Manning?'

So she'd noticed the stain and the puddle of urine.

'This isn't a bleeding hotel you know.'

Yasmine fixes the policeman with a stony glare. 'Please do not swear,' she says crisply. 'I don't care for it. Clean clothes are not a luxury. They are a human right.'

'I'll see what I can find,' he sniffs.

The door closes behind him.

Yasmine sits down on the edge of the blue mattress and indicates that Robbie should do the same. Her high heels and smart navy suit look incongruous in the setting. She opens her briefcase and takes out a notebook.

'This must be a bit of a shock.'

Her voice is softer than he'd expected.

'Yes.'

'I need to tell you that the police say they have a witness who claims he was with you at the time of the accident.'

The usual images thunder through his head like a terrifying visual mantra. *The van. The bike. The crunch.*

Stop. STOP! he tells himself.

He wants to vomit again. 'Who is it?' he asks, swallowing hard.

'Someone called Eric Sharp.'

'I've never heard of him.' Robbie feels a glimmer of hope. 'I get a lot of so-called fans doing weird things. One sent me a letter accusing me of sleeping with his wife.'

'Did you?'

'Of course not.'

'The police are looking to have you charged with grievous bodily harm with intent under Section 18 of Offences Against the Person Act 1861.'

With intent? Shock waves go through him. It hadn't been like that. But if he tells this woman what it *had* been like, his family might die. And he can't risk that. He just can't. To steady himself – and maybe stop it from all blurting out – Robbie looks at the crack in the wall behind her. The bit above is clear paint. The bit below is bubbly as if damp. It strikes Robbie that the line represents the day his life changed for ever.

'Let's start with whether you want to admit it or not,' Yasmine says, with a slight edge to her voice.

He continues staring at the line. It seems like a tight-rope now. A tightrope that he's been perching on since that terrible crunch twenty years ago.

It's hard work being a bad person. Hard work pretending to be good. And even harder when you aren't sure which side you fall into.

'I don't know,' he says. 'It's not as easy as that.'

She frowns. 'What do you mean?'

Robbie ignores the question because, let's face it, how can he explain what really happened?

Looking back, it seems so cut and dried. With hindsight, it's clear what he should have done. What he should not have done. He'd always tried his best to do the right thing. But who would believe him now?

Besides, it had all happened so fast that, at times — especially after one of his nightmares — he wasn't absolutely certain what had happened himself.

Guilty or not guilty? That's what it boiled down to. Both are right. Both are wrong. Yet he has to choose one.

6

Vanessa

If there's one thing that being a witness service volunteer had taught her, reflected Vanessa as she walked home after court (avoiding the puddles from a light summer shower), it was that each generation's actions are often responsible for how the next one behaves.

Look at Zac, the murderer whom Tyler had just helped to convict. His defence lawyer had pleaded that he'd fallen into bad ways because his father had taken him out on 'jobs', which included, in one case, dousing bank staff with petrol and threatening to set them alight if they didn't hand over the money.

He hadn't carried out his threat because those poor terrified souls had given in, but, as the lawyer argued, 'Think of the trauma that those victims suffered, and the lesson passed on to the son, who grew up thinking that this was how to earn a living.'

It made her shudder to think of it. When Jack used to say that, in his view, they ought to bring back capital punishment, she would tell him he didn't mean it.

'I bloody do,' he'd reply. 'It would make criminals think twice. Look what happened to my dad.'

Vanessa didn't like to say anything when he was in these moods. Instead, she'd put her arms around him to give him a comforting hug. But it scared her to think that he still supported the gallows.

Her mind went back, as it often did, to when she'd met her future husband on their first day at secondary school in Exeter. She'd seen Jack before, of course, messing about on the Quay. That was before they developed it and made it all fancy, with coffee shops and canoes for hire and wet-suits for sale. It had just been a place by the river where they'd hung out with their mates and thought themselves cool because they drank Pepsi Cola and munched ham-burgers from the local Wimpy or maybe had a sly cigarette. It was all quite innocent. There was the odd fight between the mods and the rockers, but there weren't the drug gangs that you saw nowadays.

Back then, Jack was a cheeky kid who used to sneak onto the platform ferry that took people from one side of the river to the other. 'Why pay when you can do it for free?' she once heard him boasting afterwards.

But when she met him properly at school, he didn't seem so cheeky anymore. He was one of the good kids. It's what had attracted her to him. Vanessa had been a shy girl. Still was, although you wouldn't believe it to look at her from the outside. 'You're one of those women who get even more confident and beautiful as you grow older,' Jack had once told her.

Vanessa found herself sitting next to Jack because their optimistic teacher thought it might cause less trouble to mix the sexes. The boys were always the loud ones in her experience, and she should know with a name like that. 'Remember Miss Widebottom?' Vanessa would some-times say to Jack when they were older, and they'd both erupt with giggles, right up to when Jack was in the hospice towards the end.

'Nice to see you've made friends with Jack,' her mother said after he'd walked back with her from school one day. 'Such a shame about his dad and little brother.'

'What do you mean?'

Of course, Vanessa knew Jack had a younger brother who had 'something wrong' with him as they referred to it in those days. Jack was always looking after him: taking him to the sweet shop for treats or to the park.

'They were run over in the summer holidays,' her mum had continued. 'Jack's dad was pushing the little lad over the road in his wheelchair and a car went right into them. I'm afraid they both died.'

A horrible cold prickly feeling went through Vanessa. She hadn't known anyone who'd died before. How awful!

'He hasn't said anything to me,' said Vanessa.

'Maybe he doesn't like to talk about it, love,' her dad chipped in.

So Vanessa took her cue from that, careful not to say much about her own parents either, in case it upset Jack. Instead, they talked about how she loved English (especially grammar) but hated maths. He told her it was the other way round for him so they helped each other out with homework, always at Vanessa's house because Jack's mum was often poorly and had to stay in bed.

'The bottle,' her dad would say darkly.

'Depression,' her mum would say sharply.

The other kids teased them for hanging out together. 'Got a boyfriend, I see,' said one of the girls in her class who wore eyeliner at twelve. 'Fancy that.'

'I don't care,' he said to Vanessa. 'I like being with you. And it's great that you're helping me with my essays. I need to pass my exams if I'm going to be a policeman.'

Vanessa felt a bit hurt by that – it almost sounded as if he was using her. But then she reminded herself how hard it must be to have lost a dad and brother and have a mum who was in bed all day. Perhaps that's why Jack was scared about getting romantically involved. He'd already had loss in his life and now his mum needed him.

Then, when they were fifteen, two things happened.

Both were as important as the other in their own way, although it was the first that made the local paper headlines.

MOTHER FOUND DEAD

Jack had come back from school one day to discover his mother was still in bed. This wasn't unusual in itself, but this time she wasn't breathing.

Both Jack and Vanessa had done a first-aid course at school – another idea from Miss Widebottom, who was ahead of her day – but try as he might, Jack couldn't bring life back to those blue lips. He called 999 and when the ambulance men arrived, they asked if he had anywhere to go. He gave them Vanessa's address. That night he stayed in their spare bedroom. And then he never left.

Jack's mum had a sister 'miles away', whom she didn't speak to and wasn't keen to take on a nephew she'd never met. His dad didn't have any family either. Vanessa's parents didn't formally adopt Jack, but they might as well have done. There weren't the rules and regulations there are today.

A few weeks later, Jack suddenly started to talk about his mum and what it had been like when he'd found her. 'I'd been waiting for her to do it,' he said. 'I knew she couldn't go on without my dad and brother. I wasn't enough for her.'

Vanessa's heart twisted when he said those words. So much so that she couldn't help but lean forward (Jack was only just her height anyway) and give him a kiss. Not on his lips but close to his mouth. Then she stepped back, horrified at what she'd done.

He looked at her with such surprise and shock on his face that she knew she'd ruined their friendship. How could she have been so stupid?

But then he gave a little moan and put his arms around her, hugging her so tightly that she could barely breathe. After that, he kissed her in return.

Three years later, Jack joined the police force and Vanessa scrapped her dream of training to be a teacher. Instead, she got a job at a fashion store in Exeter, so she could start saving immediately. Soon after that, they were married.

'We'll have kids when I'm promoted,' Jack told her. 'With any luck, we'll have a girl and a boy and we'll all live happily ever after.'

Jack was good at saying what they'd do. It made her feel safe. Most importantly, Vanessa knew it made him feel safe too.

But neither Vanessa nor Jack could have predicted that 'The Girl Who Came Back from the Dead', as the newspapers called Janie White, would, one day, change their lives for ever.

And now she was about to find out how.

7

Janie

'Help me,' I try to say again.

But I can't. I can't talk. I can't move.

The pain is a fire racing through my bones. Like a mountain that has fallen on my face and my chest and my legs, crushing me into tiny pieces.

The man is now standing over me. He's a blur but I can hear him saying 'Are you alive?' over and over again.

'Call someone,' I want to yell.

Again, nothing comes out. Perhaps this is that moment between life and death that you read about.

'Mum!' I scream.

This stranger is my only hope. 'HELP ME!'

My scream is still silent, unlike the gulls arguing furiously over-head, as if trying to decide my fate.

I'm not ready to go. It's not just because I need to find Mum. There's Dad too. I can't leave him. Not for ever. He wouldn't cope.

And that's when I hear the second pair of footsteps.

8

Robbie

It wasn't until he saw the local paper two days after the accident that Robbie realized the truth.

18-YEAR-OLD CYCLIST IN COMA AFTER BRUTAL HIT AND RUN

So she was still alive! His mouth went dry and a sharp stress pain immediately sprang up in his right temple. He retched over his cereal.

'Are you all right, love?' asked his mum.

'I don't feel well,' he managed to blurt out.

The other papers picked it up:

YET ANOTHER HIT AND RUN. STAND UP FOR CYCLISTS! IT'S TIME TO GET HEAVY

YOUNG GIRL STILL IN COMA – MIGHT NEVER RECOVER

The tabloids documented her progress on a daily basis.

DAY THREE OF JANIE'S FIGHT FOR LIFE

As time passed, 'day' became 'week'. The government was already running a national campaign against drivers' carelessness towards cyclists and Janie had, it seemed, become the perfect emblem.

Robbie read the headlines with feverish horror, unable to look at the text or the pictures below for fear it would be too real.

But it *was* real. Robbie knew that then. And he knows it now.

'Robbie,' says Yasmine, interrupting his thoughts. 'I need to structure your defence. Did you run Janie over, as the police claim?'

Janie. He doesn't want to think of her as 'Janie'. He doesn't want to think of her as anyone with a name. That way, he could almost pretend it hadn't happened.

'Maybe it will help if I remind you of some facts,' says the lawyer in a clipped tone, as if she is convinced of his guilt. 'The medics say the victim clinically died for an unknown time but they managed to restart her heart. However, as a result of oxygen starvation and the horrific physical trauma inflicted on her body, she suffered life-changing injuries. In fact, the repercussions continue. She's had several strokes in the last few years.'

He shakes his head, appalled by the horror of it all.

'There are pictures from the accident that have now gone viral online,' she continues. 'People looking at them might well include the future jurors, if this goes to trial. It's bound to influence them.'

Robbie begins to shudder. 'I haven't seen them. The police took my phone.' He doesn't add that, even if he still had his mobile, he simply couldn't look at these photographs. He couldn't take it.

Sweat has gathered on his forehead and is now trickling down his back. He's on the verge of saying something. But he can't. He mustn't. He needs to think.

'If the driver had called for help,' says the lawyer softly, 'those injuries might not have been so bad.'

Robbie puts his head in his hands. His hair feels damp.

'Look, Robbie. Is there anything you can tell me, before the police question you?'

Robbie wipes his forehead with his right sleeve. Then he rubs his eyes. The world is still there in front of him. So is the lawyer. So are the facts.

'No,' he says, his heart thudding.

Yasmine stands up and moves across the cell. She's losing patience with him, he senses. Her face suggests she despises him. Who wouldn't? He despises himself. Yet what else could he have done at the time?

Plenty.

She shakes her head. 'You haven't given me anything to work with.'

'That's because there isn't anything to say.'

Her lips tighten with clear disapproval.

'I see. In that case, Mr Manning . . .'

No more 'Robbie', he notes.

'. . . In that case I suggest that, during the interview, you respond with "no comment" to most questions. I will advise you of the exceptions when we get to them.'

Robbie thinks of the police dramas that he and Irena have watched together at her instigation. They always made him nervous and uncomfortable but he could never tell Yasmine it was because he was constantly terrified of being caught himself.

And now he knows.

'When someone says "no comment" on television,' he falters, 'I always think it looks suspicious.'

She shrugs. 'If you have nothing to say, it's best to say nothing.'

Yet what if he does but can't?

Robbie swallows. 'If it comes to trial and I am found guilty, how long do you think I'll get?'

She shrugs. 'Fifteen years perhaps.'

Fifteen?

He puts his head in his hands.

'To be blunt,' she continues, 'your fame might go against you, depending on the judge. He or she might make an example of you, to show that celebrities aren't given softer treatment.'

He can understand that.

Yasmine walks over to the door and presses a bell push to be let out. He has a sense that she wants to get away from him as soon as possible.

Robbie can barely breathe at the thought of being left alone in this cell with its piss and vomit. He feels like a small child, about to be abandoned in the middle of nowhere.

'What happens now?' he blurts out.

She turns as if reluctantly. 'The police will interview you once the room is free. Then they'll decide if they have enough evidence to charge you. If they don't, you will be released. If they do, you will be taken to the local magistrates' court tomorrow morning where you will have to indicate your plea in public.'

'What does that mean?' he cuts in.

'You tell the court whether you intend to plea guilty or not guilty. But that's not binding. It's just an intention. If you're not granted bail, you will be sent to a remand prison until you appear at the crown court where you will formally enter your guilty or not guilty plea.'

It all seems like a terrifying complicated game where he suddenly has to learn a set of rules which will decide his future.

'What's a remand prison?'

'It's where people are held while waiting trial or sentencing.'

'I *will* get bail, though, won't I?' asks Robbie, desperation in his voice.

'Not necessarily. The courts might be worried about you absconding on a private jet.'

'I don't have one.'

'It doesn't matter. The point is that you've got enough money to run away and hide.'

He can't argue with that. The prospect is tempting.

'If you plead not guilty at the crown court,' she continues, 'there will be a trial. It will probably go on for several days.'

'With lots of publicity?'

She looks stonily at him. 'Of course. You're a big name, Mr Manning.'

'And if I plead guilty?'

He already knows the answer but he needs to hear it again to make up his mind. 'Then there will be no jury.

Instead, the judge will decide how long you spend in prison.'

'Will there be press there?'

'Yes. But there won't be the sensationalism that a long-running trial would generate.'

That was something. It might help his family. But fifteen to twenty years inside a cell like this? How could he stand it?

Another horrible wave of panic overwhelms him. 'Is there anything I can do to get out of this?'

Yasmine's hostility is almost tangible. 'You can tell me if this witness, Eric Sharp, is right when he says he saw you running over the victim. You can tell me, if you weren't there, *where* you were at the time. These are the questions that the police will ask you in a minute. Your answers will determine whether they charge you.'

He turns his face away, saying nothing.

'Mr Manning, I have to ask you this. A young woman has been maimed for life. Don't you feel anything?'

He wants to speak but can't.

'I should also tell you that if this does go to trial, the victim might want to testify. You will be questioned in detail about your past, your family, everything. Trust me. The prosecution will leave no stone unturned.'

A shock wave of fear and nausea washes over him. He can't put Irena and the children through this.

'Mr Manning, I'm going to ask you one more time to tell me what happened on the day of the accident. Did you or did you not hit Janie with intent and fail to stop?'

'I can't,' he whispers.

'Can't or won't? You'll have to, sooner or later.'

But he doesn't answer.

There's only one course of action open to him now. He just has to be brave enough to take it.

9

Vanessa

Vanessa's mobile rang when she was in the garden, feeding bread to the birds. Jack had always been very particular about that.

Of course, she knew the voice immediately; she and Judge spoke nearly every day. As she kept telling herself, there was nothing romantic going on between them. Just friendship.

'I've got something to tell you, Vanessa. Your supervisor was going to call but I wanted to give you the news myself.'

Something in the tone of his voice made her skin begin to crawl; the same way it had done when the consultant had told them that Jack had cancer.

She dropped the bag of crusts, ducking as the birds swooped down, and sat on the concrete path. It was damp from the rain but she barely registered it. 'What is it?'

'That boy you sat with in court the other day. The one giving evidence against the drug runner who'd killed his cousin.'

Vanessa's knees began to shake. Side to side. Right to left. Left to right. 'The other boys from the gang have got him, haven't they?' she said shakily.

'No. He's got one of *them*.'

Vanessa couldn't help the brief wave of relief that Tyler was safe. But this was quickly followed by confusion.

'What do you mean?' she whispered.

'The stupid boy only went and got a gun and shot the new leader of the drug gang.'

'Dead?' she whispered.

'Dead,' he confirmed.

So Tyler was now a murderer himself. Vanessa began to weep. Silent tears that ran down her face and into the grass that Jack had lovingly grown from seed all those years ago. ('It will be ready by the time the baby comes,' he had promised.)

'Will he get life?' she asked, in a voice that came out as more of a croak than a whisper.

'He'll go down for a long time, that's for sure.'

Vanessa's mind was whirling. 'But can't the defence argue that –'

'The defence can argue anything, as you know,' he cut in. 'But revenge is no excuse for murder. The law has to set an example. Look, I've got to go but I hope you're all right – I wanted to prepare you, as you'll hear it sooner or later.'

As Judge rang off, Vanessa noticed the man next door looking over the fence and then back again at his cabbages. He was usually quite friendly but now he was giving her a strange look.

Embarrassed, Vanessa slunk back inside and repaired her streaked mascara.

Then she picked up the phone and asked if she could visit Tyler. After that, she went for a walk to try and clear her head. That's odd. Every now and then, she had the oddest feeling that she was being followed.

Yet every time she looked back, there was no one there.

The prison was a stern-looking Victorian brick building on the other side of Exeter with a datestone that announced it had been built in 1853. It had railings on the windows. Inside, it smelled of disinfectant and lack of hope. You'd never guess it was so close to a shopping centre where people went about their ordinary lives. Or pretended to.

Tyler had been sent here even though he hadn't been tried yet, because there wasn't room anywhere else. He looked up briefly when she came in and then down again.

Vanessa wanted to take his face in hers and force him to look into her eyes. But she wasn't his mother, who was nowhere to be seen. So she came straight out with it.

'That young man who walked past us in the lobby and gave you that horrible look – was he the new gang leader?'

'Yeah.'

'Why did you kill him?' Her voice rose up into a wail.

''Cos he helped kill Kieran too. 'Sides, he'd have got me if I hadn't got him first. Life would have been too good for him just as it is for Zac. You said that yourself.'

Had she? Was this all her fault? Or had he planned to do it before the trial, whether the defendant went down or not, to avenge his cousin? She wanted to ask but suspected she might not get the truth.

'But now you're going to prison,' she said quietly.

The boy shrugged. 'It's worth it. I'll be out before I'm thirty if I behave myself. I've done the maths.'

Vanessa thought of the stories Jack used to tell her about prison (he'd sometimes been called to disturbances

44

at their local 'clink', as he termed it). 'It will be awful inside,' she said.

'I'll cope.' His eyes were angry now. 'He needs to be taught a lesson. If you do bad, you get punished.'

Didn't he see the irony?

'But *you've* done bad,' she said, adopting his lingo.

He stared at her. There was something deep and scary and fathomless about his eyes.

'Everyone does. Haven't you ever done something wrong, Vanessa?'

Her mind flashed back to the cliff all those years ago.

'Well, have you then?' he asked, as if sensing her hesitation.

'No,' she said. 'Well, not murder, anyway.'

Then she left. After all, there was nothing she could do to help Tyler. And nothing she could do to take back that lie.

Because the truth was that her stupid, stupid actions *had*, all those years ago, been responsible for taking a life.

So in a way, she was no better than a murderer herself. Was she?

IO

Janie

There's another voice now.

It's arguing with the first.

There might be a third too. I'm not sure.

I try to block them out. I don't like arguments.

Mum and Dad used to argue all the time. It hurt me, but it's nothing like the pain I feel now. I wish I could describe it; do it justice. I feel as though my head has been sledgehammered. My legs crushed by a train.

Did I say that before? Forgive me. My mind is like tiny fragments of glass, whirling around as though they are scratching each other. And the disbelief. Oh my God, the disbelief. This can't be happening to me. It can't.

So I do what I used to do when Mum and Dad argued.

I take myself to another place. Back to where it all began.

11

Robbie

The cell door opens. It's the policeman. Empty-handed.

'You can't have chairs in case you use them as a weapon,' he says.

The thought occurs to Robbie that Yasmine should have known that.

'There aren't any clean clothes either. But the good news is that they're ready for you now in the interview room.'

He goes to put handcuffs on Robbie. 'Is this necessary?' asks Yasmine.

'Not always, but we've got a famous prisoner here. Someone might be parachuting down as we speak to ship him out.'

'Are you joking?' says Robbie.

'I never joke. Especially not when a young woman's life has been ruined.'

Robbie bows his head. He can hear the crunch in his head echoing now. That awful shudder as the van ploughed into the bike. They walk down a corridor to the interview room with plain beige walls and a window that might or might not be the kind where someone on the other side can observe him.

'Take a seat Mr Manning. My name is Detective Sergeant

Brown. I'd like to ask you some questions about 15 September 2004 when a witness claims you were driving with undue care and attention and deliberately ran over the victim, leaving her with life-changing injuries. Is this correct?'

Robbie closes his eyes. He's had time to think now. There seems to be only one way out if he's to protect his family, if not himself, from this media storm. 'Yes,' he says.

His lawyer looks startled.

He opens his eyes now and looks straight at the detective sergeant. 'It was my fault. I want to plead guilty.'

Yasmine cuts in again. 'I think my client and I would like to discuss his plea before questioning continues.'

'No,' says Robbie. 'I don't want to go on with this interview any further. I want to plead guilty as I said and face the consequences.'

He almost says more. He almost says that he deserves whatever is coming to him. That in a way it will be a relief after waking up every morning for the last twenty years with the horror of what he has done. The pain of then trying to get on with a 'normal' day. But he doesn't. Because no one can really understand how he feels unless they have been through it themselves. The only thing that helped over the years was to lose himself in music, but even that couldn't blank it out fully.

Detective Sergeant Brown gives him a hard stare. 'Oh, you will face the consequences. Don't worry, there's no doubt about that, Robert Manning.'

He finds himself being taken back to his cell. 'They've got to contact the CPS to authorize the charge.'

'What's the CPS?'

'Crown Prosecution Service. When the custody officer arrives, you'll be cautioned and formally charged.'

Everything is so bewildering.

Five hours later, he's called out of his cell to yet another room in the police station. 'Robert Manning, you are charged that, on the fifteenth of September 2004, contrary to section 18 of the Offences Against the Persons Act 1861, you did cause grievous bodily harm with intent to Janie White . . .'

None of this feels real. It's as though they are talking about someone else. He vaguely hears Yasmine requesting some time with her client.

She looks furious, exasperated and worried, all at the same time. 'If I'm to take your case and brief a barrister, I need to know exactly what happened.'

'I ran her over, OK?' he says. 'Then I drove away out of panic. End of story.'

'I've defended a lot of people in my time,' she says in a softer tone than before, 'and something doesn't feel right here.'

Robbie feels anger rising inside. 'Look, Yasmine, this is *my* life. Not yours. I appreciate your help. I was scared before when we talked. But I've had time to think. I have to take this on the chin. Or –'

He stops.

'Or what?' asks Yasmine.

'Nothing.'

But he's lying. And he suspects she knows it.

12

Vanessa

'Heard the news?' asked Carol.

Frankly it was beginning to get on Vanessa's nerves. Her supervisor always opened a conversation with this phrase when she knew darned well that Vanessa hadn't heard the news – because it was fresh off the court gossip line.

'Robbie Manning has admitted he's guilty. So he won't be going to trial after all. He'll just be sentenced.'

Vanessa couldn't help feeling disappointed. She'd been hoping to support Janie. To look after the poor girl. She might even have told her that it was her husband who'd been on the scene when they'd found her.

'The most appalling thing has happened,' Jack had told her when he'd come home from work that day, his face white. 'Some bastard knocked a young girl off her bike and then drove away. At least, it looks that way from the skid marks on the road. The lass didn't have a heartbeat when we were called to the scene but the ambulance crew managed to resuscitate her. God knows how. She's in a coma now but her injuries . . . Christ, they're horrific.'

Then he'd sobbed on her shoulder in a way that Vanessa had never known before. Usually, Jack had been tight-lipped about his cases, telling her that he wanted to leave them at the door when he came in (apart, that is, from the ones involving suspects who didn't get punished when he thought they should. Then he'd rant and rave while she made sympathetic noises.)

When Janie finally came out of her coma, Jack had been one of the first at the hospital to see if she could give them any information on the bastard who had done this.

'She can't talk,' he'd told Vanessa, his face drawn with grief. She knew he was thinking of his own father and brother. 'She can't communicate. Her life is wrecked. But I'm not giving up, Nessie. I'm going to make it my mission to find whoever did this to her.'

Jack did indeed spend years trying to find leads. But the only witness, it seemed, had been the victim herself, who couldn't talk or do very much at all. Jack had even spoken about her on his deathbed. 'I've got two regrets, Nessie,' he had told her. 'Leaving you and not being able to solve the biggest case of my career.'

Part of her wondered if Jack had been driven by all the attention it had received in the press: if he'd successfully found the evil driver, he would have really 'made it' as a detective. But she also thought Jack wanted to give that poor girl and her father the satisfaction of knowing that the culprit was behind bars.

How she'd have loved to tell Janie about her brave determined husband!

And now she couldn't. Because Robbie Manning had pleaded guilty, which meant Janie wouldn't need to give evidence. Of course, it was good that Robbie Manning had stepped up to the plate. But, in some ways, Vanessa couldn't help feeling that he deserved to go through the trauma of a trial and all the publicity it would evoke.

'Your mugging case has been cancelled today, Vanessa,' said Carol, cutting through her thoughts. 'I've just been told that the only witness no longer wants to give evidence.'

This happened occasionally and, today, Vanessa couldn't help but think that maybe it wasn't a wholly bad thing. If Tyler hadn't been called to give evidence, would he still have taken revenge on the new gang leader? Maybe. Maybe not. But now he'd be locked away for years. Vanessa's eyes pricked with tears. His words still rang round her head.

'Haven't you ever done something wrong, Vanessa?'

If only she hadn't taken that footpath walk along the cliff. If only she had listened to Jack. Then she wouldn't have made the biggest mistake of her life.

Vanessa shivered as she got ready to leave the office. Would she ever come to terms with it? No. And maybe she shouldn't. Perhaps she deserved to be punished inside for ever.

Vanessa's mind went back to when her taste buds started to change and she felt nauseous in the mornings. They'd been married for almost two years then.

In those days, it took two days for the pregnancy test result to come through from the doctor. When she told Jack, his face looked like a little boy's at Christmas. 'This baby is going to be the most precious baby in the world,' he'd whispered.

He'd spent hours just sitting next to her, stroking her tummy.

Vanessa's mum wrote to say she'd started knitting.

Then Vanessa gave up her job as a shop assistant because Jack said no wife of his was going to work when she was a mother.

'But I'm not one yet,' she'd said.

'Yes, you are. You've got my child inside you. You need to rest, love.'

So she did. But it was so boring being at home all the time! One day, Jack came back and found her painting the walls of the spare room: the baby's nursery.

'You can't do that,' he said, appalled. 'You might fall off the ladder. I was going to do it myself at the weekend, like we arranged. You just sit and rest. That's my baby you're carrying inside, love. We need to take care of it.'

By the time she was seven months pregnant, she was going stir-crazy. She knew Jack meant well, wrapping her in cotton wool like this, but she missed the girls at the shop and getting out of the house every day. The doctor had told her about a local antenatal group but Jack didn't want her going because, he said, 'you might pick up germs'. He could be very funny about that kind of thing. Most particular. He'd spend hours, for instance, scrubbing down the kitchen table after work. Privately, she wondered if this was his way of dealing with the terrible things he had to see in his job.

But one day, when Jack was working over the weekend, Vanessa couldn't take it anymore. It was a beautiful late-autumn morning and she needed to get out. So she made a sandwich and walked up the hill at the back of the bungalow, where the sea view over the cliff was stunning.

Without realizing it, she found herself straying from

53

the public footpath, towards the edge. And that's when it happened. Oh! Somehow, she stumbled on a stone and fell, stomach first, to the ground, her hands flying out in front to try and protect herself.

Stunned, Vanessa managed to haul herself to her feet. She wasn't hurt, but what about the baby? 'Come on, little one,' she pleaded aloud, putting her hand on her tummy. 'Move around a bit. Give me a kick to show me you're all right.'

Yes. There it was. Not very big but it was definitely there. She'd ring the midwife when she got home just to check.

But the minute she opened the front door, Vanessa felt a low ache in her stomach, a bit like a period pain. Hands shaking, she rang the midwife who was luckily in the area and came straight over.

Jack was on duty but his supervisor said he'd pass on the message. By the time he got home, Vanessa was in premature labour. Vanessa had always planned on having a home birth like most of her friends had, but not like this.

'Will it be all right?' she called desperately.

'Don't you worry now,' the midwife replied tersely.

When the baby arrived, there was silence.

Vanessa's mouth was almost too frozen with fear to speak. 'Why isn't it crying?' she whispered.

'Just wait a minute, love,' said the midwife. 'I need a quick word with your husband.'

After a few minutes, Jack came back alone, tears streaming down his face.

'What's happened?' Vanessa said in a voice that didn't feel like hers. 'Why did the midwife take our baby away like that?'

'Vanessa love, I'm sorry. But . . . but the little mite was so premature that she couldn't breathe.'

'She?'

He nodded, tears streaming down his face.

This couldn't be right. It just couldn't.

'Was it because I fell?' she sobbed.

'What?'

'Didn't the midwife tell you?'

'She just said you went into early labour.'

Vanessa described what happened and then waited for Jack to tell her it wasn't her fault. But he didn't.

'I want to see her,' she said.

'No, love, you don't. It will upset you too much. Trust me.'

So she went along with it, because she was too confused, too shocked, too utterly bewildered and hysterical and upset and hurt to do anything else. How can you have a baby inside you one minute and not the next? Where were those kicks that she'd felt with such joy over the preceding months, holding her hand against her stomach tenderly and calling Jack over to do the same? 'Magic,' he'd said. 'Pure bloody magic.'

But the baby had gone. In its place was her empty body, still leaking blood. Her breasts disgorging milk that now wasn't needed. The nursery with its tiny clothes beautifully folded for the daughter who was no longer here.

It made it worse, too, knowing the baby's sex. It brought up the picture of a real person.

'It will be all right,' soothed Jack, taking her into his arms. 'We'll get through this together, you and me.'

They didn't even have a funeral. In those days, pre-term

babies were sometimes 'sorted out'. In other words, disposed of.

Later, Vanessa asked herself the same question again and again. Why on earth hadn't she insisted on seeing her daughter? It might have helped her to heal if she had. Instead, Vanessa could only imagine what she had looked like. Her head came to Vanessa's dreams at night. Sometimes it was two heads. Once, three.

But it was different in those days. Women listened to their husbands. You certainly listened to someone like Jack. Especially as it was all her fault. If she hadn't been so selfish and gone for the walk, then none of this would have happened, would it?

So when Tyler had asked if she'd ever done something wrong, the answer was yes.

She had.

In her mind, she'd as good as killed her own child because of her own stupidity and carelessness.

13

Janie

When you die, you see your whole life flash before you.

At least, that's what everyone believes. But now I know it's not true.

It doesn't flash. Instead, it's like a slow film that seems at times to stop and dwell on small, seemingly unimportant details.

Yet at the same time, I sense they're much more important than they seem.

So as I try to shut out the arguments going on around me, I go back to the sea.

I think I'm about eight because I'm wearing my favourite swimsuit — the one with the turquoise mermaid pattern. Mum is next to me in the water. My feet are touching the ground. 'Look,' she's saying in that singsong voice of hers. 'Make your hands move like this and kick out your legs like me. Then you'll stay on top of the water. It's called floating.'

I can do the arms bit but when I take my legs off the bottom, I'm scared.

'I'm sinking,' I cry out.

'No, you're not,' says Mum. 'Your feet can still touch the seabed. But even if they couldn't, you'd float, like I said.'

'I want you to hold me.'

'It's all right, Janie. I'm here. I'm always here.'

It was the first lie she'd told me. The first I knew about, anyway.

Here's another. One day, when we were on the beach, we came across two heart-shaped shells. 'This one is for you and this one is for me,' said Mum. 'Yours is my heart and mine is yours. It means we'll be bound together always. Keep it safe and then we'll be together for ever.'

But that didn't happen. Did it?

Then, suddenly, a new voice interrupts my thoughts. A third one. Or is it a fourth?

'Jacob's right. We need to go before someone finds us. She's dead. Anyone can see that.'

Jacob? Who is that? I've got to remember it yet already it's slipping away. I try to hang on to it. Jason. No, that's not right. Something beginning with 'J'.

Jonathan. Was that it? I'm not sure. Why won't my brain work?

Desperately, I try to move to show them that I'm alive. But I can't.

Then snapshots of my life begin to flood into my mind. If I concentrate hard enough, it might help me hang on to life, or whatever this limbo is that I've found myself in.

'Try,' I tell myself. 'TRY.'

14

Robbie

Apparently, he has to spend another two nights in custody before he can appear at the magistrates' court.

Meanwhile, someone's washed the floor of the police station cell but it still stinks of urine.

It's not as bad as his mind, though. That feels as though he's wading through a sewer of dark thoughts and guilt and fear and God knows what else.

'Your wife brought in clean clothes for you,' says the custody sergeant.

Robbie's heart somersaults. 'Did she leave a message? Or ask to see me?'

'No.'

A shot of fear zaps through him. Does this mean Irena doesn't want anything to do with him?

'Can I ring her?'

'You have the right to make one call. It's up to you who you choose. You'll have to give me the number and I'll ring it for you.'

Robbie's heart pounds as he watches the officer punch in the numbers and then hands him the phone.

'*Hi! Sorry, we're out, but if you leave a message, someone will call back.*'

It was the chirpy recording that Irena had made months

ago. She'd insisted. 'If *you* do it, fans who've got hold of your number will just be ringing night and day to hear your voice.'

He doesn't leave a message. Nothing feels suitable.

Yasmine calls to 'see how you are'.

'Not great.'

On the day of the hearing, he is taken to court in a police car. It has tinted windows – the type you can see out of but which others can't see in. THUMP! Something yellow hits the window next to his face and streams down. Robbie winces. 'What the . . .'

'Only eggs,' says the policeman next to him. 'It's quite common, especially with people like you.' His tone is sarcastic. Then comes another thud.

Fear edges into the policeman's voice. 'That one sounded like a brick.'

Robbie ducks.

'The windows are meant to be bullet-proof,' says the policeman, as if reassuring himself.

'They might shoot me?' Robbie trembles.

'It's been known.'

There are placards too.

WE TRUSTED YOU, ROBBIE.

And HOW COULD YOU?

But there is also one that reads WE BELIEVE IN YOU, ROBBIE, and another that says I KNOW YOU COULDN'T HAVE DONE IT.

That last one hurts the most.

Yasmine is waiting for him in the cells beneath. Robbie had no idea that they existed in courts. He'd just presumed that prisoners went straight to the dock. But after the brick-throwing, he is relieved to be safe.

'I need to ring my wife,' he says. 'I was only allowed one call but it went through to the answerphone.'

'That's not right. I'll get a message to her. What do you want me to say?'

'Tell her I love her. That I love all of them.'

She looks grave. 'You know, Robbie, you don't have to indicate a guilty plea. This Eric Sharp is facing drugs charges. He's doing this to get his sentence reduced or even dropped. We can argue he's not trustworthy.'

'But I am guilty. Besides . . .'

He stops in the nick of time.

'Besides, what?' she asks.

He hesitates. 'Nothing.'

She frowns. Her eyebrows, he notices, are lasered. His daughter Daisy has been asking for them, although of course they'd told her she was too young. When he gets out of jail, she will be a grown woman. She might not want to see him again.

'Are you sure there's nothing else you want to add?'

'Quite sure,' he lies.

'There are bound to be press and fans up there . . . and people who aren't fans anymore,' warned Yasmine. 'Some people have an unhealthy interest in crime, plus the nation feels like it owns you, Robbie. You're a big name. Yes – many will be angry and shocked. They will hate you for leaving a woman to die. But some will still believe in you.'

Is this meant to be a comfort or a warning? He's not sure.

There's a knock on the door. It's a young woman constable. 'They're ready for you.'

The court is heaving. Every seat is taken. But he can't see Irena. What was it that his lawyer had said? *'Some will still believe in you.'* Will they? Why does that even matter now? Nothing is more important than his family. They're the ones he's let down. And, of course, Janie. *The van. The bike. The crunch.*

He can still see the blood on the road. Still see her bike's front wheel spinning and the crushed helmet flung onto the pavement. Still feel that strange conviction in his head, as he stands there, that she's trying to tell him something. That she's still there, alive – something he wishes every day that he'd known before the headlines.

'All rise' booms a voice.

They stand up as the judge comes in. Robbie is surprised – although he shouldn't be – to see she's female. She gives him a hard look. Judges are meant to be impartial, aren't they? But this one doesn't look as if she likes him very much. Robbie doesn't blame her. He doesn't like himself either.

Then they sit. Someone else reads out the charge against him.

Even though Yasmine has prepared him, Robbie feels as if he is whirling around in a centrifuge; the kind they'd used at school. It's as if the charge relates to someone else. If only.

'Grievous bodily harm?' Why can't they just say it in layman's terms? Why not add that he'd been driving without a licence? That he'd caused life-changing injuries to a young girl? Then again, as Yasmine had explained, all this would have come out in a trial if he'd pleaded not guilty. And more. Things that he didn't want brought into the open.

'Do you intend to plead guilty, not guilty or make no plea?' asks the judge.

'Guilty,' says Robbie firmly.

There are gasps from the public gallery. 'No, Robbie!' screams out a woman. 'You couldn't have!'

'Silence, please!' thunders the judge. He turns to face him. 'Your case will be sent to the crown court where you can formally enter your plea.'

Robbie crosses his fingers as Yasmine lodges a bail application. Please can he go home, even for a few days, he begs silently. But the judge turns it down. 'There are grounds to believe that if granted, you may refuse to appear.'

Then she nods at the officer. 'You may take the prisoner down.'

This is a nightmare with no end.

Yasmine lodges a bail application, but it is refused. 'They think you're a flight risk,' she says. 'So I'm afraid you have to go to prison until your case comes up.'

Life as he knows it is finished now, Robbie tells himself.

Yet in a weird way, it's a relief. All those awful nightmares about coming round the corner and seeing the bike. The terrifying realization that he couldn't avoid it. The jolt of the van hitting the frame. The shocked silence. Opening the heavy driver's door, his whole body shaking. The horror of the crumpled bloody mess in front of him. And then Irena shaking him gently and telling him he's had another bad dream and that it's all right when it's anything but. Because those nightmares hadn't just been nocturnal terrors. They had been true.

At least now, there's no more pretence.

But Robbie also has a horrible feeling that this is the beginning of something else. Something far worse.

15

Vanessa

'We'll have another baby,' Jack had agreed when she kept pestering him.

But it never happened.

Vanessa wanted to have the new IVF treatment but Jack said they ought to let nature take its course.

Sometimes he suggested that it might be better if they didn't try again. 'What if we lose another?' he'd said.

He spoke as though she had mislaid the baby somewhere. Behind the sofa. In the shopping centre. On the bus.

Jack was kind enough – '*No, love. You stay in bed. I'll bring you a nice cuppa*' – but she knew that he blamed her for going up to the cliff on her own when she was so heavily pregnant. So although she wanted another child desperately, she couldn't help feeling scared in case something went wrong again.

If only she could go back to work. Yet Jack said there was no need. Now he'd been promoted, he earned enough for the two of them. He certainly didn't want anyone to think he couldn't be what he called 'a good provider'.

'But I've got nothing to do,' she said.

'You've got me to cook for and look after.'

'Are you sure you won't consider adoption?'

Jack's mouth had tightened at that. His top lip was very

narrow. Vanessa's mother had always said it was a sign of meanness to oneself. But his bottom lip was full, which apparently meant he was generous to others. So that was all right, wasn't it?

'I've told you before that I'm not bringing up someone else's kid,' he said in his 'that's the end of this conversation' voice.

When Vanessa wrote to her mum, the reply wasn't as sympathetic as she'd hoped. 'Men like Jack need a lot of attention,' her mother said firmly. 'It's because he lost his family so young.'

But it hurt. So badly that Vanessa grew to accept this constant pain in her heart as something that was part of her. Even so, that overpowering maternal urge inside grew stronger and stronger, so she began doing voluntary work at a mother-and-baby centre. 'How old are your kids?' the mums would ask.

'I don't have any,' she'd reply.

Then they would look either pitying or suspicious. Why was a woman without children helping out at a place like this? So as quickly as she'd begun, Vanessa stopped working at the centre and began visiting old people instead. Then Jack put a stop to this because she caught shingles.

That's when things changed.

First, her words started coming out wrong; then she just wanted to go to bed and put the eiderdown over her. The doctor never mentioned the word 'breakdown' but Jack did. He suggested that she went away to one of 'those homes that make you better', but the doctor said that, in his view, Vanessa needed distracting and suggested a return to work.

So she went back to her job as a shop assistant, even though Jack wasn't happy about it and fussed over her terribly, insisting that he'd meet her at the end of the day or, if he was on duty, that she get a taxi home. The girls in the shop were very kind to her and didn't mention the baby.

Then they began getting a spate of thefts. It was often after the same well-dressed customer came in. Vanessa spotted her putting a cashmere jumper into her bag and they called the police.

'You're good at this,' said the manager when Vanessa found a young man stuffing a pair of boxers down his jeans a month later. 'How would you fancy being a store detective here? We were about to advertise for one.'

It was a breakthrough. The new role made Vanessa feel like she was restoring a sense of justice to the world. It also helped to keep her mind off things. But not quite everything.

Vanessa didn't want to think about any of this now. *You've done enough thinking already*, she told herself as she pushed her way through the shopping centre in Exeter after the hearing. Maybe it was the disappointment about Robbie's guilty plea, and what Jack would have thought, that brought back all those painful memories that she'd tried for so long to forget.

Then a man barged into Vanessa, startling her. 'Ouch!' she said. 'Get your hands off my bag!'

'I wasn't after your bag,' growled the man. 'I was pushed into you by the crowd.'

He avoided eye-contact as he spoke. Jack used to say that was a sign that someone was fibbing.

'I'm not stupid, you know,' she said.

'And I'm not lying,' insisted the man.

He looked innocent enough. Had she made a mistake? Just like she'd made a mistake the other day when she'd thought someone had been following her?

When she got home, the bungalow felt empty. She still half-expected Jack to be there. But at least the post had arrived – she always looked forward to that. It gave her something to do.

Mind you, there was never very much. Which was why the big white envelope caught her eye. It had a local post-mark and her name in block capitals.

Vanessa went into the lounge to open it.

At first, she thought it was a sick joke or one of those begging letters.

I'm sorry to bother you . . .

Can I take a moment of your time . . .

But the next bit made her face go hot then cold then hot again: *I've recently found out that . . .*

'No,' she gasped. 'That can't be possible.'

Her eyes raced to the next line.

Vanessa's legs buckled. She sank to her chair, trying to breathe. Then she read down to the end.

I'll be in touch soon after you've had time to let this sink in.

With love from your grandson.

16

Janie

Those voices that I heard before are still there. But they sound as though they're coming from a long way off. Nothing feels real. Least of all me.

I'm going back. I'm twelve years old. I'm sure of this because my parents are singing 'happy birthday' to me over a cake with twelve candles.

Mum's voice was like an angel's. I know people use that phrase a lot but in her case it really was true. She was so talented!

Sometimes, Mum would tell me the story of how she and Dad met. 'I was singing in a nightclub,' she'd say, with that faraway look in her eyes.

Then Dad would give us both a big warm hug and I'd breathe a sigh of relief. Everything was fine. No more arguments. We were all happy together. For now.

Suddenly I catch a voice which is louder than the others. It's a man's. 'Get a move on or I swear I'll cut your throat.'

Is he talking to me?

'Mummy!' I try to call out. 'Daddy! Help me.'

I want to be twelve again. I want to slip my hand into Dad's and feel safe. I want to feel my mother's arms around me. I want to be out of this place. I want to be able to talk. To walk. To live.

I don't want to die. Not yet. Please, someone. Help me.

17

Robbie

After he pleads guilty, Robbie is led out in handcuffs to a van at the back of the court, where the journalists are ready with their cameras and their questions.

'Why did you do it, Robbie?'

'Do you feel ashamed now the truth is coming out?' calls out another.

He keeps his head down as the lawyer has advised. All he wants to do is see Irena. To explain.

But he can't, even if she had been there. He's being handcuffed to a bench in the van. There's another man there, also in cuffs.

'Where are we going?' Robbie asks the guard, but he slams the door shut.

'To Fastlock, mate,' says his fellow companion. 'It's where we wait to get sentenced. But don't hold your breath. Last time I got sent there, I was banged up for two years before my trial came up.'

'What if you're then found innocent?' asks Robbie, appalled. 'Do they give you compensation?'

The man laughs. 'Are you kidding? If you go down, mind, the time gets taken off your sentence.'

Then his eyes narrow. 'Hey, you're that pop star, aren't

you? The one everyone's talking about. You mowed down that girl.'

A lump rises up into Robbie's throat. Tears swim in his eyes. Tears he'd tried for years to hold back in front of others so that no one suspected. He manages to nod.

The man's eyes harden. 'I never liked your music, but even if I did, I wouldn't listen to it now.'

He spits on the floor. 'That's what I think of wankers like you.'

'It's what I think of myself too,' says Robbie quietly. 'What are you in for?'

'What's it got to do with you?' snaps the man.

Robbie's skin prickles. 'Then you've probably killed someone.'

'I'm no bleeding murderer like you.' He lunges forward but is held back by the handcuffs fastened to his seat.

'Oi, stop that,' yells one of the guards, sliding back a panel dividing the body of the van from the cab. 'Or you'll be up before the governor as soon as we get there.'

Both men fall silent as the van rocks on.

There's a narrow slit for a window but Robbie can't see what's outside. He wonders instead what Irena might be doing right now. Why didn't she come to the plea hearing? Has she given up on him? Or – oh God – has something terrible happened to her or the children? Surely someone would have told him if that was the case. Then again, hasn't he already learned how bad communication is in this new world he's found himself in? This is inhumane. A man should be allowed to see his family.

A few hours later, they slow down. They stop and

there's a sound of gates opening. The van continues and then stops again. The back doors slide open. The guards are waiting. 'Out you get.'

Robbie's eyes squint in the early evening light. It had been dark in the van. A high wall meets his eyes. On top there are rolls of barbed wire. There are security cameras too. The guard sees him looking at them.

'Not the kind of cameras *you're* used to, I expect, *Mr* Manning. Come on, superstar, this way.'

The sarcasm is evident.

They're led into a room that leads into another and then another. Someone gives him a large plastic bag. 'Put all your possessions in here, Manning, including that gold watch of yours. Bet you've got a few more of those at home, haven't you?'

It's none of your business, he wants to say. But he forces himself to stay silent.

'Into this cubicle. Clothes off and put this on instead.'

He is handed a maroon tracksuit.

'Shoes too. Size?'

'Ten and a half.'

'We don't have halves here. We don't have no elevens either, so you're stuck with tens.'

'But they'll be too tight.'

'Hear that everyone? This bloke what's maimed a girl for life and kept quiet for twenty years, is complaining because his shoes are too tight. Poor little diddums. Now get in there and change before I set the dogs on you.'

He doesn't mean that, Robbie thinks. Or does he?

'When will I get my watch back?'

'When you're released in twenty years.'

He doesn't look as if he's joking.

'Can't I keep my washbag?'

The lawyer had advised him to bring it in.

'Sorry, superstar. Only regulation stuff in here, in case you're hiding something in that toothpaste tube of yours. You can get your essentials from the canteen.'

'Can I go there now?'

'It's not a shop,' says the prisoner who'd been in the van with him. 'It's the name of the form you fill in to say what you want. Then once you've paid, it comes about ten days later.'

'I need something to clean my teeth with before then,' says Robbie appalled. 'And soap and deodorant.'

'We'll see what we can find,' says another guard. 'But don't expect special treatment here.'

'If anything, you'll get worse because of who you are,' says the other man. He seems more subdued and friendly now – perhaps prisoners help each other here, Robbie hopes, although he doesn't know if he really wants help from a criminal. Then again, isn't he one himself?

'Surely this kind of treatment has got to be against the law,' says Robbie.

'And what are you going to do about that? Write to the papers?' The guard laughs. 'Doesn't look as if they're on your side anymore, mate. In fact, they bloody hate you.' He thrusts a phone screen in front of him.

BREAKING NEWS

POP STAR ROBBIE MANNING PLEADS GUILTY TO MOWING DOWN 18-YEAR-OLD CYCLIST. POLICE HAVE BEEN HUNTING THE CULPRIT FOR TWENTY YEARS.

There's another headline too, from a different paper.

DISGRACED MANNING JAILED WHILE WAITING SENTENCE. GIVE HIM LIFE – THAT'S WHAT WE SAY!

'Can't tell you how many bribes we've been offered to give these journos an interview or some tasty bit of information,' snorts the guard. 'There are plenty of folk in here who feel let down by a family man like yourself. If I were you, I'd watch my back.'

'But it's safe in here, isn't it?'

As he speaks, Robbie is acutely aware of how naive he sounds. He's read articles about prison like everyone else. Heard about overcrowding and riots and drug problems. But although he's been terrified for the last twenty years that any moment he could end up in one himself, the reality is only now dawning.

It's not just the authorities he needs to fear. It's the men behind bars with him.

'Guards can't always stop trouble,' chips in a grim-faced woman in uniform. 'Last month, one of the inmates was executed.'

'Executed?' Robbie feels his skin crawl.

'That's right. Had his head chopped off with a samurai sword.'

'WHAT?' Robbie's knees judder. 'How did a weapon like that get in?'

'Where there's a will there's a way. So like I say, superstar, keep your wits about you. You've got a target on your back. Now, let me show you to your room, sir.' He laughs. 'Sorry. I mean cell. Oh, and by the way, someone from the crowd outside the court gave the driver this for you. I should hand it in but I'm being kind to you.'

He passes over an envelope. It's already been opened. Inside is a note:

Careful what you say, Robbie. Or you'll be sorry.

18

Janie

'Cut your throat?'

That's what the voice said. I'm sure it did.

Something is flashing. It's like a blade glinting in the sunlight.

Or perhaps it's a mirror.

The pain is so bad that I almost can't feel it.

'Please,' I try to say again. 'Help me.'

But my lips won't move.

There's another voice now. A gentler one than the first. 'I don't think that . . .'

Then the harsher voice cuts in. 'I warn you, Robbie. Get back in that van or you'll never see your parents again.'

19

Vanessa

With love from your grandson.

Vanessa read and reread the final line of the letter.

But she didn't have a grandson. This had to be a joke.

Vanessa's skin came out in goose bumps. This wasn't fair. She'd have given anything for a grandchild. Clearly, the person writing it didn't know she'd lost a baby or that she hadn't been able to have any more.

Nor was there any suggestion on where they should meet. It just said he would be in touch.

This made it even more likely that it was a trick. Maybe – please, no – it was related to Tyler. The gang would surely want retaliation for the boy killing their new leader. What if they held her responsible too for 'supporting' him in court?

'*Ignore it,*' said Jack in her head. '*It's just some stupid arsehole who wants to scare you.*'

Vanessa hadn't liked it when Jack swore. He hadn't done it a lot but when he had, it felt very uncouth coming from his lips. Those warm lips that had pressed them-selves against hers so lovingly every night. 'We're a dream team, Vanessa,' he would say. 'We only need each other.'

'But you're gone, Jack,' she said out loud now. 'It's all

very well you telling me to ignore it but what if someone hurts me? Who's going to protect me?'

Then the answer came into her head.

As she sat and waited for Judge to return her call (she hadn't liked to leave a message but he'd see the missed number), Vanessa recalled the first time she'd met him, during witness service volunteer training in one of the rooms at the back of court.

They'd just got to the bit about making sure they didn't give any of their personal details away to a witness or anyone else for security reasons when the door opened and this short, rather jolly-looking man came in.

Vanessa's first thought was that this was just the kind of man who'd make a perfect Father Christmas. (Jack had once dressed up at a police charity do for kids but they'd had to bulk him up with pillows because he'd lost weight. They hadn't realized then that he was ill.)

There were about four of them in the group; some for different courts in other areas. 'Don't mind me,' said the Father Christmas lookalike as he slipped in at the back.

It was only after the session had finished that he introduced himself as a judge. Vanessa had been surprised because he'd seemed so down to earth. So normal. Jack had always described the judges in court as being 'up themselves' but this one didn't seem like that at all.

'I'd like to thank you all for volunteering for this role,' he said in a way that sounded like he really meant it.

Vanessa was always an attentive listener, but she found herself concentrating more on his wonderful deep voice than the content. The sound made her feel as though she was eating dark chocolate while listening to jazz music. She also found herself taken by his eyes as he looked at each of the volunteers, his gaze resting briefly for just the same amount of time on every recipient.

When it was Vanessa's turn, she found herself flushing, even though it was winter and the heating wasn't working very well.

'You may find that the witness becomes attached to you after the hearing,' he said, as though he was talking directly to her. 'Many will see you as their "rock" during the case. You will have sat by his or her side. You will have known the emotions that the witness is going through. You will have comforted him or her. You will have explained what is going on as if you were leading someone through a tunnel without a light, or a desert without landmarks.'

Wow! thought Vanessa. *I really want to do this job!*

But the judge was saying more. 'Whatever the outcome – whether the accused is found guilty or not – witnesses will have all kinds of conflicting emotions. Yet however much you want to continue supporting them after the trial is over, be aware that this is not part of the role. One should never get drawn in, personally.'

'Is there an actual law against that?' Vanessa heard herself asking.

That jolly face turned to something sterner. 'No, there isn't,' he said with an edge to his voice. 'But I would strongly urge you to be careful. In some ways, it's a little like being a health-care professional. You are there to help at the time. But if you carry on seeing them out of kindness once they've been discharged, there comes a point when it is not appropriate. Besides, how do you provide emotional support for everyone? And will there be enough energy left for yourself?'

'Can you put on your wig?' asked someone.

There was a ripple of laughter.

'If you like.' He did so. 'I'm glad you asked this because I can assure you that I am the same man whether I am wearing it or not. So don't be frightened about court. We are all human.'

His words made her think in a way she'd never thought before. It was so different from working in the shop and helped distract her from Jack's empty chair in the lounge.

When the training session ended, Vanessa didn't feel like going home. So she headed for a local coffee shop. It was packed. The only spare space was at her favourite table by the window, with its lovely view over the green and the cathedral.

But someone was already sitting there. The judge. Even without his wig, he was distinctive with what her dad would have called 'a strong face'.

He looked up as she stood there, hovering uncertainly. 'You're welcome to join me if you like.'

Nervously, she took a seat with her coffee. It slopped over the edge into her saucer and he promptly handed her his serviette so she could mop it up.

Vanessa flushed, feeling awkward and out of her depth. Was she really sitting next to a judge?

'How did you find the session this morning?' he asked in a kind voice.

'Very . . . er . . . very interesting.'

'Tell me, Vanessa – it is Vanessa, isn't it?'

She nodded. 'Yes, Your Honour.'

'Please call me Richard.'

She blushed. 'I can't. I mean, you're a judge.'

'I don't like standing on ceremony, Vanessa.'

Then a funny thought came to her. 'I could just call you Judge, instead, as if it's your first name.'

He laughed. It wasn't a sarcastic laugh. It was a warm, kind one. 'If you like.'

'You were going to ask me a question before all this name stuff,' Vanessa heard herself say.

'Thank you for reminding me. I'm always interested in why people sign up to be a witness service volunteer. What was your reason?'

She was about to talk about her need to do something after her husband died, although she wasn't sure she should tell him that it had been Jack's idea to apply – that would be too weird! But then her husband's voice cut in. *'Wait a minute, Nessie. Ask him a few questions first.'*

Jack hadn't called her Nessie for ages. She'd been glad about that. It hurt too much. But now the familiarity made her feel she ought to do what he said.

'Actually,' said Vanessa, not feeling as scared as she thought she would, 'I'd like to know about you first. Do you always talk to us volunteers?'

'I do if my schedule allows me to. It's not usual, I have to say. But I like to get to know everyone in court and I think your team does a fantastic job.'

Her team! Now that gave her a sense of importance. Bold enough, in fact, to ask the next question.

'What made you become a judge?'

He laughed. 'Do you know, no one has asked me that

since I was in chambers? I'm impressed. But I warn you, it's a long story. Let's save it for another day, shall we?'

Vanessa had presumed this was just a way of warning her off any more personal questions. After all, why would a judge want to confide in her – a woman with barely any schooling, let alone experience in court?

The next time she saw him there, he waved her over. A few weeks later, the same thing happened again. It felt a bit odd, having lunch with a judge, but he seemed very relaxed.

'Cheese and pickle again, I see,' he said, eyeing her choice.

She blushed. 'Looks like you're keen on tuna,' she heard herself saying.

'You're observant.'

'My husband was a policeman,' she replied. Then she told him about Jack and how much she missed him.

Over the next few months, it seemed increasingly natural to eat together every now and then. Sometimes they were joined by other people whom Judge seemed to know, including a man who cleaned windows. She liked the way he was on first-term names with the waitresses and always left a tip. In his spare time, someone said, he helped out at his local food bank. 'Man of the people' – that's how everyone referred to him.

'*You're getting too familiar,*' warned Jack in her head. '*It's not a good idea to overstep the mark. Folk like this man come from a different world.*'

But he was wrong.

20

Vanessa

That conversation had been over a year ago now. Since then, Vanessa had got to know Judge much better. She even had his phone number off pat.

Judge would understand about her so-called 'grandson'. He'd give her some advice. But he still hadn't rung her back. Maybe he was in court or in a meeting. Besides, perhaps she should handle this one herself. Judge was always telling her that she should have more faith in her decisions.

The letter must be either a spoof from some prankster or something more sinister. If this 'grandson' did contact her and suggest they met somewhere, she'd go straight to the police.

Meanwhile, she needed to do something that would clear her mind. Maybe she'd take the bus to Exmouth beach. Vanessa always preferred going there in the early evening, when there were fewer children around, because it gave her a pang watching parents helping their toddlers build sandcastles.

That feeling of loss had never left her, even if it had eased slightly as she and Jack had grown older and their own friends' children became adults. They were more like the others then – not that they socialized much. 'We only need each other,' Jack said again and again. Besides, he was always tired after work and just wanted to relax with her.

'You're lucky to have a husband who enjoys your company,' said one of the women at work whose own husband spent all his spare time in their car port, tinkering with engines. And Vanessa told herself that yes, she was. No one could take away those memories. Not everyone could boast of having such a close relationship with their husband. Besides, she still had his voice in her head.

Today was a beautiful day. It was term time, so when she reached Exmouth there were only a few little ones out with their mothers or fathers. Vanessa was frequently struck by how many men seemed to look after children nowadays. She couldn't imagine Jack being in charge of a pram – or was that unfair? He'd been tied to his job when he wasn't with her. Maybe that's why the baby emptiness hadn't hit him as hard as it had her.

Stop! she told herself. Regrets were useless. You had to live for the present. If there was one thing she'd learned during her life, it was that. Distraction. That's what she needed. Live for the present.

Her eye settled on an ice cream van parked just above the beach. On impulse, she treated herself to a raspberry-ripple cornet and sat on the beach looking out at the water. But her mind wouldn't settle. She kept thinking of Tyler, who wouldn't be out for years now after what he'd done. Stupid idiot. Wicked too. He'd taken a life. There was no excuse for that.

'You have to put each case behind you,' Judge had once told her. 'I've learned to do that.'

'How?' she'd asked.

'I imagine a metal wall coming down between me and my worries so I can't see the other side. You should try it.'

She had. Sometimes it worked. Sometimes it didn't.

Throwing away the still-crispy cone in a bin (she always did that because it showed that she had the willpower to stop while there was still some left), Vanessa took off her shoes – a rather nice pair of red kitten heels she'd treated herself to recently – and walked into the sea. The waves were flat and they seemed to stroke her feet.

With love from your grandson.

The words from the letter kept echoing round her head. How cruel of someone. It wasn't fair. She'd have loved a grandson just like that little blond boy over there, playing with his mother and laughing every time they ran back from the sea with a pail of water to fill the sandcastle's moat.

There was an older woman with them too. A granny perhaps. Vanessa's heart gave another wrench. At times, she felt like she was the only one in her circle without a grandchild to buy clothes for or look after.

'It's one of the reasons I needed to do something when I retired,' she'd told Judge during one of their chats in the coffee shop.

'I get that,' he'd said.

'Do you have children?' she'd asked.

'One,' he'd said. 'He moved to the States after my wife died.'

This was the first time he'd mentioned that he was a widower. She'd felt both sad and relieved. Vanessa didn't want anyone thinking she was having a coffee with a married man, even if it was quite innocent.

'I'm sorry for your loss,' she'd said.

'Thank you.'

She'd wanted to ask more but it was clear from the way he'd promptly changed the conversation to her old job as a store detective ('*That must have been fascinating*') that he didn't want to discuss it. Vanessa understood that. Didn't she have stuff she didn't want to talk about either?

Time to put up that metal wall, Vanessa told herself now as she walked away from the water. But she couldn't get Judge's trick to work. So instead, she took herself for a stroll into the town centre to do a spot of shopping. The old store detective in her liked to see what security was like. She might even try on a few new outfits.

The phone rang when she was in the changing room. Vanessa was at that awkward moment when she'd just put a dress over her head, which meant she had to wriggle out to find her handbag.

By that time, the caller had rung off.

Strange. She didn't recognize the number. Maybe it was one of those cold callers.

Within seconds, the phone rang again.

'Hello?' she said tentatively.

'Hello,' answered a deep voice.

Vanessa froze.

It was him. Either that or she was going stark raving crazy.

'Vanessa?' asked the voice.

She could barely get her lips to move. But she had to.

'Jack?' she whispered. 'Is that really you?'

21

Janie

*There's no sign of my mother. She's gone now. I feel a terrible empti-
ness. How can she have left me again?*

*But one of those voices is talking. I can just about hear it through
the ringing in my ears.*

'All right. Let's go.'

*'No,' I beg in my head. 'Wait!' But there's no point – I can hear
the van driving away. I'm alone again.*

*Then I hear something else. It sounds like the sea pounding
against the rocks. Yet it had been flat before the accident. Perhaps it's
angry.*

*Or maybe there's something wrong with my head. It doesn't feel
right. And I'm pretty sure I can feel blood trickling down my face.*

Somehow, I manage to move my head to look down.

A cold horror goes through me.

I can't see my left leg.

Robbie

A guard escorts Robbie and the other man from the prison van down a long wide corridor and then another. They pass groups of prisoners on the way, all in identical maroon track suits. Some glance at Robbie and then do a double take, indicating they've recognized him.

'Get a move on,' yells the guard.

'Where are they going?' Robbie asks.

'It's their gym session.'

'How can I join up?'

'Join up?' he snorts. 'It's not a bloody club with a membership scheme, Mr Manning.'

He says 'Mr' in a tone which might be polite or sarcastic. It's hard to know.

'You get one session a week unless you've broken the rules, and then you lose your privileges. Mind you, there's always chapel. There's a saying that prisoners either find God or the gym when they come inside.'

'You get hot chocolate if you change your religion,' adds his companion. 'I can't remember which religion, but I do know someone who got away with it.'

Presumably this 'chocolate' non-sequitur is somehow connected to the 'God or gym' comment. Prison conversation is beginning to make Robbie feel as if he's fallen down an *Alice in Wonderland*-style rabbit hole. That had been one of his daughter's favourite books when she'd been little. It makes his heart ache to think of her.

'Forget the gym,' says Robbie. 'I just want to ring home.' He speaks tightly so as not to cry.

'You'll have to give us the numbers you want to ring and then we approve them. Or not. After that, you get a phone card.'

'How long does that take?'

'How long is a piece of string, Mr Manning?'

'Usually a few weeks,' mutters his van companion.

Panic surges through him. 'But I've got to ring my wife!' His voice comes out as a cry.

'Everyone's got to ring someone. You have to wait. Think of the poor girl you ran over. Twenty years later and she still can't ring anyone, can she?'

They've come to a halt outside a heavy door. 'This is C wing, boys. You'll be here until you're sentenced. But we're full to the hilt now so you'll find others who are long-term. Some of them have been here for years.'

'The murderers and rapists,' whispers the other prisoner.

A cold sweat of fear breaks out on his back. 'Surely that's not right?'

'*Right?* You've been masquerading as a celebrity for years after ruining a girl's life and you want to know what's right?'

The guard is opening the door as they speak. There's a second inner door about ten centimetres away, which he unlocks too. This one is made of iron bars. Robbie can see men in maroon tracksuits loitering on the other side, staring at them curiously.

'It's him,' he hears someone saying. 'It's bloody Robbie Manning himself.'

'Calm down, boys,' shouts the guard. 'Let us through.'

'Can I have your autograph, Robbie?' says a lanky, pimply youth.

'Fuck off, Carl,' says the man next to him. 'The geezer's a murderer. Or as good as.'

'You can talk,' snorts the first.

Robbie is being walked down a long corridor to a room that looks like an office. 'Sign here,' says the officer at the desk. 'Every time you go in and out of the wing, you'll do this to show us where you are. You will only go out if you've got an activity like the gym or the chapel or education. We need to put you down for a work party too.'

'Party?'

The officer looks at him as if he's just been born yesterday. 'It's not some rave-up if that's what you're thinking. It's the name for the jobs that have got to be done round here. You can't just sit on your arse, you know. Some of the men here are on laundry duty or cleaning or cooking. There's gardening too, but everyone wants that because of the fresh air. We've got one space left so you're on toilets.'

There's a snigger from another guard. 'Bring your Marigolds, did you, Mr Manning? No? That's a shame.'

'I need to ring my wife,' he says again. 'It's got to be a human right.'

He feels a tear rolling down his cheek. Embarrassed, he wipes it away.

'I suppose I can allow you one quick call from the office now, but only to the number we have on your file.'

Robbie hopes they will give him some privacy but they show no sign of leaving him alone.

She picks up immediately.

'Irena? It's me. I've been taken to some prison in Essex. Are you all right?'

'Yes,' she says in her beautiful accent, which still makes his insides light up with a loving warmth, even after everything that's happened. 'I told them to tell you I was when I delivered your clothes.'

So the policeman had lied about his wife not leaving a message.

'Are you OK, Robbie?'

He can hear the sob in her voice.

'I'm fine. Don't worry about me. It's you I'm worried sick about, love. I'm so sorry. So very sorry . . .'

He stops because if he goes on, he will cry and that won't help. He has to be strong for his family. He definitely won't mention the anonymous threatening note.

'Please be careful,' he says, forcing himself to continue, even though he knows his voice is breaking with the strain of trying to keep it together for her. 'There are a lot of people out there who hate me now. Make sure the doors and windows are locked. Keep your wits about you when you go out. Don't answer the phone unless you recognize the number.'

'Time's up, Manning.'

'I love you,' he says urgently.

'We love you too,' says Irena. She is crying loudly now. He can hear it. He can't hold back any longer.

'I'm so sorry,' he weeps, feeling tears rolling down his cheeks. 'Tell the children I'm sorry too.'

The line goes dead.

'Couldn't you have let me have a bit more time?' Robbie says angrily. He doesn't normally get angry but hearing Irena crying has torn him apart.

'You got more than I should have given you. Now pull yourself together. I'm taking you to your cell. Watch yourself with your cellmate, mind.'

'Why?'

'Let's just say he's a bit of a funny one.'

'What's he in for?'

'Bruce? Oh, he's a double murderer. Seems harmless enough. But if you want my advice, I'd watch your step.'

23

Janie

Why has everyone left me?

The pain has become part of my body now. The knowledge that I'm going to die dawns slowly. Ironically, I feel surprisingly calm. Not only that but my previous panic has changed to determination.

'Think,' I tell myself. 'Think about your memories. Stay thinking. Hang on to life.'

My mind goes back. I'm in my school uniform and the bus has just dropped me off. I walk up the cliff so I can finish Jane Eyre before homework. If I go straight home, it will be the usual maths (ugh) and tea routine.

I sit on the bench that looks down to the beach. Not the main one – it's on the far side where no one goes because of the rip tide. And then I see her.

Mum. Walking into the sea.

Not swimming.

Just walking.

Then all of a sudden, her head submerges. And she's not coming up.

I don't know how I get down the steps so fast.

She has to be out there somewhere. She simply has to.

'Mum!' I yell. My heart beats so fast that I can't breathe. Peeling off my skirt, I plunge straight in. I don't think about the fact that I can't swim. I just do it.

'Janie!'

'Mum? Where are you?'

'Behind you!'

I turn round and there she is, bobbing on the water. Laughing.

'You did it, you clever girl!'

Afterwards, Mum said she'd seen me on the bench and had gone under to make me swim. 'You've got to, love,' she told me, her eyes bright and feverish. 'If you don't conquer your fears, the world will get you.'

What did she mean? Only later did I realize she was referring to herself.

Dad said she was nuts. He used other words too that I didn't get.

After that, life went back to 'normal' for a bit.

My parents were good at that. They had big bust-ups and then pretended everything was all right. But then came the day when none of us could pretend anymore.

The day when Mum disappeared for ever.

24

Vanessa

Jack and Vanessa had always had great sex. She'd presumed everyone else did too until she started talking to the girls at work about it. That was when she was twenty. Looking back, she could see she hadn't realized then how young that was. The way those girls spoke about it . . . well it wasn't how Jack made her feel.

'We were made for each other, baby,' he would croon.

Jack never called her baby unless they were in bed. She'd have felt embarrassed if he'd addressed her like this in public to be honest. It would have felt pretentious, like he was pretending to be a Hollywood movie star. But under the eiderdown – or against the wall or on the table – well, she could try to pretend that she really was a 'woman in a million'. That had been another of Jack's expressions.

Yet if you'd pressed her to ask what she really liked him to call her, she preferred plain 'Vanessa' to 'baby', because then she knew that he was thinking of her and no one else. Of course, Jack would never be unfaithful, but she did notice that he got aroused when they went to the cinema to see *A Star Is Born*.

So when Jack said 'I love you, Vanessa,' she melted. It wasn't just the name. It was his deep voice that caressed every syllable. The 'baby' bit would happen mid-sex. The 'Vanessa' came after, when she was lying in his arms. It was the part she liked best. It made her feel loved. Secure. Even after they'd lost the baby. *Especially* after they'd lost the baby. Even when her periods kept coming and coming without any sign of another pregnancy. Even when the menopause arrived early at forty and with it went the hope of conceiving. Even when Jack was weakening towards the end and his thin cold hand was reaching out for her.

'*Vanessa . . . Vanessa . . .*'

It was his way of saying it would all be all right.

It's why he still spoke in her head. But now here he was, talking to her on the phone, in a changing room, of all places. It was his voice – the same dark rich tone, a knowing way. Yet at the same time, this voice had an edge, as if there was a question mark hanging off it.

'Jack?' she whispered. 'Where are you?'

By now, she'd managed to pull the shop dress up and over her head. It felt faintly ridiculous sitting there on a bench, half-naked, talking to her dead husband on the phone. Had her grief over losing him finally turned her mad?

'Jack?' said the voice at the other end. 'No. It's Lewis.'

Lewis? Who was Lewis?

'Do I know you?' she asked, not wanting to sound rude but at the same time not wanting to be over-friendly to someone whose name she didn't recognize.

'I'm your grandson.'

The writer of the letter! The one that had said how glad he was to have found her. The one who'd signed off *With love from your grandson.*

Not only had this stalker got hold of her address but he'd also found her number.

Vanessa began to feel angry now. She didn't usually do anger. She was a forgiver, unlike Jack, who had always held grudges. But right now, this anger bubbled up through her, twisting and turning her guts because it wasn't just anger. It was disappointment that it wasn't her husband after all, along with fear.

Jack used to say that fear and anger were what drove him to do his job, especially the time when a bank robber shot him in the leg. The man had got twenty years for murder because Jack's partner hadn't been so lucky. He'd died the next day, leaving a widow and four children under ten. (Vanessa still sent them a Christmas card every year.)

'Stop playing games with me,' she shouted down the phone now. 'I don't know who you really are. But I'm going to tell you something. I don't have children. So I can't have grandchildren. I'm an elderly widow and I'm going to report you for harassment and causing great distress.'

There was a knock on the door then. 'Everything all right?' asked the assistant.

'Yes, thanks,' she said quickly.

'Are you still there, Vanessa?' asked the voice at the other end.

He spoke as if he knew her. Damned cheek.

She should switch off the phone. Block this unknown number, if only she could work out how to do it.

'Yes, I am still here,' she snapped. 'But not for much longer. You should be ashamed of intimidating an old lady.'

Usually, Vanessa refused to see herself as old. But recently she'd found herself playing the age card.

'I'm not intimidating you,' said Lewis, if that's what his name really was. In her experience from her shop detective days, anyone who was up to no good rarely gave their own name. 'In fact,' he added, dropping his voice, 'my mum would kill me if she knew I was talking to you.'

'Why?' asked Vanessa. This last comment sounded – and she hated to admit this – quite genuine. Was it possible that this wasn't a prankster or a con man after all?

'Because she's your daughter.'

That hadn't been in the letter. It was too much. This Lewis had gone too far this time. Now she knew he was lying.

'She can't be,' said Vanessa. 'I've already told you. I don't have any children.'

His voice was slow and steady. 'My mum was born forty-nine years ago on 12 October. It was a home birth.'

Vanessa went cold.

'What did you say?' she whispered.

He repeated it.

Vanessa's eyes flooded with tears. She could see the midwife's face when she'd asked why the baby wasn't crying. Feel Jack's arms around her. 'Vanessa, love, I'm sorry.' She could picture the empty cot that Jack had made. She could feel – as if it was yesterday – the cracking of her heart, which, despite all her jollity on the outside, had remained broken ever since.

'You gave your own daughter away for adoption,' he said quietly.

'I did NOT,' spluttered Vanessa. 'My baby died. She was too premature to live.'

'The thing is, Vanessa, I've got Mum's birth certificate, right here in my hand. It says that her father was Jack Grossmith and that he was a policeman.'

Did he think she was born yesterday? 'You can get birth certificates off the internet,' she scoffed. 'I've read about it.'

'Her mother was Vanessa June.' He continued. 'Her occupation is listed as "housewife".'

'Again, you could have got my name from the internet.'

'I know this is a bit of a shock.' His voice was softer now. Apologetic. It reminded her of Jack's when he came home late from work. 'It's why I couldn't put it in the letter I sent. I knew you wouldn't believe me but, at the same time, I wanted to prepare you.'

This didn't sound like stalker talk. Maybe the caller was mentally unwell. Perhaps he'd got her birth details from Google.

'What does this certificate say your mother is called?' she demanded.

'Molly.'

Molly? She and Jack had fixed on Sandra as a name for a girl and George if it was a boy. But the name didn't matter. The fact was that this Lewis was playing a cruel joke. He had to be.

'I've only just found out that Mum was adopted, you see,' he continued.

This wasn't possible. Was it?

'How did you get hold of my phone number and my address?' she asked.

'It wasn't difficult.' He almost sounded pleased with himself, the way Jack had when he'd solved a case. 'I went through the electoral roll to check out anyone with your name in the right sort of age group.'

'How many were there?'

'A few.'

'Then you'd better try the others, hadn't you?'

'There's no need. You're my grandmother.'

'How can you be so sure?' she whispered.

'I can sense it. Feel it. I also found your picture on the net. You were at some award dinner.'

She had certainly gone to enough of those with Jack, so it was possible.

'It gave your name and my grandad's. You were sitting next to him. He looks a bit like me.'

'You sound like him too,' Vanessa heard herself say. Her throat tightened with emotion. 'But none of this explains how you got my number.'

'If you've got someone's address, you can find their phone number on the internet if you know what to do.'

'That doesn't seem right.'

'Please,' he went on, ignoring her comment. 'I'd love to meet you. But if you don't want to, I'll respect that. I'll just have to go through the rest of my life not knowing my own grandmother.'

Vanessa hesitated. If this was true, of course she wanted to meet him too. But if it wasn't, she needed to change her number. Did that mean moving house as well? How did you escape someone like this?

'I can tell from your silence, that's a no,' said the voice. He sounded genuinely despondent.

'Wait,' she said. 'You haven't asked about your grand-father.'

'But he's dead.'

'How do you know?'

'You said just now that you were a widow.'

Of course she had. How stupid of her. She could hear Jack's voice again. *'You need to be more careful, Vanessa.'*

She could also feel herself getting more and more muddled.

'So why are you contacting me?'

'I don't know, really. To find my roots, I suppose. Look, maybe this is a mistake. Let's just leave it. Like I said, Mum would go nuts if she knew I was talking to you. When I suggested trying to find you, she went berserk and said you were nothing to us.'

Nothing?

She couldn't help feeling hurt even though Lewis's mother couldn't possibly be her daughter. Could she?

'I'll go now,' he said quietly. 'I don't blame you for not believing me. I could be a nutter for all you know.'

'Wait,' she heard herself saying. 'Yes. I mean yes, I'd like to meet you.'

Well, she had to, didn't she, Vanessa told herself. If only to rule out the remote possibility that any of this was true.

His voice lifts. 'Oh, I'm so glad. Are you free on Friday? One o'clock?'

'Yes,' she said, trying to think of her court diary.

'I'll be outside Marks & Spencer in Exeter.'

'You live near me?' she said in surprise.

'Not that far. I didn't know either until I tracked you down. Ironic, isn't it? Or maybe it's fate.'

Fate? Was that possible? It all seemed a little bit too convenient. Vanessa didn't know whether to feel terrified or excited, but Jack was roaring in her head now, hurting her ears, *'Put the phone down now.'*

So she did.

25

Robbie

Bruce is a very pale, thin man. He doesn't look like a murderer. He merely nods at Robbie when he comes in and then gesticulates towards the bottom bunk.

Robbie isn't sure if his new cellmate means he wants Robbie to sleep there or whether the bottom bed is Bruce's.

He looks at the guard for guidance but the door has slammed behind him.

Bruce stands and stares, as though appraising him from top to bottom. Robbie wants to wee. He is more scared than when he had performed in front of a certain head of state at the Royal Albert Hall. He has a sudden, urgent need for Irena to hold him. To say it will be all right. But it won't. It can't be.

His legs are wobbling so much that he feels as if he might keel over. He staggers towards the chair in the corner of the room and sits down.

Bruce shakes his head. 'Mine,' he says firmly.

Robbie stands up quickly. There's nowhere else to sit.

There isn't a basin or a toilet either, as far as he can see. As if reading his mind, Bruce points at a stained brown bowl under the bottom bunk.

'Have to share,' he says.

Is he kidding? This shouldn't be allowed. Robbie thinks of the various articles about prisons he'd seen, always turning the pages quickly to move on to lighter features.

'You should read that,' Irena had once said, noticing. 'It's interesting.'

But he couldn't because at the back of his mind was the fear that he might end up behind bars himself.

And now he has.

'You're the famous pop star,' says Bruce.

It's a statement. Not a fact.

'Yes,' says Robbie.

'Pretty girl,' says Bruce.

Robbie doesn't know if his victim was pretty; after the accident, he hadn't been able to bring himself to look at her picture. Now he can only imagine the publicity in the papers and online. At least here he can't see it even if he wanted to. Phones and computers are banned. Some prisoners have newspapers delivered but he hasn't got permission for this yet. If someone is reading at meal-times, he deliberately looks away from the headlines.

'Not pretty now,' says Bruce. 'You should see the pictures in today's *Express*.'

He frowns and takes a step towards Robbie. Then he puts his hand in his pocket. Robbie begins to shake.

What's he going to produce? A knife? A razor?

It's a pencil.

'Sign,' he says.

'Sign?'

He nods. 'Sign your name.'

Robbie has been asked for his autograph countless times over the years. But this feels different.

'What do you want me to sign?' he asks.

'The wall,' says Bruce, as if it's obvious. He indicates the section by the bottom bunk.

There are several names there already with dates next to them.

'Who are these people?' he asks.

He doesn't really want to make polite conversation but if he's going to be stuck in a cell with this man, he might as well try to get on with him.

'People I got rid of,' says Bruce solemnly.

Robbie feels his chest tightening. 'You killed them?'

'Not these ones. These are people who were in my cell until I made it so unpleasant for them that they had to be moved.'

'You hurt them?' croaks Robbie.

'Not physically.' He taps his head. 'Only in here. I talk a lot, you see. Drives people mad. You'll go crazy too.'

Robbie is already feeling that way.

'Sign,' says Bruce. His voice is louder now.

'I don't want to.'

'Sign.'

Robbie looks for an alarm bell. There isn't one.

He could refuse again but if he does, this man might attack him, even murder him. Robbie can't see a weapon, but anything seems possible right now.

Reluctantly, he squiggles a signature that might or might not be read as his name for posterity.

Bruce peers at it. 'Cool. Now write a message under it.'

Robbie feels his heart sink. 'What kind of message?'

Bruce grins again. 'How about this: "From one bad man to another"?'

So Robbie kneels down and does as he's told. Because it's true.

'What's with the scar, man?'

Bruce – who towers over him at six foot plus – is staring at the top of Robbie's head. It wasn't until his bald patch appeared in his early thirties that the scar from the accident – where he'd hit his head against the steering wheel – was exposed.

Robbie touches it awkwardly. 'Just something that happened to me as a child.'

But he hadn't been a child. He'd been eighteen. Old enough to know better. Another lie to add to all the others.

Then there's the sound of footsteps outside and something slides under the door. It's a scrap of paper addressed to him.

Remember, Robbie. We are watching you. And your family.

26

Vanessa

Somehow Vanessa managed to get herself dressed again and leave the changing room, even though she was shaking with nerves after the phone call from this Lewis.

'Any good?' asked the assistant.

Vanessa stared at her. 'Is what any good?'

'The dress.'

'Oh, no, thanks.' Then she looked down and realized it was hanging out of her bag. She must have stuffed it in there with her phone in her confusion.

'Goodness. I'm so sorry.'

She went bright pink. The sales assistant looked at her. Her expression hardened. 'It was an accident,' Vanessa said. 'I used to be a store detective myself. I'd never dream of taking anything.'

'Sure.'

As she left, she heard the girl say to a colleague, 'You never can tell, can you? Funny. She seemed so genuine when she came in.'

Vanessa would usually have been mortified, but right now her head was whirling. How could she possibly have a living daughter? Her mind went back, as it so often did, to that terrible night and Jack's words. '*Vanessa love, I'm sorry. But . . . but the little mite was so premature that she couldn't breathe.*'

Then her phone rang.

'Is something up?' asked Judge's voice. 'I had a missed call from you.'

'Yes,' she said. 'I wondered if I could run something past you.'

'Can you meet me in my chambers at around six o'clock?' He had his work voice on.

'Thanks,' she replied, relieved that he could fit her in. She had to tell someone, and Judge was the only person she could trust.

Then she caught the bus back to Exeter and made her way home towards the bungalow that she and Jack had bought fifty years ago. As she turned into their road, though, something made her turn back. Round the corner. Up another road. Into the graveyard of the church where she and Jack had been married. Where his ashes had been buried.

She knew the wording off by heart: *Jack Grossmith. Loving husband. Always missed, never forgotten.*

'We don't really have a grown-up daughter, do we, Jack? We couldn't have. Our daughter was stillborn because she was so premature. That's what you said.'

Tears blurred her eyes. 'You told me not to look at her because it would upset me too much. I was in such a state that I thought you were right. Remember how I told you later that I wished I had? But you said that the midwife had "disposed" of her.'

They did that in those days. Nowadays babies have proper funerals, even if they're premature. (She'd read a feature about that recently in a magazine. It had made her feel sad and envious.)

Right now, Vanessa's body was wracked with such emotion that she could barely draw breath. She just wept and wept, her hand against Jack's headstone as if he was squeezing hers back; assuring her that of course he hadn't misled her so cruelly.

'I don't believe you lied,' she whispered when she finally made the tears stop, 'because I love you. But if you *did* lie to me, Jack, we're over. I swear it on your stone. And you can yell at me all you like but I won't change my mind.'

He didn't answer.

If someone or something annoyed him, Jack sometimes went into a sulk. Usually, she would jolly him out of it so that he spoke to her again. But not today.

So she turned and left him.

Judge was ready for her, even though she was early. Vanessa hadn't been able to wait any longer.

'Would you mind shutting the door behind you?' he said.

He sounded very formal. Then again, he had to. They couldn't afford any gossip. Not that there was anything to gossip about, of course. But, as he said, a platonic relationship is sometimes the hardest one to explain.

You could say that again. Vanessa had often wondered what on earth it was that made Judge want to be friends with her. An ex-store detective. A witness service volunteer. A widow without the education that he must have had. It didn't add up.

'It's partly because you say what you think,' he'd said when she'd asked him. 'In my position, people usually tell me what they assume I want to hear.'

She could talk so easily to him too, and now out it came: the letter signed *With love from your grandson*; the phone call from Lewis and how he'd got her number. And then his claim that his mother was her daughter and that she was still alive.

'Did you see the child when she was born?' asked Judge.

'No,' she gulped. Then she told him about her fall on the cliff; how she went into labour early and how Jack had called the midwife for help.

'Can you give me the date of the birth?'

It was engraved on her heart.

Judge put on his glasses (a new pair, she noticed, in a fetching pale brown tortoiseshell), and switched on his computer. 'There are some things I can access that aren't available to the general public,' he said slowly. 'It's one of the perks of the job. Let's see . . .'

Vanessa sat opposite him, on the edge of the big black leather visitor's chair with studs round the front (which wasn't particularly comfortable, if she was honest), waiting. Butterflies fluttered in her stomach. What was he searching for?

Eventually he took off his glasses and rubbed his eyes. He reached across the desk and took her hand. Judge had never done that before. His hand was big. It wrapped round hers like a warm parcel.

'Vanessa,' he said. 'I've found her records. You had a daughter. And she lived. Her name is Molly. She is forty-nine years old and she has one child. A boy. He's called Lewis and he's twenty-eight.'

27

Vanessa

In her dreams, Vanessa often walked along the beach with a small child. Usually, it was a little girl called Sandra, though sometimes it was a George. If they weren't on the beach, she would be reading a bedtime story to her son or daughter. This didn't just happen at night but in daydreams too, when she'd sit and imagine because this helped to ease a pain that had never gone away.

Down the years, she'd plastered over her grief by looking after Jack, going to work and then her witness service volunteering. But now Lewis's letter and phone call had brought it all back.

'I have a daughter?' she whispered.

Judge's voice was soft. 'She was adopted by a couple called Evans. She got married when she was twenty. She's divorced and Lewis is her only child. They are listed as living together locally. Unfortunately, there's no address.'

Vanessa made a strange noise.

'Are you all right?'

He'd let go of her hand now.

'Yes. I think so.'

'How do you feel?'

'Happy. Excited. Confused. Angry.'

The words came rushing out of her mouth.

'It means Jack lied to me.'

'Sometimes,' said Judge softly, 'we tell lies to people we love because we are trying to protect them.'

'But what was he trying to protect me from?' she spluttered. 'He denied me my motherhood. I couldn't have another baby after that. We tried and tried. But now I know that we had . . . Molly . . .'

She faltered. The name didn't feel right after having 'Sandra' in her head for years.

Then she tried again. 'Now I know that we had Molly, it's different.'

'So what are you going to do about Lewis?' asked Judge.

'I'm going to meet him,' she said, surprising herself with her determined tone.

'Would you like me to come too? For support?'

Perhaps it was the anger, but she felt a new confidence flowing inside her. 'Thank you, but I think I need to do this on my own.'

'You're a good, kind woman, Vanessa,' he said as he stood up, indicating their time was over. 'Don't forget that. None of this was your fault. But sometimes life gives us the chance to make amends for other people's actions.'

He opened the door. Then he said in a loud voice. 'Thank you, Mrs Grossmith. I'm glad you feel able to continue. We appreciate your role as a witness service volunteer. The next case will indeed be challenging.'

Of course. He needed to explain to anyone who was passing why she was there.

Then she made her way to a café for a hot sweet tea, to treat her shock. When she'd gulped it down, she rang the most recent number on her call log. Surely this would show if Lewis was genuine. If he were a prankster, he wouldn't answer or it would go through to a different person. People could apparently be very clever with technology nowadays.

'Hello?'

He sounded so like Jack with that deep, husky tone, that it was almost uncanny!

'Is that Lewis?'

'Yes.' There was excitement in his voice.

'I just wanted to confirm our meeting on Friday,' she said.

28

Janie

Before Mum disappeared for ever, she did another practice run at drowning. She went into the sea when the red flag was up. Thank God, someone called the lifeguard and he got her out.

Mum claimed she'd hadn't seen the red flag and that she was 'strong enough to cope with a few high waves', but Dad wasn't having any of it.

'If you're going to try and bloody kill yourself, think of our daughter first, won't you?' he said. 'Not to mention the guard who risked his life for you.'

'Risked his life?' I asked, coming into the room after I'd been listening to all this from behind the door. 'What do you mean?'

'Nothing,' they replied simultaneously.

Then they sat down to watch TV, as if nothing had happened. Maybe I should have stayed in case it all kicked off again but the truth was that I just wanted to get out – away from all this. Besides, some girls at school had invited me to go to a gig in town.

'Be back by ten,' Dad ordered.

The others were already there when I arrived. I should say here that I wasn't one of those teenagers with a special friend or in a 'gang'. I just sort of hung on the fringe of some classmates who all knew each other really well but let me tag along.

I certainly wasn't in the 'cool set'. So I was pretty surprised when the singer of the band said 'Hi' to me at the bar where I was buying a Pepsi.

I was so embarrassed that I spilled it down my front.

'Let me get you another,' he said.

I could feel myself going very red. 'I'm all right, thanks.'

'No, honestly.'

I wanted to make small talk but I was too shy and he seemed to sense that.

'Are you local?'

'Yes,' I said. 'We're near the seafront.'

'That must be great.'

'It is. I swim almost every day.'

'Cool.'

I blushed. 'Where do you live?'

He named a town a few miles away. 'My family and I have lived there since I was born.'

'I thought pop stars lived on their own or with friends,' I heard myself saying.

He smiled but not in a 'don't be daft' way. It was a kind smile. 'I'm not a pop star yet.'

'Yet?' I repeated. 'But you want to be, right?'

'Yes, I do. What about you? What do you want to do in life?'

'I've applied for a job in publishing so I can learn all about books. Then I want to write a novel.'

'Wow, that sounds amazing.'

'I've never told anyone else about the novel bit,' I admitted.

'I'm flattered,' he said, smiling.

That made me feel bolder. 'I love the lyrics to your songs.'

'I wrote them.'

I sat forward in interest. 'Do you like poetry?'

'Definitely.'

Then we started discussing Keats. He was so easy to talk to. I liked him – he was modest, kind. He didn't just go on about himself, he wanted to know about me too. That's when the interval music started.

We danced together for a little while. It was a fast one but then went into a slower rhythm. I looked up and our eyes locked. This might sound like a cliché but it's the only way I can describe it.

His mouth came down towards mine and then stopped as if asking permission. I tilted my face up as if to say 'Yes'. And then he kissed me.

I should say here that I'd never been kissed before. His mouth felt surprisingly soft but at the same time, warm and loving and right, even though we didn't know each other. I wanted it to go on for ever.

Then someone with a red and blue tattoo and a straggly beard (ugh!) said he had to go back on stage. 'Get a move on, man, or I'll take your place.'

I didn't like the angry sound of this man's voice. It was as if he was jealous. I've described him as a man but he wasn't 'old, old'. More like in his twenties.

The singer clutched my hand as if he didn't want to leave me. Then this man dragged him back towards the stage. 'I'm Robbie, by the way,' he called as if I didn't know that already from the band introductions earlier. 'What's your –'

But his voice was swallowed up by the cheers for the second half.

Dad was very strict about curfews, so I had to leave before the gig ended. I felt so excited – and yet also anxious in case I didn't see Robbie again – that I couldn't sleep. I tried telling myself that the band might play again round here.

At least, that's how I remember that evening, but my head might have got it all wrong. Because then something happened that took my mind off everything else.

Not long after the gig, my mother walked into the sea again. And this time she didn't come back.

29

Robbie

That first night in prison, Robbie doesn't sleep. He tosses and turns on the upper bunk (Bruce had made it clear that he 'owned' the bottom bunk) and has nightmares in technicolour. It is always the same. *The van. The bike. The crunch.*

He's had them ever since the accident, but over the years, when Irena woke him and said he was having a bad dream again, he always pretended it was about something different.

And now there are the threatening notes to worry about. Was it Jacob? Or one of the others in the band? None of them would want the truth to come out. But if so, where were they?

On the other hand, it might be a disgruntled fan trying to weird him out. Usually his fan mail was of the *We love you, Robbie!* variety, though occasionally he got messages telling him that his music was 'crap'. But no one had actually threatened him or his family before.

Which narrows the odds to one. That's if he's right. And he might not be. After all, that person wouldn't want the truth to come out either.

Whoever the writer is, Robbie isn't sure if he should warn Irena or whether that might spook her. Yet how can he, if he isn't able to ring her or arrange a visit? Robbie wants to scream, using words he doesn't allow from his kids' mouths, let alone his own. Why is communication so fucking awful in prison? It isn't civilized. It isn't safe. Supposing someone, right now, is forcing their way into his home and attacking his family?

'Stop beating your pillow like that. You're doing my head in,' thunders Bruce from below.

At 6:30 a.m. there's a loud electronic bleep and a clicking sound from the door.

His cellmate springs out of bed within seconds.

'Where are you going?' asks Robbie.

'The washroom, mate. You need to be fast.'

Robbie soon sees why. Within minutes, a long queue has formed of men with towels round their waists and bare chests, even though it's 'fucking freezing' as one of them puts it.

People are looking at him, nudging each other. Others are more vocal.

'Bet your fancy house has got better bathrooms than this.'

And, 'Give us a song then, Robbie.'

He doesn't tell them that he can't sing anymore. Not since the police knocked on his door.

'Yeah. How about something from *Death on the Road*?' someone sniggers.

'That's no laughing matter,' snarls another. 'My sister's lad got killed by a drunk driver.' He eyeballs Robbie. 'Scum like you should be stoned.'

I wasn't drunk, Robbie wants to say, but instinct tells him to keep quiet in case he provokes more anger.

Then, when it's his turn, the man whose nephew died,

barges past and hijacks his place. *Don't say anything*, Robbie tells himself.

When the man comes out, he knocks sideways into Robbie, elbowing him hard. Again, Robbie forces himself to ignore it. At last, he's in. The water is lukewarm, and dribbles rather than gushes, but at least it's a chance to get clean.

Oh my God. What is this? Robbie can feel something squidgy under his right foot. He looks down. It's brown. To his horror, he realizes it's a turd.

'Enjoying the bath bomb, I left yer, are you, Robbie?'

There's a wave of laughter. Clearly, they're all in on it.

Robbie tries to wash it off but he hasn't got a flannel. He has to use his hands and the muck has gone into his fingernails. The water is now freezing cold. Then his towel, which he'd hung on the wobbly hook inside the shower, falls into the brown soggy mess. Unless he wants to get out starkers and walk naked back to his cell, he has no option but to put the soiled towel round his waist.

'Bloody hell, he smells worse than when he went in,' snorts a young inmate.

'It's the smell of the devil,' says a man with piercing blue eyes.

'You won't get a clean towel for a week,' says the officer outside curtly.

'This isn't humane.'

'You're the one who's not humane,' hissed the man whose nephew had been killed in a hit and run. 'What kind of bastard doesn't stop when he drives into a young girl?'

Robbie winces.

'Don't act all high and mighty, Lee,' spits another. 'How many young girls did you rape?'

'Fuck off. They got the wrong man.'

'Sure they did.'

'Say that again and I'll –'

A bell sounds. 'Roll call,' says the officer. 'Cool it off, lads, and get dressed quick or you'll get a strike. Three and you lose a privilege.'

'What kind of privilege?' asks Robbie, desperately hoping he won't lose his visiting rights. He couldn't cope if Irena wasn't allowed to see him.

'Breakfast for starters.'

'That can't be allowed,' he hears himself saying. Perhaps he shouldn't be talking to the guard like this but prison is so confusing. Some rules are explained. Others aren't until you've broken them. It's like finding your way through a maze.

'You'd be surprised, Manning, what can and can't be allowed in prison. After the delights of cold toast this morning, you need to get to work. You're on toilets, remember.'

'Yeah. Watch out for more shit,' someone laughs.

By the time it gets to lunchtime, Robbie has thrown up three times. He has washed his hands so often that they are red raw. His voice is sore with stress and grief. The voice that made his fortune is now his downfall. If he wasn't famous, he wouldn't be getting this treatment.

If only he could speak to Irena again. But apparently his requested numbers for the phone card still haven't been approved and today's officers won't let him make any more calls.

'I want to see the governor,' he says.

'Hear that, Joe? Mr Manning wants to see the guv. Which one do you want? Let's see. There's number one guv. He's the top man. Then there's two, three, four and five.'

'Any of them,' snaps Robbie. His blood is boiling now. 'I want to complain that I'm not allowed to ring my wife. If you don't let me, my lawyer will be telling the press how you're treating me.'

The two officers exchange looks. 'Go on, then. You've got three minutes and we're staying here next to you. No funny stuff like arranging an escape.'

Robbie ignores what he presumes is a joke. There's no escaping this place. He dials his home number.

'Irena?'

'Robbie?'

She sounds frightened.

'Are you all right?' he asks desperately.

'No,' she says. 'We are not. There is hate mail. People knock all the time on the security gates and ring the intercom. They are shouting nasty things about you. Someone threw a stone through a window at the back of the house.'

'How did they get into the grounds?'

'I don't know.'

His heart thumps. He wants to tell her about the threatening notes but she's scared enough already, and, besides, the guards are listening. It might even have been one of them who put the note under his door. 'I need to find you somewhere safe to go,' he says. 'But I'm not allowed to contact anyone. They only allowed me to ring you because I kicked up a fuss. Try Paul or Yasmine. They might be able to help.'

He feels helpless. A useless husband and father.

'There is something else, Robbie. Your agent calls. He says he cannot represent you anymore. The record people too. They say that if you go to jail, they are cancelling the next album and tour and terminating your contract.'

Robbie feels his world sinking. He knew this would come eventually but the probability that he'll never make music again is like a punch in the stomach.

Yet none of that's as important as his family. 'I need to see you,' Irena,' he pleads.

'I apply for the visiting paperwork but it has not come in yet.'

'I'll ask at this end,' he says desperately. 'Are the children all right?'

'No. The kids at school, they are horrible to them. They say bad things.'

His chest tightens. 'I'm sorry.'

'Why, Robbie? Why didn't you call the ambulance after the accident?'

His throat is almost too choked to speak. 'I thought she was dead.'

'But you were wrong. The papers say that if you had, that girl's life could have been different.'

How can he tell her the truth? He'd made a promise to the old man, hadn't he? If he breaks that, his family could be hurt. Besides, this isn't a private place to speak. The officer puts his hand on the phone.

'That's it, Manning. Your time is up.'

30

Vanessa

Friday at one o'clock outside Marks & Spencer in Exeter, Lewis had said.

But the hours and minutes went so slowly before she left the bungalow that Vanessa found herself looking at her phone every few seconds in case he'd changed his mind. She didn't want that. In fact, it wasn't until now that she realized that it would finish her off if he cancelled. Devastate her entirely. Wreck this artificial 'I'm fine' life she'd built up for herself over the years by destroying this hope he'd given her.

He was her grandson!

'*But you don't know for certain,*' said Jack in her head.

'Shut up,' she said, turning one of their 'couple photographs' upside down on her mantelpiece so his face couldn't smile at her anymore. 'You don't get a say in this. Not after you lied to me.'

Vanessa wouldn't have dreamed of speaking to Jack like that in real life. But then again, when he'd been alive, she wouldn't have dreamed he could have done what he had. She'd rather he had slept with another woman. Robbed a bank, even. But to take her child from her – that was wicked. Cruel. Unforgivable.

Now she had another chance.

She checked the time again. What if he doesn't turn up? Perhaps she shouldn't have been so formal when she'd told Lewis that she wanted to 'confirm' their appointment. But she'd been nervous. That sometimes made her voice sound stiff. He might have interpreted it as cold and told himself not to bother with a grandmother who was so offhand.

Please, no. She couldn't bear that.

Vanessa was in such a spin that her thoughts kept rushing around as if they didn't know what to do with themselves. Stupid inconsequential things insisted on thrusting themselves into her head; things that didn't matter, like what she should wear.

Nothing too bright, because that might suggest she saw this as a day out in town instead of meeting her grandson for the first time. Honestly, if it wasn't for Judge finding the evidence online, she'd never have believed any of this in a month of Sundays.

What would Lewis be like? He'd said he looked a bit like Jack in the photo he'd found and he certainly sounded like him.

But what she really wanted to know was what her grandson was like on the inside. He'd sounded very polite on the phone. He sounded caring too. He didn't want to upset his mum. That was good, wasn't it?

Then her phone rang, sending her into spasms of panic, thinking it was Lewis cancelling. But it was Judge. 'I could still come with you, if you've changed your mind?'

'No, thanks,' she said, thankful that it was only him. 'That's very nice of you but I've a feeling this is something I need to do on my own.'

'I understand that,' he said.

She'd known he would. Finding out that Jack had hidden this huge secret for all those years had made Vanessa feel even more determined that she wasn't going to rely on another person ever again. How could she trust anyone after this? Apart, of course, from Judge.

Despite her earlier dismissive thoughts about what she was going to wear, Vanessa found herself dilly-dallying in front of the mirror, trying on one outfit after the other. The blue pencil skirt looked like she was trying to be twenty years younger. Let's face it, she hadn't worn it for years but it was there because it still fitted her. Vanessa couldn't bear to throw away clothes. Some still had their price tags on them. They'd become an obsession.

She'd told Jack she needed to look good because of her job but now she realized it was because she was desperate to be a different woman from the one whose baby had died and had never managed to have another. Jack seemed to accept their childless situation. Not like her.

'You've always had your heart pinned to your sleeve, love,' said her mother in a letter from Tenerife after one of Vanessa's 'I don't know how to cope without children' letters. 'But if you want to keep your marriage going, you'll just have to get on with it.'

Mum was known for being tough, perhaps because she'd lost her own parents in the Blitz. But she had a point. Vanessa needed to be jolly, almost as if not having kids had been her choice. But it was so difficult.

'*Do you have children?*'

How many times had she been asked that question over the years? Vanessa was not a violent woman – of course she wasn't – but sometimes she felt she could punch the next person who asked that on the nose.

Now if someone asked her, she could say, 'Yes, I do. A daughter.'

How amazing was that?

In the end she was late leaving the bungalow. She had to run to get the bus and even then she had to hurry down Exeter's high street, avoiding the 'end-of-summer sales' crowds.

'We'll try one more shoe shop,' she heard a woman saying, rushing past holding a little girl's hand. 'But we've got to find something you like before school starts.'

Vanessa winced. That could have been her. She could have been buying Molly new shoes and a school uniform all those years ago if Jack hadn't cruelly given her away.

Her heart was beginning to pound now. It banged inside her like a stone swinging from a string. She was almost at Marks & Spencer. Would Lewis be outside? How would she recognize him? She should have asked for more details.

And then she saw him. The initial stab of disappointment that he hadn't brought her daughter with him was followed by the shock of his appearance. This was a younger Jack. Tall. Slim. Hands in pockets (except that this young man's trousers were denims; Jack had hated jeans, declaring they were for 'slobs'). A nose that was slightly Roman, giving him an imposing manner. He was looking around with that same expression that Jack used to have. A searching look that said '*I don't miss anything*'.

Yet there was also something peculiarly vulnerable about this young man's face. It took a second for Vanessa to recognize it. Of course! It was fear. Fear trying to pretend it wasn't fear. Didn't she know all about that?

It must, she realized, have taken guts for him to have contacted her. He was also risking his mother's fury. Just as she was risking Jack's, who was still bawling in her head. '*You're making a big mistake, girl. Leave it. Go home.*'

'Get lost!' she heard herself say.

The young man turned round. Vanessa went red. 'No,' she said. 'I didn't mean you. I . . . Dear God.'

She stopped because the resemblance close-up was uncanny. 'You have your grandfather's nose,' she said. And then, to her embarrassment, she burst out crying. 'I'm so sorry,' she wept.

But she couldn't stop. The tears just came and came. People were looking. She heard her breath gasping. Then she felt a tissue in her hand. Not just a square of loo paper, which people always seemed to use nowadays. This was a proper tissue from a packet that Lewis was holding out to her.

'It's all right,' he said. Then he put his arm around her as if they already knew each other and shepherded her inside. 'Let's go upstairs to the restaurant, shall we? You can go to the Ladies and sort yourself out while I find us a table.' His eyes locked with hers. 'Then we can finally get to know each other.'

'I'd like that,' she whispered.

His eyes were still on hers. 'So would I.'

While she was trying to calm down in her cubicle (she could hear an irritated queue forming outside), Jack kept going on and on. '*Get evidence, Vanessa. Make him show you some proof. This young man could be anyone.*'

'But he's not', Vanessa hissed. 'He's our grandson. He looks like you.'

Jack went silent after that. Someone knocked on the door. 'Are you all right in there, love?'

'Yes, thanks,' she called out. 'Just coming.'

Vanessa washed her hands and stared with horror at the mirror over the basin. How could she meet her grandson with streaked mascara? Quickly, she got her face wipes and make-up case out of her bag before running a brush through her hair.

Where was he sitting? Her eyes skirted the tables. Once. Twice.

He'd gone. She knew it. She'd wasted that precious chance by going to the Ladies. He'd suggested it, hadn't he? Maybe he'd taken one look at her and decided he didn't want a hysterical grandmother after all. That she wasn't worth upsetting his mother for.

She'd lost him. Frightened him off. And now she'd never find her daughter.

How could life be so cruel?

'This is your fault, Jack,' she burst out crying, to the clear dismay and shock of the shoppers around her. 'If it hadn't been for you, none of this would have happened.'

Then she sank down to the floor of the restaurant and wept.

31

Vanessa

As she sobbed, she felt a hand on her shoulder. 'Vanessa,' Lewis said. 'Are you all right?'

Relief and shame in equal measure shot through her as he helped her to her feet. 'I thought you'd gone,' she sobbed, 'just as I'd found you.'

He gave her a hug. A hug!

'I'm so sorry you're upset. I understand this is all a shock. I found us a table just here.'

That table? In her distress, she must have gone past it without noticing him. Just as she might have walked past him in the streets over the previous years, without knowing. Maybe his mother – her own daughter – had even been there. Tearfully she hung on to his arm as he led her to the table. 'I'm sorry about getting so upset,' she said, sitting down gratefully. 'It's because I'm furious with my husband for telling such a wicked lie about my baby.'

He nodded gravely. 'It was a dreadful thing to do.'

'I've got so many questions,' she sniffed, 'that I don't know where to start.'

'So have I,' he said. 'But let's have that cuppa first, shall we? I got you a slice of Dundee cake too.'

'My favourite! How did you know?'

'I didn't. But it's mine, so . . .'

The cake looked delicious, but she couldn't eat anything. Her unanswered questions were too important. 'I want you to tell me exactly how all this started. Step by step.'

'Of course.' He was looking at her straight, directly in her eyes. 'I was going through some old documents at the house. Mum needed help with clearing stuff out from my grandparents' house. Her adoptive parents, I mean. She gets tired easily because of her breathing problems.'

'Breathing problems?' she repeated.

'She's always been chesty because she was born so premature, but she manages really well.'

His voice trailed off and Vanessa looked away because the pain and the guilt were rising up again and she didn't know how to manage them.

'I'm sorry.' He looked as though he was going to reach out and touch her hand before thinking better of it and withdrawing his arm. 'I didn't mean to upset you even more.'

'It's all right,' she said thickly. Then, to give herself some time, she added 'Do you live with your mum?'

'For now, yes. I've been on gardening so I've been giving her a hand.'

'Gardening leave?'

He nodded. 'I'm an accountant. I've just got a new job, but because it's in a similar field to my old one, I've had to wait six months before I could start. They've been paying me, so . . .'

Goodness! Vanessa had never heard of this before. 'That sounds marvellous.'

'*Cushy, you mean*,' growled Jack in her head. '*These pen pushers have it easy.*'

She ignored him. An accountant! That was really something.

'Then I came across this file with my mum's birth certificate in it.'

Vanessa gave a little moan.

'There were medical papers referring to all the problems she'd had when she'd been born prematurely, like respiratory issues. One referred to her "astonishing recovery". There were also medical records from the hospital where she had to stay for three months . . .'

'Three months?' Vanessa gasped, picturing this poor little thing lying in the neonatal unit, tubes poking out of her, all without her mother by her side.

Lewis's voice tightened. 'Then she was fostered by a couple for a year and after that she was adopted by another family.'

Vanessa's eyes blurred. What kind of emotional scarring would that leave on a child?

'I always thought my mum's parents were my natural grandparents,' said Lewis wistfully. 'Mum had never said she was adopted. She wasn't very pleased when I told her I'd found the papers and asked her why.'

'And why didn't she?'

'She said she was ashamed and wanted to pretend it had never happened. But that's not all. There was also a letter in the file from a man called Jack Grossmith, who described himself as the 'baby's father'.'

Vanessa's mouth dried. So Jack had written a letter to their baby's adoptive parents while pretending to her that their child had died. The bastard.

'What did he say?' she whispered.

He reached inside his jacket and brought out an envelope. 'You can read it if you like.'

Shaking, she drew out the sheet of paper. There was her husband's large, almost childish sloping writing.

My wife and I have reluctantly decided that we cannot look after our daughter.

'That's a lie!' she burst out. 'It sounds like a joint decision, but he didn't tell me.'

'Please,' said Lewis. 'Read the rest of it.'

When our daughter was born, she was very tiny due to her prematurity and she didn't cry. We thought she was dead. Then, when I was comforting my wife, who had understandably become hysterical, the midwife managed to revive her but told us that she didn't think the child would live more than a few hours. She took her to hospital, where doctors confirmed she was unlikely to survive. She had multiple organ failures and breathing difficulties. I visited daily, but was told that a lack of oxygen at birth might well have led to cerebral palsy or other complications and that we wouldn't know for certain until she was older. My much-loved brother had suffered brain damage at birth. He was everything to me but I did not want my wife to go through the terrible worry that I remember as a child. So we have made this difficult decision, in the hope that she will be adopted one day. I am writing this because I want our daughter to know that she was loved by her parents. We are sorry to have let her down.

Vanessa flung the letter on the table. 'We? *We?* Lewis, please believe me, I knew none of this. He must have taken the decision for me because he knew I'd never have let our daughter go.'

The women at the next table were staring but Vanessa didn't care. 'You do believe me, don't you?'

Lewis didn't answer. His eyes had gone cold, just like Jack's used to. One minute warm, the next disapproving. She'd had to manage that all her life. And now she was seeing it across the table.

'The irony is that Mum pulled through. Apart from her weak chest, you'd never think she'd had any problems.'

Fuck you, Jack! The swear word took her by surprise but she couldn't help it. Yes, it had been hard for him trying to look after his brother, but he should have allowed her to make the decision too. As for special needs, well they'd have managed. She would have coped with anything if it meant having a child of her own.

'But I didn't know that then,' said Vanessa. 'I just believed what my husband told me.'

Lewis's eyes were still hard. 'But there are two signatures on the adoption papers. His and yours.'

'Then he must have forged mine. I remember him getting me to sign something but Jack said it was part of the . . . the disposal arrangements.'

'So you had a funeral?'

'No.'

She was beginning to feel more and more stupid now. Actually, worse than stupid. As though she was lying. When she wasn't.

'Jack said he didn't want a stone for us to grieve by. He said it would make the pain worse.'

'And you went along with that?'

That prickly heat feeling that she always used to get when Jack challenged her was starting. 'It was a different era, Lewis. You've got to believe me. Things have changed so much in the world.'

He looked away silently and a cold feeling snaked round Vanessa's heart. Had she just found her grandson only for him to push her away?

'Did your mum have a good childhood?' she asked haltingly.

'Oh, yes.' His eyes were back on her now. 'Her adoptive parents treasured her.'

Was there an unsaid 'when you didn't'?

'And she got married . . . ?'

'Yes, although she and my dad broke up when I was three. It was messy. She reverted to her maiden name and changed mine too. I suppose that's why I'm so protective of her.'

'Do you still see him, your dad?'

'No.'

There was another silence. She needed to fill it or he might leave.

'Your grandfather – my husband – died three years ago,' she said.

'After what you've told me about him rejecting my mum, you'll have to forgive me for not shedding any tears,' he said coldly.

'I get that,' she gulped.

He made a 'really?' face. 'I'm sorry but I don't think anyone can get it unless they've been adopted. It made you stand out in those days. People knew. They whispered. Made fun of her, sometimes. Mum always said she felt different. It can't be easy to go through life knowing that the people who gave you breath didn't want you.'

Tears were beginning to run down Vanessa's face again. 'But I would have wanted her if I'd known she was alive. Is that why you tracked me down? To tell me how angry you are?'

'I can understand why you might think that, but it's not the reason.'

'*I told you,*' said Jack. '*He's after your widow's pension and the bungalow.*'

'Is it money you want?' she blurted out.

'Money? Is that what you think?' He looked wounded. 'Why would I want your money? I earn plenty. I've just told you. I'm an accountant.'

'I'm sorry,' she said. 'But why exactly did you get in touch?'

'To find out why you gave my mum away and . . .'

He stopped.

'What?'

'I don't know. To see what you looked like, I think,' he said, more softly this time.

A tear was running down his face now. 'The thing is, Vanessa, that this might sound daft at my age. But when I found out about you and Jack, I was curious as well as angry. I wanted to ask you how you could have done this. And now, after hearing your side of the story, well . . .'

He paused.

'Well, what?' asked Vanessa in a whisper.

He gave her what seemed like an almost-shy look. 'Well, now I'd like to get to know you better.'

32

Janie

The memory I can't remember is still niggling away in my head. I'm glad of it because I want to distract myself from the pain.

Not just the pain that is wracking my body.

But the pain of losing Mum.

I didn't believe Mum had gone for good. That's what everyone said. But I knew better.

She had to be out there somewhere. Mum wouldn't have left me like that. She couldn't have.

On the day she disappeared for good, I swam up and down; again and again.

The coastguards scoured the beaches and sea. The lifeboat went out. So did the seaplanes.

Searching. Searching.

Three police cars turned up.

People huddled in groups silently. Pointing to the sea. Walking up and down the beach. Glancing at me every now and then.

My dad's eyes were red and raw. 'I'm sorry, Janie, but we've got to accept it.'

Then I heard him talking to one of the police officers.

'Depression . . . Ask the doctor . . . Done it before . . . We've tried . . .'

After that, the policeman wanted to interview me. 'Do you know why your mum was depressed?'

He seemed a kind man. His name was Detective Inspector Grossmith, although he said I could call him Jack.

'No,' I said. 'She always seemed quite happy to me.'

'We found an empty bottle of pills under your mother's pillow. Do you know what happened to them?'

A flash of fear shot through me. 'Of course not,' I said.

If Mum had taken an overdose and then gone into the sea, she might find it difficult to get out. But it wasn't impossible.

My only remaining hope was that they hadn't found a body.

'That means she must still be alive then,' I said.

'I'm afraid not,' said Dad. 'If people go missing at sea, it can take ages for them to turn up. Sometimes they never do.'

'That doesn't mean they won't,' I said.

He gave me a hug. 'It's OK, Janie. We'll manage.'

But we didn't. Otherwise, I might not be here now, in the road with blood pooling on the ground beside me.

That's when I hear something.

At first I think someone is screaming. Then I realize it's a siren.

'I'm here,' I try to say. 'Help me. Please, I need to live. I can't die – not before I've found my mother.'

33

Robbie

How much longer does he have to wait in this hellhole?

'The court schedules are running behind because of illness,' says the lawyer when she comes to visit him. He's going crazy with the not-knowing and his phone card still hasn't arrived. It's been six days since he spoke to Irena.

'Why are you allowed to visit and my wife isn't?'

'Paperwork is being delayed for non-legal visits.' She gives a small sigh. 'Prisons aren't always as organized as one might hope.'

Yasmine seems kinder than before. Maybe it's because she's shocked by his appearance. When Robbie stares at himself in the cracked mirror of the communal bathroom, he looks older. Drawn. Haggard. His eyes are bloodshot. His hair is greyer and thinner. His once upright posture has been replaced by a dejected slouch.

How can all this happen in three weeks? He looks more like his elderly dad had done than his thirty-eight-year-old self.

'I need to know my wife and children are all right.'

'They've been taken to a safe house,' says the lawyer. She looks uneasy. 'Someone climbed over the wall the day before yesterday and painted "JUSTICE FOR JANIE" on the side of the house.'

'What?'

'A conservatory window was also smashed while the children were in there,' she continues. 'Irena called the police, who came round immediately, but the culprit got away. No one was hurt, but they were all obviously shaken. I'm sorry.'

His stomach is freefalling with shock and horror. 'Why didn't anyone tell me?'

'I left a message with the prison. Didn't you get it?'

'No. This is outrageous.' His hands are shaking with anger. His knuckles are white. 'Where exactly is my family?'

'You can't know.'

'But I *must* know.'

'It's better this way, Robbie. You might say something in your sleep. Your cellmate might hear. Or someone in here might force you to tell them. The fewer people who know, the safer they'll be.'

There's a short silence as he digests this. 'Thank you,' he says finally.

'That's all right.' Her voice softens. 'I understand how hard it is for you, Robbie, and for Irena and the children.'

'Do you? Have you ever been in this position?'

'No. But I've seen a lot of people who have.'

'It's hardly the same.'

'True. But it has given me experience in advising people on what to do and what not to do. I'm your lawyer, Robbie. I have your interests at heart.'

'Then . . .'

He stops.

'Then what, Robbie?'

I received a threatening note.

That's what he wants to say. But he daren't. She might tell the police. Word will get out. The sender of the note – if it's who Robbie thinks it is – might take it out on his family. It was just his style. He can't risk that.

'Why do I get the feeling that there's something you're not telling me, Robbie?'

The van. The bike. The crunch.

'I've told you everything.'

'Have you? You've said you thought Janie was dead and that you drove off. We can argue that you panicked at the time and now deeply regret your actions. But there might be some mitigating factors – something that means you could get out earlier to be with your family – if you can think of anything else.'

He's tempted. Oh, so tempted. But if he does, he knows that there is someone out there – the man whose name he doesn't dare to say out loud – who will harm the three people he loves most in the world.

'I'm guilty,' he bursts out. 'I deserve to be punished.'

'Guilt is more complicated than that, Robbie. It's never black and white. I can help you find the grey that might reduce your sentence. But I can only do that if you are totally transparent with me.'

'I don't want to talk anymore,' Robbie says. 'I've said all there is to be said. Just look after my family for me, Yasmine. Please.'

'I'll do my best, Robbie. You have my word on that.'

An hour later, he is called out to the exercise yard. Only the guard and one man from another wing go with him. Usually there's a crowd of them, jogging round in single file.

When the guard leaves, Robbie feels a tremor of apprehension.

The chap in front is going faster. So fast that he is sprinting round the yard, coming up behind him now.

The blow hits the back of his head with such force that his vision blurs. He is vaguely aware of the ground coming up towards him. He throws up. Blood comes out as well as vomit. So does one of his front teeth.

'That's a warning,' says the other man, chucking a stone on the ground. 'It comes with the compliments of someone you used to know. That person's also got a message for you. Keep quiet if you want to see your family again.'

34

Vanessa

Lewis wanted to get to know her better?

'I've always wanted a grandson,' Vanessa said, the emotion choking her throat. 'Or a granddaughter. And, of course, I was desperate for a child before that. Most of my friends had kids. I can't explain the terrible ache in my heart for all the years we spent trying for another baby, not knowing I had one the whole time.'

Her fists clenched under the table as she spoke. 'I would kill Jack if he wasn't already dead.'

'I'd feel the same if I was you,' says Lewis. 'Actually, it would be quite cool, having a gran behind bars.'

For a minute she thought he was serious. Then she saw the smile on his face. 'It's not a laughing matter, is it?' she said, trying not to giggle.

'No, it's not,' he agreed.

But then he began to laugh and so did she, and for a while, they just couldn't stop. 'We're like a pair of kids,' she said, and that's when her laughter turned to tears, because the last forty-odd years had all been such a waste.

'No, they haven't,' said Lewis when she blurted this out. 'It's never too late to start again.' His hand closed around hers. She gripped it gratefully.

Then he took his hand back and glanced at his watch.

'I'm really sorry but I have to go now. I promised to get some shopping for Mum. It's not good for her to carry heavy bags with her breathing issues.'

Vanessa's heart lurched. 'That's kind of you.'

'Not really,' he said. 'She's my mum. I'd do anything for her.'

Wasn't that what Molly might have been saying about Vanessa too, if Jack hadn't given her away? The pain was almost too much to bear.

'Have you got any photographs of her?' she asked.

Lewis clapped his hand to his jacket pocket. Vanessa thought he was going to say he'd left them behind but instead he said, 'I almost forgot to show you.'

Then he brought out his phone. Of course. This generation didn't do proper photos anymore, did they?

'Here she is, sitting in the garden. And there's another with her stroking the cat.'

Her daughter! This was her daughter! But she didn't look anything like her. Or Jack. Her hair was light brown – not blonde like hers or black like Jack's had been. She was small, in a delicate, petite way, with sharply outlined cheekbones.

Vanessa had expected to feel a rush of emotion but she didn't. Was that because of the guilt?

'She's got a nice smile,' she said.

'Mum's smile lights up her face,' said Lewis as if she'd said the right thing. 'But if she gets upset, she goes on and on about it. When I found her adoption papers, she was furious. Said I didn't have any right going through her private stuff and that you were nothing to her.'

Vanessa flinched.

'Sorry, but it's true. She'd kill me if she knew I was here with you.'

'But what if I met her and explained I didn't know anything about it?' she pleaded. 'Or if you told her?'

Lewis shook his head. 'She wouldn't believe me, Vanessa. I mean, it's a bit far-fetched, isn't it? A woman not knowing her baby was alive and then unwittingly signing adoption papers.'

His voice had developed a harsh edge. Maybe he was angry too – that was understandable.

Her throat thickened with sadness. 'Things were very different in my day,' she said. 'So much has changed now.'

'Certainly seems that way.' Lewis was looking at his watch again. 'I'm sorry but I really do have to go.'

'*Clever*,' said Jack in her head. '*He's bailing when you still want him to stay. Don't you see, Nessie? He's trying to keep you keen.*'

Her grandson was standing up and helping her to do the same. Even though she didn't need any help (thank you very much!) she appreciated the chivalry.

Then he hesitated. 'I don't want to leave you,' he said.

Thank goodness! For a minute, she'd thought that cold tone and his declaration that he had to go meant he didn't want any more to do with her. But now his attitude had changed again and he seemed genuinely caring. Still, wasn't that what happened when you'd been hurt?

'I don't want you to go either,' she said.

'Are you free next Tuesday?' he asked.

She could feel her own face falling. 'I'm afraid not. I've got to go to court.'

'Court?' he repeated. 'What have you done?'

'Nothing.' She laughed. 'I'm what's called a witness service volunteer. I accompany witnesses who feel a bit nervous about giving evidence. Show them where to go. That sort of thing.'

Of course, there was a lot more to it than that, but she didn't want to waste the few precious minutes they had left by talking about her work.

'How very noble of you.'

Was he being sarcastic? 'I just see it as giving something back.'

'I think that's amazing.'

No, he was genuinely impressed. Vanessa could feel herself blushing.

'How about Wednesday, then? We could have lunch at this great hotel I know. You'll love the views from the terrace.'

Vanessa's body was flooded with a happiness she hadn't known existed. 'That would be lovely,' she said.

'I could pick you up from your house.'

'How do you ... ?' Then she remembered the letter he'd sent.

'Number 60 Green Lane, isn't it?' He grinned. 'I've got a good head for names and figures.'

Vanessa's memory had become less sharp since Jack's death, but then again, this often happened after a loss. That's what the bereavement leaflet at her GP's surgery said. Still, this wasn't something she wanted to share with Lewis. Not now, anyway. Maybe when they got to know each other better.

Then Lewis gave her a lovely warm smile. 'This has been one of the best days of my life.'

Her eyes swam with tears. 'Mine too. I'm so sorry, dear, that Jack was so wicked.'

The 'dear' bit slipped out unintentionally. But he didn't seem to mind.

'It's not your fault,' he said, giving her a quick hug, which sent a wave of love – yes, love! – through her from top to bottom. 'Until Wednesday, then.'

35

Vanessa

Vanessa was a bit hurt that Judge hadn't rung so she could tell him about her meeting with Lewis. They had agreed long ago that she wouldn't phone him at work except in an emergency. When she rang his mobile in the evening, it went straight to voicemail.

The following morning, Vanessa was supporting a young man who was so nervous about giving evidence against his boss in a fraud case that she didn't know whether to hold his hand or tell him to get a grip. 'If you don't stand up against bullies, they win,' she said. 'Trust me, I know.'

'How?' he asked, his voice shaking.

Vanessa tried not to share personal information with the people she helped, but sometimes she couldn't stop herself. 'My husband was a bully and I should have stood up against him. He . . .'

She hesitated for a moment. 'He wouldn't let me see our daughter.'

He looked shocked. 'That's awful.'

'I know. But now that's all changed. My grandson is taking me out to lunch tomorrow,' she added proudly.

'That's nice,' he said.

'It is. But do you know what the best thing is? I've got

my self-worth back. Standing up against a bully can help you do that too . . . But I'm not trying to pressurize you.'

Yet as soon as the words came out of her mouth she realized that's exactly what she *was* doing.

'Look, I am going to give you some advice,' she continued quickly. 'Don't let yourself be trampled on.'

He fell silent, as if absorbing her words.

'Thanks,' he said, finally.

He gave his evidence confidently and the bullying boss was found guilty of inappropriate behaviour, resulting in a suspended jail sentence and a heavy fine. Relief was written all over her charge's face.

Vanessa had hoped the boss would go to prison. Supposing he tried to avenge himself on the young man who had given evidence? Or what if the newly self-assured young man tried to get his own back on the bullying boss? That awful experience with Tyler had shown her that you could never tell what someone was going to do.

She was still worried the following day when her grandson – how wonderful it was to use that word! – turned up outside her house in the flashiest car she'd ever seen.

Jack would've loved it. But unusually for him, he wasn't saying anything. Maybe he was jealous.

'How was court yesterday?' Lewis asked as they headed for the coast.

So she told him. 'It's not a dangerous job, is it?' he asked.

Vanessa was rather flattered by the concern in his voice. So he cared! 'No,' she said. 'Besides, I'd do it even if it was.'

Glancing across, she saw him nodding. 'It's important

that we do what's right.' Then she fell silent for a bit, thinking about Jack's behaviour.

'It wasn't your fault that Mum was given away,' he said, as if reading her thoughts. 'I've been thinking about what you said and it sounds as though you were married to a rather controlling man.'

'Maybe I was,' said Vanessa. 'But it didn't feel like it at the time. It was more like he was protecting me.'

'Hah!' snorted Lewis. 'I've come across plenty of blokes like that.'

'Where?' she asked curiously. How she wanted to know everything about her grandson's life!

'At work,' he replied in a clipped tone, suggesting he didn't want to discuss it. 'By the way, I told Mum that I'd tracked you down and that we'd met up.'

'You did?' she gasped. 'Was she as angry as you thought she would be?'

'Actually, she wasn't. She said that she understood why I was curious.'

Vanessa sat forward, her words tumbling over themselves. 'Will she agree to meet me, do you think?'

'I'm afraid not. She didn't buy your story about it all being your husband's fault. She thought you must have known something.'

'But I didn't!'

'I know, I believe you. Let's hope Mum changes her mind.'

Vanessa felt tears in her eyes but didn't want to spoil this precious time with her grandson. Besides, as Lewis said, maybe Molly would have a rethink. After all, this must be a big shock for her too.

But, as the car turned left down a steep hill, Vanessa's disappointment was replaced with a gasp of delight. 'What a view!'

Lewis sounded pleased. 'Just wait until you see the restaurant. It's amazing.'

Wow! It certainly was! He'd reserved a table that looked out over the sea. Someone was playing the piano in the corner. He told her to choose anything she wanted from the menu.

'I'll just have fish and chips,' she said shyly.

'What about the scallops?'

'But they're so expensive!'

He leaned towards her, brushing his arm against hers. It sent delicious tingles down her. How she'd have loved to have held him as a baby. To have held his mother too. Her daughter . . .

'I think they're good value, actually,' he insisted. 'Go on. I want you to have the best. You're my granny, after all.'

His granny! It felt so good to hear this!

'*Careful*,' said Jack in her head. '*He's spinning you along. Don't you see?*'

'*Rubbish*,' she retorted silently.

'I want to know all about you,' she said while they were eating. He dabbed his mouth delicately with a napkin, she observed. Clearly he had been brought up to have good manners.

'There's not much to tell. Like I said, it was just me and Mum from when I was three. Mum's parents were pretty old so they didn't play a big part in my life.'

Mum's parents.

The scallops suddenly stopped tasting quite so delicious as the guilt flooded in again.

'What about your work?' she said quietly. 'I'm very proud of having a mathematician in the family.'

'I've always liked numbers,' he replied. She could hear the passion in his voice.

'I don't think that particular gene came from my side,' she said, laughing. 'I was hopeless at maths.'

She didn't like to mention how good Jack had been. In fact, she tried hard not to mention him at all.

'Well, I think your genes are amazing,' said Lewis. 'You look too young to be my granny.'

'Nonsense,' she said blushing.

But when the waiter came to clear their plates, he asked whether 'your mum' would like a dessert.

Vanessa felt chuffed at that and, when Lewis drove her home, after leaving a generous tip, she was happier than she'd been for a very long time.

'I'd love to do this again,' said Lewis.

'So would I,' she said excitedly.

'My new job is keeping me really busy, but when I can, it would be great to take you out again.'

'I'm going to be pretty busy shortly myself,' she said, keen not to sound like one of those women who had nothing to do.

'Really?' said Lewis. 'Going away with your boyfriend, are you?'

She laughed gaily. 'I don't have one.'

'You surprise me!'

There was a ping on his phone. 'Sorry,' he said. 'I forgot

to put it on silent. It's just my news app . . . Wow! Robbie Manning has been attacked in prison.'

Something like a 'serves-him-right' thrill shot through her. 'Goodness! Is he all right?'

'It doesn't give any details.'

'Jack was on duty when his victim was run over,' she heard herself saying, despite her earlier resolution not to mention his name too often. But for some reason, she now felt the need to absolve him. If nothing else, her husband had been good at his job. 'He spent years trying to track down the person who did it.'

'I don't know how anyone can live with themselves when they've committed a terrible crime,' Lewis said, shaking his head.

'I agree. In fact, I was a bit disappointed when Robbie pleaded guilty. I'd rather hoped I might be needed if there was a trial. There was a possibility that Janie might be a witness.'

'But I thought she couldn't talk. How would she have given evidence?' he asked.

Vanessa leaned towards him. 'She can't talk, but apparently, she can sing!'

'What? That's extraordinary. How does that work, then?'

'She had a stroke – in fact she's had several – but after the last one, she burst out in song! Something to do with a new speech therapy, Carol said.'

'Who's Carol?'

Vanessa suddenly remembered that her supervisor had told her this in confidence. Oh dear! She'd got carried away in her enthusiasm. But it was so nice to be able to confide in someone about her job. Apart from her brief and sometimes infrequent chats with Judge, there was no one else to talk to now Jack had gone, and she'd never been one of those women who had close girlfriends. Jack had liked her to be at home when he was off duty.

'My boss,' she said. 'But I shouldn't really have told you,' she added hastily. 'I'd get into trouble at work for that.'

'Don't worry. I'll keep my mouth shut. Poor woman.'

Lewis's face darkened. It was only for a minute, but it reminded her of Jack. There was a definite similarity between the two. 'Blokes like Robbie Manning need to be banged up for a long time. At least, that's what we all used to say in the office. Anyway, I can't tell you how special this day has been for me. Even more than the last, because now we've got to know each other properly.'

'I feel the same,' she blushed.

Then he kissed her on her cheek, making her blush even more.

'See you soon, Granny. Can't wait for next time!'

36

Janie

No! The siren is fading. Don't go. I need you.

But it's not coming here. It's off to save someone else.

To be honest, the pain is so bad that if it weren't for the fact I have to find Mum, death would be a relief. It's as if someone's holding a red-hot iron against every part of my body.

I need to distract myself from this teeth-clenching agony – if I think about something really powerful, maybe I can replace it.

So I go back to before, back to when Mum 'drowned'.

At least, that's what they told me. But I've never believed a word of it. She was a strong swimmer. And despite that empty bottle of pills, I know she wouldn't have taken an overdose. Mum loves me too much. It had to have been one of her games, like before.

Since then, I've looked for her everywhere.

In town. On the bus. On the beach.

If she'd had friends to talk to, I'd have asked them. But Mum kept herself to herself.

She used to work in the library but had to stop because of the black clouds that kept coming into her head. 'You're the only one that makes the sun shine for me, Janie,' she used to say.

Dad put flowers on the cliff, above the spot where she was seen going into the sea.

But when we were clearing out Mum's things, I found something in one of her handbags – a receipt for an advance train ticket to Waterloo for the day she went missing.

'Look,' I said, rushing to Dad excitedly. 'She went to London instead!'

Dad gave me a quick hug. 'She probably bought it intending to go but didn't, love.'

Then I realized that the shell wasn't there. The one she kept by her side of the bed that matches mine.

'See that?' I said, pointing to the empty space. 'When you leave somewhere, you take your precious things with you. It proves she's not dead.'

'Janie, darling, she was seen walking into the sea. Perhaps she took the shell with her.'

I got angry then. 'She isn't dead, Dad. Why won't you listen to me? I just know she isn't.'

His voice had grown impatient. 'Then why did she walk into the sea all those times and give us scares? They were practice runs for going in and not coming out again. I'm sorry, but we have to accept the truth, Janie. I don't know how else to say this. Your mother killed herself.'

'But she didn't,' I yelled. 'She loves me. She wouldn't leave me.'

My mind forces itself back to the present. Mum wouldn't leave me any more than I can leave Dad. If I die now, who will he have left? I've got to hold on, in the middle of this road, even if the pain is killing me.

And that's when I hear a different kind of siren. It's getting closer. Yes! A police car has pulled up.

37

Robbie

Robbie told the guard that he'd tripped while running and hit his head on a loose stone that happened to be lying in the yard.

'You're sure of that?' asked the guard. 'We take prisoners' safety very seriously.'

'Quite sure,' he said.

He was beginning to know the rules. No one blagged to anyone – not unless they wanted to be beaten up again.

But the news got out anyway, crediting an 'unknown source'. Someone wanted it to be common knowledge. Perhaps it was the writer of the notes, sending out another warning.

'It's in the paper,' says Bruce the next morning. 'You'll be for it now.'

'I didn't tell anyone.'

'Course you didn't. You'd better watch out, mate.'

'Honestly I didn't.'

'Then maybe it was one of the guards, making a bit of money on the side. From a tip-off.'

Bruce fixes him with a stare that chills his very bones. 'You give me half your food at every meal and I'll put out the word that I'll protect you.'

Robbie never thought he'd make a deal with a murderer but he finds himself agreeing.

A week later, Robbie is told he has a visitor. It has to be Irena. His heart pounds. Desperately he tries to make himself look more like the old Robbie, but it's impossible.

The toiletries he'd ordered through the canteen list haven't arrived. He's aware that he stinks and that a beard doesn't suit him.

'You got a visitor?' asks Bruce, watching him comb his hair with his fingers. 'I haven't had one since 1985.'

Robbie tries not to think about the murders that must have led to such a long sentence.

'May I borrow your deodorant?' he asks.

Bruce seems to think about it. 'OK. Only one spray, mind.'

It's a cheap, sweet-smelling brand but it's better than stale sweat. Then it dawns on Robbie that he's just asked a murderer for a favour. His skin goes cold. What had he been thinking? Bruce will want something back now. That's how it works here.

He is led with the other prisoners into the visitors' room. There are individual tables with chairs like parents' evenings at the children's school. He slumps down on one, trying to pick a dried egg stain off his tracksuit bottoms.

The visitors file in.

So many people. No one he recognizes. Women. Men. Children. Please let Irena bring the children. On second thoughts, no. It would be too much for them.

Then he sees her. Tall and slim. Her lovely auburn hair flowing onto her shoulders. Dressed in expensive jeans and cowboy boots. She comes straight to him. His beautiful wife does not belong in a place like this.

She tries to kiss him. 'No touching,' warns the guard.

She sits opposite him. He blinks away the tears.

'You look older,' she says bluntly. One of the reasons he fell in love with Irena was that, unlike the fawning fans, or the agent who used to be so keen to please, or even the obsequious record-label people who had wanted to make sure no one else poached him, she spoke her mind. But is it his imagination or is she being cool with him now? There are no tears in *her* eyes.

'I *feel* older,' he says. 'But, please, I want to know about you and the children. My lawyer said they've taken you and the kids somewhere safe?'

She nods. 'It is OK, but it is not home.'

'I'm sorry,' he says, feeling dreadful that he has done this to them. 'Are the children all right?'

'They are coping.'

Her sentences are short and to the point. They often are, he reminds himself, but this feels different. Of course, it does. She knows he's a criminal now. It changes everything.

'I want you to hire a bodyguard.'

'No, Robbie. I am not having a stranger living with us. It will unnerve the children.'

'But it's not safe for you to be alone.'

'The police are outside. We are fine.'

Robbie had learned over the years that when Irena had made up her mind, that was it. He didn't want to upset her any more than she was already. She might refuse to have anything to do with him.

'How are they getting on at school?'

'They have moved to a different one. They are adjusting.'

But her eyes say otherwise.

'No one told me that! Do the other kids know who they are?'

'We use a different surname.'

'What is it?'

'I am not allowed to tell you.'

Not allowed to know his family's new name? 'I've ruined all your lives,' he sobs.

Irena leans forwards across the table.

'You ruined that girl's life,' she says. 'You ran into her and drove away. This is not the husband I know.' Her lips tighten. 'It makes me want to leave you.'

'No!' he cries. 'NO! Please.' He lets out a loud sob. Then he lowers his voice. 'There were reasons.'

'What reasons?' she says, a hopeful lilt to her voice.

'I can't say. It's too risky.'

Her face darkens. She stands up. 'If you cannot tell your wife, I definitely go.'

He leaps to his feet. Then he whispers in her ear. 'Irena, please, you have to understand. If I tell you, you'll be in even more danger. We might never see each other again.'

Her voice almost hisses. 'My family and I were in the worst possible danger when we travelled here all those years ago. I am not scared of anything, Robbie. So if you want me to stay, you'd better tell me everything.' She looks up, her violet eyes drilling into his. 'And I mean everything.'

38

Janie

At first, I think it's the same voices again. But these sound older. More official.

'Bloody hell. Look at all that blood.'

'And her face. Oh my God, her face.'

'Is she alive? She can't be, no one could survive that.'

They're scaring me. What do I look like?

'Can you hear me, love? What's your name?'

Another chips in. 'It's no good, Sarge. There's no pulse.'

'I'm alive! I can hear you!'

At least that's what I want to say. But once more, my lips won't move.

'Better record the time of death.'

'How long do you think she's been here?'

'We'll have to make do with the time now. The pathologist will need something.'

No. NO! What if they bury me or – God forbid – cremate me while I'm still alive?

'Someone's been drinking, Sarge. Look, there's an empty gin bottle in the gutter. I'll bag it up as evidence.'

A gin bottle? All of a sudden, a memory flashes into my head. One night – shortly before she disappeared – Mum had gone to hit me with a gin bottle because I'd told her she'd drunk enough.

She didn't mean to. She'd just had too much. She didn't know

160

what she was doing. Luckily Dad stopped her in time. 'You crazy bitch. You're not fit to be a mother. I could kill you.'

Later, she told me how sorry she was. 'I didn't mean to, Janie. You're the whole world to me.'

I'd blocked all this out because that's what you do when something is too much to take on board. I'd also dismissed Dad's response as a figure of speech. But now, as I hear the voices around me, a horrible thought comes into my head.

What if my father had murdered my mother and pretended she had drowned?

No, that's crazy. Isn't it?

'Please,' I cry out in my mind to these men. 'Do something. Get me to hospital. Make me better. I need to be well enough to get to London and find out what really happened to Mum.'

39

Vanessa

Vanessa's heart hummed happily for the rest of the day. And the day after that. It was a tune she'd heard on Radio 2. (She liked to keep up with modern music.) 'What a Beautiful Day.'

And it was. Every day was going to be beautiful from now on, thanks to Lewis and her second chance.

'I have a grandson,' she wanted to tell a neighbour over the road when he came round with some gladioli from the allotment. (He'd started bringing little gifts after Jack had died and sometimes she wondered if he had a bit of a soft spot for her.)

But she couldn't, because he'd known her and Jack for years. He knew they didn't have any children. How could she possibly tell him what had happened? It all seemed a bit, well, embarrassing. Even though it was also wonderful.

Vanessa wanted to talk about Lewis to Carol, and to the cheery young man in charge of checking their passes in court. (She was rather proud of the 'witness service volunteer' badge that hung round her neck. It made her feel as though she was doing something useful.) But Vanessa managed to keep mum, in case it led to awkward questions.

Vanessa was a friendly person. Everyone said so. She

knew it to be true – she liked people. It's why she was so good at her role. This wasn't her being immodest; it was what the supervisor had said in her last appraisal.

Since Jack had died, she'd started to be more sociable because there was no one to question whether she really wanted to go out on a cold winter's day to have a coffee with a friend when there was 'actually rather a lot of housework for you to finish, love' and wouldn't she 'rather stay at home so we can have time together'?

Vanessa now realized that Lewis was right. Jack had been controlling: jealous of anything and anyone that didn't involve him. 'I just want to look after you,' he'd said. 'There are a lot of bad people out there. I deal with them every day.' But it was more than that. If he'd had his way, she wouldn't have gone back to work after their baby had died. Then she wouldn't have become a store detective.

'I earn enough for you to be at home,' he'd argued.

'But Jack, I want to be out and about.'

He'd grudgingly agreed.

But now he was gone, she could do what she liked. Or could she?

'I'm my own woman now,' Vanessa said out loud to Jack. 'I'm a mother. I'm a grandmother. I want to tell the world. But because of your lies, I can't.'

Well, she could. But what would everyone think? The more she thought about it, the more foolish she would look. Why hadn't she insisted on seeing her baby? *'No love, you don't. It will upset you too much. Trust me'* still rang in her ears.

But now she had a grandson! He'd be calling any day to make arrangements for their next meeting.

Yet the days passed and he didn't.

Vanessa's initial euphoria had turned to anger. She found herself slamming cupboard doors. Being cross with herself. Stubbing her toe and then swearing out loud, which was something she rarely did. And shouting at Jack.

'This is your fault. All of it!'

But deep down she knew it was her fury speaking because, after all, wasn't she the one who had been so flipping naive?

Vanessa saw naive people all the time. She came across them day after day in court. They were the ones who said things like 'I trusted her'. Or 'I didn't think he was the type to rape me/steal from me/rob my house/smash into my car'.

Yet she was no better. She'd trusted her husband, and look what he had done. She should have known.

Had Lewis betrayed her trust too?

What had his parting words been? *'See you soon, Granny. Can't wait for next time!'*

A vague promise, she realized now. Rather like a boy might make to a girl he didn't intend to see again.

What had she done wrong? He'd seemed so pleased to be in her company. So genuinely loving and affectionate. 'Granny,' he'd called her. And then those wonderful words that she kept repeating to herself. *'I'd like to get to know you better.'*

So why hadn't he called to fix another meeting?

She'd been hoping that, when they next got together, Lewis might be able to persuade her daughter (it still felt unreal saying that!) to come along, despite everything.

It felt as though her life depended on it.

To find you had a forty-nine-year-old child you thought

had died at birth and then learn that she was alive but didn't want to see you . . . Well, it was too much to bear. It really was.

'I simply have to meet her,' Vanessa muttered to herself, 'and explain why it happened.'

She couldn't even talk this over with Judge. Vanessa knew he was sitting on some big case. It was a complicated one, she'd gathered from the papers, about blackmail and fraud. Usually it gave Vanessa a bit of a thrill to read about cases she was part of (well, present in the court, anyway) or which she knew Judge was presiding over, as he put it. 'Sometimes I feel like we're in a play,' she said.

Judge looked solemn. 'You have a point, Vanessa. What I like about you is that you often see things in a different light from others.'

'What else do you like?' she'd teased.

'Your sense of humour. It's very uplifting.'

That was a front she'd built up over the years to hide the pain of childlessness buried inside her. But right now, she didn't feel jolly at all. Out of the people she knew, Judge would be the one who'd understand. Who'd have thought when she'd been working as a shop girl that a judge would be her closest confidant? Oh, Lewis, where are you?

But still her mobile didn't ring.

Then another thought occurred to her. What if her grandson had had a terrible accident? Instantly Vanessa had visions of his car going over a cliff or him having a heart attack. She might have lost her grandson when she'd only just found him and there was no one who would know how to contact her. Of course, she could ring him but supposing he was with his mum? That would put him in a very awkward situation, wouldn't it?

The weekend was here now. Vanessa used to dread Saturdays and Sundays even when Jack was alive. He'd often be working anyway, so she'd go out for a walk on her own and all around her would be families. Parents pushing prams. Grandmothers holding hands of little ones. Couples arm in arm. If Jack wasn't working, he liked to slump in his chair. '*Make me one of your Victoria sponges, would you love? I really fancy a slice.*'

And she would.

That's what you did in those days. That's what she'd been brought up to do.

And all the time Jack had been lying. All the time he'd known darn well that their daughter – *their daughter!* – was being brought up by someone else. At some point, unknown to her, their child would have met her husband. Got married. Given birth to Lewis, her grandson. And then she'd have got divorced without the comfort and support of her parents.

'You stole all this from me, you bastard.'

SMASH!

Vanessa looked down on the floor. At Jack's face grinning at her through the shattered glass of the frame. That was a photo from when he'd won an award for bravery. He'd chased a robber out of a shop and caught him. But he hadn't been brave enough to tell him about their daughter, had he? Had he known anything about her life? Had he ever tried to track her down?

The pain had been bad enough, Vanessa told herself, when Judge had first shown her what he'd found on the internet. But meeting her grandson in the flesh – not once but twice – had made it worse. He was living proof of what she'd lost. What she'd missed out on. All those years of birthdays and first days at school and Christmases and . . .

SMASH!

Another photograph hit the floor. Their wedding picture. A bright, hopeful younger self stared up at her.

'Fuck you, Jack. Fuck you!' she shouted, shocked by the words that were coming out of her mouth.

Just as well the bungalow was detached.

If Jack had lied about Molly, what else had he lied about? 'Go on, Jack,' she yelled. 'Tell me!'

Then something made her go to the back of the cupboard and yank out the box where she kept everything. Their marriage certificate. Precious letters like the one from her mum just before she'd died. A postcard that Jack had sent her from some swanky police convention in Canada, where he'd been sent to talk about his work as a DI. That had really been something at the time but now she wondered what he'd been getting up to.

If Jack was a liar, maybe he'd had some woman on the side. What – oh God – what if he'd had a love child with her? 'Stop,' she told herself. 'You're letting your imagination run away with you.'

But she couldn't help it.

Vanessa threw the box on the floor and began rifling through Jack's chest of drawers. She'd never been able to summon the courage to do that, even though he'd been gone for three years now. It had helped her to know that part of him was still there. But not now.

Nothing. Except this – his medical files. The ones the

hospital had given her when he'd passed. She'd hidden them in his underwear drawer herself. Seemed a funny place to keep them, but she hadn't wanted them on view to remind her of the pain. The cancer. The ending.

She sat down. Leafing through notes that chronicled an early appendectomy, a broken leg (in the line of duty), a heart murmur that was deemed to be 'innocent'. Why was she doing this? What was she looking for? Vanessa wasn't sure. All she knew was that she needed to comb through this man's life. Find everything she could. Because, clearly, she hadn't known her husband at all.

And there it was. An official letter from a clinic. A vasectomy clinic.

Vanessa read it incredulously. She checked the date at the top, then she took another look at the person it was addressed to, just in case there'd been a mistake. After that, she read it again, to be totally sure. Why had he kept it? Then again, Jack had always been meticulous about keeping paperwork. Whatever the reason, everything suddenly everything seemed to fall into place.

'You bastard,' she whispered.

Jack had had a vasectomy the month after their baby had 'died'. All that trying for babies. All that 'maybe it will happen next month, love'.

All that had been a con on his part. Not just a con – a betrayal of the deepest kind. She'd rather he'd had ten fancy women than this.

'Why, Jack? Why?' she whimpered.

'Because I was scared we'd have another child like the first. Like my poor little brother. We were enough for each other, Vanessa. At least, you were enough for me.'

His voice in her head was quieter than before. But she still recognized it.

'You bloody, bloody fool,' she said, bursting into tears. 'You're a control freak. Do you know that?'

Silence.

Stumbling to her feet, Vanessa kicked the chest of drawers that had contained the file, as if it was personally responsible for hiding this secret that had blown her world apart.

Then, her foot throbbing with pain, she put the vasectomy letter in her handbag.

Lewis would understand.

She could call him, despite her earlier reservations. This was a huge thing that surely needed a face-to-face meeting. In fact, thought Vanessa, maybe it would show Molly how deceitful Jack had been. It might persuade her daughter that the mother she so despised really *had* been in the dark about the adoption.

In fact, she could take it to her in person. After all, she had the address.

'I wasn't a policeman's wife for nothing,' Vanessa told herself. When Lewis had driven her home from that lovely lunch, they'd stopped at a garage for petrol and while her grandson went in to pay, Vanessa had needed to blow her nose. Usually, she had a tissue to hand but not on that day. Remembering how Lewis had produced one at their first meeting, she'd opened the glove box.

There weren't any tissues but there had been an owners' manual with an address on it: 101 Acres Road.

What was stopping her from going there right now?

40

Vanessa

Acres Road was a thirty-three-minute walk from Green Lane according to Google maps. The irony cut through her chest as painfully as if she'd taken a knife to it herself.

To think her own daughter lived so close and she hadn't known.

She might even have seen Molly pushing Lewis in a pram. Perhaps he'd been one of those babies she used to look at longingly.

'If you were still alive, I'd give you the chop myself,' she told Jack as she made her way towards her daughter's street. 'I'm never going to forgive you for this. Never.'

She was getting a bit out of breath now. Maybe it was the stress. Or maybe it was because it was hot: an Indian summer, as the papers called it. Vanessa might have driven if not for the fact that her hands wouldn't stop shaking with shock. She'd seen too many people in court who had hurt someone when they'd been at the wheel. 'I was tired,' they'd plead. Or 'I was upset.' She'd felt a certain sympathy for them, although never for the ones who'd killed people because they were drunk or on drugs.

She thought of Robbie Manning, banged up in prison just as he deserved to be, and wondered what his story was. How could he have mowed that young girl down and left her for dead? Some people were so wicked.

Meanwhile, right now, all she wanted was to see her daughter. Eleven more minutes if she walked at a steady pace, according to her phone.

Vanessa's neck began to sweat. It used to do that when she'd been a store detective. There was nothing quite like that moment just before she approached someone. You had to be sure of your ground otherwise an innocent shopper could try to sue her or the shop for distress.

So she always waited until there was definite proof. The dress in the bag. The jumper that a customer would put on in the fitting room, slip her own top over it and then quietly walk out. She'd often told the manageress they needed to buy security tags but been told that head office was 'looking into it'.

But she wasn't going to confront a shoplifter now. She was about to see her daughter! The child who had been stolen from her.

Nearly there now. Was she doing the right thing? Vanessa felt her heart racing along with the house numbers: 93, 95, 97, 99 . . .

Was this it?

Number 101 was a modern semi-detached with a privet hedge dividing it from its identical twin. All she had to do was to walk up the path.

'*Stop hesitating, Nessie,*' Jack snapped. '*If you're going to make this mistake, just do it. But I'm not watching.*'

The net curtains twitched. At least she thought they had. There was a small gap in the middle. Someone was there, watching. Someone small. Was it a child? The shadows made it hard to see. Lewis had said his mother wasn't very tall; something confirmed by the pictures on his phone. The figure waved to her.

Her throat tightened with fear and also excitement. Could this be her daughter? Did she want to see her? Then again, how would she know Vanessa was coming?

The doorbell was a white button set in a black case. It didn't make a sound when she pressed it. Was it one of those that only sounded on the inside? If so, how could she be certain it had been heard?

Molly – if this really was her daughter – was still waving at her. But then someone came up behind her and the gap in the net curtains closed. She had been seen.

Vanessa pressed the bell again.

She noticed a knocker and tried that.

Through the frosted-glass panel of the front door she could see a blurred figure approaching.

'Who's there?' asked a voice.

'My name's Vanessa Grossmith,' she said nervously.

'What are you selling?'

'I'm not selling anything. I need to speak to you.'

'What about?'

'It's complicated. Look, would you mind opening the door so I can explain?'

There was the sound of bolts being drawn. A short, middle-aged woman with hair drawn back from her face in a tight ponytail took one look at her and stepped back, as if shocked.

'What do you want?' she asked sharply, leaning awkwardly against the door.

'I'm . . . that is . . . well, I was looking for Lewis.'

That was only partly true, but it would help if her grandson was there. He could explain.

'Lewis? Who's he?'

'Lewis Evans.'

'Never heard of him.'

The woman's face had turned hard with a 'don't mess with me' air. Vanessa had seen that kind of look in court.

'He lives here,' Vanessa heard herself sounding increasingly hesitant. 'With his mother.'

'I don't know what you're talking about. I've got enough on my plate without this sort of thing. Go away.'

Then she shut the door in Vanessa's face.

Vanessa waited for a few seconds, looking at the net curtains.

They were closed again now.

Had she made a mistake? Was it possible that the address she'd found in Lewis's car belonged to someone else? She couldn't ask him because that would mean confessing that she'd been snooping in his glove box and then admitting that she'd visited his mother, even though he had clearly said she didn't want to see her.

And who was the person at the window? Maybe she had got it all wrong. 'You silly idiot,' she told herself.

But as she made her way home, Vanessa realized that another thing was also bothering her. Something about that woman's face and harsh voice was ringing bells.

She'd met her somewhere before.

Vanessa usually prided herself on remembering faces.

But she couldn't for the life of her remember where or when she'd seen the woman who lived at 101 Acres Road.

41

Robbie

'I don't understand,' says Irena, after he's finished explaining what happened on the day of the accident. It's the closest he has ever come to confessing. But he's horribly aware that he hasn't told her everything. He can't. Not if he's going to protect her and the children.

'Why didn't you confide in me before?' she continues. 'How could you *not*? You ran a girl over. Left her for dead.'

His wife's eyes fill with tears. Not angry tears – Robbie would have preferred that – but sorrowful tears that say she doesn't know this man she's married. This man who is him but not him.

Tears are streaming down his face too.

'You are the father of my children. You have let down not just me but them too.'

'I know,' he sobs.

'We can't have secrets from each other. Is that everything now?'

He nods, hoping she can't see the guilt on his face.

'Then you must tell the court and the lawyers what you tell me.'

'I can't, Irena. You don't understand.'

She gives him one of her hardball stares that manages to be kittenish at the same time. 'Why?'

He swallows hard.

'Why?' she repeats.

She twists her slim gold wedding band up and down her finger as if threatening to take it off. You don't mess with Irena. He'd known that from the beginning. She and her family had been through hell when they'd fled to the UK. His wife was stronger than anyone he knew. Including himself.

'Because,' he whispers, looking around at the other prisoners and their visitors, 'he gave me no choice. He swore me to secrecy.'

Irena sits forward on her chair. '*Who* did?'

Robbie glances round the room again. Then he leans across and whispers the name in her ear.

'How can he make you swear this?'

'He was blackmailing me,' he whispers. 'He said that if I didn't swear to keep quiet, he would kill my parents.'

Irena frowns. 'But they have passed now. So there is nothing to be scared about.'

Sometimes Irena could be very smart. At other times, she was very naive. 'Don't you see,' he says, his eyes filling with tears, 'he'll hurt you or the children instead if this gets out.'

'You really think so?'

He nods. 'This man could have been behind the people who vandalized the house. He might try to get to you in the place you're in now.'

Irena makes a 'tss' sound, as if his suggestion is ridiculous. 'We have protection. There are police on guard, Robbie. No one can hurt us.'

'But we can't be sure of that.'

She looks at him and shakes her head. 'We must trust them, my love.'

He feels a shot of relief at the word 'love'. So she still cares for him despite the terrible thing he's just told her.

She folds her arms. 'I cannot have our children thinking you are a wicked man who just runs down a girl in cold blood and leaves her to die. They need to know exactly what happened.'

'Shhh,' he says, looking around nervously.

Her beautiful violet eyes harden. 'I will not shush, Robbie. You have to tell the judge what really happened.'

'But I can't,' he groans. 'I won't risk the three most precious people in my life.'

Irena stands up.

'I am leaving now.'

Terror grabs his chest. 'Leaving the prison or leaving me?'

'That,' she says, 'depends on what you do. If you do not tell the court, I will leave you.'

42

Robbie

He thinks about Irena's ultimatum, day and night. He turns it over and over while scrubbing brown stains in the toilets – he's almost got used to his job now – and mopping up piss from the floor.

He thinks about it at night when he goes to his cell and tries to shut out his cellmate's constant talking. ('Did I tell you about the time that I knifed this chap in the eye because he was coming on to my girl?')

He thinks about it so much that his head feels as if it might explode. So he tries to distract himself by making up songs in his head.

Before he was arrested, the music and the lyrics would come to him instinctively as if someone had just placed them in his mind.

But no longer.

'Gi's a tune, then, Robbie,' his cellmate is always saying.

He's scared of what Bruce might do if he doesn't, so he tries. But nothing comes out.

Bruce isn't happy. 'Did you mime all that stuff on stage, then?' asks Bruce.

'No. I . . . I just can't sing anymore.'

At night he has vivid dreams about being stuck on a train going in one direction, while Irena and the children travel in the other. He yells out for them as their carriages pass. Sometimes he finds himself being shaken awake by Bruce. 'Shut the fuck up, man. Some of us are trying to sleep.'

Yasmine comes to visit. He can tell from her face that something has happened. 'Your crown court plea hearing is in two weeks. There's a gap, so they've brought you forward.'

'Good.' He just wants to get it over with now.

'There's still nothing you want to tell me?' she asks.

Has she been talking to Irena? No. His wife had promised not to repeat what he'd told her, even to the children. He trusts her. More than she trusts him, probably. She hasn't visited since he told her what had happened. When he rings her (that precious phone card has finally come through) there is a distant air to her voice.

On the day of the plea hearing in the crown court, Yasmine brings a suit for him to wear. He'd given her his usual measurements, but it hangs off his frame after all the weight he's lost in prison. It doesn't help that he's still giving Bruce half of every meal in return for protection from the other prisoners, who apparently want to chop off his testicles.

'It didn't seem a good idea to go back to the house to get one of your own,' says Yasmine. 'There are still people nosing around at the gate and it might make things worse for your family.'

None of the other prisoners give him the customary 'good luck' or thumbs-up as he is placed in handcuffs and escorted by officers out through the wing. Instead, they stare at him with steely eyes.

Then he is taken out through a side entrance and towards an armoured prison van.

As he gets in, Robbie looks up at the high wall with the barbed wire on top. He recalls a rumour he'd heard on the wing about someone doing a runner at this point and trying to vault the wall. The coils of wire had caught an artery and the bloke had bled out before the ambulance arrived. He wants to throw up.

After a long, bumpy drive, he feels the van slowing down. He can hear people banging on the side. There's a narrow band of daylight above the tinted window, through which Robbie can see crowds of people, shouting angrily. There are placards, the same as last time, but now they read: PUT HIM AWAY FOR LIFE.

The van stops. They are in a small walled car park. Maybe because the traffic and the crowds have delayed them, he isn't taken to the cells. Instead, he's led straight up into the courtroom. His whole body is shaking.

The press is there. He knows they are journalists from their notebooks and iPads and furious scribbling.

So is Irena. Thank God. And so too – oh no – are the children. He doesn't want them to hear any of this.

They look at him with doubtful eyes. Their father. The man who left a girl to die. A girl who wasn't much older than Daisy is now.

Robbie is suddenly aware that Irena is giving him a little wave. At first he thinks it's a supportive gesture. Then he realizes she is trying to tell him something.

Yasmine notices too. She gets up – clipping her office heels smartly on the floor – and goes to Irena. Robbie can see his wife handing over a piece of paper.

The lawyer looks at it and frowns.

She comes up to him in the dock and gives it to him. 'I've no idea what this means,' she says, 'but your wife says she has found something out that you should know.'

Then she returns to her seat.

Robbie reads the words in Irena's beautiful sloping writing.

I looked up this man you tell me about on the computer. He died last month.

Robbie freezes.

Is she right? How can this be true? He glances across at her and she nods as if she knows exactly what he's asking. She'd written something else too.

This changes everything.

It does. But it poses another question. If he's dead, who has been sending him those threatening letters?

The judge enters and everyone stands.

Official words run over him, asking how he is going to plead.

He gets to his feet.

A sea of faces turn to look at him.

They remind Robbie of the first big crowd that came to see the band play after they'd been signed up. How long ago that seems now.

'Not guilty,' he says.

There are gasps around the court.

The judge turns to look at his barrister. 'I believe the

defendant indicated at the magistrates' court that he wanted to plead guilty. Can you confirm that this new "not guilty" plea is correct?'

'Yes, Your Honour.'

The court is in uproar.

PART TWO

43

Vanessa

'Heard the news?' asked Carol excitedly when Vanessa arrived at the office. 'Everyone's talking about it.'

'About what?' Vanessa asked dully. Her head was still reeling from her discovery about Jack's vasectomy and the woman at 101 Acres Road. Who *was* she?

'Robbie Manning has changed his mind and pleaded not guilty.'

'You're kidding.'

Vanessa's anger bubbled up inside her. How dare he? What if he gets off? If Jack were here, he'd be furious. She waited for him to say something in her head but he was strangely silent. Her husband had been quiet for a while now. Maybe he was angry that she'd discovered his secret. Or perhaps he was finally feeling guilty.

'So now we're just waiting to see if Janie is prepared to give evidence,' Carol continued. 'If she does, I won't forget what I said before. Providing she wants witness support, you'll be my first choice. But she might not ask for it.'

How ironic that she had dreamed of being by Janie's side so she could tell her how Jack had tried to hunt down her assailant. She'd imagined the girl – now a woman – looking grateful. She'd imagined herself telling Jack in her head and him saying, '*Well done, Vanessa. I might not be there but you are. We're a team.*'

But they hadn't been a bloody team, had they? (Oh dear – more swearing.) Jack had hidden his vasectomy, giving her false hope, month after month, that she might conceive.

Why, Jack? Why?

Sometimes Vanessa wondered about the voice in her head. Jack didn't always talk when she expected him to. Before now, she'd really felt he was communicating with her from wherever he was. But maybe she'd subconsciously been making it up because she couldn't accept he was gone.

And she still couldn't, dammit, despite everything.

The confusion in her head almost distracted her from worrying over Lewis. Why was that address in his glove box if he didn't live there? And why did that woman who had answered the door seem so familiar?

'I'll let you know as soon as I hear,' said her supervisor, cutting through her thoughts. 'Are you OK, love? You look as though you're in another world. I said I'll let you know as soon as I hear if Janie wants support in court.'

'Thanks,' said Vanessa. A few days ago, she'd have felt honoured. But right now, her heart just wasn't in it.

44

Robbie

'What made you do an about-turn, man?' asks Bruce when they take him back to prison.

'I just did,' says Robbie.

His cellmate and the others are clearly disappointed, like a bloodthirsty crowd who've suddenly been denied the spectacle of a hanging. 'We was expecting you to get twenty years,' he says. 'You made me lose a fiver to one of the guards.'

Now a defence has to be built, which will involve long conversations with his lawyer in the Legal Visits room. The trial and prosecution costs all apparently come from the public purse. 'Won't go down well in the press, mate,' warns Bruce, who seems highly knowledgeable about these things.

Yasmine appears both hacked off and, at the same time, relieved that he has given himself 'a chance'. He wonders why she cares. Perhaps it's because she saw the same look on his wife's face that he did. Hope. Fear. Desperation. All bound up in a ball of confusion.

'It would have helped if you had told me about this man from the beginning,' says Yasmine during their 'strategy meeting', as she calls it.

'I was scared he was going to hurt my family.'

'And now he's dead.' This is a statement rather than a question.

She has checked Irena's Google research and found it to be true.

'I need you to tell me everything else,' she says.

Robbie closes his eyes. 'It's hard. It will bring it all back.'

'I know,' she says. 'But it's imperative that we put the jury in the whole picture. I want them to see you as a young man who made a mistake. To see that boy grow up into a responsible father – maybe the same age as some of the jurors – who carries this terrible weight on his shoulders. I want them to think that they, by the grace of God, might have been terrified into making that same mistake themselves. You will still go down, Robbie. But it might help to cut my estimate of fifteen years by a year or two.'

'I don't know where to start,' he says.

She hands him an exercise book; the lined type he used to have at school. He'd often been told off for writing down song lyrics instead of working.

'A lot of people find it hard to begin,' she says. 'It can be helpful to jot down some notes instead. Think of it as writing your life story. I want to give the jury some background. At the moment, the world sees you as a rich, privileged rock star who wrecked a young girl's life.'

'I'll try,' he says.

45

Robbie

But he can't. It's not just that he's knackered after a day of cleaning toilets which he now finds peculiarly therapeutic. Nor is it because he's exhausted from the other men's jibes ('Couldn't face up to what you did then, Robbie?') or the cold faces of the officers who clearly feel the same. It isn't even that he's worn out by his cellmate, who sees Robbie as 'one of us', insisting on giving him lurid details of his own crimes.

It's because writing down his life story will make it too real. For years, Robbie has tried to pretend it didn't happen while at the same time never being able to put it out of his head.

Now he's waiting for a trial date, when he will have to stand up in court and try to persuade the jury that, yes, he ran that poor girl over but he didn't mean to harm her.

But try as he does, he can't put pencil to paper. The guilt is too huge.

And then something happens.

'You're not doing the toilets today, Manning,' says one of the officers who clearly loathes him. 'You're going to Education.'

When Robbie had first come to prison, he'd been surprised to find that there were classes in maths and English at GCSE level. Some of the men went along even if they already had academic qualifications (Bruce, to his surprise, had an A-level in geography). Some also did distance-learning courses from the Open University.

Education was meant to be a compulsory part of prison but, somehow, Robbie had slipped through the net. He suspected the officers were punishing him by making him 'stick to the toilets' (words that were horribly accurate at times).

As his lawyer had said, an historic case involving a beautiful girl who is now broken had touched the nation's pulse. 'The fact that a famous rock star has been charged is the icing on the cake for the headlines.'

But now it seems Robbie has to go to the classroom and face even more hostility.

'Come on, man,' says Bruce. 'It will be a change from all the shit. There are digestive biscuits. Chocolate, if we're lucky. And the teacher's OK.'

At least it will give him someone else to talk to apart from his cellmate.

So he joins the line of men queuing up by the door of the wing, ready to be escorted by the officer through to the Education block. They'd been chatting until he got there, Robbie notices. When they see him, they give him stony faces.

'Going to learn how to run someone over and escape, are you?' says the man whose nephew had been killed in a hit and run.

'Nah,' says someone else. 'He's already passed his exams at that.'

'Won't be so good at getting the jury to let you off,' says another.

'Couldn't just give them a guilty plea, could you? Cowardly, that's what I call it.'

'That's enough,' says the officer. 'Get a move on, you lot.'

The classroom was surprisingly normal-looking. There was nothing to show that this was part of a prison apart from the bars on the window and a clock that had a somewhat ironic DO NOT REMOVE sticker below. On the walls were posters with facts about nutrition and alcohol units as well as a world map. There were examples of writing, too. Someone had made up a poem about missing his gran's scrambled eggs.

The teacher was a man nudging his sixties, at a guess. He reminded Robbie of his dad, which made his chest lurch. Thank God he wasn't still alive to see what his son had turned into.

'We have a new student today,' he says.

'Yeah,' snarls someone. 'The famous rock star who was too shit-scared to plead guilty.'

'That's enough of that, Carl.' The man turns to Robbie. 'My name's Martin. Welcome to the class. Today we're going to write our life stories.'

A groan goes round the room. 'Not again.'

'Robbie, have you heard about the Koestler awards?'

He shakes his head.

'It's a writing and artistic competition for men and women in prison. One of the categories is life stories and I'm proud to say that we have had a high level of silver and bronze stars in the past. Eight years ago, one of our men actually got a gold.'

'Proud?' This isn't a word Robbie has heard before in prison.

'I'd like you to start by writing about something important that has happened to you in life.'

Another wave of groans. Some men pick up their pen-
cils. Others stare gloomily into space. Martin walks around,
making suggestions in an encouraging voice. Then he
reaches Robbie's desk.

'I can't,' he says, looking up. 'I've tried – my lawyer
wants me to make notes about what happened – but I just
can't do it. It's like it wasn't me who . . . who did it. Even
though it was.'

'Then write it down in the third person. Don't use the
"I" word. Call yourself another name if you want. Some
of the men do that here because they can't face what they
did either.'

But Robbie can't find another name. It doesn't feel
right. He was the one who'd been driving, after all. 'Be a
man,' his wife would say if she was next to him. 'Face up
to what you did.'

'Begin by talking about how you got into music,' Martin
suggests. 'That might help.'

So he has another go. And somehow he finds himself
writing a sentence.

'It started when Robbie and the lads won a music competition at school,' he began. 'Mr Brown, their music
teacher, entered them for it.'

He stops. Actually, it went further back than that. It had
started when he'd spotted that small blue guitar in the toy
shop. He can still see it now . . .

46

Janie

My body is being moved. I can feel it, although I still can't get my words out. I think I'm being lifted onto a stretcher and then put down again. Then an engine starts.

'Careful,' says someone.

'How fast do you want me to go?' says someone else. It sounds like a woman.

'This one's a blue light,' says the first voice. 'I'm going to try the resuscitation pump again.'

Something cold is being put against my chest.

'Nothing,' says a third voice.

'Try again.'

There's a distinct note of panic, which makes me panic too. Am I dead? I don't feel it. What if I'm stuck in this no-man's land for ever?

'There isn't any point.'

'Yes, there is,' *I want to scream.*

'There's always a point,' says the first voice.

'Exactly,' *I try to say.*

'Still nothing,' says the third voice.

I'm here, I want to yell. I wouldn't be able to remember things if I was dead. So I keep going. I keep bringing back my memories to stay with it . . .

After I found Mum's train ticket and discovered the shell had gone, I knew Mum had to be alive. Every bone in my body told me.

That's why I bought a ticket to Waterloo, using the remains of my Christmas money.

I walked over all the Thames bridges, looking at everyone I passed.

I knew this was crazy. There must be zillions of people in London. But coincidences happen. Who's to say that my mother might not be in one of these crowds?

I went to the Royal Academy and the National Gallery and the Tate, because Mum loved art and used to talk about all the galleries she'd like to visit in London one day. I walked round the Royal Albert Hall too because she loved listening to concerts on the radio.

And then I walked to some more places I didn't know and someone under a dirty railway arch asked if I wanted a spliff.

I said no.

My feet hurt and it was getting dark – the nights were drawing in now. Dejected, I got back on the last train home.

I walked back from Exeter St David's station, tears streaming down my cheeks. How was I going to find Mum in a place that big?

'WHERE THE FUCK HAVE YOU BEEN?'

Dad rarely swore.

He took me by the shoulders and shook me. Then he put his arms around me and wept.

'I thought you'd gone. We've been looking for you everywhere. They've even started searching the sea.'

All this was said with such awful wracking sobs, I felt terrible for putting him through this.

'I've got to ring the police,' he said, letting me go. 'Tell them you're safe.'

But as he spoke, someone knocked on the door. It was the nice policeman from before. The one who had told me to call him Jack.

I'll never forget the relief on his face.

'So you're back, young lady. Thank the Good Lord for that. Your dad has been out of his mind with worry. Officially, we're not meant to start a missing persons search so soon, but in view of what happened to your mum, we've had all hands on deck, so to speak.'

'I'm sorry to put you to all this trouble,' I said.

He looked serious. 'Hunts like this cost the public a lot of money. But the main thing is that you're all right. Where did you go?'

'To London . . .'

I stopped.

But it was too late. Dad knew why I'd gone.

'Janie,' he said, pulling me to him. 'Don't you realize? She's not going to come back. I'm sorry. I really am.'

But in my heart, I kept feeling that Mum was out there somewhere. I'd just have to wait for her to come to me because there was no way I'd find her in a city like London.

So I worked hard for my A-levels. I went to concerts. I often looked out for the band I'd seen before and the dishy singer. But I never saw him again.

Then the job in London came up and I got it! Surely this was a sign! In my spare time, I could wander the streets. I would find Mum one day. I just knew it.

'Try this one instead,' says someone.

There's another heavy weight on my chest. A big jolt goes through me.

Suddenly that white light that has been around me starts to recede. I feel different.

'You've done it,' says the second voice, his tone a mixture of excitement and trepidation. 'My God, you've done it. There's a pulse.'

'Yes,' says another voice I hadn't heard before. 'But how long has this young woman been starved of oxygen?'

47

Robbie

Robbie tries to keep on writing despite the memory of the bike with its wheels going round and the crushed cyclist with her bloodstained hair. *The van. The bike. The crunch.*

But it's so difficult. His mind keeps going back to the days when his children had been little. He had held each one from the second they were born. Had breathed them in.

Someone out there had given birth to the girl he had run over. Someone out there was her father and mother. He hadn't 'just' wrecked the girl's life. He had wrecked her parents' lives too.

What would he have done if someone had run down Daisy or Simon? He would have killed them, that's what.

He wouldn't blame Janie's family if they wanted to do the same to him. Janie . . . He wished he didn't know her name. It made her too real. It made his crime too real.

'Birth joy,' he wrote down. 'Death guilt.'

Then he crossed out both pairs of words. 'Focus on the music,' he reminded himself. And suddenly his pencil picked up speed.

Robbie had always been music-mad. He'd seen his first guitar in a toy shop and apparently had a tantrum until his mother had bought it, even though he later learned it had cost her a week's wages.

At secondary school, he made friends with some boys called Sam and Matt who were music-mad too. At first Robbie felt embarrassed because his parents were skint and most of the others had dads with cars and their own houses with 'downstairs cloakrooms'. He couldn't ask them back to his place. It would have been too embarrassing to show them his tiny bedroom, dominated by the narrow single bed.

But music brought them together. They practised for hours in Sam's dad's factory. Robbie wrote the lyrics and Sam composed. They both sang and played the guitar. Matt let the drums do what his hands and head made them do and it sounded cool. Then their music teacher heard them. 'I reckon you boys have potential,' he said. 'There's this great music competition I know of. I could help you make a recording and send it in.'

When Mr Brown received a letter saying they'd got into the finals, none of them could believe it. The headmaster actually mentioned it in assembly and they had to walk across the platform. 'Even if you don't win,' said the head in a voice that suggested he didn't expect them to, 'this is a big feather in your cap, lads. And for our school too.'

The day they received the letter, they were due to play a gig in a town about twenty miles away. Robbie and his mates were still on a high with excitement. At the interval, he went to the bar (just for an orange juice as he wanted to stay sober) and saw a girl with stunning shoulder-length auburn hair. She glanced at him and then looked away shyly. As she did so, she knocked over her drink.

The girl was clearly embarrassed. 'I do things like that too,' Robbie said. 'Let me get you another.'

'I'm all right thanks.'

'No, honestly. It's no trouble. What are you drinking?'

'A Pepsi, please.'

She ducked her chin down as she spoke as if she was talking to the beer-stained carpet.

'Are you local?' Robbie asked.

'Yes. We're near the seafront.'

'I'm about half an hour away but inland. I'd like to live by the sea.'

Her face lit up. 'I swim every day.'

'That must be amazing!'

'It is.'

Then they started talking about what she did and how she hoped to work in publishing but that eventually she wanted to be a novelist.

'I love the lyrics to your songs,' she said.

'I wrote them.'

Her eyes widened. 'Wow! You must be really talented.'

'Not really. They just sort of drop into my head.'

'I love poetry,' she said. 'My favourite poet is Keats.'

'Mine too!' he said. 'Season of mists and mellow fruitfulness . . .'

She joined in, 'Close bosom-friend of the maturing sun . . .'

Then she stopped, blushing furiously at the word 'bosom'.

'I love nature,' she said.

'Me too.' Then he blushed as well because he'd actually used a similar phrase seconds earlier. It made him sound like a parrot.

'Will you dance with me?' he asked as the interval music started.

She hesitated. 'Please,' he said.

After a lively number, the pace slowed down. Other couples were moving towards each other.

Robbie held out his arms, unable to stop himself. She slotted into them as if she had been made for him. Halfway through, he looked down at her. It seemed natural – oh how natural – to kiss her.

Her lips were so soft.

When the dance finished, they stood there on the dance floor staring at each other. 'I feel as if I've always known you,' he said.

'Me too.'

'I'm Robbie.'

'I'm –'

But then Robbie felt himself being pulled away by Jacob, who had grabbed his T-shirt. 'Come on mate. You've got to get back on stage.'

'I'll come and find you afterwards,' he said, calling out over his shoulder. 'What's your name?'

But the music drowned out the last word. He'd find her after the concert, he told himself. As soon as they finished their last number, he leaped off the stage. But she was nowhere to be seen.

Robbie had had the strangest feeling that he'd lost something very precious that night. There was another band playing the following week. Maybe she'd be there! 'I'll go back and try to find her,' Robbie vowed. In the meantime, the boys were practising madly for the competition final.

On the day, Mr Brown drove them in his big van all the way up to the NEC in Birmingham. Robbie knew he should be excited but instead he felt sick with nerves. So did the others.

'I'm scared,' Sam finally admitted in a small voice.

'So am I,' said Matt, who had turned very pale.

'Don't be,' said their teacher. 'Forget there's a crowd out there. Pretend you're playing in a small room to someone you really care for.'

So when Robbie saw the sea of faces in front of him, he distracted himself from the overwhelming fear by thinking of the shy girl who loved both Keats and his own lyrics. He thought of how he was going to try to find her again. He would! He was sure of it. He loved her. That might sound a bit too quick, considering he hardly knew her. But how else could he describe that yearning ache in his heart?

As Robbie played in front of all these people who would decide his future, he heard his voice soften at times and gain power at others. In his head, he was back at the gig with her. He was stroking her hair. He was asking her name when, in his imagination, the music was quiet enough to hear her reply. All the things he should have done at the time.

The applause came as a shock. He was still there with the girl in his head. Not in a stadium with these kids bopping around and the judges on the side.

When they announced their decision, Robbie couldn't believe it.

'We've won!' said Sam leaping into the air.

Matt just stood there, looking shocked.

'You've won!' repeated Mr Brown. 'Do you realize what this means, boys? You're going to be big. Someone's bound to sign you up after this.'

'Don't be so bleeding daft,' said Robbie's dad when he went back home. 'That teacher has no right to put all those dreams into your head. People like us need to do jobs that pay the bills.'

Robbie's dad had just been made redundant from his warehouse job and was now working in the local wood yard. But there was talk of redundancies there too (he'd heard his parents' anxious conversations through the bedroom wall), and once he came back to find his father mending a broken window at the back of the house.

'What happened?' he'd asked.

His dad had looked angry and hurt at the same time.

'Someone who thinks we should "go back to our own country".'

'But you were born here.'

His father shook his head. 'Folk can be bigoted, son. You'll have to get used to it. It's why I want you to have a steady job where people look up to you, like a teacher.'

A teacher? He wanted to be a musician! Why couldn't his dad understand? That girl had done. The one with the auburn hair, who he couldn't get out of his head. It would be so nice to share the competition news with her. 'That's amazing,' he could imagine her saying. 'I'm so proud of you, Robbie!'

The next day (a Saturday), he went back to where he'd done the gig and wandered round the town hoping to see her. No such luck.

Eventually, he caught the bus home, head down,

feeling as though he'd missed something huge, even though part of his heart was tingling with excitement at having won the competition.

But then on the Monday – he'd always remember that day – a letter arrived. Addressed to him.

'Someone wants to meet us,' he told his dad. 'Look.'

Sam and Matt had got similar letters.

It was from a music promoter who they'd never heard of but who Mr Brown said was 'quite a big fish'. He wanted to sign them up! They all went to the meeting, including Robbie's dad and the other parents too. His mum couldn't change her shift at the supermarket so she stayed behind.

'I'm sorry,' said his dad, 'but there's no way my boy is signing a contract. How do we know you're not just making money out of them?'

'This is a fantastic chance for them,' pleaded Mr Brown.

'I can do what I like,' said Robbie. He'd never stood up to his dad as firmly as this before. It felt scary but at the same time, empowering. Besides, if he did well, he could help his family. He couldn't say that out loud though – he knew it would embarrass them.

'No you can't, son. Not till you're eighteen.'

'But that's only next month, Dad. Why not now?'

'I can wait,' said the promoter eagerly.

Robbie put his pen down. If only he'd listened to his dad, then the accident might not have happened.

48

Vanessa

Lewis rang that evening. As soon as she heard his voice, Vanessa knew he was going to be cross with her.

'Why did you visit my mother?' she expected him to say, because part of her had a feeling that that woman had been Lewis's mum but was hiding it for some reason.

'How has your week been?' he said instead in a friendly, almost jaunty tone.

So she *had* got it wrong then. How silly of her.

'All right, thank you,' she replied cautiously.

'All right?' he repeated in what sounded like a concerned manner. 'That doesn't sound convincing. Has something happened?'

He was so intuitive!

Vanessa drew a gasp. 'Actually, I went through Jack's papers and found he'd had a vasectomy without telling me, just after your mum was born.'

There was the sound of a deep breath at the other end. 'That's terrible.'

Vanessa's voice was thick with grief. 'I know.'

'What a bastard. Sorry, I know I shouldn't say that.'

'It's OK. You're right.' She felt comforted, as if they were on the same side.

'I can see now,' said Lewis, 'what kind of man you were dealing with.'

So he understood!

There was a beat of silence then, which she felt she needed to fill. 'How was *your* week?' she asked, even though that seemed a rather frivolous question after the vasectomy revelation.

'Sorry? I didn't hear that.'

There was quite a lot of noise at his end with men talking loudly. Maybe he was at the new office. Vanessa rather liked the idea of her grandson ringing her from work. Perhaps he'd said to his boss (or maybe Lewis *was* the boss!) that he was just going to call his grandmother.

'Great, thanks. I was just ringing to see if I could take you out for lunch again on Saturday.'

The relief made her laugh, rather girlishly, she realized. How stupid of her. 'That would be lovely,' she said. 'But you must let me treat you.'

'Nonsense. It's on me. I insist. Now, how does twelve o'clock suit you? I know of another lovely restaurant you might like, near Dartmouth.'

She couldn't wait. Meanwhile, Jack had come back again, as his usual suspicious self. '*What's he up to, Ness? That's what I want to know.*'

'Cut the "Ness" bit,' she retorted sharply. 'I never liked it. Stick to Nessie if you have to. But I'd rather be Vanessa to you now. You don't deserve to be familiar with me anymore.'

That shut him up. Now, what should she wear? The blue dress with little white spots would be perfect, especially as the weather was so mild.

On Saturday, Vanessa was ready and waiting at the end of the front path outside her house. She looked at the wrought-iron gate, which Jack used to paint every year. It needed doing badly now and it struck her that perhaps she could ask Lewis if he knew of a handyman. Maybe not yet, though. He might think she was asking him to do it and, clearly, he was a busy man. She'd wait until they knew each other better.

When the yellow sports car pulled up, Vanessa thought it was someone asking for directions. People often got lost around here with the maze of roads.

But then the driver leaned across and opened the passenger door from the inside. It was Lewis.

'You've got a different car!' she said excitedly.

'Yes, I often do. I lease them out. It's a clever scheme, really. It's much cheaper than owning your own and it means you can drive all kinds of models.'

So that explained the address on the logbook. It would be the name of the person who leased out the car. The same woman she'd called on, thinking Lewis had lived there!

Yet it still didn't explain why she had looked familiar.

Vanessa tried to put this out of her head as they drove along, Lewis telling her about a party he'd been to (one of the girls in his office was leaving, so they'd all had a bit of a knees-up last night). But she still felt very stupid for jumping to the wrong conclusions about the house.

'You said you and your mum lived nearby,' she said. 'But where, exactly?'

'On the other side of Exeter.'

There were a lot of places fitting that description.

Vanessa would have liked Lewis to be more specific, but perhaps he was worried in case she turned up, which was exactly what she'd done.

'Look over there,' he said, pointing ahead. 'If you follow the coastline, you'll see where I'm taking you.'

It turned out to be a fish restaurant right on the beach. 'How did you know I like seafood?' asked Vanessa, looking at the menu.

'You had scallops last time. Remember?'

Oh dear. Of course. How silly of her.

'Sorry,' she said. 'I sometimes forget things.'

'It's understandable,' he said, but his tone was kindly. Not patronizing at all like Jack's had sometimes been.

Recently, Vanessa had discovered that her short-term memory wasn't quite what it had been. But she could easily remember things from long ago.

Like the time Jack had got a fishbone stuck in his throat and she'd done the Heimlich manoeuvre, which she'd learned in the shop as part of their first-aid course.

'I owe you my life,' he'd said afterwards.

If she'd known then what she knew now, she might not have bothered.

Still, that was the past, Vanessa told herself. Right now was the present. And – fingers crossed – her life had suddenly brightened up. All she needed to do was speak to her daughter. To persuade her that she had known nothing about Jack's wicked behaviour and ask her – please – could they now start to build a relationship?

'*You daft woman*,' Jack said.

Vanessa didn't dignify this with a reply.

She knew he was wrong. Molly would understand when she met her face to face.

And somehow, by hook or by crook, she had to make that happen.

49

Robbie

Robbie's dad said he'd throw him out of the house if he signed the contract. 'Your schoolwork is suffering with all this practice,' he pointed out.

It was true. Robbie's parents had received a warning letter from the head to say that if their son didn't pull his socks up, he was in danger of failing his exams.

'But I might not get this chance again,' he pleaded. 'I want to be a musician. I don't care about going to college.'

Robbie's dad's face was puckered up with fury, his eyes narrowing. 'You don't know what you're saying. You've got the chance to make something of yourself – not like me. Why do you think I've worked my arse off to put a roof over your head? It's because my father came to this country with nothing and had to live in a shitty hostel with one meal a day until he could get a job. When I was a kid, it wasn't much better. The prejudice was just as bad. And it hasn't really improved now. You're a bright lad, Robbie. You could do well. But if you're not going to bother, you can get out of this house. I'm not feeding and clothing you any longer.'

'Just give me a bit of time to show you. Please.'

'Go on, love,' said his mum. 'It's a great opportunity for him.'

Later he heard his parents arguing. 'I just want our boy

to have a steady job that's more skilled and better paid than mine. Robbie has a chance to get qualifications. He needs to make the most of that.'

'I know, love, but what if he makes it big in music one day? Someone has to. And if he doesn't, he can still do his exams and get a proper job.'

A proper job? Music *was* a proper job. But Robbie was grateful to mum for sticking up for him – and for bringing dad round to the idea.

Two weeks later, when he turned eighteen, he and Sam signed the contract with the music promoter, who also turned out to be an agent. Matt needed a bit of convincing ('I want to sing, but not in front of everyone') yet he signed his part too.

'Nothing will come of it, mark my words,' his dad said. 'It's not like you've got a label interested in you. I just don't want you to get your dreams dashed. I'm worried for you. That's all.'

Robbie knew that his dad meant the best for him. He understood that, for Dad, the weekly pay packet at the wood yard represented some kind of safety in a country that didn't always want you. But Robbie wanted to make music his life.

So he tried to revise for his exams and practise at the same time. Lyrics kept coming into his head about the shy auburn-haired girl with the soft lips.

He began getting worse and worse marks at school; something he managed to keep from his parents.

Time and time again, Robbie went back to the hall where they'd played and walked round the seaside town. There was no sign of her, yet he still couldn't give up.

Then the agent rang Sam's house and all the lads met up there after school. Sam's dad, Old Man Senior as he was known, seemed really excited.

'Your agent has been approached by a record company,' he said.

Sam was the only one who could find a voice. 'We've got a contract?'

'Not exactly. You've got to audition for them first.'

They couldn't believe it. None of them could. Wasn't this something they'd been dreaming of for years? And now it was happening!

'My dad's not very happy about this,' Robbie admitted to Sam's dad. 'He thinks it will interfere with my school-work.'

Old Man Senior gave him a wink. 'Don't worry about that, lad. I'll have a word with him. This is too good an opportunity to turn down. Anyway, the band needs you with your fancy words. I'm behind you lads, all the way. You lot could be the next Beatles!'

Mr Brown was excited too. 'This is your big break, lads. It's how it starts! You might only get one chance. So play the very best that you can.'

No pressure then.

They needed to get there under their own steam, along with all their gear, but none of them had a driving licence. Robbie couldn't afford lessons and the others hadn't taken their tests yet.

'It's a long way to London,' said their teacher. 'I would take you but the wife and I have booked a fortnight in the Isle of Wight.'

Sam's dad was going away on a 'business trip' so he arranged for Sam's older brother, Jacob, to take them instead in one of the family's company vans.

They were all set to go.

50

Robbie

Jacob didn't hang around when he drove, claiming he needed to be home fast that night. He made it clear that he had only agreed with his dad's command to take the 'kids' in case they 'made it' one day. Then they'd 'owe' him.

This both scared Robbie and excited him. If Jacob, who was always so scathing of his brother and his mates, thought they had a chance of becoming famous, maybe they really did! But at the same time, Robbie knew that six-foot-plus Jacob would try to muscle in somehow. Jacob also hung around with people who were rumoured to be dealing drugs. Not good.

The drums rattled next to him as they swerved round corners. There was a diversion, taking them closer to the sea. 'It's going to make us late,' snapped Jacob thumping the wheel with his fist in frustration. His driving grew even more erratic as Robbie clung on to his guitar case for safety. He could barely see out of the windows because the gear obstructed his view but soon the roads began to look familiar – this was her town! Heart racing, he pressed his nose to the window but still there was no sign of the girl with the auburn hair.

Eventually, they got to London. The music producers

had these swish offices in a place called Tottenham Court Road. They'd told Jacob he could park round the back.

When they got out of the van, their legs ached from hours cramped in the back and nerves at what lay ahead.

'Bloody hell,' said Sam under his breath as they took in the glass and chrome studio. 'Pretty posh, isn't it?'

Then a man with a ponytail and ripped jeans came in. 'Which one of you is the songwriter, then?'

Robbie tried to answer but his mouth was too dry.

'Him,' said the others.

'I like your stuff, but I need to know you can keep it coming. Give me something new. Now.'

Now? Robbie wasn't sure he could do that. But then he thought of his dad, who didn't believe in him, and of the crisp tenner his mother had given him for the trip and which must have taken her a long time to save up for. He thought of the girl from the gig. He thought of their teacher, who had found the competition in the first place.

But while all this was going on in his head, his heart was doing its own thinking and words came out of Robbie's mouth that he'd never heard before. They certainly weren't the type of lyrics they'd agreed would suit the band. It was like some kind of spirit had got into him and taken him over.

Sam and Matt looked at him as if to say, 'What the fuck?'

But the man with the ponytail, and then some more 'label people' who came in and asked him to do it again, seemed to like it. 'Let's hear the whole band now, shall we?'

So they set up their instruments and played a few tracks, following his lead.

'Sheer bloody genius, lads,' they said. Then they signed them up on the spot! Was this really happening?

'The first thing we're going to do is get you to record your debut album. While you're doing that, you can also go on tour. We want to get your name out there so that by the time the record comes out, people will have heard of you. Robbie – you can keep your surname. "Manning" works. It sounds strong.' They gestured at Sam and Matt. 'But we need something different for you two.'

'How about Senior?' Sam suggested. 'Dad'll be pleased – it's a kind of nickname that came down from our grandad.'

'Sounds good to me,' said the promoter. 'Let's say "Young" for you then, Matt. It will resonate with our demographic.'

Matt nodded but didn't say anything. Maybe he feels shocked like I do, thought Robbie: good-shocked, but still shocked.

Robbie couldn't wait to tell his parents.

'But what about your exams?' demanded his dad as soon as he got back.

'I'll do them as well,' said Robbie.

'Well done,' said his mum, glancing nervously at Robbie's father. There was a dark bruise on her elbow, Robbie noticed.

'Are you OK, Mum?' he asked when they were alone in the kitchen.

'Fine love, thanks.'

'What happened to your elbow?'

'Oh that. I just bumped into a door the other day, that's all.'

But Robbie felt an uneasy tremor running through his bones. It wasn't the first time this had happened. What if his parents were still arguing about his future? Dad sometimes had a bit of a temper when people didn't do what he thought they should. Supposing he'd hurt Mum?

51

Janie

I'd like to be able to tell you about what happened next. It went something like this. At least, I think it did.

Voices were all around me.

Words floated in and out of my head.

'The survival statistics aren't good, I'm afraid.'

'Her spine is crushed and it's likely Janie has suffered severe brain damage.'

'There's no other way of saying this, Mr White. Janie has life-changing injuries.'

'Janie . . . my darling Janie. Wake up. Please.'

Was that Dad's voice or Mum's? It was hard to say. It would be worth going through all this if it meant she'd come back again.

'She's come out of the coma.'

I didn't even know I'd been in one. In fact, I felt as though I'd been having a deep dream. I kept my eyes closed. My eyelids were too heavy to open.

The voices kept firing questions at me.

'Janie? Can you tell us what happened?'

'A big white van hit me,' I try to say. But the words won't come out.

'Let her rest,' says someone.

Later – I've no idea when – I hear a deeper voice.

'Janie has suffered catastrophic injuries, Mr White. I'm afraid she might never speak or walk again.'

Never speak or walk? That's impossible. They must have muddled me up with someone else.

And on top of all this were the terrible, blinding headaches; the searing agony which had me thrashing with silent screams for more painkillers; and the constant bleeping of hospital machines.

But worst of all was Dad's voice.

'Oh my God, Janie,' he would sob over and over again.

He thought I couldn't hear him, but I could.

Be careful what you say in front of someone you think is unconscious. They might hear more than you realize.

'Who did this to you?' he kept asking.

'A van,' I tried to say.

But the words still wouldn't come out. It was as if they were stuck in my throat. Never to be freed.

52

Vanessa

Vanessa chose Dover sole at the restaurant. It melted in her mouth. So did their conversation. *That's corny*, she told herself, but it was true. She wanted to know everything about Lewis. Did he have a girlfriend? Not at the moment. Had he gone to university? No, but he'd studied accountancy at a local college. Of course, what she really wanted to know was more about her daughter, Molly.

But she needed to be subtle. Maybe talk about herself for a bit and try to find a way in.

'I've got a big case coming up,' she said.

His eyes lit with interest. 'That one you mentioned before with the girl who came back from the dead?'

'Yes,' she said. Then, because she couldn't help it, she added, 'I'm going to be sitting next to her as a witness supporter.'

His face beamed. 'That's great! You were hoping to do that, weren't you?'

So he remembered! Vanessa felt a flush of pleasure, thinking how he really listened, unlike some people she knew.

'That poor girl,' he added, looking more reflective. 'Her life has been changed for ever.'

'Yes. It has.' Vanessa was glad to see that her grandson was clearly a sympathetic person.

'Still, at least she'll be getting justice.'

'Only if Robbie Manning gets convicted,' said Vanessa in a rather sharp tone that wasn't usually hers.

'You sound doubtful.'

'Well,' she said, fuelled by the glass of wine she'd just had, 'I'm always amazed by folk who get off when your gut instinct tells you they're guilty.'

'Wow!' Lewis's eyes widened. 'Have you had cases like that?'

'I shouldn't really say.'

'Of course not.'

But Vanessa was already wondering if she'd said too much. So she changed the subject by asking where he'd gone for his summer holidays. 'I like to take a break in winter,' he said. 'I'm thinking about the Bahamas this year.'

The Bahamas. My goodness! He must be rolling in it.

'I love the look of those white beaches you see in magazines,' she said. 'Will you be going with friends?'

'Maybe. I'm still finalizing my plans. What about you?'

'I like being at home at this time of the year,' she said. 'But I started having a regular little spring break after my husband died – he wasn't a big one for travelling. Earlier this year, I went to the Scillies. It was gorgeous with all those flowers! Next spring, I'm planning a break in Sorrento.'

'That sounds nice.'

He had half an eye on his mobile, which was on his side plate. She must be boring him again. Oh dear.

'Yes,' she continued, less certainly. 'I thought I'd treat

myself. It's being organized by a company that specializes in holidays for people on their own.' She flushed. 'Of course, I'm not going in order to meet someone.'

Lewis wasn't looking at his phone now. He was looking at her. 'Why not? You're a very attractive woman for your age.'

She flushed again. 'Thank you.'

Was her daughter as charming as him, she wondered. How she yearned to meet her! But she didn't want to push too much in case she frightened Lewis off. She'd try to gain his confidence and then have another go.

But then he looked down at his watch. 'I'd better be making tracks. I promised to mow mum's lawn. Excuse me a minute while I pay the bill.' Then he reached inside his jacket pocket and took out his wallet. 'That's odd.'

'What is?'

'I don't seem to have my card on me.'

'*Hah*,' crowed Jack. '*I thought this might be coming.*'

'I'll pay,' said Vanessa, taking out her debit card and pushing Jack's protestations aside.

He looked troubled. 'Only if you let me pay you back.'

'There's no need, honestly.'

'Really, I insist.'

He took the card from her and went to the till.

When he came back, he handed it to her with the receipt. 'I'm so sorry about that,' he said.

'Don't think about it.'

He frowned. 'I'm worried about where my own card is. I'm sure I put it in my wallet this morning.'

But when they got back to the car, he let out a cry. 'There it is. On the floor by my seat. How daft of me.

Still at least I can stop off at a machine and get you some cash out.'

'You really don't have to. It was my turn anyway.'

But he wouldn't take no for an answer. He also bought her a bunch of yellow roses at the same time.

'Do you like art?' he asked.

'I'm useless myself but I love *looking* at paintings,' she said. 'I used to visit the museum in Exeter when I wasn't working.'

'That's funny. I was going to suggest that myself. How about going in a couple of weeks? I'm going to be working away for a bit doing an audit.'

'Sounds great,' she said, hiding her disappointment that it wouldn't be sooner.

'How's it going?' asked Judge in the café the next day.

'Fine, thanks' she said briefly.

Vanessa had been avoiding him, to be honest, partly because she hadn't wanted to tell him about turning up at a stranger's house to track down her grandson. It made her feel silly.

He cleared his throat. 'I wondered if . . .'

Then someone stopped to talk to him. It was a lawyer she knew by sight. Vanessa didn't want to be in the way, so she made an 'excuse me' noise and slipped away.

The following weekend she was out in the centre of Exeter, shopping. She needed to fill the hours. Although they'd only had lunch together twice, every day now felt flat without Lewis.

And then she stopped. On the other side of the road was Lewis, and next to him was the woman from 101

Acres Road. Vanessa was sure of it. She was limping, which would explain why she'd been leaning against the door in that awkward way.

So they'd been lying. Both of them. The woman and her grandson.

As if sensing she'd been recognized, the woman turned and stared at her. And suddenly, it all came flooding back to Vanessa. So *that's* why her face had seemed so familiar.

August 30th. Five years ago. The day she'd been let go as a store detective.

53

Robbie

It was 2004. The first gig on the tour was going to be in Brighton in six weeks' time, which meant a long drive with Sam's brother's Jacob. He was cock-a-hoop now they'd been signed up but there was something unnerving about his excitement – it seemed to verge on jealousy at the same time.

'I could do what *you* do.'

Jacob even got them to ask the label people if they could take on another band member but they said no; three was a good number.

So he carried on being a roadie, although it was clear he wanted to do more. 'Reckon I bring you luck,' he said after their practices went brilliantly.

'Reckon you do, bro,' said Sam, slapping him on the back, and everyone agreed.

Jacob might not be particularly nice but Robbie couldn't help feeling a bit envious of Sam, who could clearly see past his brother's faults. How he'd have loved someone to support him with Dad. If he ever had a kid of his own, he'd make sure it had at least one brother or sister. It was lonely being an 'only'. Then again, the band were his brothers now.

He also harboured a secret hope that maybe, just

maybe, if they did loads of gigs round the country, he might see that beautiful auburn-haired girl again. After all, she liked music, didn't she? She might travel to see bands. He could tell she had an ear from the way she'd danced and moved.

His brief recollection of her still inspired his lyrics. 'Poetry,' said the chap with the ponytail who turned out to be in charge of the label company. 'Pure bloody poetry.'

They practised for hours after school and at the weekends too – the Brighton gig wasn't like the small local gigs they'd been doing before. This was a milestone for them, a really important event, the promoter had said, as if they weren't feeling nervous enough. And all the while, they recorded songs at a studio in Exeter that the album people would be funding.

Everyone was knackered by the time the day arrived. Matt was physically sick with nerves, making them late for their 5 a.m. start. But they were excited too. They used a different van this time with brand-new numberplates. 'It's a dream to drive,' Jacob said, as if it was his own and not his dad's.

'What happened to the last one?' one of the others asked.

'Went to scrap.'

'He reversed it into a wall in the yard,' said Sam softly when Jacob went for a pee. 'Dad wasn't too pleased. Jacob's been out all night too. Only just got back. He and Dad had another row about him bumming around and not getting a proper job.'

Jacob had left school before taking his A-levels and had since flitted from one job to the next.

'Couldn't he work for your dad?' asked Robbie.

'Dad says he's got to prove himself first. That's why Jacob's taking us today. Dad reckons it might give him a purpose if he gets more involved in the band.'

'But it's *our* band.'

Sam made a 'what can I do?' gesture. 'If we don't agree, my dad won't let us practise in the factory or support us like he does.'

That was it then. What Old Man Senior wanted, he got. Everyone in town knew the way he worked. He was too wealthy and too influential to upset.

'What are you two talking about?' snarled Jacob, coming back.

'Nothing, bro,' said Sam.

When they all piled into the van, Jacob reeked of whisky. There was also, he noticed, a bottle of vodka in the pocket on the driver's side.

'You've been drinking,' said Sam.

'So what?' Jacob snapped back.

The rest of them looked at each other worriedly.

'You can't drive if you're over the limit,' said Robbie.

'Don't you tell me what I can and can't do, you little shit. You're getting a free lift, aren't you?'

But Robbie didn't like the way that Sam's brother was weaving all over the road.

'Maybe we should find someone else to drive,' said Matt.

There was a screech.

Jacob had slammed on the brakes. He was turning round now and glaring at them. 'Any more from you three and I'll chuck the lot of you out. You won't get another driver at this short notice and you'll never get all this stuff on a train and then across London.'

'You're right. Sorry, bro,' said Sam nervously.

'Damn right, I am.'

Then, when Jacob turned back to the wheel, Sam whispered to the others. 'We can't miss this opportunity.'

So they drove on.

54

Robbie

Jacob was a bad 'un. They all knew that. Ever since Robbie had known him, there'd been whispers – the rumours becoming worse as they got older. It was another reason why Robbie's parents didn't like him being in the band. But Sam was different. He was like Robbie. Or so Robbie had thought at the time.

New stories bubbled up every now and again, including one rumour of Jacob 'taking advantage' of a girl in his year at school.

But it died down as quickly as it had appeared – the girl had withdrawn her claim just before it reached the court. Some said that Jacob's dad had paid her off.

Not long after that came another rumour. This time it was a whisper that Jacob was selling drugs to fifth-formers. An investigation was launched and someone else was held responsible. Nothing could be proved but the 'culprit' was expelled.

'His old man will have bailed him out,' observed Robbie's dad over tea (fish fingers again). 'Watch them, Robbie. I know you're friends with Sam but that family sticks together.'

Sam's dad was small and scary. It was said that he'd killed a man during a pub brawl in his youth but got off thanks to a good lawyer. He had beady black eyes that bored into you. But he'd always been good to Robbie and good to the band. He'd let them practise in his factory, hadn't he? Let them use the van.

Old Man Senior seemed to have a soft spot for Robbie. 'You're a good lad,' he often said to him. 'You work hard at school too, I've heard. Your parents must be proud of you. I've also heard money's tight at home. Take this.' He pressed a fifty-pound note into his hand. 'Use it to help your mum out with the food bill. Don't tell her it came from me – just say you earned it doing some odd jobs. And do a bit more to involve my Jacob in the band, will you? He needs a purpose right now. Maybe you could help him write songs like you do.'

'But I can't,' Robbie wanted to say. You couldn't simply teach someone. The words just came into his head. He didn't have to think about them. It was like someone had put them there, laid them out in advance for him to find. He didn't want any interference with that.

Of course, he didn't say any of this – he couldn't get on the wrong side of Old Man Senior.

So he just nodded. Meanwhile, his dislike of Jacob grew and grew until it became a big black cloud of foreboding hanging over him.

It wasn't only because of all the bad things people said Jacob had done to others. It was because Robbie knew – or rather felt in his heart – that Jacob was capable of doing something even worse one day.

If only he'd listened more carefully to that gut feeling, everything would have been different. Because there was another reason why Robbie was scared of Jacob. A reason that went back to when he had just turned sixteen.

It started when Jacob caught up with him one day, walking home from school. 'Want a cigarette?' he asked.

He said it in the kind of voice that made Robbie feel like he'd be offending him if he said no.

The cigarette made Robbie cough, but it also made him feel like he was one of the lads.

'That'll be fifty quid,' Sam's brother had said after Robbie had taken a few reluctant puffs.

'Ha ha,' Robbie said.

'I mean it,' Jacob replied. 'That wasn't just any old cigarette you know. It's good-quality weed.'

Back then Robbie didn't know what the smell of cannabis was like, let alone the taste. But now he thought about it, he was beginning to feel a bit . . . different.

'I didn't know –' he began. But Sam's brother was taking a flick knife out of his pocket and running his finger along the blade.

Now he was scared. 'But I don't have fifty quid.'

Jacob grinned. He had perfect white teeth – they all did in his family. Rumour had it that they'd gone to America to get them done. 'Then you'll have to do me a little favour . . .'

'OK,' Robbie heard himself saying when Jacob had finished. Well, what else could he do? You didn't want to mess with someone like Jacob.

Anyway, it only meant dropping off a package at some bloke's house the next night. And then the same for four more weeks.

'You've paid off your debt now,' Jacob said after the final drop. 'But why don't you carry on and earn yourself a bit more?'

Robbie was about to say no but then he thought about how exhausted Mum looked from working all hours, and the strain his dad felt too. He'd just do it for a bit, he told himself. After all, it was only a few packages. He tried not to think about the contents. The less he knew, the better, he reasoned. Besides, the niggling doubts in his head were outweighed by the relief on his mother's face when he gave her a hundred quid that he'd 'put aside from some extra paper rounds'.

'You're a good lad,' she said, giving him a hug.

Then, one night when Robbie was doing a run, the rain was so bad that the seal on the package came loose. Inside was a packet of white powder. Robbie did some searching on the internet. Bloody hell!

'I can't drop off your packages anymore,' he told Sam's brother. 'I'll go down if I get nicked.'

'Too late, I'm afraid, mate. You're up to your neck in it already. Even if you don't get caught, I might. Then I'd have to tell the cops you were one of my mules.'

Robbie felt bile rising into his mouth from fear. 'That's not fair.'

Jacob's black eyes narrowed. 'Isn't it? You knew what you were doing.'

'No, I didn't.'

'Come on. Don't be so naive. What did you think you've been carrying all these months? Avon Lady make-up? 'Sides, it doesn't matter if you knew or not. The fact is that you took it. That means you owe me.'

Robbie swallowed the lump of fear rising into his throat.

'It's OK,' said Jacob. 'You don't have to do it all the time but, every now and then I'll be asking you a favour. And you'll do it because you don't want to end up in a YOI, do you?'

'What's that?'

'Don't be so naïve. A Young Offender Institution.'

'No,' whispered Robbie. 'I don't.'

'Good. Besides, from what I hear, your parents are skint. Don't they need all the help they can get?'

He couldn't deny it. Wasn't that why he'd carried on anyway? It had been OK until that padded envelope had opened . . .

'All right then,' said Robbie. But it didn't feel right. He knew it didn't. Oh, why hadn't he listened to that little voice inside?

55

Vanessa

Vanessa had loved being a store detective She was good at her job – everyone said so. She was pleasant but firm and never approached a customer unless she was certain they had taken something.

But the woman with the limp had got the better of her.

Vanessa had seen her stuff a £70 blue angora jumper in her large handbag – as clear as day! – and then leave without paying.

Yet when she got to the door and Vanessa asked her to stop, the bag was empty.

The woman had then lodged a complaint against Vanessa, claiming discrimination because she had a limp.

'That's ridiculous,' Vanessa said. 'How can that have anything to do with it?'

But apparently it had. She had other 'related' medical issues, said her lawyer, including stress and breathing problems. The 'wholly unfair' accusation had caused her client extreme mental anxiety.

Then it got into the local paper. The shop was made out to have been discriminatory. It was suggested to Vanessa that she take early retirement (which more or less meant she was being sacked) and a substantial settlement was made to the woman with the limp providing she dropped charges.

'But I saw her put it in her bag,' she said to Jack.

'Maybe it had a false bottom,' he said.

Maybe it had. She should have thought of that. But it was too late to prove it.

'You don't need to work, love,' he said. 'I'll take care of you, and you'll get your pension soon.'

But she *wanted* to work. She needed something to do.

Then Jack got ill and she put all her energy into nursing him. When he died – sooner than they'd expected – she wasn't only shocked and grieving. She was also rudderless.

That was when she applied for the voluntary job at the court which – rather surprisingly – the Jack-in-her-head was all for.

Now the terrible truth began to dawn as she walked in a daze towards Southern Hay, where she'd parked the car. Vanessa *had* met her daughter before. Not only that, but she had also tried to get her arrested! How ironic and awful was that, on so many different levels?

She needed to talk to someone. Judge. But before she could dial his number, her mobile rang.

'Vanessa?'

It was Lewis. Her heart began to pound.

'I saw you just now in the street. I know you saw us too. You're probably wondering what's going on.'

Instantly she felt relieved, both by his candour and by the kindness in his voice. 'Yes, I am.'

'May I take you out tomorrow and explain?'

'*Don't be so bloody daft,*' Jack cut in.

'Yes,' said Vanessa firmly, as if she was addressing her husband rather than Lewis. 'I think that would be a very good idea.'

56

Robbie

Jacob asked him to deliver more packages. This time it was to scarier areas; parts of Exeter Robbie hadn't known existed: dark, shady patches further down the river away from the Quay, with used needles in the bushes.

The people terrified him too, especially on the grass outside the cathedral – a favourite night-time spot. 'Gi's some money,' they'd often call out. 'There's a good boy, sonny.' Often, they stank of meths or urine. The smell made him want to vomit.

One night, near Exeter prison – a grim stern-faced building not far from the high street – a man stepped out of the bushes and held a knife to his throat. 'Give me that packet you're carrying,' he'd growled.

Robbie had been so terrified that he'd just dropped it to the ground and ran for dear life. He didn't stop until he reached the street next to his. Then, looking back to make sure he hadn't been followed, he raced into his own house and shut the door behind him, leaning against it, gasping. This could bring his family more trouble than good.

'You stupid little . . .' Jacob had said later, using a word that Robbie's father would have thrown him out of the house for uttering. 'Do you know what that's cost me? You'll have to pay me back.'

'But I don't have it,' Robbie had pleaded.

'Then you'll have to do extra jobs for me, won't you?'

A cold scared feeling snaked through Robbie. He knew – just knew – that he was becoming more and more involved. How was he ever going to get out of this?

Then, one night, Jacob sent him to Plymouth. At first, despite his reservations, Robbie felt quite excited. He'd never been to the city before. Even though it was only an hour on the bus from Exeter, his family weren't great travellers. He told his mum he was meeting friends in town. His parents were having another row about how they were going to meet the bills; too distracted to ask questions.

But he followed Sam's brother's instructions and found himself in a horrible fourteen-storey block of flats in Devonport that stank of urine and worse; where kids younger than him, dressed in ragged jeans, gave him hard stares and swung pocket knives as they walked with casually defiant 'what you going to do about it?' expressions. How he wished from the bottom of his soul that he'd never accepted the reefer that had put him in Jacob's debt.

'I want to quit,' he told him when he got back.

'You can't,' Jacob snorted. 'If you try, I'll make sure you get busted as a dealer.'

Robbie felt as though the world was crashing in on top of his head. It was surely only a matter of time before he got caught by the police. His parents would be deeply ashamed. He'd go to prison. So he carried on.

After they'd had signed the recording contract, Jacob became increasingly jealous of the band, teasing them and calling them 'top of the flops'.

When he got Robbie on his own, he became really

nasty. 'What are you going to do if the police find out you're a criminal, Robbie? Your career will be over.'

It reached the point when Robbie couldn't take it anymore. He was going to confess. That's what he'd do. Screw the contract. It might be his dream but he couldn't live with this all his life. His parents would never forgive him but it was better than this weight, breaking his soul.

So, heart in mouth, he went into the police station.

'I want to report a crime,' he said.

He told the officer on the desk everything and was then interviewed by a male detective. Shaking but determined to do the right thing, Robbie gave him Jacob's name and address. 'He forced me into being a carrier,' he sobbed.

By the time he finished confessing, his legs had stopped shaking. He felt better. Purer. 'Are you going to charge me?' he asked.

'Nah, son. You were just an innocent victim.'

'But Jacob will go to prison, won't he?'

'Should do.'

Robbie sat and waited. Days passed. Then weeks. Then a month.

But nothing happened. Jacob wasn't arrested. Far from it. Instead, he became even cockier.

'Heard you tried to grass me up, Robbie lad,' he said, those black eyes narrowing. 'You'd better watch out. Anyone who tries to shaft me isn't safe. I hope you know that.'

'How did you find out?' he asked trembling.

'My old man controls everything that goes on around here, Robbie. So I'd watch your step if I were you.'

His words made Robbie shiver. There was no getting

out now. Old Man Senior had the whole town gripped in his hand.

But when Jacob took the wheel on that fateful day, Robbie knew he had to stop him. Not just because of the bad driving. Or because of the alcohol on his breath. But because of his other smell.

'You've been smoking weed again,' he hissed to Sam's brother.

Jacob smirked. 'And what if I have?'

'It will affect your judgement.'

'Ooh, affect my judgement,' echoed Jacob in a mocking, squeaky voice. 'And what are you going to do about that?'

No one else was around to hear the conversation. Robbie had two options. He could tell everyone and then miss the gig and end his career – or he could stay quiet and hope everything would be all right.

57

Vanessa

Lewis picked up Vanessa in the yellow sports car and they drove to a beach before walking up to the top of a sandy cliff.

'*Are you completely mad, Ness?*' Jack kept saying. '*He could push you over the edge. And I don't just mean physically.*'

I've told you to cut out the Ness, she retorted silently. *Anyway, Lewis wouldn't do that. He's our grandson.*

'*Are you sure about that?*' asked Jack.

Yes. She had to be.

'You know,' said Lewis, indicating that she should take his arm (so he still cared for her!), 'when Mum said you'd come round to the house, I didn't know how you'd found the address. Then I realized you must have seen the owner's manual.'

'So your car wasn't leased.'

'I just swap cars around. I borrow them from friends. We all do it. That one happened to be mine.'

'I see,' she said slowly.

'*Dodgy*,' muttered Jack.

'I'm sorry I turned up like that,' she added, ignoring her husband. 'I just wanted to see your mum. My daughter.'

'Of course you did, Granny. But you see, that put me in a tricky position. I told you before that Mum doesn't want you in our lives. She's hurt and angry because you gave her away.'

'But I didn't! It was Jack. And how did she know it was me when I went to your house?'

'I'd told her we'd met up and I guess she knew you'd try and find her. But the good news is that I've persuaded Mum to change her mind. She says she'll see you for a short time and hear you out about what happened.'

Her daughter would see her? Vanessa wanted to cry with excitement but also fear. Supposing Molly recognized her as the woman who'd tried to have her arrested? With any luck, she might not. After all, it was years ago. She looked a bit older now. Vanessa certainly wasn't going to bring it up. She'd only lose her daughter as soon as she'd found her. Of course, Vanessa couldn't help feeling shocked. She'd never imagined her daughter as a criminal.

'I don't know how to thank you.' Tears streamed down her face. 'I can't tell you what this feels like. Until you came into my life, I thought my daughter was dead. Since finding out she's alive, all I've wanted to do is to see her and hold her and . . .'

Overcome with emotion, she threw herself into Lewis's arms, hugging him.

But then she felt him gripping her arm. Somehow their positions had changed so that he was holding *her* rather than her holding *him*.

'The bad news, Granny, is that she wants you to pay.'

He said this so smoothly at first that she didn't realize the significance.

'I don't understand.'

'It's like this, Vanessa. Don't you think you owe her – and me too?'

Was this really the same Lewis talking? The grandson who had told her he wanted to get to know her better?

'Do you mean pay *money*?' she asked incredulously.

'Ten thousand pounds should do it,' continued Lewis equably.

'*Ten grand?*' roared Jack in her ear.

'You've got more than enough,' said Lewis smoothly. 'I know you have.'

Her mind shot back to when he'd taken her debit card to the bar. She'd checked her balance after that as she always did every evening. Correct to the penny. The cost of the meal had come off it but nothing else. And he'd paid her back in cash. But somehow he'd found out she had over £10,000 in the account.

'*I told you not to hand over your card,*' Jack snapped. '*I bet he took a photograph of it and got one of his dodgy friends to check your balance. You work in a court, Vanessa. You must know how clever fraudsters are.*'

She was so stunned she couldn't speak. Besides, Jack's telling-off meant she couldn't get a word in edgeways anyway.

They were standing too close to the edge of the cliff. The wind was whipping up and the sea was dashing on the rocks below. It reminded her of that terrible day when she'd fallen on the cliff path.

'Don't worry, Gran,' Lewis said, as if reading her mind. 'I'm not going to push you over the edge. Now let me take you back to the car. The sooner you pay, the sooner you can see Mum.'

'So that's why you contacted me in the first place,' she said numbly.

He held up his hands. 'It's part of the reason, but I must admit that I was also curious to see what kind of people could give my mother away.'

'Jack did,' she butted in. 'Not me.'

'Whatever. The thing is that the result was the same, wasn't it? Think how it must feel to know your parents didn't want you. You've got a lot of making up to do, if you ask me. Now, let me get the car door for you.'

He was so charming. So outwardly thoughtful. So deceitful. So wicked.

'*Told you so,*' said Jack.

The wind was getting stronger. Sharp needles of rain began to fall, stinging her face. Below them, strong waves thrashed. The sky had gone black.

Lewis came towards her. His face was set. Vanessa could hear her chest thudding with terror. Then he moved to one side to open the car door. Her heart pounded with relief.

As he stepped back to let her in, he slipped on the mud and fell. 'Shit!'

'Are you all right?' she asked, leaning down towards him, concerned, despite everything.

'Leave me alone,' he hissed.

He was lying on the ground. One of his trouser legs had ridden up, exposing his ankle. That's when she noticed. An emotional electric shock zapped through her.

'Oh my God,' she gasped. 'You're wearing a Peckham Rolex.'

Jack had shown her one once. '*It's the nickname for a prison monitoring tag,*' he'd said.

242

'That's why you're away so much,' she said shakily, as the truth dawned. 'You're in prison. Every now and then you get day release and that's when you see me . . .'

Again, Jack had told her about this. It was meant to help prisoners 'reintegrate' back into the community.

'That's none of your fucking business.'

Her mouth was dry with fear. 'You're meant to have a probation officer with you.'

'Not always,' he smirked. 'They trust you after a while. But don't go thinking about reporting me. Or you'll be sorry.'

Courage, fuelled by anger, took over. 'How dare you? It's very much my business! You're trying to extort money from me.'

Then a terrifying thought struck her. She stepped back. 'Why are you in prison? Did you hurt someone?'

He was hauling himself to his feet. 'Of course not. It was just fraud. I readjusted some figures at work. It wasn't like the client couldn't afford it.'

'Stealing is wrong,' she thundered. 'You told me you earned plenty but you've just taken it from others. I should turn you in. Then you'll be back in jail full-time. That nonsense about gardening leave and new jobs was all lies, wasn't it. Your "office" was actually your cell.'

He was on his feet now, his face close to hers. She could smell his sweat.

'If you say anything to anyone, you'll never meet your daughter. I'll tell her that you've changed your mind and that you're not having anything to do with her. Is that what you want?'

Never meet her daughter? Never get a chance to explain

what had happened at the birth in her own words? Not hug the person who had haunted her dreams for all these years? Not find out about her daughter's life and maybe, if she was brave enough, ask why on earth she'd become a shoplifter?

Then another awful thought occurred to her. Had Molly turned to crime because of her – or, more accurately, Jack? Had her daughter felt rejected because she'd been adopted?

Vanessa knew from her work in court that some people committed crimes because they had low self-esteem. 'Some people go on offending because they've hit rock-bottom and don't feel it can get any worse,' Carol had once explained.

She had to see Molly. She had to explain it all.

How could she allow this opportunity, possibly the only one she'd ever get, to slip through her fingers?

'*For God's sake,*' growled Jack. '*Don't do this. Can't you see this man is dangerous?*'

'All right,' said Vanessa, pushing Jack's voice out of her head and facing Lewis square on, trying to sound braver than she felt. 'You win.'

58

Vanessa

It would be worth it. Worth every penny of £10,000.

You have enough, Vanessa told herself. Besides, she had nothing else to spend her money on now she was on her own.

So she paid it into the account Lewis gave her, ignoring Jack's pleas in her head. '*You honestly think he'll fulfil his part of the bargain? Why should he? He's got the money, hasn't he?*'

But what else could she do? This might be her only chance.

Lewis was going to bring Molly to a coffee shop at twelve o'clock on the following Wednesday. It was more 'neutral ground' than their house, he'd said coldly, without his former warmth or niceties. Clearly he was showing his true colours. 'Mum doesn't want you there.'

Vanessa arrived early. There was a clock on the wall which saved her the embarrassment of constantly checking her watch. 12.10. 12.20. 12.30.

'*I told you*,' Jack's voice persisted. But he sounded sad for her rather than smug.

Vanessa felt physically sick. Where were they? Maybe something had happened to them? But, deep down, she knew Jack was right. Lewis had double-crossed her.

Then her phone rang: number withheld.

'Granny?'

'He's probably changed his number,' said Jack. *'Clever.'*

'Where are you?' she asked, her words falling over themselves.

'Unfortunately, there's been a bit of a hitch.'

Her voice was almost too choked to speak. 'I knew I shouldn't have trusted you.'

'Don't be like that, Granny.'

'Just tell me what's happened,' she pleaded, ignoring his sarcastic tone.

'The thing is, Mum's had second thoughts. She wants more time to think about it. But I've got another idea. I can introduce you to someone else. Someone you'll want to see.'

'Who?'

'You'll find out when we get there. Meanwhile, I'm afraid I'll need an extra five thousand for the introduction fee.'

'Are you kidding?' said Jack.

'Are you kidding?' said Vanessa.

'Deadly serious, actually.' His tone was grim.

Blow the money. She'd come this far. She couldn't stop now.

'All right then,' she said quickly, fearful he might change his mind.

'Good. You'll find it's worth it when you meet this person. How about next Wednesday to fit in with my day release? Same time. Same coffee shop. But only, of course, when you've paid the money. By the way, in case anyone asks, you gave it to me as a gift because, after all, you're my granny. Grannies do that kind of thing. Don't they?'

'Fine,' said Vanessa. Then a terrible thought crossed her mind. Lewis had lied about so many things. What if he had been lying about his crime? Supposing it hadn't been fraud after all.

'Just tell me you're not in prison for hurting anyone are you?' she faltered, her voice tailing away with terror.

'Scared that I'm going to kill you after you've handed over the money, are you?' He gave a short laugh. 'Funnily enough, I did meet someone inside who's become a good friend. He has contacts who'd do anything for the right price.'

Vanessa felt her voice trembling. She tried to calm it but failed.

'Is that a threat?'

'What do you think, Granny? See you next week then. Oh, and don't go telling anyone about this. Or you'll be sorry.'

Then the line went dead.

59

Janie

As I lie here in hospital, all I hear is one word.

Rehab. Short for 'Rehabilitation'.

There is nothing short about my rehab treatment. It seems to go on for ever.

There are machines to strengthen my body. Machines to strengthen my arms.

Machines to ease the strange phantom pain of my amputated left leg.

The gym where I just flopped down on the ground because I couldn't stay upright, despite the crutches and my prosthetic.

Kind people in white coats who tell me they've 'seen worse' and that I'll 'get there'.

But I keep having what they call 'setbacks'.

My body doesn't take kindly to these efforts to repair it.

Nor does my mind, which isn't to be trusted. One minute I know I'm in hospital, the next I think I'm by the sea or at school or at home.

I want my mother more than ever.

I yearn for the white light to take me back and carry me to her.

In the meantime, I grin and bear it. Dad visits every day with a smile that doesn't match the sadness in his eyes. Between him and the well-meaning staff, I have no choice but to continue with this gruelling routine. 'It will be worth it, Janie. You'll see!'

But no one can know for sure, can they?

And then, something happens that changes everything.

60

Robbie

Writing everything down, thinks Robbie, isn't such a bad idea. It's quite cathartic. It helps him to see himself object-ively, especially as he's doing it in the third person, looking inwards to a teenager he's almost beginning to feel sorry for. The young Robbie had been in a difficult place. He'd been understandably terrified by Jacob, a bully and a crim-inal. No wonder he'd made wrong decisions.

Yet nothing excuses his final crime. He's dreading get-ting to that part. But when he does, he has to describe it as it was. Word for word. Otherwise, what's the point in doing this?

'How's it going?' asks the prison tutor, stopping by Robbie's desk for a minute.

'OK, thanks,' he replies.

Then he picks up his pen again. It's taken a few weeks to get this far, even though he writes it in his cell at night as well as in class. But he's almost there now. It's the morn-ing of the accident. They're on their way to the gig in Brighton. The promoter says this is their chance to really launch their career. And Jacob – high on drink and drugs and God knows what else – is at the wheel of the van.

It was all right at first, or so Robbie told himself. Jacob was driving steadily. He stopped when the lights turned amber instead of trying to beat them to red as he often did. He waited at junctions. He didn't exceed the speed limits.

Then Sam and Matt began talking about the album they were going to record for the label at the posh glass-and-chrome London studio. 'Imagine if it gets to the top ten! We'll be rich,' Sam said excitedly.

Robbie, sitting up front, couldn't miss Jacob's hands tightening on the wheel. He could almost smell the jealousy; it felt dangerous.

'I'm going to buy a sports car,' said Matt.

'I'm going to get one too.'

'Mine will be red.'

'What would you get Robbie?' asked Jacob, glancing across at him with one of his sardonic smiles plastered across his face. His eyes were slits. He wasn't looking at the road.

'A house on a nice estate with a big bathroom and three bedrooms,' said Robbie. It was his mother's dream. She was always saying so.

Jacob guffawed. Spit flew out of his mouth and onto the wheel. 'That's sweet, isn't it, boys? Then again, your dad's black, isn't he? Did he grow up in a mud hut and wear a grass skirt?'

'No, he didn't,' said Robbie tightly. 'But even if he had, there'd be nothing wrong with that. So don't talk like that.'

'I'll talk however I want.'

Thud. One of the wheels caught the edge of the pavement.

'Be careful, bruv,' Sam said from the back.

'Be careful?' Another guffaw. More spitting on the floor of the van. Eye rolling too. A swigging of the vodka from the bottle to hand. 'Is that my little bruv telling me to be careful?' Jacob's voice hardened. 'Since when do you get to tell me what to do?'

'Sorry,' said Sam quickly.

'Sorry? You'll have to do better than that if you want me to get you to your "very important gig" on time.'

Sarcasm dripped off the words. Then Jacob took his hand off the wheel again, reaching into the glove compartment. Taking a pinch of white powder, he snorted it up his nose, his shaky hands dropping bits onto his jeans.

The others shifted uncomfortably. Thank God the road was straight, thought Robbie. He didn't know this area very well. And from the way he was driving, Jacob clearly didn't either.

'Dad will smell it,' said Sam, his voice wobbling.

'Cocaine doesn't smell, you idiot. 'Sides, no one's going to tell the old man. Are they?'

There was a silence.

'ARE they?' he roared.

'No.'

There was a puking sound from the back – Matt was being sick.

'Great. You'd better clear that up before we get there. My dad doesn't like a mess.'

Then Jacob turned sideways to face Robbie. 'What about you? Are you going to split?'

'No,' Robbie said quietly.

'Didn't think so. After all, you're up to your neck in this with the little jobs you do for me, aren't you?'

'What do you mean?' asked Sam, confused.

'Why don't you tell them, Robbie?'

Robbie could feel himself getting very red. 'Shut up, Jacob.'

'SHUT UP?' His voice was scorching with fury. It burned Robbie's ears and made his chest beat so hard he thought he was going to have a heart attack. 'Who do you think you're talking to, you little creep?'

THUD.

Jacob's driving was berserk now. Zigzagging across the road. They were going – once more – through the same town where Robbie had met the auburn-haired girl. The sea was on their right. It looked so beautiful. So flat, so peaceful compared to the tight, toxic atmosphere in the van.

He was taking a left now. Past a lifeboat station, towards a bend.

Jacob was going to kill them all at this rate. He had to do something!

Jumping up, Robbie leaned across and grabbed the wheel, attempting to steer the van safely.

'What the fuck are you doing?' yelled Jacob.

Robbie was too busy concentrating to answer. The sun was in his eyes. He couldn't see properly. Where was the road going?

The safest thing to do was to stop. But the handbrake was so stiff and Jacob, still in the driver's seat, was pressing down on the accelerator.

Then they took a corner. 'Anyone got sunglasses?' Robbie screamed.

That's when they felt the bump and the horrible sound as metal hit the front of the van.

There was a screech of tyres and the van stopped.

'Oh my God,' whispered Robbie. 'We've hit something.'

61

Robbie

Yasmine sits opposite him in the prison's Legal Visits room, his notebook in her hand. Robbie shifts uncomfortably in his seat. His lawyer has been reading solidly for the last hour. Robbie's mouth is dry. What is she going to think of him? For some reason, amongst everything else going on, her opinion matters.

The notebook is a written record of everything he's already told Irena. But, somehow, seeing someone else reading his life story makes it feel even more real. Even more terrifying.

The lawyer looks at him. Her face is a mixture of astonishment and hope. That's what it looks like, but how can there be hope when he's ruined a girl's life?

'So you took the wheel from a man who was incapable of driving?' she says.

He nods. 'I'd never driven before but I knew I had to do something or we'd all die.'

'And what happened after that? Did you get out of the van to see what you'd hit?'

He hesitates. He'd been unable to write this bit down. But now, he realizes, he can't hide anymore. So he tells her everything that happened when they got out of the van. Well, almost everything.

Her questions come falling out, one after the other.

He tries to answer them as best he can as she furiously makes notes.

Then he tells her the very last piece of the nightmare jigsaw. Old Man Senior.

Yasmine sits forward attentively. 'This is gold, Robbie. Don't you see? If we can get the jury on side, we can win this case, especially if we can provide proof that this man Jacob has a criminal history. Why didn't you tell me this before?'

Robbie hesitates. He thinks of Irena's face and her words. '*If you do not tell the court, I will leave you.*'

'I wanted to protect my family from the media frenzy that would come from a long trial,' he says. 'I felt it was best if I simply pleaded guilty and went down as quietly as possible . . . Besides, I always felt I was guilty anyway,' he finishes, almost in a whisper.

Yasmine's facial expressions go from shock to anger and, finally, to determination. 'But I think we've got a very strong defence here,' she says. 'And I'm going to do my darnedest to convince the jury of your innocence.'

Robbie's eyes fill with tears. 'It won't bring back Janie. Not the girl she once was.'

'No,' she says. 'It won't. Yet it will bring justice down upon the people who were really responsible.'

'But the old man is dead.'

'What about the others?'

'Disappeared off the face of the earth – and before you ask, I didn't have anything to do with that.'

'I'm not saying you did.'

He puts his face in his hands. 'I'm still scared that one

of them might read about the case and come after my family.'

'I can't say that won't happen, Robbie. But you might be able to get police protection. And even if you can't, you can make a new life for you and your family somewhere else.'

'It will mean changing our lives,' he says.

'Hasn't that already happened?'

Yes, it has, he realizes. Not as much as Janie's life has changed, of course. But the main thing is that the chief perpetrator is dead. As for the others, Robbie really doesn't know where they are, despite the various online searches he's desperately made over the years.

'So you'll tell the court everything?' she asks.

He thinks back to Irena's ultimatum.

He nods.

'Good,' she says. 'Now let's get cracking. We've got one month to build a case.'

62

Janie

'Ready, Janie?'

The voice comes at me like a wave. I hear several waves a day. There's my dad's voice, which is soothing, but which carries with it an air of tragedy at times, and amazement that I'm alive at others.

There's the physio's voice, which lifts me up, telling me not to worry because she's 'got' me and I'm not going to fall.

There's the carer's kind voice when she suggests that I might need the commode.

When you've had injuries like mine, you see and feel and hear things in a different way.

You also talk differently. At least I do. After the first stroke, which apparently happened soon after the accident, I couldn't speak at all. Not a sound.

But I could still see and hear.

My brain, on the other hand, seems to turn on and off. It's a bit like an old car: sometimes it starts in the morning, sometimes it doesn't. I've heard someone say that 'no two cases are ever the same'.

Then the physio taught me to sign, so I can now reply to people when they speak to me.

The first thing I did was to tell him what had happened.

'A white van hit you?' gasped the physio.

Before I knew it, the police arrived at the hospital.

'Can you give us any more details, Janie?' asked a man. I vaguely recognized him from when Mum had gone missing. I think he said his name was Jack.

'There were voices,' I signalled. 'One of them wanted to stay but the others wanted to go.'

Dad was there too. 'If it's any consolation, Mr White,' the policeman said, 'I'm going to make sure we catch the bastards who did this to your daughter.'

63

Vanessa

The following Wednesday took forever to come. Vanessa didn't have high hopes – she didn't need Jack to tell her that Lewis would come up with another excuse.

So she didn't bother getting there early. When she did arrive, Vanessa pretended to read the news feed on her iPad, resisting the temptation to look up every time she heard the ping of the coffee-shop door opening.

So when she sensed someone walking towards her table and pulling up a chair opposite, she felt a tingle of shock and relief, and something else she couldn't place.

'Hello, Vanessa,' said Lewis. 'This is Thomas.'

Vanessa stared and stared.

'I don't understand,' she whispered.

'Sorry. I should have introduced you properly. Thomas is my son. He's four, almost five. He lives with his mum but I have access twice a month, providing I'm accompanied by my probation officer. She's sitting over there so we can have some privacy.'

Vanessa glanced briefly at a woman in a black anorak, who gave her a brief nod. Then she turned back to take Thomas in. What a beautiful little boy! He was so like Lewis. So like Jack. 'So this . . . this is my great-grandson?'

'Yes.' Lewis looked pleased. 'You see, I do keep my promises, Granny. Well, some of them.'

Vanessa wanted to hold this little boy in her arms. To cuddle him. To feel the warmth of this miracle. Her great-grandson! She wanted to say how she'd never, in her life, imagined this. But how could you explain such a complicated situation to a child? How could she just leap in and play great-grandma when they didn't know each other?

'Would you like something to eat?' she tried instead.

'Yes please.'

What beautiful manners!

'Are you allowed to have a chocolate biscuit?'

Thomas looked up at Lewis. 'May I, Daddy? Granny and I made biscuits this morning, so I've already had one.'

Granny? Her daughter? Vanessa's heart flipped.

'I would say it's all right, love.'

Lewis had a different look about him, Vanessa noticed. His face was softer. He was genuinely proud and loving of his little boy. This was a side she hadn't seen before. Was it possible that she had been too harsh on him?

No. He was extorting money from her, after all.

'It's not too late to turn over a new leaf, Lewis,' she said gently. 'Wouldn't it be better for your little boy if you did that?'

His expression darkened. 'What do you know about that? You don't know what it's like to bring up a child.'

She winced. 'I do know that it's wrong to steal. Besides, you're an accountant. You could earn an honest living.'

'Yes – but that doesn't mean I earn a fortune. Instead,

I get to see how much others earn. I wanted to make sure that Mum had everything she needed.'

'But surely this is the wrong way to go about it?'

'Is it? Have you any idea how hard it is for some people who don't have fancy bungalows to live in and widows' pensions?'

'Daddy.' Thomas was tugging at his father's sleeve. 'Don't argue.'

'We're not, love,' Lewis said quickly. Then he whispered to Vanessa, 'Stop preaching right now, or I'll leave with Thomas and you'll never see him again.'

64

Janie

The policeman had promised he'd find the people who ran me over.

But he couldn't.

'They've tried, Janie,' said Dad with tears in his eyes. 'But they don't have enough details to go on. There weren't any witnesses, unfortunately.'

Of course, I was disappointed, but part of me also felt that, even if they did find those responsible, it wasn't going to help. I might as well just get on with trying to live as normal a life as possible.

One of my fingers seemed to work better than any of the others. It was still weak, but with the physio's encouragement and the exercises she gave me, I finally managed to type with this 'good' finger. It took ages, but it helped. By then, I was out of residential rehab and into a specially converted apartment on the outskirts of Exeter.

I was worried in case Mum came back to the old house and didn't know where I was. But when I wrote this down, Dad looked sad. 'Maybe you don't remember this, Janie, but Mum drowned. I'm sorry.'

It's what everyone thought. Everyone but me.

I know – don't ask me how – that Mum is still alive.

PART THREE

65

Judge

Richard Baker hadn't always wanted to be a judge. He hadn't come from that sort of family. The job description had not figured in the '*Which Career Is Best for You?*' booklet that they were each given at grammar school.

But he'd seen enough unfairness, in class and at home, to know that he didn't like injustice. And that he wasn't afraid of an argument.

'You hold your own well in debates, Baker,' one of the masters had observed after Richard's team had thrashed the opposition from a minor public school, who then went home in their smart uniforms, heads bowed in shame.

'Thank you, sir.'

'Ever thought of being a lawyer?'

'No. To be honest, I'm not entirely sure what that entails.'

'There are different kinds. Some do what's called conveyancing. That's . . .'

'Buying houses,' cut in Richard.

'Exactly.'

'Apologies for interrupting, sir. It's just that I read a lot – and I've learned a new word from the dictionary every night since I was a child.'

'Very commendable. Apology accepted. Lawyers might also handle areas such as divorce, employment disputes and crime,' he continued.

Richard found his interest being piqued.

'Then there are barristers, who argue in court. They could be defending or prosecuting someone who is suspected of having committed a crime.'

'But how do they know if the person they are arguing for is innocent?'

'Good point. Some barristers might say it doesn't matter.'

'But it should.'

'Maybe.' The teacher had waved his hand as if this need not bother them. 'And then, Baker, there are judges, who preside over the court and give the jury advice on the law.'

'By the way, there are very few female judges.'

'Why?'

'Excellent question. In my view, there should be far more.'

'And what gives judges the right to give the jury guidance? They're not God.'

The master patted Richard on the shoulder. 'I think this might well be the career for you. My uncle is a barrister, as a matter of fact. I could have a word if you like and arrange a meeting. You could also sit in the public gallery at the local court and see what happens for yourself.'

Richard was always looking for ways to get out of the house and away from his stepmother and father. The prospect of hiding away in a court was appealing.

At first, he felt a fraud as he walked from home to the Old Bailey and told the man on the door that he was going into the public gallery. He was allowed into a case that had already started but he soon picked it up. A woman was accused of murdering her stepmother. He couldn't help feeling a certain sympathy for her.

The jury took thirty minutes to find her guilty.

'But I didn't do it!' she called out when the verdict was given. Then she looked up at the public gallery and seemed to stare right into Richard's eyes, as if she knew he'd wanted her to get off. 'I didn't do it,' she repeated. 'You've got to believe me.'

Richard did.

On Monday, he sought out the careers master and said that yes, he wanted to read law.

'Good. I would suggest applying to Balliol. That was my old college. I think it would suit you down to the ground.'

And it did. Richard loved the sharp debates at Oxford. The way you were treated as an adult. The freedom from home. Certain things irritated him, such as having a 'scout' to clean your room. Why should students like him have such ridiculous privileges?

Often he wondered about the woman in court. When they began to study precedents in lectures, he looked her up. Richard's blood froze. A year after she'd been sentenced, she had strangled herself in prison with shoelaces.

It was then that Richard decided he didn't only want a career as a barrister. He wanted eventually to become a judge.

It was also about the same time that he met Ian. Not that long before his stepmother died.

But if he'd known then about Janie White and how the case was going to change his life, none of this might have happened.

At least, that's what he pretended. The truth was that he just hadn't been able to stop himself.

66

Janie

Time went by. Don't ask me to tell you how many days or months or even years. My brain doesn't work like that anymore.

I can tell you that I am going to be in a wheelchair for ever now but that I can move myself around the apartment quite speedily when I want to. I miss the sea and the gulls and the smell of the salty air, but at least I have a view of the quay here.

Meanwhile, my new computer is amazing! I can tell Dad what I want for tea – scampi and chips please! (He's very patient at feeding me.)

But the best thing is that I'm writing a diary.

I'm trying to remember everything that happened but there are some big blanks too. Because of my memory, I have to keep rereading the bits I've already written before I can start the next part.

I was doing it every day until I had another stroke.

At least that's what they told me. I don't remember much about it. It was quite a mild one, they said, although it set me back considerably.

Then Outpatients sent a new physio round.

'Ready, Janie?'

She was a jolly person who hummed while helping me do my exercises.

And, somehow, I found myself humming along with her. It was rather comforting.

'Janie?' She used my name as if she had known me for as long as the old physio had, but I didn't mind. 'I didn't realize you could hum.'

I shrugged in a sort of 'Nor did I' way.

She seemed to get it. They're quite intuitive, some of these caring people. I suppose you have to be.

'Have you ever tried singing?'

I gave her an 'Are you kidding?' look.

'There's some new research, Janie, that says people who can't talk after strokes sometimes have better luck singing instead.'

I pointed to my iPad.

'Want to write something down?'

I nodded.

'I can't sing,' I typed. 'I have a terrible voice. I couldn't even get into the school choir.'

It was true. 'I tried again and again every year,' I wrote, 'but I never got in. I blame "Greensleeves". This was the song we had to sing for the audition. Have you ever tried it? Those notes are higher than a house.'

She laughed as if this was funny. Actually it wasn't, because I'd been desperate to be in the choir. Mum had a lovely voice. Even when she was crying.

'Case studies show that you don't need to have been good at singing before, Janie,' she said. 'Strokes can change all kinds of things. Not just voices but personalities too.'

Had my personality changed, I wondered. Difficult to tell. I'm not sure what the old 'before the accident' me was like.

Anyway, all this was making me a bit tired, to be honest. So to keep her quiet, I opened my mouth. I pretended I was back at school, auditioning for the choir. I steeled myself for that first bloody line.

'Alas my love, you do me wrong . . .'

270

But nothing happened.

'Try again,' said the physio, who was beginning to get on my nerves now. It felt like she was nagging. 'Copy me. Open your mouth wide. Imagine you're breathing from your throat.'

'Alas my love . . .'

It's hoarse and scratchy, like rough sand or rocks as you clamber out of the sea. But, nevertheless, something is coming out.

'Your voice needs oiling,' said the physio, giving me a beaker of water with a straw in it. 'Don't be put off. It's not surprising – you haven't used it for so long. Try singing this after me.'

'A spoonful of sugar helps the medicine go down.'

If I could have gasped, I would have. My mother used to sing that when I was a child!

'A spoonful of sugar . . .' I began.

Then I stopped. Something else had just come into my head.

'After the white van hit me, I heard voices,' I sang croakily.

'I know, dear,' said the physio. 'You wrote that down. Remember?'

'One was called Robbie and the other was called Jacob.'

'Hang on. I need to tell someone this.'

And that's when the second half of my life started. The part I'm going to tell you about now.

67

Janie

'It happens occasionally,' said one of the doctors. 'Stroke victims can sometimes find they have a singing voice even if they can't speak. Did she sing before?'

'No,' said Dad.

'Mum did!'

Dad flinched.

'I gather that your wife is no longer with us,' said the doctor gently.

'That's right,' Dad replied.

'We don't know for sure,' I sang.

Dad flinched again. 'My wife drowned but they never found the body.'

'I'm sorry.'

Despite me remembering the names Robbie and Jacob, the police are still no closer to finding the people who hit me. I also told them that I thought I'd seen someone with a red-and-blue tattoo, although I couldn't be sure so maybe I imagined it. They contacted the press and lots of papers put out appeals for information. But no one came forward.

Dad showed me all the newspaper headlines from the time of my accident. 'Why did people care so much?' I asked.

'You were . . . are . . . so young and beautiful. Plus,' he continued, 'the government were running a campaign to make drivers more aware of cyclists. You caught their attention.'

I tried to act as if I hadn't noticed his change of tense.

Meanwhile, life just goes on with my reading and my diary, and now my singing.

I love listening to music too. One of my favourite singers is Robbie Manning. I have his picture on the wall. His face reminds me of someone but I can't think who.

I don't like looking in the mirror because my own face has changed so much.

I try not to think about what could have happened in my life if I hadn't ridden my bike down the road that sunny morning. If I'd got out of the sea even a minute later, everything might have been different.

But I can't help it. If it weren't for that van, I might have been a famous writer, or a publisher. I might have been a mother, had children. But most of all, I might have found Mum.

More years go by. I count them with the help of my computer. Fifteen. Sixteen. Seventeen. Eighteen. Nineteen. Twenty.

Twenty whole years since the accident.

And that's when a policeman calls. He and Dad talk together in low voices in the room next door. After that, Dad comes into the kitchen where I'm writing my story. It's not easy because I'm doing it retrospectively. You see, the present only makes sense if I go back to the beginning. To make it more difficult, I can only write what I remember. And that changes all the time.

Dad's face is still. Silent. Serious. 'Janie, they've got the man who did this to you.'

Then he tells me his name.

68

Vanessa

'I have a great-grandson.' Vanessa didn't know whether to laugh with happiness or cry.

Unlike his father, Thomas was an innocent child. He might, in time, learn to love her. She already felt like she loved him, even though they'd barely spent an hour together.

Then she'd made the mistake of trying to get Lewis to see the error of his ways. Shortly after that, Lewis had said they had to go. He glanced nervously at the probation officer as he spoke.

'When can I see my daughter?' Vanessa asked desperately.

'I'll be in touch,' he said curtly.

'*No doubt there'll be more money involved*,' Jack had sniffed. But her husband's voice wasn't as hard as usual. Perhaps he'd been touched by the child too.

Vanessa couldn't help giving Thomas a little kiss on his cheek as they left. It felt so soft! So warm. It was agony, letting him go.

'Please let me see him again,' she implored Lewis.

'Like I said, I'll be in touch.'

Then she watched the lovely little boy slip his hand into his father's, turning to give her a small shy wave as he left.

After they'd gone, she could barely move for the terrible aching hole he'd left in her heart.

The next day, she received a call from the office, summoning her to a meeting about the 'Girl Who Returned from the Dead' (as the papers kept calling her) and the special arrangements that needed to be made for her appearance in court.

'I have to stress that this may be one of the most difficult cases you've ever had,' said her supervisor. 'Going to court will be a very big thing for Janie White and reassuring her will be a big challenge. I know you can do it though, Vanessa.'

Of course, she would do whatever she could to ease the poor girl's nerves. But, right now, all she could think about was her beautiful great-grandson. How cruel it would be if Lewis never allowed her to see him again. If necessary, she'd give away all her money just to spend a few more minutes in his company.

'Oh,' said Carol, 'I almost forgot. They've changed the forms. This is just an update. Can you have a read-through and sign at the bottom?'

One of the paragraphs asked her to confirm that she didn't have a criminal record.

Of course not, unless you counted being daft enough to be duped by your husband and then again by your grandson.

She also had to declare any personal connection with the witness. Should she say, wondered Vanessa, that Jack had tried to find the evil monster who had knocked down Janie White all those years ago? Surely not. Besides, she didn't want to stand down from this case. For some reason, it felt important to her. More than any other.

She picked up a pen and signed.

'Just one last thing,' added the supervisor. 'I know I don't need to remind you of this, but don't give out any details of the case to anyone, will you?'

Vanessa thought of how she'd told Lewis she'd be looking after Janie.

'Of course not,' she said, feeling slightly sick.

'Good, because it's not common knowledge that Janie can sing. Remember how I told you not to mention it to anyone?'

Oh God, thought Vanessa. How stupid she'd been to tell Lewis, in her desperation to impress him.

The supervisor beamed at her. 'You're the perfect support, Vanessa. That poor woman is going to be in safe hands.'

69

Robbie

Prison makes grown men cry. Not just him but others too.

Robbie had learned this the day after the lawyer's visit. 'I'll be back next week so we can keep prepping,' she'd told him.

Prepping? She made it sound like homework, rather than dissecting a terrible crime. Even so, he found himself going over and over the facts again, which was what he was doing when he passed Big Jim sobbing in the pod. The pod was the kitchen. Robbie had been 'promoted' there from the toilets, thank God. Some other poor bastard had that job now.

But then he realized that the pod was just as bad, only scarier: they were allowed to use knives. Sometimes the contradictions in prison were ridiculous. How could you give a murderer a sharp knife and tell him to slice up potatoes for lunch when he could easily use the very same knife to slice the limb off a fellow prisoner who hadn't shown him respect?

'Respect' was a big word in prison, Robbie discovered. You might show someone a lack of respect by accidentally brushing against them in the queue for food. Someone had done that before he'd got here, his cellmate told him shortly after he'd arrived. The victim was still in intensive care.

'What about the man who did it?'

'No one owned up.'

'Didn't the others split?'

His cellmate had looked at him like he was stark raving mad. 'And that would be showing respect, would it? Think about it, mate.'

'What's wrong?' Robbie now asked Big Jim.

Big Jim wasn't just big. He was enormous. His feet were twice the size of Robbie's, or at least looked as though they were. When someone had anonymously deposited a used condom in one of his shoes last week (not an unusual occurrence), it had seemed quite small.

'I can't find my cat.'

This had been another surprise when Robbie had arrived. Cats roamed the grounds. They were feral, apparently. It had started when an officer had brought in his pet moggy (without permission) and it had turned out to be pregnant.

The prison cats walked around as if they were patrolling officers themselves, though they soon skedaddled if anyone tried to pick them up. But they brought out a soft side in some of the most hardened prisoners and security guards.

Some, like Big Jim, formed particular attachments to them – he'd managed to coax a white-pawed black cat into his cell. The officers turned a blind eye because Big Jim's behaviour had improved significantly as a result, or so Robbie had heard.

'When did you see him last?'

'Two bleeding days ago.'

Robbie sat down next to him. He'd had a cat when he was a kid; he understood the pain. 'It's OK. I'm sure he'll turn up. He'll want feeding.'

Just what his mother had said when his cat had gone. But he hadn't come back. Years later, his mother admitted that she'd found him by the roadside soon after he'd vanished. She hadn't told him, she said, because she didn't want him to be upset.

Robbie kept that to himself. Big Jim was sobbing enough as it was. When men inside began to cry, they could get angry pretty quick. And Big Jim was holding a knife.

'Do you want me to cut these potatoes?'

More sobbing, although at least he let Robbie take the knife. But as Robbie started to peel the potatoes, he found himself crying along with Big Jim. He began weeping for everything. Being away from the kids. From Irena. From life.

But most of all, Robbie was crying because he had destroyed an innocent girl's life.

Then the men started to come in for breakfast.

'Stop bloody whimpering,' said one of the accompanying officers. 'You'll make them all kick off.'

Robbie had noticed that it didn't take much for men to ally themselves to someone's cause. Not necessarily because they believed in it but because they wanted to fuel the disturbance.

The last thing Robbie wanted was to be labelled as a troublemaker. So he moved away and quietly thought about Irena and the children and the trial, and how he had to be strong for them. But Big Jim was still sobbing.

'Right,' said the officer. 'Let's get you away from here before you cause even more trouble.'

Big Jim resisted all the way to the gates of the wing, thrashing with his fists and feet so hard that another officer had to be called in to help.

The next day Robbie learned that he'd been taken to Solitary.

The day after that, they found Big Jim's cat in the freezer. No one would admit responsibility.

That night, Big Jim was found dead in his cell. He must have hidden one of the kitchen knives.

When Irena visits, Robbie's head is still messed up from Big Jim's death but he tries to hide it.

'You didn't come last week,' he says. 'I was worried.'

She shrugs. 'We have been ill.'

'But you didn't tell me.'

'I write.'

'I didn't get it.'

'You don't believe me?' Her face is very pale.

'Of course, I do.'

Letters went astray in prison. Cats got put in freezers. Grown men like Big Jim topped themselves over a stray even though he'd been in prison for garrotting the leader of a rival gang.

A tear runs down his face.

'Stop.' Irena's hand is on his wrist and then away again, before a guard can see it and tell them off. 'I need you to be strong like us.'

Suddenly, he finds himself bursting into uncontrollable tears – something he's managed not to do since coming here. But now the court case is coming up, he is terrified by the thought of being in prison for the rest of his life. 'You don't know what it's like,' he sobs. 'You didn't nearly kill someone. Leave her for dead. Now she can't talk or walk. The jury is going to hate me.'

'But it was not all your fault,' Irena soothes.

'The jury might not think so. What if I'm found guilty? I'll be in prison for years and years with murderers and rapists. You and the children will be on your own and –'

'The jury will understand,' she cuts in. 'When you tell them what you tell me and the lawyer, they will feel sorry for you. You were a young boy who was misled.' She stands up. 'I must go now. I have to take Daisy to her ballet class. I am trying to keep our normal routine going for the children's sake. Besides, you need time to prepare your mind.'

But what if the jury convicts him?

Robbie starts to gasp for breath. He feels himself swallowing huge gulps of air in panic.

'Breathe,' says Irena in a voice that is sympathetic but tough at the same time. 'That's better. Please, Robbie. Pull yourself together. We will survive as a family. I know we will.'

From the *Daily Mail*:

WOULD YOU STAY BY YOUR MAN IF HE WAS GUILTY?

The trial of Robbie Manning – the singer who, in a dramatic twist of events last month, changed his mind and pleaded not guilty – is to start shortly.

We can't help wondering how his wife feels. Would you trust him if you were in her shoes?

A quick straw poll round the office says no.

Yet at the same time, some of us might have a grudging admiration for Irena, who met Robbie at one of his performances back in the early days. It's said that they fell in love when she gazed up at him from the front row.

Sceptics thought that this young woman – an unknown who had just moved to the UK – was after his money.

But the years have proved them wrong. They have built a solid family base; an example to look up to until the shocking news of Robbie's arrest.

Sources say that Irena is visiting her disgraced husband in prison. But what will she do if he's found guilty?

The nation is holding its breath.

Some readers might wonder why Janie White, The Girl Who Came Back from the Dead, is so important. But older readers will remember how Janie's story captivated the nation at the time. The government was campaigning for drivers to take more care over cyclists following a series of tragic incidents. Janie was a beautiful young woman whose future was cruelly snatched from her. She was, and remains, symbolic of all the innocent cyclists who have been maimed or killed over the years.

Now we all hope that justice will be done. For Janie. And for any decent person who believes in doing right.

70

Robbie

Robbie can't sleep. He can't eat. He goes over and over the things he had told Irena. The things that happened after the accident. He writes them down in his journal, but that only makes it worse.

'Your fucking nightmares are keeping me awake,' complains Bruce. 'What's going on inside your head, man?'

And without meaning to – or perhaps because he really will go mad if he doesn't – he tells this man. A murderer. Because unlike Irena, whose eyes had shown such horror when he'd told her, Bruce is evil. He might understand. So he reads his latest entry out loud to his cellmate . . .

The first thing he saw after the accident was a heap of mangled metal. Then a bicycle wheel, still spinning. Twisted handlebars with a wicker basket still attached.

Only then did he see the body, lying just to the right of the bike. Motionless.

'No. NO!' he cried.

'Fuck!' said Sam softly from behind him.

Robbie's chest lurched, the same way it had when Jacob said he had to keep delivering those packages. But this was worse. Far worse. He felt sick. Weak. The victim, he saw, had long hair, streaked with blood.

Robbie had blood streaming down his face too from hitting his forehead on the windscreen when Jacob had slammed on the brakes.

He knelt on the ground next to her. Her face was turned away from him. He didn't like to touch it so he went round to the other side. My God! It was smashed in like a broken mask, eyes closed. And her leg – the left one – oh my God, her leg!

'Please tell me you're alive,' he whimpered. At least he thinks that's what he said, but his mind was in such a state that he couldn't really know if he'd spoken at all.

He felt for a pulse. Her arm was crushed too. Blood was all over his hand now. Was he doing it right? He certainly couldn't feel a beat.

'She's dead!' he cried out, stumbling to his feet.

Jacob was looking around as if working out the lay of the land, just like when he was planning the drug dropoffs. There was a fixed, determined expression on his face, just like Old Man Senior's. 'We've got to get out of here,' he said.

Robbie felt as though he was standing in concrete. His legs were fixed. 'We can't, Jacob. We've got to report this to the police.'

'Sure you want to do that? You were the one who grabbed the wheel, remember? You'll go to jail.'

'You're just scared they'll do you for being high,' Robbie retorted.

'They will,' whispered Sam, who was shaking so hard that his jaw was juddering. 'Like you said, Robbie. She's dead. If we report this, you and Jacob could get banged up. You shouldn't have been driving without a licence and

Jacob was drunk and on drugs. Telling the cops about this won't bring her back. We've got a future. We haven't worked this hard for nothing. Who's going to want a band that killed someone?'

Matt began to cry.

Robbie was terrified. His parents wouldn't cope if he went to prison. But it hadn't been his fault, had it? He'd just tried to take over from Jacob, who hadn't been fit to drive. Surely the police would understand that?

'I've still got to do the right thing,' he heard himself saying. 'I'm going to tell someone what's happened.'

'No you're not,' snarled Jacob. 'Or you'll make me use this.'

To Robbie's horror, Jacob pulled a flick knife from his pocket. It glinted in the early morning sunlight as he held it against Robbie's throat. 'Be quiet or I'll kill you. I'll kill the rest of you too if you don't listen to me. We need to get out of here right now, before anyone comes along.'

'Put that down, bro,' said Sam pleadingly. 'We agree with you, don't we, boys?'

'What about the van?' whimpered Matt.

But there was hardly any damage. Just a few scratches. A big van like that and a bike? Well, there was no contest.

'We need to get rid of it in case the police get forensics,' said Sam, his voice trembling.

'I'll ring Dad to tell him what's happened,' said Jacob firmly, although Robbie could sense a quiver in his voice too. 'He'll sort it. He always does.'

And that's exactly what happened. They drove straight home and Old Man Senior took them into his factory office, closed the door and told them that this had 'never happened'.

'Sometimes,' he said, 'you have to put things like this out of your head or else you don't get over them.'

Things like this? thought Robbie. A girl had died, and it was all his fault. Well, not all, because he wouldn't have had to take the wheel if Jacob hadn't been high. The sun had blinded him, too. He hadn't expected the corner because he didn't know the area that well. But at the end of the day, he was the one responsible.

The cut on his head was still bleeding. 'I fell off my bike,' he told his mother.

'Robbie! That's bad. I'll take you to A & E.'

'No,' he said, scared that someone might ask him questions there and get suspicious. 'I don't have the time. I ought to practise.'

She gave him a worried look. 'You need to look after yourself more, love. Here, let me see what I can do myself.'

Then she cleaned the wound and put some dressings on.

Meanwhile, Old Man Senior rang the promoter to say that the band had gone down with a bug.

'They were pretty pissed off at being cancelled at such short notice,' Sam told Robbie, 'but Dad worked his charm and they agreed to rearrange the gig for a few weeks' time.'

'I can't do it,' Robbie sobbed.

'You've got to. We need your lyrics, and we need your voice. Come on, Robbie, do you really want to turn down this chance of a lifetime?'

But he couldn't eat. He couldn't drink. He kept retching, bringing up bile. No need to pretend he had a bug – he felt worse than he'd ever felt in his life. He watched the news obsessively over the next two days on TV but nothing came up. Then, on his way to band practice, he saw the cover of the weekly local paper, which had come out that morning. His stomach plummeted.

18-YEAR-OLD-CYCLIST IN COMA AFTER BRUTAL HIT AND RUN.

POLICE SEARCHING FOR DRIVER. APPEAL FOR WITNESSES.

My God! He sprinted to the factory unit where Old Man Senior allowed them to rehearse. 'She's still alive!' he said, bursting in. 'We should have rung for the ambulance!'

'You're the one who couldn't feel the pulse,' hissed Jacob. 'It must have still been there. Now shut the fuck up before someone hears you.'

Robbie stared at him, incredulous. 'Don't you have any feelings?'

'Not if it's a choice between some stranger and me being sent down.'

Robbie turned for the door.

'Where are you going?'

'I can't stay and practise as if this hasn't happened.'

He ran through the streets feeling sick to the core. Then he vomited on the ground to the tut-tutting of a couple passing by. They watched disapprovingly as Robbie threw up again. 'Had too much to drink, I suppose?' the man said.

'I've done something terrible,' Robbie blurted out.

The woman clutched her husband's arm. 'What?'

For a crazy second, he wanted to tell them but then he ran on.

'Is it nerves about performing on a big stage?' asked his mum when he arrived home, running upstairs to lock himself in his bedroom. Her voice came through the door. 'You'll be all right, Robbie. Your dad and I are really proud of you. I know we wanted you to go to college but we've come round.'

The next morning, he heard the soft thud of his dad's *Daily Express* being delivered. He crept downstairs before anyone else was up. And there it was. As he'd feared, the nationals had picked up on the local paper's story.

Earlier this week, 18-year-old Janie White was mown down by a hit-and-run driver near her Devon coastal home. She is now in a coma, fighting for her life. When will the government act to curtail this continued violence towards cyclists on our roads? Recent statistics show that, in the previous 12 months, 111 pedal cyclists were killed in Great Britain while 4,353 were critically injured and a further 11,994 sustained other types of injuries. It is time for this to stop.

Robbie couldn't read any more. Instead, he went back to his room and stayed there. When his mum knocked on the door, he yelled out: 'If Sam calls, tell him I've quit the band.'

71

Robbie

His mum brought food and left it by the door. He shot out to use the toilet every now and then before dashing back again.

On the sixth day, there was a knock. 'You've someone to see you,' said Robbie's mother in a different voice from usual.

'I said I didn't want to see anyone.'

Then a deep, scratchy voice cut in. 'It's me. Jacob.'

Robbie shook. If he didn't let him in, Jacob might grass.

'Heard you're chucking in the band,' he said after Robbie's mother had gone downstairs. 'But you won't do that, will you? We need you. If you don't play, I'll tell the police what happened.'

'I can't anymore, Jacob. Plus, if you do that, they'll get you too.'

'My dad will sort it for me. He always does. But he won't help you if you tell the truth.'

Jacob's face was white. Robbie had never seen him look so terrified. 'It's in every single bleeding newspaper now,' he hissed, spit flying out of his mouth. 'My dad says they'll hang, draw and quarter the person who did this. And we all know who that is, don't we?'

'Then I'll hand myself in and face the consequences,' said Robbie dully.

'And name us?'

Robbie hesitated for a vital second.

Jacob grabbed the collar of his shirt so hard that he could barely breathe. 'If you are stupid enough to do that, I'll deny everything and so will the others. You've got no proof, but I'm not taking that risk. So that means you are not bloody well going to hand yourself in. Got it?'

Robbie could only make gasping noises to show he agreed.

The grip released. 'Glad you see sense. Besides, I want this band to continue. While you've been sobbing in your room, I've been taking your place. I can't write the stuff you do but I can sing. The producers like me. And I've got the guts to do anything and be famous, even if you haven't.'

His voice was packed with emotion. Robbie had never heard it like this before. Jacob, he realized, was dead serious about worming his way into the band.

'What about Matt?'

'He's moved away.'

'Because of this?'

'I don't know, do I? Who cares? Look, Robbie. That girl Janie, or whatever her name is, might die. And even if she survives, what's she going to say? She might remember that a van hit her but my dad has got rid of it now. There are hundreds, probably thousands, of white vans in this country. If there had been any witnesses, they'd have come forward by now. We're safe as long as no one blabs. So are you going to come back to the band or are you going to hand yourself in and ruin your future? Not to mention break your parents' hearts?'

'Get out,' said Robbie, regretting now that he hadn't said this earlier. 'How can I live with this guilt for the rest of my life? I'm going to the cops whether you like it or not.'

Jacob's face darkened. 'You're going to regret this.'

He'd hand himself in the next day, Robbie decided. He'd have one last evening at home. And then he'd take his courage in both hands and do the right thing.

But in the morning, his mother knocked on the door and told him he had another visitor.

It was Old Man Senior. 'I'm going to get straight to the point, lad. You were the one who was driving. But my Jacob was responsible too. I try to help my family. But drunk and on drugs while he was driving? Nearly killing a beautiful young girl like that? The press will make mince-meat out of you all – it's all over the headlines. None of you stand a chance if we don't play our cards right.'

Robbie had been avoiding the recent news. He knew there would be pictures and he couldn't deal with that. He just couldn't. The fact that the victim was 'beautiful' shouldn't be important. But he'd delivered enough news-papers to know that looks mattered to people.

'All this,' continued Old Man Senior, 'is going to be a tough one for me to handle if you go to the police. So I've got a proposition for you, Robbie. If you keep quiet, I'll make sure you want for nothing.'

'I don't want anything anyway,' said Robbie to the wall. Why couldn't everyone just leave him alone?

'Look at me, lad.' He felt a pair of hands grip his head and twist it so he was forced to gaze into Old Man

Senior's unsmiling eyes. 'Be sensible like Matt and his parents. Get out of here and live a new life.'

'You paid them off, didn't you?'

'My Jacob needs a mission in life,' he continued, ignoring the question. 'This band could be the making of him. It could help him go steady. And, I don't mind admitting it, I rather like the idea of my lads being famous. But they tell me that they need your lyrics. Apparently, no one else can write like you. So if you don't go back to this effing band, I am going to make it very difficult for your parents.'

A shot of terror ploughed through him.

'What do you mean?'

'Do I have to spell it out? Your dad works at the wood yard, doesn't he?'

'So?'

'I know the bloke who runs it. We're old chums. We wouldn't want your dad to lose his job, would we? You might all be out on the streets then. And your mum. Got a pretty face, that one. It would be a shame if anything happened to it.'

Robbie felt a rush of fear grabbing his heart and twisting it. 'You wouldn't do that.'

'Wouldn't I? I tell you, son, there's nothing I wouldn't do for my family. This could be the making of my lads, Robbie. But we need you in it too if we're going to be big.'

He patted Robbie on the back. Robbie wanted to move away but his feet were glued to the ground with fear.

'Think about it. You've got twenty-four hours to decide. If you make the right decision, I might even be able to persuade my mate to give your dad a promotion.'

'And if I don't do what you want?'

Old Man Senior's face hardened. 'Then you might wake up one day and find you don't have a mum or dad anymore.'

'I'll think about it,' said Robbie, hardly daring to believe he was standing up to Old Man Senior. But he had to do the right thing, didn't he? Besides, these might just be empty threats.

The following day, Robbie finally left his bedroom. He came downstairs to find his mother's arm in plaster.

'I tripped on the pavement and fell,' she said, when she saw the look on his face.

'What really happened, Mum?' he whispered.

She looked terrified. 'Quiet or your father will hear. Some man knocked into me. As I fell, he said to tell you that this would be the beginning of something far worse if you didn't do what you had been told. What did he mean, Robbie?'

'It doesn't matter.'

Then he remembered the purple bruise on her elbow from before. 'Were you lying about that too?' he asked.

She flushed. 'It was when we wanted you to give up the band and focus on your schoolwork. Someone cornered me and told me that you had to keep singing, otherwise they'd tell the police what you'd done.'

His mum paused and looked at him as if she didn't know him. 'What *did* you do, Robbie?'

How could he tell her he'd been a drug mule for Jacob? And that now he'd mowed down an innocent girl?

'Nothing,' he said. 'It's all right. You won't get hurt again.'

Then, hating himself, he went back to Old Man Senior. 'All right,' he said grimly. 'You win. But if you or any of

294

your thugs lay a hand on either of my parents, I'm going straight to the police.'

Robbie stops. He looks up from his journal at his cell-mate's face.

'Bloody hell,' says Bruce, who, for once, had listened to every word without interrupting. 'I'd have fucking killed that Jacob and his dad there and then.'

'I'm not like you,' says Robbie.

Bruce snorts with laughter. 'Come off it, man. Under-neath, you're as bad as the rest of us. If you'd helped that girl, she might have lived.' He reaches across, grabbing Robbie's sleeve and then wipes his nose on it. 'That's what I reckon the jury will think, anyway.'

72

Janie

Robbie Manning. The man whose poster I had on the wall until Dad ripped it off.

He did this to me?

Did Dad really say that? Or is my mind playing tricks on me again?

But as the days go by, it seems all this is for real.

'Are you sure you want to give evidence in court, love?' Dad asks. 'It's going to be really stressful, you know. It might affect your health. And think of the publicity. It's going to bring it all back again.'

'I have to, Dad,' I sing.

'You don't have to. Remember what the lawyers said – we can do a televised recording instead.'

'I want to be there,' I reply.

But I don't tell him the real reason why.

Mum will be in court. I'm sure of it. She'll have heard about the trial and she'll want to see me. I know it. Then finally we can be together again.

And don't tell me I've got false hopes. Because when you're in my position, a false hope is better than no hope at all.

Then, a few days later, a note flutters through the door. Usually Dad gets the post but he's in the bathroom and I manage to pick it up with this long stick they've given me. It's only one line, but it's enough: *'IF YOU GIVE EVIDENCE YOU WILL DIE.'*

'Right,' says Dad when I show him. 'That's it. I don't want you risking it. Someone's already hurt you. I'm not letting them do it again.'

But it's not his decision. It's mine. And no one's going to stop me. I want to face the man who did this to me. But most of all, it could be my only chance of finding Mum.

73

Vanessa

Today is the day that Janie White finally gets justice.

That was Vanessa's first thought when she woke. At last!

Normally, she put out tomorrow's clothes on the spare bed the night before. It was a habit from her store-detective days. It saved time so she could get Jack's breakfast and see him out of the door (or in, depending on his shifts) before going out herself.

Vanessa's eye was usually drawn to the outfit that felt right for that day. She never hesitated. It was as if something was telling her that the sky-blue blouse was perfect for a Monday because it was the start of a new week.

But last night had been different. What did you wear when you're looking after a woman whose face had been plastered over the front pages of every newspaper in the land?

A woman whose story was enough to wrench the heart of any living soul.

She needed something soothing. Something that might make Janie feel at ease. Certain colours could do that: yellow was good at raising people's spirits; soft blue could be comforting; red could be too vibrant or in-your-face.

But right now, Vanessa was facing an even more difficult challenge. After all, what colours would disguise a woman who had made a terrible mistake? Who had signed legal forms to say that she neither had any personal connection to the case, nor had discussed it with anyone else.

The form had also asked her to declare anything that might be relevant. Did that include being the victim of extortion by a grandson on remand? Possibly. But what about her great-grandson?

Vanessa's body positively melted when she thought of little Thomas. His sweet face. That innocence. The way he had so clearly loved his dad. One day, maybe, he would learn to love her like that. It wouldn't make up for all those years as a mother that Jack had deprived her of. But it would help. It might even help the little boy, too, to have another person in his life.

No. She couldn't tell anyone about Lewis or he might be taken back to prison full-time, and then she'd never see Thomas again. It was bad enough not seeing her daughter. But to meet her great-grandson and then lose him? It was too awful to think about.

Meanwhile, she had to concentrate on helping Janie. Now, what could she wear that would give the poor girl some hope?

Flicking through her wardrobe, Vanessa's fingers finally settled on a pale pink skirt suit from Jaeger. Subtle enough to calm both her and the witness; stylish enough to show she meant business; soft enough (just feel the texture!) for comfort. It was as if the suit was putting its arms around her, saying everything would be all right. But would it?

Get a grip, she told herself, looking in the mirror. *It's not you who you need to be thinking of. It's Janie. How must she be feeling?*

Vanessa had never supported a witness like this before. How would it all work? Presumably Janie would write it down on her keyboard if she wanted some water. Or maybe sing. It was intriguing! Rather exciting, in fact.

She was still mulling this over while eating her usual breakfast of fruit and toast, when her phone pinged.

It was a message from Carol.

Emergency. Janie's dad has got in touch to say Janie's received an anonymous threat, telling her that if she gives evidence she'll die. Shocking, isn't it? Janie still wants to go ahead but is understandably shaky. Can you go round and talk to them both? Maybe show them round the court before the case starts? You're the best person for the job, Vanessa.

Her supervisor sounded even more complimentary than usual. But behind the words, Vanessa could sniff desperation.

It had taken them years to catch this bastard Robbie Manning. Years during which this poor woman had been trying to piece her life together. Vanessa had read all the reports in the paper, and in her gut, she knew he was guilty.

Life was fragile. Fleeting. It could end in the click of a finger. Or it could change into something completely different. It could work the other way too. One minute you might be mourning the child you lost nearly fifty years ago; the next you find she's alive with a son and a grandson. A human heart might be whole one second and fractured into a million pieces the next.

As she got up to put her plate in the sink (Jack had always fussed about the right way to stack the dishwasher so she hadn't used it since he'd died), Vanessa felt a surge of powerful determination shooting through her.

She was going to help Janie in whatever way she could. She'd show the young woman that the court could actually be a friendlier place than it seemed. She'd familiarize her with the layout; show her who sat where; explain some of its ridiculously yet also strangely comforting archaic processes. But most of all, she'd prove to Janie that she, Vanessa, was there for her.

It was, after all, the least she could do. She had made mistakes in her own life – including a terrible one – but she could try and restore right to other people's lives as compensation.

While she was slipping into her light beige coat, her mobile rang.

'I'm on my way,' she said, assuming it was her superior.

'Just me, Granny.'

Vanessa froze.

'I want to wish you luck for the case today. I do hope The Girl from the Dead gets justice.' He landed on the word 'dead' with a chilling emphasis. 'Those things you confided in me? Maybe you shouldn't have done.'

Would Lewis tell on her? Or was he just trying to scare her?

'Don't worry, Granny. I won't say anything if you don't. By the way, I'm still trying to talk Mum round to meeting up. I reckon a £5,000 deposit should do it.'

More money? She was almost beyond counting. But she couldn't lose her daughter again.

'And you think she'll definitely see me?'

'I can't guarantee that, Granny. But it's worth it to find

out, don't you think? Or, to put it another way, she'll *definitely* say no if you don't pay up. Just put it in the usual account.'

Her savings would be depleted to nothing at this rate. But Lewis was right, damn him. It was worth it.

'When will you know for certain?' she whispered.

'I'll be in touch.'

And then he put down the phone.

74

Robbie

The cell door opens with an electronic bleep and the usual heavy bang, as it slams against the wall.

'Wake up, mate. You're in court today.'

Robbie doesn't need waking up. He hasn't slept a wink. His mother used to use that expression. He'd had this vision of her trying to wink in the night as a child. Now he knows what it feels like. Thank God she isn't alive to see this. He is almost grateful that his parents, who both passed away some years ago, are no longer here.

It was going to be a long drive from London to Exeter. Yasmine had already explained that defendants were generally tried in the crown court nearest to their crime.

'Thank you,' Robbie now says to the guard. He is unfailingly polite to everyone. You had to be when you were in the public eye. He'd learned that early on in his career – you couldn't have an off day like normal people. Any sign of irritability or tiredness or, well, anything, really, would be on the front page. He'd seen it all.

So Robbie always tried to appear respectful, even if he didn't feel it in his soul. This guard was unpleasant. He clearly enjoyed bossing others around. And he had his own opinions before the verdict.

'Going all the way down to Devon, I hear.'

'Yes.' Robbie isn't looking forward to this. He doesn't want to go anywhere near the place where it happened.

'Ready to face the music, are you, sonny?' The man guffaws at his own joke. 'Not the kind of music you've been used to, I expect. Let's hope you get everything you deserve.'

Robbie ignores him. Best not to rise to the provocation. Instead, he heads for the showers to be first in the queue.

But someone has got there before him. On the mirror, in what looks like red lipstick, are the words: *Still think you're a star, do you? You deserve to die for what you did. I hope you go to hell.*

No fear of that.

He's in hell already.

But Robbie has a feeling it's going to get a whole lot worse.

75

Vanessa

Was she crazy to have given in to Lewis again?

Maybe. But she'd rather do that than spend the rest of her life wondering if she'd missed her only chance to meet her daughter.

In the meantime, she needed to concentrate on the case.

Janie's home wasn't what Vanessa had expected. For some reason, she'd assumed the interior would be fairly bland, to fit the traditional red-brick block with its 'Homes for Assisted Living' sign outside.

But each wall was a different colour: turquoise, scarlet, azure blue.

'My daughter loves bright colours,' said Janie's father, leading her through the apartment towards the back.

You're not kidding, Vanessa thought. It was like a rainbow, jumping out to greet anyone who came inside. It excited her – Janie felt like her sort of person!

'Thank you so much for coming,' he said.

'It's a pleasure.'

Derek White was one of those men who seemed kind but who also gave the impression that they'd been 'through the mill', as Vanessa's mother used to say.

'The letter has really unsettled us both. Of course, the

police are investigating but to be honest, I'm beginning to think this is all getting too much for Janie. I'm not sure she should give evidence at all.'

'What does Janie think?' Vanessa asked.

'She wants to go ahead but she doesn't know what she's letting herself in for. I was called up to sit on a jury once and felt so uncomfortable. Goodness knows what it must have been like for the witnesses.'

He had a point, thought Vanessa, just as her phone bleeped with another text. Lewis. A shot of fear, excitement and apprehension zapped through her but she couldn't read it now.

'Quite a lot of people give video evidence,' said Vanessa, trying to bring herself back to the moment.

'I still think it's too much for her. Surely the lawyers have got enough to nail this bastard without upsetting my daughter even more? They have her written statement, after all.'

'A written statement isn't the same as seeing someone,' Vanessa said gently. She was aware her job wasn't to persuade witnesses to be there but she couldn't help it. Robbie Manning must not be allowed to get off. 'Do you live here with Janie?'

'Yes. We have a rota of full-time carers and a physio.'

'What sort of things does Janie like doing?' she asked, wondering if this might help in some way.

'Well, there's a craft room in the building and table tennis too for those who are capable. I wasn't sure how we'd cope after having our own house for so long but this is quite an amazing place.

'Everyone has their own entrance. There's also a

residents' lounge if people want company, but my Janie's quite a loner. She loves listening to music, of course, and we go for walks. Well, I walk and she's in her wheelchair. But most of the time, she likes writing stuff on her computer.' He gave a little laugh. 'Not that she ever shows me.'

'Oh well,' Vanessa said, trying to make a joke out of it. 'We all have our secrets, don't we?'

She glanced up at him in time to see him biting his lip. 'I suppose so.'

They were coming into another section of the apartment. Above was a skylight. The whole room was light, in fact. The walls here were sunflower yellow.

A woman was sitting in a wheelchair, her slouched back facing them. She was wearing a bright blue jumper.

'Janie,' said Derek. 'I've brought you a visitor. She's called Vanessa and she's from the court.'

The motorized wheelchair turned with a gentle whirr. Vanessa had seen all kinds of people in her time but Janie's face required every ounce of her strength not to look away. It was hideously scarred. The left eye was lower than the right. Her arms hung loosely by her side. One leg appeared twisted. So did her mouth. The other leg ended in a stump above the knee.

Vanessa found herself frozen. All the things she'd decided to say; all the words to explain why court wasn't actually as scary as it might seem, went completely out of her head.

Anger pounded through her blood. Hatred. Fury towards the man who had done this to the woman in front of her. Disgust at whoever had sent her that note.

No wonder Janie was upset about going to court.

But just as Vanessa searched for the right words to say, the most beautiful, angelic voice rose into the air.

It wasn't like anything Vanessa had ever heard before. It sailed to the ceiling and transformed Janie's fallen face into what looked like utter joy.

'Hello,' she sang. 'How lovely to meet you.'

76

Judge

'Morning, Your Honour,' says his clerk.

'Good morning, Stuart.'

Even now he felt like an imposter when someone called him that. In his head, he was still Richard Baker whose stepmother hated him and whose father didn't have the guts to stop her mentally whipping a small boy. Anything for a quiet life. That had been his father's unspoken motto.

Was that why he, himself, had deliberately chosen to lead a life that was anything but quiet and uneventful? A lie to cover another lie.

'Your papers are all ready in your office,' said his clerk.

'Thank you, Stuart.'

Judge sat down. His usual morning decaf coffee was on his desk in his fine bone-china mug. Alongside it was a plate of the wafer-thin ginger biscuits that Ian had introduced him to all those years ago. Everything was in its place. It was the way he liked it.

But today was different. Today was the Janie White case, or, as some newspapers called her, 'The Girl Who Came Back from the Dead'.

He'd done enough high-profile cases before without feeling nervous, so why should this one be any different? Usually, he relished the chance to mete out justice to the man and woman on the street who had been wronged, like this poor girl. Wasn't this why he had become a judge in the first place? To put the world to rights?

But there was something about this particular case that gave him a bad feeling. Perhaps it was because Robbie Manning – whose modern music even *he* had heard of – had suddenly changed his mind and pleaded not guilty. There was always something suspicious about defendants who did that. It smacked of someone who panicked at the last minute when faced with telling the truth.

He'd like to talk about this with Vanessa but it wouldn't be professional. Judge's heart always lifted when he thought of her. She was the only woman who had ever made him feel that way. Not in *that* way, of course. But a different way.

'Can you just take me as I am?' he'd asked Vanessa when she'd tried to find out more about his childhood and 'what makes you tick'.

'Don't be daft,' she'd said. 'That's what friends are for, isn't it? Just as long as you can take me as I am.'

He'd doubted whether she had as much to hide as he did, but her answer had reassured him.

'Of course,' he'd agreed, feeling a warmth spreading through him.

Ignore it, he'd tell himself when people gave them second glances if they sat together in the coffee shop. This wasn't a regular occurrence but he could see the question 'What's a judge doing with a voluntary worker?' written on their faces.

They'd been out to dinner a few times, and to the cinema too (though not since they found out they were going to be on the same case together). Vanessa had loved that film with Jim Broadbent. 'Bill Nighy is another favourite of mine,' she'd chirped. He hadn't known much about either of them, but he'd rather enjoyed their performances anyway.

Once her hand crept into his during a psychological thriller she'd wanted to see.

'Sorry,' she'd said afterwards. 'I was scared.'

But he hadn't minded – he'd actually rather liked the feel of her hand in his. It was different from Ian's, but that was good because no one could replace him.

He was glad Vanessa would be there today. That poor Janie White needed someone like her, with that cheery smile, matter-of-factness and down-to-earth kindness. A real tonic! It had certainly helped him . . .

'Excuse me, Your Honour,' said his clerk, cutting into his thoughts. 'This has just been delivered by a courier.'

Judge opened it. Later, when he looked back, he couldn't remember anything out of the ordinary about the envelope. It was sealed and his name on the front was typed like the brief note inside.

Send Robbie Manning down or else the world will find out what you did to your stepmother.

Judge's blood froze. There was only one person in the world who knew that.

And he was dead.

77

Vanessa

'It's lovely to meet you too,' said Vanessa to Janie, but her eyes blurred with tears.

What kind of evil person could have done this to her? She'd only had one other 'client' in a wheelchair before and he had had an assistance dog. It struck Vanessa that maybe Janie might benefit from one, but this was hardly the time or the place to mention it.

Vanessa's phone pinged. It was her supervisor telling her that the trial was due to begin in two hours.

But Vanessa sensed she couldn't rush this.

'Is this yours?' she asked, gesturing to the computer at Janie's side.

'She writes stories on it,' said Janie's dad.

'That's brilliant. Has Janie always done that?'

'Yes!' she says, breaking in with a trill. 'I can answer myself, you know!'

There was a laugh as she sang, yet at the same time there was also a hint of 'I'm not an idiot'.

'Of course,' said Vanessa, thinking back to Jack's comment about the girl being a 'blooming cabbage'. This clearly wasn't true – at least not anymore. 'I'm so sorry. You've got such a beautiful voice. Could you sing before the . . .'

She stopped.

'Before the accident?' sang Janie. 'Not very well. But Mum had a lovely voice, didn't she, Dad?'

Derek nodded. He was a handsome man, Vanessa thought. Around sixty, at a guess, but with mostly silver hair. Maybe it was the stress.

'Yes. My wife had always wanted to be a professional.'

There was a short, awkward silence, which Vanessa filled by talking Janie through the order of events at the trial, hoping it might reassure her.

'Would you like me to take you into the court now before everyone arrives? I can show you the screen you could sit behind, to give evidence where no one will see you. My supervisor thought you might feel more comfortable that way.'

'OK,' sang Janie.

That was quick for someone who'd been having second thoughts.

'You're sure, love?' Derek threw a worried glance at Vanessa. 'I'm concerned that a court appearance might be too stressful for her.'

'I want to do it, Dad.'

Strange. Her supervisor had given the impression that it was Janie who had been having doubts, not her father. But it didn't seem that way.

'I want to show you something first,' Janie continued.

Vanessa glanced at her watch. Time was tight, but Janie seemed insistent.

Janie wheeled herself to the bedroom and pointed to a shell by her bed. Then she touched her heart. 'My mother gave that to me,' she sang.

'It's beautiful,' said Vanessa. 'I'd love a proper tour, Janie, but I think we're going to have to go now.'

Derek looked nervous. 'Do you honestly think this is a good idea?'

The poor man was obviously spooked by that anonymous note. What father wouldn't be? Vanessa suddenly had a very bad feeling about this.

'It's your choice,' she said. 'You don't have to give evidence.'

Janie's mouth tightened. 'I want to,' she sang. 'I've made up my mind. No nasty letter is going to stop me. If I can survive my accident, I can survive anything.'

78

Robbie

He feels as sick as a dog as the van heads towards his inevitable destiny. The journey, he knows, will take about five hours. Through the slit window, he spots the odd recognizable landmark. Stonehenge. Bridport. Lyme Regis. They must be taking the coastal route. He catches sight of the sea slapping against rocks. It's furious. Angry.

He hopes they won't go through the small seaside town where the accident happened, but they do. It's not on the direct route so Robbie can't help wondering if the driver has been told to do it on purpose to spook him out. And there it is. The exact spot. The same sharp corner.

He retches.

'Bringing back memories, Manning?' asks the guard.

So he was right – the diversion *was* intentional. Maybe the prosecution had bribed the driver to do it. Nothing, he was beginning to learn, was impossible in prison.

When they get to the court, there are crowds outside. This is nothing new for Robbie. After all, there had been crowds waiting ever since the band got big.

Jacob used to like that. He'd revelled in fame. So had Sam. But crowds had always made Robbie feel sick with nerves, especially when he went solo. All those people waiting to hear him sing and play the guitar! Supposing they came away disappointed?

Yet they never seemed to, judging from the roars for more and the music sales reaching heights he'd never even dreamed of.

But now he was facing a different crowd. These people wanted something else. They were demanding blood, judging from the posters they were carrying.

JUSTICE FOR THE GIRL WHO CAME BACK FROM THE DEAD.

YOU DESERVE TO DIE TOO!

And then the phrase that always breaks his heart: ROBBIE, HOW COULD YOU?

Where was Irena? He could only hope she was safe inside the court. He hadn't wanted her to come at all but she'd insisted. 'We do things together,' she'd said in that 'don't argue with me' voice.

He is being led out of the van.

Seagulls are screaming overhead. 'Guilty. Guilty,' they seem to hiss.

They've entered the court now and he's being led down the stairs to a cell, where he'll wait until the case begins. He starts to shake. He can still hear the fury outside.

'Your fans don't seem to like you much, mate, do they?' says the officer before slamming the door behind him.

The defence barrister, whom Yasmine has briefed, arrives shortly afterwards. She is, apparently, 'skilled in her field'.

'Now remember what we talked about, Robbie,' she says. 'Just tell the truth.'

'I will,' he says, trembling. But would they believe him?

Changing his mind and pleading not guilty at the last minute can't have looked good. And even now that he knows Old Man Senior is dead, Robbie's terrified. His lawyer had told him that this witness Eric Sharp was going to be there. He'd never heard of the man. Is he a nutter? Or had he really seen the accident with his own eyes?

What if the jury believes this stranger?

What if he's made a mistake, going down the trial route? Can he go back again to guilty? He doesn't know but it feels too late now.

There's a knock on the door. It's the prison officer.

'They're ready for you,' he says.

79

Vanessa

They were in court now, with half an hour to go before the case began.

'You don't have to do this, love,' said Derek again.

Janie looked around. 'It's smaller than I thought,' she sang softly, as if relieved.

Vanessa was glad they hadn't been put in one of the bigger, more intimidating courts.

'This is the screen I was telling you about.'

'Is it bullet-proof?' asked Derek.

'No,' admitted Vanessa. "It's not meant to be a physical defence. More of a mental one.'

'Dad, stop worrying.'

'Someone's been threatening you, Janie. Of course I'm worried.'

'What can they do to me? There are police here, aren't there?'

'Yes but . . . They might not stop someone trying to hurt you *after* the case, love.'

Janie shook her head. 'If I don't do this, it will be a message to other drivers that they can get away with near-murder. I've been waiting twenty years for justice. I'm not backing down now.'

Her voice had lost that bright, tuneful quality.

A clerk came up to them. 'The case is due to start. I believe you have special dispensation to go into court now behind a screen so you are in place before giving your evidence.'

'Yes,' said Vanessa. She touched Janie gently on the shoulder. 'Shall we make our way?'

Derek shot her a hard look. 'You're trying to push my daughter into this.'

'No, Dad,' sang Janie softly. 'She isn't. I want to do it.'

80

Robbie

Robbie's legs are trembling, as the guard leads him to the dock. He looks around, searching for Irena in the public gallery on the opposite side of the room.

There she is, in dark glasses with a scarf around her head, even though it's hot. She gives him a slight nod. He'd hoped for a gesture showing more affection. Then again, Irena often kept her feelings to herself.

In some ways, Robbie is grateful he can't see Janie White. His lawyer had told him that she'd be giving evidence behind a screen so no one could see her. 'Perhaps she's ashamed of her injuries.'

Robbie winces. Injuries he is responsible for.

'All rise.'

The judge comes in. He is short and solid, with an appearance that reminds Robbie of a barrel. Their eyes meet briefly. It isn't a condemning expression, Robbie realizes. Yet it almost looks fearful. Maybe even judges get scared by criminals, despite seeing them every day.

Robbie's barrister had told him how the trial would start. The prosecution would outline the case. They'd make it sound as though Robbie was guilty from the beginning. The jury might be swayed by this. So it was up to the defence – Robbie's barrister – to put forward the other side.

'But won't the jury have made up their minds by then?' he'd asked.

'If they have, they will hopefully change them when you describe what really happened.'

But will they? He'll soon find out.

The case begins.

The prosecution lawyer is young (about forty at a guess) and confidence gushes out of her.

'We are here today to decide whether the accused, Robbie Manning – who did not have a driving licence and had never driven a vehicle before – is guilty of deliberately running over a young girl in the prime of her youth and leaving her for dead.'

She pauses for dramatic effect.

'You will, no doubt, have read of many such cases over the years. Perhaps you have allowed yourself a little sigh and moment of regret for the victim. But today you have a chance to see, at first hand, the terrible impact of what the defence might later claim was "a moment of madness" or "a lack of concentration". Maybe even sunlight obstructing the driver's view. In my career, I have heard them all.'

She's looking straight at the jury now. 'But the effect is just the same. Death. Traumatic injury. Devastation. Not only for the victim but also for the victim's family. Loved ones. And an end to the victim's hopes and dreams.'

The jury is spellbound. Robbie can see that. This barrister seems more like an actor in a film. He, Robbie, is the villain. Even though Yasmine had warned him that the prosecution would try to demolish him before the other side had its say, he knows he doesn't stand a chance. He who goes first must surely get the upper hand by making the initial impression.

'I could,' continues the barrister, 'describe the scene to you in words. I could describe how critical injuries have changed Janie White's life. I could also tell you that she has received an anonymous note, threatening her very life if she gives evidence.'

Robbie stiffens. He didn't know that. Who had sent Janie's note? Could it be the same person who sent his? Are they both being targeted?

'But in my view, nothing tells the truth more accurately than pictures. I would like to show you exactly what Robbie Manning has done. Please turn to the monitor on the wall. This is a picture of Janie shortly after the accused ran her over and left her for dead.'

There are gasps from both the spectators' gallery and the jury.

Robbie forces himself to look at the bloody mess that has haunted him for twenty years. He is back there now, in his head. Shaking. Desperately asking if she is still alive.

'And here is a picture of Janie as she is today.'

Oh my God! Robbie goes cold at the slumped body in the wheelchair. The face that droops on one side. If he could, he would willingly take her place, to purge this terrible guilt inside. He's a monster, he tells himself. An evil monster. Running someone over by mistake was one thing. Not staying and not calling for help was another.

'And here,' continues the barrister, 'is a picture of Janie, a few months before the accident, taken by a friend at a gig they went to. Little did Janie know that her life was about to change for ever.'

Robbie's body begins to break out in sweat. His hands are so slippery that he cannot grip the rail. His vision blurs. He rubs his eyes, unable to believe what he's seeing.

Janie is the girl from the gig. The girl with the pale auburn hair. The first girl he'd ever kissed. The girl he'd searched for, all those years ago.

81

Vanessa

'Are you all right, love?' whispered Vanessa. Sometimes she just couldn't help using words that others might consider too friendly.

Janie nodded. Maybe she was saving her singing voice for later, or maybe she was nervous. Derek must be in the public gallery, although they couldn't see him from behind the screen.

Vanessa saw tears in Janie's eyes as the prosecution outlined to the court how Robbie Manning, now one of the most famous singers in the world, had left her for dead.

They couldn't see the pictures on the monitor that the barrister just mentioned, but they could hear the jury's gasps. Janie began to hum, obviously distressed, rocking herself back and forth in the chair. There was a computer in front of her on which she could type her thoughts. *How could he have done this?* she wrote. *What kind of person could be so cruel?*

'I know, love. I'm sorry. Would you like some water?'

No, thank you, she wrote. *I want to get out from behind this screen. I've changed my mind. I want him to see me.*

But what if it freaked Janie out to see all eyes on her in court?

'They've already shown him pictures of what you look like,' Vanessa reminded her.

No. I want to him to see me in the flesh. I want to shame him. Please, Vanessa. Get rid of this.

Lashing out, she tried to push the screen away.

Vanessa began to panic. This had never happened to her before. She caught the eye of one of the court officials and he came over. Briefly, she explained the problem.

'We can sort it,' he said.

Someone must have told someone something because the judge – *her* Judge – called for a brief adjournment so the screen could be removed. Everyone else was requested to leave the court while it happened.

'Is that better?' asked Vanessa, concerned this would be too much for her to handle. Everyone would be looking at them.

Janie nodded. *I feel freer*, she typed.

You're a brave woman, Vanessa almost said. But she didn't want Janie to think she was being condescending.

People filed back. All eyes were on them. There were gasps of shock. What must Janie feel like, to be on show like this?

There were some police at the exit doors too, including that younger cop whom Jack had worked with. It made her feel upset. Even though she was angry with him, Jack had died too young. Vanessa thought for a moment about their plans to go on a cruise after his retirement. He'd always wanted to see the Norwegian fjords. She'd fancied the Caribbean. Many other women of her age still had their husbands. Why not her? Was it better to have a cheating living husband than a dead one?

Yes, she couldn't help thinking. Then she'd really give him a piece of her mind. *Do you hear that, Jack?* she asked silently.

But Jack's voice was conspicuously absent in her head.

Meanwhile, Vanessa almost took Janie's hand to give her comfort, but she sensed the steel behind the woman's eyes. The Girl Who Came Back from the Dead wanted to do this on her own. And who was she to interfere?

82

Janie

'You're going to be asked to give evidence in a minute, love,' whispers the nice lady next to me. I think her name is Vanessa, but I can't quite be sure. My mind's like that. It pretends to take in things but then loses them.

Her voice comes through the fog which is wrapping itself round my brain. This is normal for me too. There are moments when I can think clearly and moments when I can't.

Right now, I can't.

Maybe it's the sea of faces gawping at me. Staring. I'm used to that. When Dad takes me shopping in my wheelchair, there'll always be someone who takes a good hard look. Or there'll be a whisper from a child. 'Mum, what's wrong with that lady?' Or, worse, there'll be pity.

I can read all these expressions on the jury's faces. Then I see a man behind a glass screen with guards either side of him. His face looks familiar.

'Who is that?'

'He's the man who's accused of running you over, love.'

Memories of what Dad had told me come back. 'He's a famous pop star.'

'That's right,' says Vanessa softly.

'He was on my wall! But then Dad tore him down because he said he'd hurt me.'

'That's why we're here,' says Vanessa kindly. 'We're hoping to find out if that's true.'

I search the man's face and body for clues.

What about the blue-and-red tattoo I'm sure I saw after the accident? Maybe it's under his suit.

How could he have left me?

83

Vanessa

She glanced up at the public gallery, at the crowds jostling for space. Then she thought of the note Janie had received. Could someone try to hurt her from there?

'Calling Janie White,' said an official voice.

Vanessa couldn't help it. She looked at Judge. He glanced at her and then away. Something wasn't right with him. She could feel it.

Something wasn't right in this court either. There was an uneasy atmosphere. Still, that wasn't surprising, she supposed. Janie's story was a tragedy. It was also a modern-day parable: your old wrongs will find you out. It was making them all feel uneasy. Janie's father, she could see, was patting his face with a handkerchief.

'Can you tell me, Janie, what you remember about the day of the accident?' asked the prosecution barrister softly. Vanessa had often thought that the levels of voices used – especially by the lawyers – were like conflicting instruments in a symphony. Deliberately misleading. Soft voices could be kindly like this one. Or they might be deadly; a precursor to the thunder.

Then again, her job right now was not to make observations like this but to read out loud the words Janie was going to type on the screen. That's what they'd agreed.

'It's more reliable than your singing voice, isn't it, love?' her father had said during the visit this morning. 'Sometimes it cracks a bit under strain.'

Janie had nodded, although she'd seemed rather hurt. Or had that been Vanessa's imagination?

But now, in court, Janie was waving her hand at the keyboard in a 'take it away' gesture. She was opening her mouth. She was singing. Not the beautiful tune Vanessa had been treated to in Janie's apartment but an angry tirade like a violent opera. The betrayed heroine, on stage, avenging her attacker through furious song.

Judge had once taken her to an opera. 'It's not for me,' Vanessa had told him. She always said what she thought to him and he to her. As he said, it was one reason why they got on so well. 'I need to understand the language and know what they're saying to get the story.'

Janie's words were crystal clear. Yet they stung the air as if laced with vitriol. Vanessa's ears rang, as the fury poured out.

'Yes,' she sang. 'I can tell you, but first I want to ask Robbie Manning something. How could you? You were my hero. I've listened to your music for years and now I find out that you're the wicked man who left me to die.'

Robbie was hanging his head. Tears were running down his face. *Well may he be ashamed*, thought Vanessa.

'I died on a Tuesday,' continued Janie. 'The sun was so beautiful! I was cycling back from the sea, where I loved to swim. I was going to start my dream job at a publishing house in London. I was worried about leaving my dad but I was excited.'

Vanessa could see more than one of the jurors leaning forward in curiosity.

'And then I heard this terrible noise. A van was coming towards me. It had these metal bars on the front as though it was grinning at me.'

Then she stopped. It was too much. Her voice was giving way.

Vanessa leaned across. 'Write it down on your screen, love. I'll read it out for you.'

But even though she'd been given official permission to do this, Vanessa couldn't help but shake with nerves. You could hear a pin drop in court. Everyone was watching her.

Vanessa cleared her throat and began to read as Janie typed.

'I felt a pain like nothing I'd ever felt before. That's when I saw a white light. I knew that if I walked towards it, my pain would go. But I also knew that if I did that, I would die.'

There was a gasp from a young girl in the jury. She looked about the age that Janie would have been at the time of the accident.

The typing was getting slower. 'But then I heard a voice asking me if I was all right and after that, well . . . There was something else. But I can't remember.'

Then Janie put her face in her hands, as if to shut out everything around her.

The court was silent, before someone from the public gallery called out, 'You're a brave woman, Janie!'

Usually, Judge would have reprimanded someone for such an interruption, but not this time.

Someone – maybe the person who had called out – began clapping. Someone else took it up. And another.

Within seconds, it became a wave of applause. Many were crying too.

Robbie is toast, Vanessa told herself. He'd never get off now. Janie might not have said much. And what she had said might not be reliable, by her own admission. But her physical presence had slaughtered her aggressor as clearly as if she had shot him dead in court.

Exactly what the bastard deserved.

84

Robbie

Robbie can't take his eyes off Janie. She's almost unrecognizable from the girl he'd kissed, yet it is her. He knows it in his bones. He knows it from the 'before' pictures. He has mutilated her body. Her brain. He is responsible for this.

The van. The bike. The crunch.

He is thrown. Traumatized. So he almost misses the words announcing the next witness.

'Calling Eric Sharp.'

For a minute, his attention is deflected. His head snaps up. Who *is* this Eric Sharp?

And then, as a tall, lanky man with short hair enters the court, Robbie realizes. Shock waves spark through him. There, standing in the witness box, is Jacob.

A whirlwind of emotions flash through Robbie's head. How can this be? Jacob's clearly changed his name. Why weren't they told? He glares at Yasmine, who returns a 'What's wrong?' expression. They'd discussed this before, of course. She'd asked him if he remembered an Eric Sharp. But he hadn't. Clearly, 'Eric' was the one who had written those threatening notes to him in prison.

'Mr Sharp, can you tell me why you changed your name?'

'Because I wanted a fresh start after the band broke up. I also needed to leave behind the memories of the accident. I was getting nightmares because of Robbie leaving that girl to die. I needed to separate myself from it.'

'Let me get this right, Mr Sharp. You're saying that Robbie left Janie to die?'

'I am. It wouldn't have happened if he hadn't been driving. Said he wanted to see what it was like. Right little cocky bastard he was, even back in those days.'

'Please avoid profanity, Mr Sharp,' says the lawyer.

'Sorry. But I'm telling you – Robbie here thought he could do it better. He always did. Didn't like anyone doing something he couldn't. He just leapt in and grabbed the wheel, shoving me out of the way. Knocked the wind out of me, it did. It was like he was high. Maybe he was. Even said he felt like "getting someone" that day.'

A male juror lets out a sound of disgust.

Robbie leaps to his feet. 'That's not true!' he calls out.

'Mr Manning,' says the judge. 'Please remain silent.'

'But it's just a pack of lies!' he shouts. 'He was the one driving. He should be standing here, not me.'

'MR MANNING!' roars the judge.

Reluctantly, Robbie sits down and the prosecution lawyer gives a small smile before continuing. 'Why didn't you ring the police, Mr Sharp?'

'We should have done but Robbie wouldn't let us. He said there was no way he was going to prison. When I pleaded with him to get help for the girl, he put a knife to my throat and said he'd cut me open unless I did what he said.'

Robbie jumps up again. Instantly, a dock officer puts

his hand on Robbie's shoulder to keep him seated but he manages to shout out, 'That's a lie too!'

'Mr Manning, I shan't warn you again.'

'What about the van?' continues the barrister. 'We understand that the defence will claim that your father disposed of it.'

'Yes, he did – but only because Robbie begged him to. He said his parents couldn't cope with the shame of him killing someone. My dad felt sorry for Robbie's dad. He said it wasn't easy for people starting again in a new country.'

'And is it true that you had previously hired Robbie to distribute drugs, as the defence will claim?'

'Of course, it's not.'

'But you, by your own admission in a statement to the police, are a drug dealer.'

'Yes.' He looks down at the floor. 'I've made some mistakes that I'm not proud of. But I intend to go straight now if I'm given a chance.'

Robbie listens to this with mounting incredulity. Hadn't Yasmine already said that the witness was hoping to get a possible drug sentence reduced by giving evidence against him? Clearly Jacob's 'clean stage' had ended.

It was all falling into place. Now Jacob no longer had the protection of his father, he'd been forced to take the gamble of telling outrageous lies in court to save his own skin.

'Your brother Sam was also present when the offence occurred. Where is he now?'

'No idea. We haven't seen each other for years.'

'And your father?'

'Sadly, Dad passed away recently. He was a good man.'

'No, he wasn't,' yelled Robbie. 'He was evil.'

'Silence! One more outburst and I will hold you in contempt of court.'

Contempt? thinks Robbie. There's enough contempt on the faces of the jurors to land him in prison for multiple life sentences.

Is there a chance they'll change their minds when they hear his part of the story? Maybe. But if he tells them what happened and he gets off, Jacob might go for Irena and the children in revenge.

He has to protect them. Whatever it takes.

85

Robbie

Robbie beckons Yasmine over. 'I need to talk to you,' Robbie whispers. 'It's urgent.'

Somehow – although it causes some consternation – his barrister succeeds in asking the judge for a brief adjournment.

'I didn't know Eric Sharp was Jacob,' he says angrily.

'Nor did I,' she says. 'There was nothing in the disclosures – that's any material that could undermine the prosecution or help the defence which the other side has to hand over – to show Jacob changed his name unless . . .'

Yasmine hesitates. 'Unless I missed it.' She looks awkward. 'There are boxes and boxes of information. When the disclosures arrived, I was off sick for a fortnight. I asked my junior to look through some of the papers. I suppose it's possible that she missed something. It happens sometimes. The other side might hide vital information amongst files that aren't very important.'

'Didn't you double-check her work?' demanded Robbie.

'There isn't always time . . .'

'That's not good enough,' roars Robbie. He's aware of his fists clenching as he speaks. 'I was told I'd be in safe hands with you.'

'I could ask for the judge to confer in chambers along with the prosecution,' she suggests.

'What might that achieve?'

'Well, it would bring it to his attention that you weren't informed beforehand of Sharp's previous identity. It's possible that he might order a retrial.'

'But that wouldn't help!' Robbie cries out. 'Jacob knows where I am now. More importantly, he could get to my family.'

'We'll step up security.'

'But you can't guarantee that they'll be safe. Can you?'

Her silence is answer enough.

There's a knock on the door. It's Irena. 'They gave me permission,' she says. 'I know what you are asking the lawyer, Robbie. I can see it in your face. I knew from the moment that I saw Jacob. You do not want to give evidence in case he harms us.'

'No. It's not that I don't want to. I *can't.*'

'Yes you can, Robbie,' she says. 'Remember what I say before. It is a greater shame for our children and for me if you do not tell them what happened. So if you say nothing, the children and I will never see you again.'

'You don't mean that.'

'I do.' She puts her arms round his neck. 'I love you very much. When we married, we promised each other to be open and honest. But you were not honest. It is only when the police come that I find out about this poor girl. Now is your chance to make this up. To redeem yourself. You give evidence, Robbie. You tell them it was Jacob and not you. Somehow you have to persuade them you are speaking the truth. Or our marriage is over.'

86

Vanessa

'Seems like Robbie Manning is for it,' Vanessa told Janie during the adjournment, hoping it might cheer her up.

But Janie just looked blank.

'There are times when she goes into a dream world of her own,' whispered Derek, who'd walked down the corridor with them.

She'd hoped to catch sight of Judge but he was nowhere to be seen. Probably in his chambers.

Sometimes Vanessa got a quiet thrill of satisfaction from what she saw as their 'special relationship'. If some of these clerks knew that not that long ago she'd been enjoying a cosy dinner with Judge at his place, they might be very surprised. He'd roasted a nice piece of salmon and she'd brought some strong Stinking Bishop cheese, which they both preferred to what he called 'pudding' and she called 'sweet'.

They'd talked about the case, of course, but only in general terms. 'If you ever get into trouble, Vanessa,' Judge had said, 'make sure you get one of the best lawyers.'

'But I'm a good girl,' she'd laughed. 'I don't intend to get into trouble.'

Then he'd turned very serious. 'The thing is, Vanessa,

that none of us knows when we're going to be in that position. So it's good to be prepared.'

But right now, Judge didn't seem as prepared as he usually was. When he'd reprimanded this Eric Sharp for swearing, she could tell from her friend's voice that something wasn't right. It didn't have that clear detached authority to it. In fact, unless she was mistaken, Judge sounded almost . . . well . . . afraid.

Mind you, Vanessa was often surprised he wasn't more afraid at times. He dealt with some very unpleasant people. There was always the danger that someone might try to wreak revenge. Look at that judge who'd found a bomb under his car a few years ago. Thank God it hadn't gone off.

Meanwhile, although she didn't like him, Vanessa had to admit that Sharp was very convincing. The jury certainly looked as though they agreed.

Despite herself, Vanessa felt a little tremor in her stomach. She wanted Robbie to be guilty. She wanted someone to pay. She wanted justice for Janie.

But at the same time, she had a feeling that wouldn't go away. A feeling that Robbie, with his face that looked so believable and had been plastered on goodness knows how many teenagers' bedroom walls, might just be as innocent as he looked.

Then again, it didn't matter what she thought.

It didn't even really matter what Judge thought.

That was the thing about a trial. You could never predict which way it would go. So much of it depended on character: the defendant's character, the jurors' characters. And the barristers' characters.

How could you ever trust a lawyer in real life, Vanessa had often asked herself.

'You can't always,' Judge said when she put the same question to him. She'd wanted him to add that he was an exception. But he hadn't. It had made her feel slightly uneasy ever since.

Vanessa took Janie and Derek down to one of the private rooms at the back of the court to get a cup of tea.

'It's the defence's turn now,' she said. 'They will try to argue that Robbie Manning didn't do it – that it was an accident or something like that.'

'That's appalling,' thundered Derek.

'Try not to worry – it's just part of the process,' she continued, unsure whether she was persuading him or herself.

Then Janie made a sudden spluttering noise. Saliva dribbled out of her mouth.

'Are you all right?' Vanessa asked urgently, hoping the poor girl wasn't going to have a fit. (She was prone to those as well, apparently.)

'It's OK,' said Derek, tenderly wiping his daughter's mouth. 'This happens sometimes.'

Janie nodded.

Derek took her hand. 'You don't have to go on with this, love, if you don't want to.'

'But I do want to,' she typed on her iPad, fingers shaking.

'If you're tired, we could ask for a longer break, or even for the trial to be adjourned until tomorrow,' suggested Vanessa gently. The case had taken it out of them all – and it was only just beginning.

'When this is over, Derek,' she said hesitantly, 'I've got a suggestion for you. It's just an idea I've had which might bring some joy in Janie's life – and yours too.'

'What?' he asked.

Then a message pinged up on Vanessa's phone.

'Excuse me,' she said, feeling the energy drain out of her.

You're doing great, Granny. I'm really proud of you. Cool outfit – that pink colour really suits you.

A shock wave went through her. Lewis! If he knew what she was wearing, he must be in court. Why? Was he trying to spook her out? Get more money off her somehow?

Vanessa attempted to put her own problems on hold and concentrate on Janie but she couldn't get one burning question out of her mind: what other tricks did her scheming grandson have up his sleeve?

And – although it had nothing to do with the case – was he going to let her see little Thomas again?

Even if her daughter refused to meet her, she'd still found her great-grandson. Please could she keep *one* child, at least?

87

Robbie

'Calling Robbie Manning.'

His legs judder as he stands up. He tries to avoid eye-contact with Janie but he can't.

The van. The bike. The crunch.

'I'm so sorry,' he wants to call out. But he mustn't speak out of turn – the judge has made that clear.

'Mr Manning,' begins the defence barrister. 'Can you tell us your version of what happened on September the 15th, 2004?'

She says 'your version' in a way that suggests Robbie will be telling a lie.

'Yes.' His voice comes out in a whisper as if it isn't his own. 'I was in a van with the band. It was being driven by the brother of one of the members. His name was Jacob then, although he now calls himself Eric Sharp – the witness who spoke earlier.'

Some of the jury members sit forward in interest.

'Jacob was the only one of us who had a driving licence. But he was drunk and on drugs. He was veering all over the place. So I leaned over and took the wheel.'

'You took the wheel?' repeats the barrister. 'Even though, as you've just admitted, you didn't have a licence?'

'I thought he was going to kill someone.'

'And you wanted to prevent that?'

Robbie can feel himself burning. 'Yes. I mean, I thought I stood a better chance because he was off his head. Then we went round this corner and suddenly . . .'

He puts his head in his hands.

'Suddenly what, Mr Manning?'

Robbie forces himself to look up. 'Suddenly I heard – and felt – this awful thump. There was nothing I could do.'

'Nothing you could do? Did you get out to see what had happened?'

'Yes.' Robbie is gasping now, drawing in huge gulps of air. He feels like he might be having a heart attack.

All of them – every man and woman – are now staring at him with cold hostile eyes.

'There was a bike on the ground and a . . . mess of blood and . . . long hair.'

'So you knew you'd run someone over?'

He nods.

'Please speak instead of making gestures, Mr Manning.'

'Sorry. Yes.'

'Did you call the police or try to give the victim artificial respiration?'

'I forced myself to take her pulse.'

Robbie shudders as he remembers the bloody pulp in his hand.

'You "forced yourself to take her pulse"? Then what happened?'

'I couldn't feel a beat.'

'Are you medically trained, Mr Manning?'

'No,' he says quietly.

'Is it possible that Janie White might have had a pulse and you didn't realize?'

'I suppose so.'

'You *suppose* so. I see. So did you then call 999?'

How often had Robbie been through this in his head? Telling himself again and again that he should have rung for an ambulance.

'No.'

'Why not?'

'Because Jacob wouldn't let me.'

'He wouldn't let you? Why?'

'He said that if I did, he'd go to prison.'

'And did you think of disobeying him?'

'I did but then he put a knife to my throat.'

'He claims it was you who put a knife to *his* throat.'

'Well it wasn't. I would never have carried one, but he did, especially when he was doing drug runs.'

'You seem to know a lot about him. Were you involved in some of those drug runs yourself by any chance?'

'Yes.' There's a ripple through the court. 'When I was a teenager, he made me.'

'He *made* you. I see.'

Robbie felt anger surging through him. 'You don't understand. That family – they ran the town where we lived. Or rather the father did. You didn't want to upset him.'

One of the jurors nodded as though he understood that. Maybe he'd had a similar experience himself. Or could it be that he had known Jacob's father?

'So what happened after that?'

'Sam – he was my friend and also Jacob's younger brother – said I should listen to Jacob. Matt, the other boy in the band, was frightened and wanted to run too. I thought she, the girl, was dead. So we . . . We drove away.'

'Where did you go?'

'To Sam and Jacob's dad's factory. Old Man Senior – that's what he was known as – got rid of the van and told Matt and me that we had to keep our mouths shut, or something bad would happen to our families.'

'So you're saying he threatened you?'

'Yes. He meant it too.'

'How do you know?'

'A few days later, my mum broke her arm on the way to work. She told me a man had pushed into her and said that if I didn't do as I'd been told, worse would happen. She'd been hurt before when I wanted to leave the band and Jacob's father threatened us. So I told Old Man Senior I'd keep quiet. I didn't have any choice.'

'I see.' The lawyer gave the jury a 'can you believe this?' look. 'And then what happened?'

'I discovered from the news that Janie was still alive.' He can't help looking at the woman in the wheelchair as he speaks. 'I'm so sorry. If I'd known, I'd have stayed and . . .'

She stares at him. Her expression is unreadable.

For a few moments, Robbie is silent. Frozen. Unable to finish his sentence. Then he tries to speak again but his mouth is too dry. Someone puts a plastic bottle of water in his hands. He gulps it gratefully.

'But you didn't stay, did you?' says the barrister coldly. 'Nor did you even try to call for the help that might have reduced Janie White's injuries. And that is why the jury might feel you should be punished. What happened next?'

'I wanted to leave the band, but Old Man Senior threatened to hurt my family if I did. So we just carried on making music and doing gigs.'

'You "just carried on"?'

'It was difficult.'

'I'm sure it *was* difficult to carry on after you'd almost killed someone,' the barrister replied, wryly.

Robbie can see the whole court staring at him in horror.

He wants to tell them what really happened. As he stands there, his mind goes back all those years. He's his younger self again. His eyes glaze over.

'Mr Manning, are you feeling unwell?'

'Let me explain what it was really like . . .' he whispers. 'I wrote it all down in prison.'

88

Robbie

After his mum's broken arm, Robbie knew he had to continue in the band. They'd signed a contract. If he left, everyone would want to know why. If he told the truth, his parents might be murdered. Old Man Senior was capable of anything.

Besides, what else could Robbie do in life? Lie in bed all day? Feeling sick to his core because he'd injured a girl so badly that he hadn't even realized she was alive?

Yes. That's exactly what he wanted to do.

He told his mother he felt ill. When she insisted, he went to the doctor. The GP, who'd read about their up-and-coming band, suggested it was nerves.

'Sometimes, when big opportunities come our way, we feel scared,' she said.

But she had no idea how scared he felt. Or why.

The other reason Robbie hated the band was that, after Matt left town, Old Man Senior suggested to the record label that Jacob took his place. To Robbie's horror, they agreed. Perhaps he paid them a great deal of money or threatened them too. You never could tell with Old Man Senior.

This meant Robbie and Jacob spent even more time together and, every day, he had the reminder that, if Jacob hadn't been drunk or drugged up or both, there would have been no need for Robbie to have taken the wheel. No one would have been horrifically injured. He wouldn't have had to lie. Every time he looked at Jacob, he felt rage, but it was also anger and disgust towards himself. And it was that which was killing him.

The other thing – although it was nothing compared to a young girl's life – was that Jacob couldn't sing. It was agony to listen to. Robbie and Sam cringed when he opened his mouth but, bizarrely, the record label and the public lapped it up.

They tried out some demos on what they called a 'proportional representation of the intended demographic'. To Robbie's shock, they loved it. Jacob's voice made people laugh – it sounded like gravel when a car went over it, yet it could also screech. Apparently, it made 'the man on the street' think that you didn't have to be a brilliant singer to make it. It was unique at a time when so many bands were just doing the same old thing. Jacob was their USP. When they did their encores, the crowd screamed for him.

'See,' Jacob said to Robbie when they came off stage. 'They love me. Suck that one up, kiddo.'

'How can you enjoy all this when we ran over –'

Jacob grabbed him by the collar of his shirt. 'Never, ever say that again,' he hissed. 'Besides, you were the one driving.'

And it was true, wasn't it?

Their first album got into the top ten. They were invited on to *Top of the Pops* and chat shows – everyone seemed to love this new band that had emerged from nowhere. 'We can't do TV,' Robbie had pleaded with the others when the invitations came in via their agent. 'Millions of viewers will see us. What if one of them witnessed the crash?'

'What crash?' said Jacob. 'It. Didn't. Happen.'

As always, Sam took his side.

Before and after every show, Robbie would be physically sick. But Jacob was right. No one came forward. It seemed a miracle, especially as those headlines weren't going away.

At first, they'd been across the front page almost every day.

DAY THREE OF JANIE'S COMA – STILL NO SIGN OF IMPROVEMENT

Then every few weeks.

WEEK FOUR OF JANIE'S COMA – DOCTORS SAY NO CHANGE

Then came week twelve.

JANIE EMERGES FROM COMA – BUT CANNOT TALK OR MOVE

'Let's hope it stays that way,' Jacob had said.

Robbie wanted to punch him for that but, to his shame, he also found himself hoping the girl would never be able to speak. Then they might be safe.

After that, the headlines got fewer and further between, although every now and then they'd crop up again in a smaller news item or at the back of the paper.

Janie White, The Girl Who Came Back from the Dead, moves from hospital to a rehab unit. She still cannot talk or walk. Doctors say severe head injuries may be permanent.

Every morning when Robbie woke up, there was a brief moment when everything seemed all right in the world. And then it came back. *The van. The bike. The crunch.*

Meanwhile, the band got bigger and bigger. They were invited to Japan. America. Canada. Places that Robbie had only dreamed of visiting. Money kept coming in. Thousands. More thousands. More than he could deal with. He gave a large amount to his parents. He made regular and enormous donations to charities.

'You can't keep doing that,' their financial adviser warned. 'You need to save. This won't go on for ever. Most bands peak.'

Yet they didn't. And, even more amazingly, Jacob went clean. 'I'm getting sober,' he'd said. 'I want to set a good example to the young people of today.'

'A good example?' Robbie had scoffed. 'A bit late for that, isn't it?'

But, for once, Jacob hadn't risen to the bait.

Meanwhile, Old Man Senior was over the moon. He thrived on the fame and kept telling his sons how 'proud' he was that they'd 'made good'.

And Robbie? He ploughed all his grief and remorse and fears into his lyrics. 'You write lyrics and music like no one I've ever known,' said their agent. 'You make it seem so easy.'

But the difficult bit was hearing Jacob, the man he hated

most in the world, singing his songs. 'Can You Ever Forgive Me for Breaking Your Heart?' – one of their biggest hits – sounded false in Jacob's voice.

'You've got to watch it with the words,' Sam said to him when no one else was around. 'They're getting too close to the line.'

'But I can't help it,' said Robbie truthfully.

In 2007, they were in Milton Keynes. At least he thought it was Milton Keynes. Or maybe that had been last week . . .

He went out to the front of the stage, like he always did, as Jacob's back-up singer. Back-up! What a joke. How could Jacob get away with that high-pitched screech?

It was three years to the day since the accident. Robbie could barely open his mouth. He felt like the vomit was going to come out any second. *I can't do this anymore*, he told himself. *I just can't.*

But then he looked down at the rows of fans waving their flags and singing along to the words. His words.

And that's when he saw her. The girl from the village hall. The girl with the pale auburn hair. The girl he'd met before his life had changed for ever. Robbie had the distinct feeling that, if he could talk to her, he'd be able to get back to his old self. He could start again.

She was looking at him too. She recognized him as well. He just knew it.

When they finished their finale, Robbie couldn't help himself. He jumped off the stage and took her hand. 'It's me,' he said. 'You do remember, don't you? I've been looking for you everywhere.'

She looked confused. 'What is it you mean?'

And then he realized. This was someone else: similar but different. Part of him was disappointed but, underneath, he had an instinctive feeling that this meeting was meant to happen. That this woman was special.

'Sorry. What's your name?' he asked.

'Irena,' she replied.

'Irena,' he repeated slowly. It felt so natural to say it. 'Will you have dinner with me tonight?'

89

Robbie

Robbie wants to tell all this to the jury. That every day since the accident, he's woken by the same questions going round in his mind. What if today is the day he's arrested? How could he have done this to an innocent girl? And how will he ever redeem himself?

'You have bad dreams,' Irena would tell him after they got together. They would be lying in their favourite position, her head resting on his upper chest. His warmth against hers.

'Do I?' he asked.

'Most nights. Why is that?'

'I don't know.'

Of course, he did know, but he couldn't tell Irena then and he can't tell the court now either. It's all too much. Too personal. So he comes out with a shortened version of what happened before and after the crash. He's aware it doesn't have the same impact, and that it doesn't reflect the turmoil in his heart. But it's the best he can do without completely falling to pieces.

'I couldn't stand playing with Jacob after what he did. Besides, more bands came on the scene and ours began to get less popular. So I left and went solo. I married Irena and we had our children. But all the time, I was waiting for a policeman to knock on my door.'

'And now that knock has come, Mr Manning,' says the lawyer. 'I put it to you that it was you who threatened Jacob with a knife and not the other way round. I would argue that it was your cowardice – pure and simple – that made you drive off. Is that true?'

'No,' he whimpers. 'I wanted to tell the truth. But I was scared that Jacob's father would hurt my family.'

'What about now?' Are your parents still alive?'

'Sadly, they've passed away, but I was worried he might go after my wife and children. I still am.'

'So why did you change your mind and plead not guilty?'

Robbie thinks back to the note Irena had passed him at the crown court hearing – *I looked up this man you tell me about on the computer. He died last month.* – and the confirmation which Yasmine had provided.

'I changed it because I found out that Old Man Senior had recently died. Jacob had disappeared, or so I thought. So had Sam, although I knew my friend would never do anything to hurt my family. I thought we were no longer at risk.'

'It wasn't that you thought you'd change your story in the hope the jury would let you off the hook?'

'No,' he says firmly.

But he can tell no one believes him.

He is finished.

90

Janie

There's no doubt in my mind.

Not now I've heard him in court.

I'd have recognized that voice anywhere, asking if I was all right when I was caught in that white tunnel. What kind of man does that and then leaves you to die?

For years I've wanted to ask him that. And now I have. But it didn't feel as good as I had thought it would.

There is something in his eyes that makes me feel he isn't a bad person. They remind me of someone but I'm not sure who.

Then again, my brain does that to me sometimes. Just as I think it's behaving itself, it tricks me. To be honest, it did that before the accident when I thought I kept seeing Mum. But it's been much worse since.

I'm feeling tired now. All I want is to go home and sleep.

But I need to know what will happen to this man who left me to die.

For some reason, I still can't help feeling that there's something that I've forgotten or got wrong.

But what?

Judge

Judge can feel a muscle twitching in his jaw, as it always does when something doesn't seem right in court.

In theory, his blackmailer needn't worry. From the jurors' faces, it looks as though Robbie's going down for life.

My career will be safe then, Judge thinks to himself.

Yet something doesn't sit properly. This Robbie Manning, with tears streaming down his face as he hears the victim's statement, doesn't look like the type to walk away from a dying girl. Judge knows appearances can be deceptive but there's something about the agony in this man's eyes that suggests he knows real sorrow.

The kind of sorrow that Judge understands all too well.

Open your minds as well as your hearts, Judge wants to tell the jury. There are sometimes three sides to a story.

Maybe he needs to tell them in his summing up. Even if it ruins his own life. Even if the blackmailer tells everyone his secret.

If only he could confide in Vanessa. She would hold his hand and tell him what he should do.

Yet that wouldn't solve anything. Not really. He already knows what he should do. His relationship with Ian is no longer going to cause public condemnation like it might have done a few years ago. The world is more forgiving now.

But his stepmother matters. If the blackmailer does what he threatens – reveals the truth – police might look back through the visitor notes. To the day when he visited the bitch. To the day when she died.

92

Vanessa

Never had Vanessa felt so upset by a case. Not even when Tyler had killed the new gang leader. After Robbie's evidence, she found herself shaking with fury. He should have called for help after the accident.

She looked at Judge. For a brief moment he looked back at her. He *was* scared, she realized. Really scared. But she couldn't think why – she knew so little of his personal life, after all. People forgot that judges were just like anyone else: sometimes things happened to them at home that affected the way they worked. It was natural.

Something made her glance up to the spectators' gallery. She was right. Lewis *was* there, waving down at her as if enjoying a play at the theatre. How dare he?

Both lawyers were being called to the judge now – the prosecution and the defence. There were urgent whisperings. Something was happening. The judge was nodding. The prosecution looked annoyed; the defence pleased.

She caught rumblings from the clerk. A new witness was being summoned.

'Calling Sam Senior.'

A man in a long sack-like tunic came in, dressed as though he belonged to some kind of cult. His head was shaved. Despite his look, Vanessa immediately warmed to his kind face.

'Is it true that you are the brother of Eric Sharp, formerly known as Jacob Senior?' asks the defence lawyer.

'It is.'

'And is it also true that you were present on the day that Janie White was injured?'

'It is.'

'Can you tell the court what happened?'

'Yes. Everything that Robbie has said is true: my brother was drunk and high and unable to drive safely. Robbie was the only one who had the balls to take over. It was impossible to steer properly – the van was already going fast. We went round a corner and, well . . . we hit something. It certainly wasn't intentional.'

The jurors looked shocked. Clearly, they had been siding with Jacob, but now here was someone corroborating Robbie's version of events.

'We all got out,' continued Sam. 'We were stunned. Dazed. Robbie wanted to call the police but Jacob held a knife to Robbie's throat and said we had to get out of there.'

There was a gasp from one of the jurors.

'I see. What did you do?'

'I should have stepped in but I was too scared. Jacob, well, he took after our dad. I loved them both, but you didn't want to get on the wrong side of either of them.'

'What about the other boy, Matt Watson?'

'He seemed too shocked to talk much.'

'What happened next?'

'We drove back. My dad got rid of the van like Robbie

said. He told us we weren't to tell anyone about it and that he'd fix it. Then he said he wanted a private word with Robbie but I listened in through the door. He said he'd kill Robbie's parents and everyone he loved if he told anyone what really happened. "If it ever comes out, you take the blame. Get it?" Those were his words.'

There was an uneasy stirring amongst the jury. 'Matt and his family did a moonlight flit that night,' continued Sam. 'I have no idea where and I haven't heard from him since. Either they were scared or Dad paid them to leave and keep their mouths shut. It was how he worked. Jacob took Matt's place. At first our fans liked him but then a reviewer criticized his voice and our sales plummeted. New bands came along and it all went downhill from there. Our contract ended and, not long after that, the record company signed up Robbie as a solo artist.'

Sam carried on rapidly as if scared someone might stop him. 'Jacob was livid when Robbie got big. No one wanted to sign us up on our own, you see. We were nothing without him. Our dad had another word and said that his threat still stood. So Robbie swore that he wouldn't tell anyone about the accident. But Jacob has never forgiven him for going out on his own and doing so well.'

'That's complete bullshit,' Jacob interrupted furiously.

'Silence,' said Judge.

'Of course he'd say that,' Sam continued. 'But it's the truth. It's why I left to join a group of people who believe in peace and doing the right thing. I have nothing to gain from this.' Sam faced the jury. 'I'm telling the truth.'

Something had changed in their attitudes, observed

Vanessa. The jurors were clearly shocked and confused. In fact, she feared, they weren't sure who to believe.

Outside the court, while Derek looked after Janie, Vanessa checked her phone.

It was all over the internet.

Recluse musician Sam Senior pleads for Robbie's release in shock reappearance. Older brother Jacob — now known as Eric Sharp — claims Robbie is guilty.

Where did that leave Janie? It wasn't fair. She needed justice. Vanessa simmered with white-hot rage.

Someone had to do something about this.

93

Judge

Send Robbie Manning down or else the world will find out what you did to your stepmother.

The words go round and round in his head, as they have done since he first read them. He tries to think it through rationally.

The whispers in court say that Jacob, who'd been in a remand prison for a drugs offence, had somehow escaped a custodial sentence by shopping his former bandmate Robbie. Deals were not uncommon, although Judge has always felt they were wrong. Part of the agreement was that neither Jacob nor his brother Sam would be prosecuted for not reporting the accident.

Apparently, Jacob had insisted that Sam should be included in this. Perhaps Jacob, despite seeming completely obnoxious, had a brotherly conscience.

And now yet another witness has come forward. A woman this time.

He could, of course, turn down the application. But there is no legal reason to do so – plenty of witnesses have been permitted to speak at the last minute over the years. But there is a chance, Judge tells himself, that she might overturn Jacob's statement and that Robbie could go free without him – Judge – doing anything. It might be the right decision. After all, Robbie had been a young man who had made a bad choice. Now he's sorry. Who does that sound like?

'You can dress yourself up in fancy robes and words, Richard Baker,' he tells himself. 'But at the end of the day, you deserve to go down for life yourself.'

Usually, it comforts Judge to arrive home after a case. But not today. As he sits down in his favourite chair by the fire, everything around him seems to scream 'murderer'. The glass of whisky that isn't doing its usual knock-out trick. The leather chair that's making his back ache in a way it's never done before. The old photograph on the walnut-inlaid side table, of him and Ian on holiday in Skye.

Ian. The only person who knew the truth about his stepmother. Or so he'd thought.

For two pins, Judge would have picked up the phone to ring Vanessa. In fact, his hand with those bloody liver spots (a sign of age, if anything was) is hovering over it right now. But he can't. It isn't ethical. They've worked on the same court cases before, of course. But they've never ever discussed them until after the verdict.

But then, of all the people Judge knew, Vanessa would understand. Or would she? Suppose she was shocked by what he'd done? Horrified? She was an upright person. He was meant to be upright too.

'What should I do?' he asks Ian's photograph.

The young man with the striped scarf smiles back at him. If they'd known then about the cancer, would they have defied society and just moved in together as Ian had always wanted?

And then it comes to him.

Ian always used to tease him about worrying too much and 'letting your imagination run away with you'.

And he was right.

Facts. That's what he needed. Facts about that blackmail note for starters.

Judge reaches for the phone. 'Gary? I hope I'm not disturbing your evening. I have a job for you. I'm sure I don't need to mention that it's highly confidential . . .'

94

Robbie

Robbie's heart went into overtime when Sam turned up to give evidence. Or so it felt.

It wasn't just his old friend's reappearance after all these years. It was what he'd then said in court, which went entirely against everything he'd said before. Hadn't Sam always told him to forget the accident? To 'pretend it hadn't happened'?

Then after the band broke up and Robbie had gone solo, Sam had just disappeared.

And now what was with the sack-like robe? Had Sam found religion? If so, could that be the reason behind his change of heart?

And as for Jacob's evidence, that had been a pack of lies. Of course he'd been drunk and high. Otherwise, Robbie would never have taken the wheel. But Jacob had been so persuasive in his arguments. He'd come across as charming and convincing. It was clear that the jury believed him.

Guilty. That's what they'll say. Guilty.

Now, Robbie sits in his cell and weeps. He weeps for poor Janie. He weeps for his wife and children. And a small part – the part he doesn't like – weeps for himself.

There's an electronic bleep as the door opens, revealing

a different prison guard from before. He seems, Robbie observes, like one of those weary middle-aged men whose face reveals more experience of life than the sum of his years might allow for.

'Got a message,' he says. 'I'm not meant to give it to you but I've always liked your music.' He looks down at the stack of CDs under his arm. 'Thought you might sign some of my albums first.'

He doesn't actually add the words 'in exchange for this message' but the meaning is implicit.

'Of course,' says Robbie, going into automatic celebrity mode despite the fear and dread running through him. 'Got a pen?'

They didn't allow him to have one here, no doubt in case he'd use it to poke out someone's eye or do some other terrible injury.

When he finishes, the guard gives him an odd look. 'You don't remember me, do you?'

Robbie feels a cold shiver going through him. This man didn't look very different from one of the drug addicts he used to deliver to in Plymouth.

'Just kidding,' says the guard. 'The thing is, we all thought we knew you. It's always the same with celebrities. We cheer for them like a football team until someone does something bad or stupid and then we feel we've wasted all our time and money and stuff. 'Cos you're just like us.'

'Right,' said Robbie, handing back the pen.

'Except you're not. You're downright evil.'

'I'm sorry,' Robbie mumbles.

'My problem is that I don't know which side to believe.

If you're telling the truth, I can see why you might have driven off. But if you're lying, then I don't want to give you the message after all.'

'Please,' says Robbie.

'Say it one more time,' says the guard.

'Please.'

'Kneel and repeat.'

Robbie is beyond dignity. He'll do anything to get a message from Irena.

'Fancy,' says the guard. 'The famous Robbie Manning is kneeling down in front of me. Can't wait to tell the boys at the Horse and Slipper tonight.'

He passes Robbie the note.

Irena's distinctive writing jumps out at him.

You told the truth. It was the correct thing to do. It's going to be all right. XXX

Robbie's heart soars. So she still loves him! But how does she know it will be all right? Has she rooted up some more evidence somehow? Or is she just trying to be supportive?

'Your wife's correct,' says the guard. 'Afraid I couldn't resist reading the message first. Always best to tell the truth. Mind you, if I was a betting man – which I am – I'd say the jury will send you down. Maybe they'd be right to.'

Anger bursts out of him. 'Why did you want me to sign your CDs, then, if you think I did it?'

'Are you kidding, mate? They'll be worth even more if you're found guilty. I guess we'll see what happens tomorrow.'

'What do you mean? *What's* happening tomorrow?'

'Haven't you heard?'

The guard obviously knows darned well that Robbie hasn't heard. 'The prosecution is bringing in another witness.'

'Who?' Robbie asks, feeling his chest thump.

'I'll let your lawyer tell you that one, shall I?'

Then he leaves, the cell door clicking ominously behind him.

95

Vanessa

Something was up with Judge. She could tell. When she'd passed him in one of the long court corridors before the case, he had deliberately looked the other way as if he didn't know her, let alone recently shared supper with her.

Usually when they were doing a case together, he'd smile at her in a slightly different way from how he smiled at others. The kindly judge. That's what he was known as.

But today his eyes had been cold, the way Jack's used to be if she'd displeased him.

She had enough to worry about as it was. That message from Lewis had unnerved her. She kept expecting another, asking for something more, but it didn't come.

It would, though. She was sure of that.

If she didn't hear from him by the weekend, she'd need to get in touch about seeing little Thomas, and hopefully her daughter.

Wasn't that why she'd paid all that money?

'*You silly idiot*,' said Jack. '*Did you honestly think that fraudster would keep his part of the deal?*'

Yes, actually. Despite everything, she still had faith in Lewis. Should Vanessa feel stupid for that? She wasn't sure.

'You have no right to speak, Jack,' she shot back. 'Not after what you did.'

Meanwhile, Janie had asked if she could watch the rest of the court proceedings. Witnesses were allowed to do that after they'd given evidence.

But Janie didn't wish to sit in the courtroom. She was too tired, her father had explained. Yesterday's proceedings had taken it out of her. She wanted to watch it on the monitor in one of the small rooms at the back. And she wanted Vanessa to be there too.

Usually Vanessa would have been keen to find out what really happened. To guess what the outcome might be. She always felt this about cases because in a way, she had been part of the action. Sometimes it was as though she was a wardrobe mistress or a companion to someone who was acting in a play.

But now, as she sat next to Janie, who was looking pale and exhausted, her mind was spinning in circles. When would Lewis introduce her to Molly? What if he didn't? Supposing he wouldn't let her see little Thomas again? How cruel would it be to finally find her family and then lose them all over again?

I don't think I could bear that, Vanessa thought. For a minute, she wanted to run right out of this room, find Lewis and get him to – make him, somehow – take her to his mother. Her daughter.

What was she doing here in court, trying to help others when she needed to fix her own life?

But she couldn't. Not without causing a scene, anyway. They were calling someone now to take the witness stand. It was a woman of about fifty at a guess. Despite her distress, Vanessa felt herself going into outfit appraisal mode, out of habit from her old job. It also helped to calm her down. The new witness was probably a size 16. She would suit spring colours like a warm green or orangey red, or maybe a peachy pink.

'I believe you were walking a little further down the road at the time the accident took place,' said the defence barrister. Her face was rather sweaty, Vanessa noticed. She'd always thought those heavy wigs must be uncomfortable.

'Yes,' the woman answered, trembling. 'It was very early in the morning. There weren't any houses on that stretch and no one else was around. I was a few yards away when I heard this terrible screech of brakes as this huge white van ploughed into a girl on a bike. I was in such shock that I just stood there. I don't think the young men saw me. They were too busy arguing about what to do. I heard every word.'

'Can you tell me why you didn't go to help, or even report the accident?'

She looked embarrassed.

'I wasn't meant to be there. I just ducked round a corner and hid, I'm afraid.'

'And why was that?'

'I had told my husband that I was staying with a girlfriend. Instead I . . . Well I was staying with a different sort of girlfriend, if you know what I mean.'

'And what made you come forward now?'

'I read about the case in the papers and felt it was my duty.'

'Yet you didn't feel it was your duty before?'

The woman was getting redder. 'I was young and . . . and I didn't make the decision I should have done. I was scared I'd get caught if I made a 999 call. I knew I might have to make a statement and then my husband would find out . . .'

Her voice tailed away.

'But you don't mind coming clean now?'

'No. I feel I owe it to Janie White. You see, her accident made me think. I realized how short life could be. So five years later – it took me that long to pluck up the courage – I left my husband and moved in with Angie. We've been very happy ever since. But I've always felt guilty about not reporting the accident. When I read about the trial in the papers, I decided I needed to come forward to tell the jury about the argument I'd heard.'

'And what exactly did you hear?' asked the barrister.

She took an audible breath.

'Robbie said he wanted to call the police. Then Jacob took this knife out of his pocket – I saw it glinting in the sun – and said that if Robbie did that, he'd kill him. Then they all climbed back into the van. I should have rung the police but I thought the girl was dead. I went over and looked. It was horrible. It certainly seemed like she'd gone.' Tears were running down her face. 'I'm so sorry.'

'You appear to have overheard quite a lot,' said the prosecution barrister, cross-examining.

'The road was empty and their voices were loud,' the woman replied defensively 'Jacob's was particularly distinctive. It was rasping and growly.'

'She's right!' sang Janie, in the monitor room. 'I remember now hearing a second voice like the one she describes. It's coming back to me. It was arguing with Robbie, saying they couldn't call the police and had to get out of here.'

'That doesn't change anything,' Derek snapped, putting his arm around her. 'They abandoned you, didn't they?'

'Actually,' said Vanessa, 'I think it's really significant that Janie agrees with this witness. Can you wait there for a few minutes while I find someone?'

Yet as she did so, she couldn't stop the doubt that she was trying to kick into submission. What if Janie was wrong? What if she'd been influenced by the woman's evidence to 'suddenly remember'?

In short, how much could they believe of that troubled, tragic broken mind?

96

Jacob

Jacob hadn't bothered listening to the new witness. What was the point? With any luck, the jurors wouldn't be fooled by his little brother's evidence and Robbie would still go down. Instead, he took himself out for a few celebratory pints at the pub next door, congratulating himself on two scores. First, it looked like he was going to avoid a jail sentence for his drug business, which really wasn't as big as the police had made out. Not when you compared it with others. Just enough for a five-bedroom villa in Malaga and a tidy little pension. It might have been different if his dad had left him anything but the mean bastard had cut him out of his will because of his 'lifestyle'. Talk about pot calling kettle black.

And secondly, he'd finally got that little shit Robbie Manning out the way.

Jacob had always been worried that, one day, someone was going to say it was his fault. Now, when Robbie was convicted – it was a no-brainer after the evidence – he would be safe.

Frankly, Jacob admitted to himself over a third pint, he'd never got over the success that Robbie had enjoyed after he'd gone solo. It wasn't fucking fair. Well, now the wheel had turned full circle. It was Robbie who was going to be behind bars while he, Jacob, would be on the first flight back to Spain before the police changed their mind.

That's when he'd felt a tap on his shoulder. 'Thought I might find you here.'

It was Irena, that woman Robbie had married. That was another thing Jacob resented – how had someone like Robbie managed to nab her? She was a stunner. In fact, Jacob wouldn't mind getting together with her himself. He was pretty sure she fancied him too. Everyone knew that when a woman ignored a man, she had the hots for him.

'You are a liar,' she'd hissed. 'You must stand up in court and tell everyone the truth.'

She looked even more amazing when she was angry! 'Come on, love,' he wheedled. 'You weren't even there. You don't know what happened.'

Then she'd given him a chilling look. It was a real turn-on when women pretended to hate him!

'I'm not your love, you miserable little worm. Life will come back at you, Jacob. One day, you will have to repay the universe for your sins.'

'Is that right?' he said, laughing as she stormed off.

Then he felt another tap on his shoulder. 'Can't be without me, can you?' he said, turning round.

But it was his lawyer. 'Why are you still here?' he said. 'Trying to bill me for extra time, are you?'

It was meant to be a joke but her expression gave him a sinking feeling.

'It's lucky for you that I happened to be in the building for another case. You need to get back into court, Jacob. There's been a development.'

'It's not going to mean they'll charge me, is it?' he said, half-jokingly.

His lawyer's face was dead straight. Until then Jacob thought she was on his side. It was why he'd hired a good-looking lawyer of his own age, one who might have swooned at his music. And yes, she had been star-struck for a while. But not now, apparently.

'It depends,' she said coolly. 'Is there anything you haven't told me?'

Jacob felt his insides plummet with a conscience that he thought he'd left way behind in primary school.

'No,' he said. 'Nothing at all.'

97

Janie

We watched the new witness give her statement on a screen in a different room in the court. She said she'd been there when the van ran me over.

I knew I'd sensed someone when I'd been lying on the ground, hovering between life and death. If this woman had called 999, I might have got help sooner.

But she couldn't because she'd been staying with a friend and didn't want her husband to know.

I used to have friends. Some of them came to see me when I was in rehab, but then they gave up.

Yet there's something else too. Something more important to me.

I can see the public gallery on the video screen and I study it carefully. I looked while I was giving evidence in court too.

Mum isn't there.

Deep down, I knew she wouldn't be even though it breaks my heart to say that.

Then I see a man coming into the gallery. He's got rolled-up shirt-sleeves and I can see red and blue tattoos.

My heart starts pounding.

'Who's that?' I write down on my screen.

'Jacob, love. Do you remember him talking before in court? He's also called Eric.'

My hands are shaking too much to write. My voice is tired but I have to get it out. 'Vanessa,' I sing. 'I've remembered something else.'

98

Robbie

Why is Janie being called back again?

Jacob's here too, swaying a bit in the gallery. He's definitely just had a drink or two. So much for the clean living.

'All rise,' says the clerk as the judge enters. His face suggests a certain fairness, senses Robbie. Still, as Yasmine has warned him, anything can happen in court. He shivers with the horror of apprehension.

Janie is being wheeled to the stand. He can't take his eyes off those terrible scars on her face. But there's something beautiful, yet haunting, about the way she stares at the jury. Suddenly, she turns to him. Her eyes are steely. 'I'm sorry,' he mouths.

Instantly, she looks away. Of course she does. What had he expected? Forgiveness? Get real, Robbie.

'There's something else I want to say,' she sings. 'Something that has come back to me.'

She pauses for a split second. It's like being on stage, he thinks. That split second of fear when you see thousands of expectant faces in front of you. Then the first chord, like you're diving in. The first line of the song, which feels like swimming in words. And then that wonderful feeling that it's going to be all right after all because, really, you are singing for yourself and no one else.

That's when the court air fills with a clear descant.

'My memory . . . People tell me it's not as good anymore. Sometimes, I think of things too late. But, just now, I remembered something about that man.'

Janie is pointing towards Jacob up in the gallery. 'He's the one who spoke before in a voice that sounds like a car going over gravel. It's his tattoo I remember. That blue-and-red flaming skull and crossbones on his arm with a 'J'. I saw it on the man who told the others that he'd kill them if they didn't leave me. It's him you should be talking to, not Robbie. Robbie was the one who wanted to stay and help. I recognize his voice.'

Then she slumps in her chair. Exhausted.

But something is happening. Jacob is being called back into court.

'Jacob Senior,' orders the judge. 'Will you please roll up your sleeves.'

The blue-and-red flamed tattoo looks angrier than ever.

'She's right,' calls out the woman who had been staying with her friend. 'I saw it too. I told you. This is the man who was threatening Robbie. He is the one who should go to prison.'

Relief washes over Robbie. It's going to be all right. He just knows it.

99

Vanessa

But how *could* she have seen it, Vanessa asked herself. Janie hadn't even had a pulse, according to the ambulance team. That's why she was called The Girl Who Came Back from the Dead.

Yet who knew how much people could hear or see when they were hovering between life and death? It could be much more than we think. She'd read a lot about that in magazines.

Meanwhile, the courtroom had burst into chaos. She'd never seen anything like it before, or rather, heard. The noise was deafening.

Judge called for an adjournment. He was clearly worried, but Vanessa couldn't think why. Usually he relished these dramas. She looked forward to the debates they sometimes had afterwards, over a glass of good wine. Yet something was telling her that it wasn't going to happen this time.

Then there came another sound – her mobile was bleeping. It felt ominous even before she read the text.

Be careful, Granny. Robbie has to go down. You need to have a word with your judge friend. Otherwise, something could happen to Janie. And to you.

A cold chill went through her. Was this why Lewis had been watching from the public gallery? Yet why was he so interested in the case? Was it possible that somehow there was a connection between her grandson and Robbie Manning?

Vanessa

There had been four earlier times in her life when Vanessa's knees had juddered so badly that she couldn't stop them. The first was when they told her that her baby had died and that, 'It will upset you too much' to see it.

The second was when Jack had died. Before she'd discovered what he'd done.

The third was when she heard that Tyler had committed murder.

The fourth was when she discovered her baby hadn't really died. She was a mother after all, with a child of her own.

And now there was this. Lewis's text. Threatening her was one thing. But threatening a girl whose life had already been ruined was another.

Judge was the man to go to now, Vanessa decided. She'd have to confess that she'd told Lewis more than she should have done about the case. But enough was enough. If it meant her losing her job, or even going to prison, so be it.

Summoning up her courage, she left Janie with her dad and made her way tentatively along the court corridors.

It was only the second time she'd been to his room or – as they called it – judge's chambers. Vanessa felt like a schoolgirl or an imposter. Maybe both.

Of course, she was neither, but maybe that's how other people would see her. Why else might a woman without any education to speak of be knocking on the door that was reserved for men and women who decided the fate of the rest of them? You couldn't get power much greater than that (unless you were royalty, and maybe not even then). Thank God she was neither. What a responsibility that would be.

But knock she did. Because, quite frankly, Vanessa wasn't sure what else to do.

'Come in,' said a voice she knew well.

Emboldened, she turned the handle, quickly glancing round the room. Thankfully, she saw there was no one else there. Just walls and walls of books and a desk piled high with more books and several files.

'Vanessa,' he said. His voice was flat and his face dark. There was a tumbler of whisky by his side. Judge never drank whisky. At least, she'd never seen him do so. He certainly didn't drink alcohol when he was on a case, either during the day or in the evening. He didn't want his judgement clouded. Or so he'd said.

'What's wrong?' she asked.

He rubbed his jawline as though it itched. It wasn't a gesture of his that she was familiar with. It was as though she'd found a new Judge. One who drank whisky during the day. One who was distinctly nervous.

'You wouldn't understand,' he said.

'Try me,' prompted Vanessa, sitting down in one of the two upright chairs opposite him.

He leaned forward. 'Why don't you start by telling me why you're here?'

He wasn't being accusatory, Vanessa knew that. She also knew him well enough to see that this was a diversionary tactic to deflect her from her 'try me' invitation.

'I'd like you to look at this text,' she said, holding out the phone.

She watched him read it.

His eyebrows rose when he saw the sender's name. 'This is the same Lewis as your grandson?'

'Unfortunately, yes.'

Judge was rubbing his chin again. 'Do you know why he wants Robbie Manning to go to prison so badly?'

'I have no idea.'

'Interesting.'

His face looked more alert now. He pushed the whisky glass away. 'Vanessa, did you ever know the real name of the man who was mentioned in court as Old Man Senior?'

'No.'

'Think hard.'

Could this be some kind of test? Judge enjoyed cryptic crosswords and quiz questions. He'd taught her some of the tricks to deciphering them, and to her surprise she quite enjoyed it. 'No,' said Vanessa.

'He ran several businesses, including factories, garages and a care home.'

'Is this relevant?'

Even as she spoke, she knew it must be. *Stupid question, Vanessa*, she told herself. But Judge nodded as though she'd said exactly the right thing.

'You might well ask.' He sighed and then got up and sat in a chair next to hers. To her surprise he took her hands. Judge had only once done this before, when he'd looked up Lewis and Molly's details online. She'd felt comforted then. Now it was her turn to comfort him. She squeezed his hands as he continued his story.

'It turns out that I had the misfortune to know him under his real name.'

'What *was* his real name?' asked Vanessa.

'I'm just coming to that.'

Not for the first time, Vanessa thought that she wouldn't want to get on the wrong side of Judge.

'I've just paid an investigator to look into Sam and Jacob Senior. Turns out that their surname is really Brooks. The record company got them to change Brooks to something that stood out more. So they took part of their father's nickname.'

'Senior,' said Vanessa, just wanting to make sure she'd got this right.

'Exactly,' said Judge. 'But their father was christened Arthur Brooks.'

'I see,' said Vanessa, trying to get it all sorted in her mind.

Judge is looking her straight in the eyes. 'There's more. When I was a young man, Vanessa, I fell in love with my scout.'

'Your scout?' she repeated, confused.

'It's what we called people who cleaned our rooms at college. He was called Ian.'

Vanessa was only partly surprised. Hadn't she always wondered why a man like Judge had never remarried? The most likely reason, she'd decided, was that he'd never got over his wife and had dedicated himself to his career instead. But she hadn't considered *this*. Vanessa tried to keep her expression neutral.

'That must have been difficult in those days,' she heard herself saying.

'It was. We had to keep it quiet.'

'But you were married.'

'Not then. After I met Ian, I had a panic. I thought I ought to get married to prove to myself I wasn't . . . well . . . that way inclined. People weren't so accepting. So I chose a young woman from my chambers who worked as a legal secretary. I tried very hard. But it swiftly became clear that, as my wife put it, we weren't compatible. Not long after our marriage, we divorced.'

'So you weren't widowed?'

'No. I'm afraid I haven't been entirely open about that. In my earlier days, it didn't always go down well if a barrister was divorced. It looked as though one had failed in some way. Of course, I made sure my ex was well looked after financially.'

Vanessa couldn't help feeling disappointed in Judge. Didn't he see that it wasn't money that was important? Even though it helped, of course.

'Did you tell her about Ian?'

'No, I didn't have the courage. But, well, it was pretty clear I wasn't sexually attracted to her.'

The poor wife must have wondered if she'd done something wrong. Had she tiptoed around him just as she, Vanessa, had with Jack?

'What about your son?' she asked.

He shook his head. 'There is no son. I'm sorry, Vanessa. I tell people there is so they don't suspect I'm . . .'

He paused, as if still unable to voice the words.

'And your friend Ian?'

'We kept separate houses near each other, but we were together regularly until . . .'

She waited. Judge's eyes blurred with tears.

'Until he died,' he finished quietly.

'I'm so sorry.'

'Thank you.'

There was a brief silence during which Vanessa wondered if she should just leave. But then he spoke again.

'The thing is, Vanessa, that I used to feel more comfortable in male company, until I met you. And do you know why?'

Vanessa was flattered by the compliment but couldn't help feeling sad for Judge's ex-wife. It sounded as though she'd had no idea what she'd got into. 'No. Why?'

'My real mother died giving birth to me, and my step-mother, Stella, was such a bitch that she put me off women.'

Vanessa had never heard Judge use a word like that before. It shocked her. Not because of the word itself but because it went against the man she knew. Or rather, against the man she thought she'd known.

'She would play mind games, Vanessa. She divided me and my father by telling us lies about each other. Then she'd tell other people that I was an impossible child. Sometimes she'd be really nice to me for a while. And then she'd go back to her old ways. It was to lull me into a false sense of security.'

'How did it end?'

Judge made an almost bird-like gesture of putting his head on one side quizzically. 'You assume there was an ending.'

'Well, I . . .'

'You're right. There was. Stella developed dementia at quite a young age. At first, I thought it was a way of getting out of caring for my father, who was much older than her. Sometimes she was perfectly lucid and at other times she said some terrible things to me.'

'That's dementia for you,' Vanessa said softly.

'Anyway, the doctor suggested she went to a care home. I occasionally visited her there out of a sense of duty.'

'That was good of you.'

'Too good, as it turned out. One day when I was there, she tried to get up and knocked her head on the bedrail. She died instantly.'

Vanessa tried to stifle a gasp and failed. 'You didn't . . .'

'No. I didn't have anything to do it. Luckily, I had gone outside for a breath of fresh air when the tragedy happened. However, I couldn't help feeling relieved. Her death meant she could never again hurt me.'

'Did anyone see you going out?'

'No.'

Judge looked at her. 'You honestly don't think . . .'

'Of course, I don't,' said Vanessa, flustered. 'I just wondered, that's all.'

Vanessa reproached herself silently. How could she even dream that her friend would do something so awful? Perhaps she'd seen too many court cases.

'It turned out,' continued Judge, 'that the care home had erected the bedrails without written permission from me – her only remaining relative. So I threatened action against the care-home owners.'

Vanessa was used to Judge's long stories, which sometimes led to an unexpected conclusion, but she couldn't work out the connection here. 'I don't see what this has got to do with Janie's case.'

'Nor should you.' Judge took a swig of whisky and then stopped as if he'd just realized something. 'I'm so sorry. I ought to have offered you a drink too.'

'No, thank you. Please. No more distraction ploys. Just get on with it.'

A glimmer of a smile touched his lips. Then it went.

'Arthur Brooks, or Old Man Senior, as you know him, the care-home owner, had heard me arguing with Stella just before she died. In fact, I was defending myself from horrible things she was saying to me. Brooks wrote to me, telling me that if I didn't drop my case, he'd stand up in court and say he'd heard me threatening to smash her head in.'

'But you didn't hurt her.'

This was intended as a confirmation of her belief in his innocence. But he took it as a question.

'Of course not. But I was scared in case no one believed me. Brooks also suspected I was in a relationship with Ian because he would occasionally come with me to see Stella for moral support. I was hoping to take silk in the future. Homosexuality might have been legal, but it was not always approved of in the judiciary because it could be used for blackmail.'

'Is that what Mr Brooks did to you?'

Judge nodded glumly into his glass. 'So I dropped the case and heard nothing from him for years. Then I received an anonymous note to say that I had to make sure that Robbie Manning went down or else the writer would tell the world what happened on the night my step-mother died.'

'But her death wasn't your fault!'

'It didn't matter. The scandal might have ruined my career. So I got a private investigator to check out my hunch that Brooks might be behind this and I was right. He wanted to make sure that Robbie Manning took the blame for Jacob. Or so I thought.'

Vanessa's mind was spinning. 'But this can't be Arthur Brooks blackmailing you. He's dead.'

'Precisely. That's why I said "Or so I thought". I didn't know about the old man's death until Robbie Manning brought it up in court.'

'So if it's not Brooks, who is behind it?'

'I'm still trying to find that out. Or rather my investigator is. Meanwhile, I could be exposed any day as having a personal connection with the father of two witnesses in a trial I am currently presiding over.'

Vanessa stared at him. 'It will be everywhere. All over the papers. Your career could be jeopardized.'

'It would be over,' he said crisply. 'It was what I was mulling over when you knocked on the door. I have to admit that I felt quite depressed about it but now you've shown me the text from your charming grandson, it would be a pleasure to see someone else put two criminals behind bars.'

'*Two?*'

'Jacob and Lewis.'

She felt her jaw drop. 'Jacob *and* Lewis?'

Judge moved the computer screen towards her. It showed Lewis's profile.

'Jacob was in the same prison as your grandson when he was on remand for his drugs charge. My investigator paid one of the guards to find out more. Apparently, Lewis and Jacob became friends when they were cell-mates. That's when they found out that Lewis's newly discovered gran would be a witness supporter for Janie White. Without his dad to protect him, Jacob would have been terrified that the truth would come out. They hoped that, somehow, you would persuade Janie not to give evidence.'

Vanessa gasped. 'I let slip to Lewis that she could sing. I'm so sorry.'

Judge shook his head. 'We all make mistakes. She could have written down her evidence on her computer, but I grant you that singing in court definitely made an impact on the jury. No wonder Jacob was scared. My guess is that he looked up the judge who was going to be presiding over the trial. Then I would bet my last fiver that he recognized my name from things his father had told him.'

Vanessa chipped in. 'So Jacob thought he could turn the screws even more and persuade you to direct the jury towards a guilty verdict for Robbie Manning so he was off the hook.'

'Actually, that's not possible in law. But I do think someone was behind him.'

'Who?'

'Well, I've got a hunch, Vanessa, but if I'm right, the law can sort out this whole bloody mess once and for all.'

'And what about the case?'

'My gut feeling is that the jury is going to find Robbie

392

innocent. So I'm going to stay mum and hope I don't get exposed until that happens. Then I'm going to have a word with a chief constable friend of mine about Lewis Evans and Jacob Senior. After that, I plan on retiring. I've had enough of the law. And it looks like the law has had enough of me.'

IOI

Two Days Later

SHOCK AS JURY DECLARES ROBBIE MANNING INNOCENT

'THE GIRL WHO CAME BACK FROM THE DEAD' CASE TO BE RE-TRIED AS NEW EVIDENCE EMERGES – JACOB SENIOR AND LEWIS EVANS ARRESTED

From the *Daily Mail*:

JANIE: MEMORY OR ILLUSION?

Of all the questions concerning the case that everyone's talking about, there is one that poses a dilemma for many of us.

What can we see or hear when we are on the brink of death?

Janie insists she remembers Jacob Senior's red-and-blue tattoo. Yet she was clinically dead at the time.

We know that Janie's mental faculties were affected by the accident. So how much can she really recall of the events on that fateful day in 2004? Senior's lawyers will no doubt argue that her memory is impaired, but if that is true, how did she know about the tattoo?

394

As for Robbie Manning, some readers may be relieved by the jury's decision that our once-favourite pop star is, in fact, innocent. Some might call him a hero in his attempt to save lives by taking the wheel, only to be blackmailed by the Senior family into keeping their terrible secret.

Others might be disappointed that Robbie had lacked the courage to go to the police – whatever the consequences.

Meanwhile, all eyes are on Jacob Senior, who is due to appear in court shortly.

We wait with bated breath for what some are calling the trial of the year.

102

Robbie

Sitting as a spectator in the public gallery is very different from being on trial. He wasn't going to come but he can't bring himself to stay away.

Even now, he can barely believe that the jury had declared him not guilty. He is a free man, legally speaking, although not in his head. Who could be when you saw what Janie was like now? It made Robbie feel like an imposter.

And now Jacob is on trial for dangerous driving, possession of Class A drugs, perjury, attempting to pervert the course of justice and forcing Robbie, at knifepoint, to leave a young girl for dead. It also transpires that Jacob had lost his licence for drink-driving and shouldn't have been at the wheel at all.

Lewis, who is being tried at the same time, is being charged with conspiracy to pervert the course of justice.

Janie is here too. He'd thought she might be too exhausted by all this to give evidence again but no, there she is. 'Brave woman,' says Irena, who insisted on coming with him.

'You would like to talk to Janie afterwards, yes?' she asks.

He's told her everything, of course. He's explained that Janie had been the young girl who he'd met at that gig all those years ago. Before they were famous. Before any of this happened.

'Still,' Irena had said with her usual perception, 'she stays in your head.'

'Yes.' What a relief it was to live a life without secrets.

It doesn't take long to convict Jacob. He gets nine years. It doesn't feel enough.

'Let's go,' Robbie says. He can't wait to get out of the courtroom; these walls are closing in on him. He puts his arm around Irena and she snuggles up. Thank goodness she still loves him. He can barely believe that they've survived this. That they've come through as a family.

'I go to the Ladies?' his wife says. Her statements still sometimes ended in a question mark. He found it sweet, even after all these years. 'See you outside.' She gives him a kiss. 'It has ended well, yes? Justice has been done.'

But *has* it? Robbie can't help asking himself. He was the one who had been in control of the van without a licence, even if his motive had been, ultimately, to protect people. He bore responsibility for poor Janie's injuries. Shouldn't he be punished too, if there was any justice in the world?

BANG!

There is the sudden, earth-shattering sound of a gun being fired. Then silence.

Robbie stops dead.

Even before someone starts screaming, Robbie knows what has happened.

Even before there are more screams followed by uniforms rushing past him, he begins shaking.

Even before the police rush into the Ladies, he can see Irena's slumped body in his head.

Even before they cordon off the area while he tries to fight his way in, he knows what he will find.

When they carry out a body covered in tarpaulin from head to toe, he knows his wife is dead.

'Please, please,' he weeps. 'I just need to hold her one last time.'

Then they bring out a man with a defiant expression and hands cuffed behind his back. 'You bastard!' Robbie shouts. 'Jacob put you up to this, didn't he?'

The man spat at him as he passed. 'You've only got yourself to blame, Manning.'

It's true. Not only had he left Janie to die. But he should have pleaded guilty at the beginning, even if it meant Irena walking out. He should have let Jacob get off scot-free.

But now it is too late.

Robbie slumps to the ground, his head in his hands. What is he going to tell the children?

This is not just his life sentence. It's Daisy's and Simon's too. And it is all his fault.

103

Vanessa

'That poor mother,' Vanessa whispered.

She and Judge were at her place. He'd never been there before – somehow it had seemed too familiar to take him back to the home where Jack still lived in her head.

Even though there was nothing physical between them, Vanessa had often thought that the emotional support she got from Judge was much stronger and superior to the things that she and Jack had done in bed.

So when he'd rung straight after the news of the shooting and asked if she was all right, she knew that she needed him.

'No,' she'd said, numbly. 'I'm not all right. Can you come round?'

Now they sat together, hand in hand, on her new sofa. She'd never liked the old beige one but Jack had insisted on it, saying it was 'a safe colour'. This one was bright purple.

She wanted to cry but it was too big a thing to cry about. 'Why would anyone do something like that?' she asked.

He took his hand out of hers and put his arm around her instead. Vanessa found herself snuggling in. 'There could be all sorts of reasons.'

'You know why it happened, don't you?' she said, looking up at him. 'You have friends in the right places.'

'Yes,' he said quietly.

'Yes to why it happened or yes to the right places?'

'Yes to both.'

'Tell me . . .' she whispered.

His arm loosened. 'It wouldn't be right.'

She had to be content with that – Judge wouldn't budge, Vanessa knew that. Instinctively, she trusted this man far more than she trusted Jack, although that wasn't hard now she knew about the secrets he'd kept from her for all those years.

She glanced at Judge, suddenly realizing he was wearing one black sock and one brown. He caught her look. 'I couldn't find a matching pair this morning,' he said, shrugging.

That didn't fit with his usually very tidy appearance. Then again, his life had changed since he'd stopped working. Just as hers had. Vanessa was safe now that Lewis was back in prison, after being convicted.

'What about you?' he asked. 'Are you going to be able to see little Thomas again and meet your daughter at last?'

'I don't think so,' she sighed. 'I thought I might put a note through Molly's door but I don't have much hope without Lewis as a go-between. He said she was adamant she didn't want to see me. Maybe she holds me responsible for Lewis's behaviour. After all, she's not a stranger to breaking the law.' She'd already told Judge about the shoplifting.

'Why don't you just go round and knock on her door?'

suggested Judge. 'Sometimes it's best to do these things in person. I'll come too, if you like.'

'Why?' she asked, even though she'd been hoping he might say that.

'Because that's what friends do. Isn't it?'

'Thank you,' she said, resting her head on his shoulder before she even knew what she was doing.

'That's all right,' he said, putting his arm around her again. 'You'd do the same for me, I'm sure.'

'Actually,' she said, 'if our positions were reversed, I might suggest you go alone to prove you can do it.'

He looked down on her, smiling. 'Now there's an idea.'

'And that,' she said, feeling an unexpected shot of courage, 'is exactly what I'm going to do.'

From the *Daily Mail*:

EXCLUSIVE: TRAGIC ROBBIE HITS HEADLINES AGAIN – WIFE'S MURDER WAS A 'REVENGE KILLING'

The *Daily Mail* understands that Robbie Manning made a powerful enemy in prison while he was awaiting trial.

Lee Smith, whose nephew had been killed in a hit and run, arranged for an outside contact to shoot Robbie's innocent wife Irena after the trial of Jacob Senior.

Smith – who is serving a life sentence – then boasted about the murder to another inmate. A prison source revealed that Smith remained convinced of Manning's guilt and 'wanted to send a warning to others'.

From the *Daily Express*:

ROBBIE MANNING – A STAR FORLORN

Our hearts go out to fallen hero Robbie Manning and his children. Here is a man who seemed to have it all. Then lost it. Before proving himself innocent, and then losing it all again.

Robbie – we are thinking of you.

104

Vanessa

The last time she had been to this house, Vanessa reminded herself, was when a woman had come to the door and told her – in no uncertain terms – that Lewis didn't live there.

She'd been lying. In fact, she'd been her daughter. Her daughter! Even now Vanessa could barely believe it.

A daughter who didn't want to see her mother.

So why, Vanessa asked herself as she parked outside 101 Acres Road, did she think things were going to be any different now?

They wouldn't be. But at least she could say she'd tried.

That's when she heard the peal of laughter. It seemed to be coming from the garden. 'My turn! My turn!'

It sounded like a child. Vanessa's heart leapt. Could it be Thomas? Her sweet great-grandson? Again, it didn't feel real to say, but it was true.

Nervously, she rang the front bell, embarrassed about going straight into the garden. It worked this time – presumably someone had mended it. But there was no answer. What should she do now?

'Hello?' she called through the side gate.

'Your go now, Thomas,' said a jolly voice.

They couldn't hear her. What should she do? Open the gate or go home?

There was no choice. Or so it seemed. So she opened the latch and went through.

'I'm sorry to bother you,' she trembled.

'Hello,' chirped the little boy. Did he recognize her or was he just being friendly?

'You came here before, didn't you?' said the woman. She was putting her arm around Thomas protectively as if Vanessa might hurt him. 'And you were watching me in Exeter that time when I was shopping with my son. Why are you pestering me? I know who you are. It was all finished with a long time ago.'

'It's why I'm here.' Vanessa's voice was shaky with nerves. 'You see, I didn't realize you were alive! Lewis will have told you that, but I needed you to hear it from my own mouth.'

'What are you talking about?' The woman looks scared now.

'You said you knew who I was,' said Vanessa.

'I do. You're that store detective. You caught me in the shop all those years ago. When you turned up at my door the other month, I recognized you immediately. But, well, I suppose you did me a favour when you almost got me arrested. I was so scared, I told my husband I couldn't do it anymore and I left him. It was about time. He'd threaten me, making me steal things so we could pay the rent, beating me up if I didn't do it. It's why I've got this limp. Lewis and I managed all right on our own until he started following his dad's bad ways . . .' she tailed off.

Vanessa looked on, stunned, as Thomas tugged at the woman's trousers.

'It's all right, love,' she said, bending down to cuddle him. 'Granny's just talking to this lady.'

'I'm not a store detective anymore. Molly, I'm your *mother*. I know Lewis said you didn't want to meet me but . . .'

The woman's mouth was open in astonishment. 'What do you mean, you're my mother? She died last year . . . Unless . . .'

Vanessa could almost see the cogs turning in her mind.

'I'm the woman who gave birth to you,' Vanessa said gently. 'Lewis tracked me down. It's why I gave him money. A lot of it. He said you wouldn't see me otherwise.'

'He didn't tell me any of this.' Molly was shaking her head. Then she looked Vanessa up and down slowly. 'You're really my mother? The one who didn't want me?'

'It wasn't like that,' said Vanessa desperately. 'Let me explain.'

'Granny!' chipped in Thomas. 'I'm hungry.'

'It's all right, sweetie. We'll have some lunch now. You'd better come in, too. It sounds to me as though our Lewis has been telling a pack of lies again.' Molly shot her a hard look. 'You'd better not be doing the same to me.'

'I'm not,' said Vanessa. 'I promise. I would never do that.'

She tried to explain as best as she could while Molly dished up home-made cottage pie to Thomas. The kitchen work surfaces gleamed, Vanessa noticed. She could even see her reflection in the coffee percolator. Her face looked worried. Nervous.

'I know it sounds very naive,' Vanessa said after reaching the end of the story. 'But it was like that in those days. At least, it was for me.'

'And your husband – my birth father – is dead, you say?'

'Yes.'

'Pity. I'd have liked to have told him exactly what I thought of him.'

'I've already done that,' said Vanessa.

Molly frowned. 'What do you mean?'

'I still talk to him in my head sometimes.' Vanessa didn't mean to be so open, but the words just came out. It felt strangely comforting to confide in her daughter, even though they barely knew each other.

'I get that,' nodded Molly. 'I'm always talking to myself, asking how I ended up with a criminal husband and son. The truth was, I had low self-esteem. My adoptive parents were kind but I always felt hurt that my birth parents had rejected me. It's why I did what my ex told me to do, so I'd please him.'

'I didn't reject you,' said Vanessa quickly. 'I didn't even know you were alive.'

'I think I believe you, but I can't just wipe out all that pain in a few minutes. I didn't even know about your husband's letter until Lewis found it when he helped me clear out Mum and Dad's house. I was going to rip it up but my son told me we should keep it just in case we ever needed it one day.'

She gave a hoarse laugh. 'I should have known he was up to something. As for you and your husband – my so-called parents – I wanted nothing to do with either of you.'

'I'm sorry,' said Vanessa, hanging her head.

Molly shrugged. 'It's why I'm going to make sure that Thomas here is always loved and looked after by his own. Lewis's ex is a nice girl. She saw sense and left my boy before Thomas was even born. But she allows me to help look after him while she's at work. Her mum does a lot too.'

'You're the lady I saw with Daddy,' said Thomas, interrupting and pointing at her.

Molly looked confused, so Vanessa explained how Lewis had brought him along to the coffee shop, even though he'd actually promised to bring Molly.

Her face looked thunderous. 'He probably did it as a sweetener, hoping to get more money out of you. I'm glad he's back in prison again. I know that sounds tough, but with any luck it will teach him a lesson. One more mouthful, Thomas.'

Vanessa watched as the little boy dutifully obeyed. How she'd have loved to have done that! How she wished she could have brought up a child.

'Can I get down to play now?' he asked.

Such lovely manners!

'You've done a great job with him,' Vanessa said admiringly.

'Thanks. But like I said, we've all helped out. You can do some playdough with him, if you like, while I clear up.'

'That would be wonderful!'

'This is a circle,' said Thomas, handing a plastic shape to her. 'Push it down like this. See?'

After that, Molly got out something called pick-up sticks. The trick, she explained, was to move one of the sticks without disturbing the other.

'It helps their hand–eye coordination,' she said.

'It's very kind of you,' said Vanessa humbly, 'to be so understanding.'

Molly gave a little sigh. 'The thing is, now you've told me what happened, I feel something has slotted into place.'

'But I haven't given you any proof.'

'You don't need to. I can see you're telling the truth. And, to be honest, the important thing right now in my life is Thomas.' She lowered her voice. 'I need to make sure he doesn't suffer from having a dad in prison. I also need to try and stop him from going off the rails as he grows up. Not like his dad or grandad, or me as a young woman.'

She gave Vanessa a sharp look. 'How much money did my Lewis fleece you out of, if you don't mind me asking?'

Vanessa hesitated.

'Was it thousands?'

'Yes.'

Molly sighed. 'He owed money everywhere. Of course, he never gave me details, but there were always people turning up here – shady types. They used to scare me.'

'I'm sorry.'

Vanessa wanted to add that the money she'd paid Lewis didn't matter now she'd found Molly but stopped when there was a knock on the door.

'That'll be your other nan,' said Molly to Thomas as she got up.

A woman came in wearing some rather cool leggings that Vanessa herself had admired in Zara the other day. Thomas flung himself round her legs and, once more, Vanessa had an incredible yearning to feel his arms around her too.

'Hi,' she said. 'I'm Grace.'

'I'm Vanessa,' she said. 'I'm . . .'

She stopped. Molly might not want her to be so open.

'Remember me telling you I was adopted?' said Molly, cutting in. 'This is my birth mother, believe it or not. It's a long story . . .'

'Wow,' said Grace in a surprised but friendly manner. 'Well, it's nice to meet you, Vanessa.'

'I ought to go,' she said awkwardly.

'Don't be daft,' Molly replied. 'There's so much I want to ask you about but I haven't been able to with this little one around. Do you mind looking after him for a bit, Grace?'

'Sure.'

'Let's go back into the garden, shall we?' Molly said to Vanessa.

'That would be lovely.' But she couldn't help giving Thomas a wistful glance.

'Don't worry. There'll be plenty of time for you to get to know each other.'

Plenty of time? Vanessa felt as if she could float with joy.

'*Be careful*,' said Jack in her head. '*There's bound to be a catch*.'

105

Robbie

Robbie's heart is beating faster than it has ever done before. Faster than when he'd appeared at Glastonbury for the first time. Faster than it had in Madison Square Garden.

It gets even faster as he walks up to the red-bricked building with the 'Homes for Assisted Living' sign outside and presses the keypad button labelled 'White'.

'Who is it?' says a voice through the intercom.

'Robbie Manning.'

'Robbie Manning?' says the voice, laden with sarcasm. 'The same Robbie Manning who left my daughter in the road to die?'

The van. The bike. The crunch.

'Yes,' whispers Robbie.

'You've got a bloody cheek, I'll say.'

Robbie had asked his solicitor to contact Derek White and explain why he'd like to visit. Janie's father had given permission but he is clearly still furious. Robbie doesn't blame him.

'Please,' he says. 'May I come in?'

'Not if I have a say in it,' replies the man gruffly. 'But my daughter wants to see you for some reason. Wait there.'

He's taking his time. Robbie glances behind nervously,

wondering if someone is going to shoot him as they had shot Irena. The police had warned him to be careful. It was possible, they told him, that Lee Smith might hire another assassin to get them. The man had nothing to lose.

Robbie can only hope that Daisy and Simon are all right. He's had to leave them with an officer at home. He can't be long. Their flight is in a few hours.

There's a click as the entrance door opens. Robbie steps into the lobby and enters a long corridor with doors on either side. A man is standing at one, waiting. Robbie hadn't seen Janie's father in court. He must have been one of many in the public gallery.

'In here,' instructs Derek White curtly.

Robbie is shaking now. This is a mistake. He should have just left for the airport with his children in case someone else tried to hurt them. But at the same time, he knows Irena would want him to do this.

Janie is sitting at her desk, a computer in front of her. By her side is a brown Labrador with an 'Assistance Dog' collar on him.

She'd been some distance away from him in court. Now he's almost as close to her as they had been at the gig all those years ago.

'Thank you for seeing me, Janie,' he says, dropping to his knees so they are on the same level. 'I want to tell you in person how sorry I am. I should have ignored Jacob and his dad. I should have been brave enough to call the police.'

Janie is looking at him in such a way that it's like her eyes are X-raying him.

Then she starts to sing. It isn't as loud as it had been in court, and it's soft. Less angry.

'You couldn't have changed the injuries,' she sings.

'But I could have got you help. I shouldn't have grabbed the wheel either.'

'You only did it to stop that horrible man doing something awful.'

'Yes,' he sobs. 'But something awful *did* happen, didn't it?'

Not just to this innocent girl. But to his Irena too.

Her voice grows even gentler, 'I'm sorry about your wife.'

Her notes and words bathe his soul, yet at the same time they scald him.

He tries to speak again but the words won't come out. Then he manages to whisper, 'Thank you.'

She's looking at him now as if she can see inside his heart. 'Your children don't deserve to lose their mother. How are they?'

He shakes his head, thinking of their stunned disbelief when he'd told them that Mummy was dead. Daisy has hardly spoken since. Simon follows his sister everywhere. 'There are no words to describe how they feel,' Robbie manages to say, in answer to her question. 'I need to protect them,' he adds, 'to make sure it doesn't happen again.'

Janie moves her wheelchair towards him. She touches his arm. The dog sits by her side, gazing up at her.

'Do I know you from somewhere a long time ago?' she sings in the same soft tone. 'When I saw you in court, you reminded me of someone I met before the accident. But I might have got that wrong.'

Robbie nods and forces his voice to speak again. 'I met you at a gig where the boys and I were playing. It was before we got signed up. You and I, well, we danced and . . .'

He wants to add 'kissed' but that feels too familiar.

'We danced!' she sings with what sounds like delight. 'How lovely. I wish I could remember that part.' She looks down at her leg and the stump. 'I can't dance now, as you can see.'

Robbie swallows the huge lump in his throat. 'I said I'd come back to find you after my set but you'd gone.'

Janie's face seems to clear. 'Yes! I had to leave because it was getting late and my father would have been worried. I went back to the hall a few times to see if your band was performing again but I couldn't see a poster.'

Tears are streaming down Robbie's face. 'You did? I went back too, hoping to bump into you. I never forgot you – well you don't forget your first kiss, do you . . .'

He blushed.

'Your first kiss?' repeated Janie. 'It was mine too. At least, I think it was.'

'I promise you,' he sobs. 'I didn't know you were the girl who I . . .'

He stops, unable to say the words 'ran over'. But she seems to understand.

'Would it have made a difference if you had known it was me?' she sings softly.

Hasn't he asked himself the same question over and over since the trial?

'Yes,' he chokes. 'I know that's terrible. I'll never forgive myself, but it's the truth.'

She gives him a look that chills his soul. 'You should have stayed, regardless of who I was. But now I know the whole story, I forgive you. You were young and scared and trying to protect your family.'

Janie's father's voice cuts in. 'My daughter might forgive you, but I certainly don't.'

'I understand that,' Robbie replies. 'I can't tell you how sorry I am.'

Derek's voice shakes with rage. 'Do you think "sorry" is going to help my daughter now?'

Then he lowered his voice. 'My daughter even had your bloody picture on the wall until I tore it down. You're lucky her memory is so unreliable or else she'd be throwing you out of the house like I am doing right now.'

Robbie stands up. 'Please. Wait. I came here for another reason too.'

And then he tells them.

106

Vanessa

When Vanessa had first applied for the role of a witness service volunteer, she was warned against developing too close a personal relationship with the people she looked after.

'It's easy to do that,' her supervisor had warned. 'But it's not professional.'

That was all very well, but you'd need a heart of stone not to form an attachment. After all, it had happened before: just look at Tyler, who was now serving a life sentence for murder. Vanessa had applied to visit him again but he'd turned down her request. It had hurt her at first but, she told herself, perhaps he didn't want her to go through the trauma of visiting him inside.

For all that, Vanessa had never experienced the sort of emotions that she had for Janie now.

So when she received a letter through the office from Derek White, asking if she'd drop round when it was 'convenient', she felt a mixture of apprehension and excitement.

'*Are you sure you should go?*' asked Jack.

'Why ever not?' she retorted, cross that he was back in her head.

'*You need to keep those boundaries.*'

'Like you did when you didn't tell me about our daughter?' she shot back.

That shut him up.

When she arrived at Janie's flat, her father answered the door immediately, as if he'd been waiting.

'I thought you were Robbie Manning coming back,' he said.

'Robbie?'

'Cheek of it. He came round, asking for our Janie's forgiveness and trying to make it up to her.'

'Did he now?'

'Said she had the most beautiful voice he'd ever heard – out of this world, he called it – and that he could put her in touch with some music-producer contact of his.' Derek snorted. 'As if that could ever compensate for what he did.'

Tears glistened in his eyes. 'Do you have any idea what it's like to have the police knocking on your door to say your daughter has been in a terrible accident? My first thought was that it couldn't be real – she was all I had left. It was like the world was closing in around me. I couldn't breathe. I felt like I was drowning. Then when I saw her in hospital . . .'

His voice cracked briefly, tears rolling down his face. 'I didn't even recognize my little girl. I've got to say, I'm not religious but I found myself making a bargain with God. If he could keep her alive, I'd do anything – anything – to help her get back to a normal life. But that's never going to happen now, is it? And the person responsible is let off when, in my opinion, he should be locked up with the other one. Scum, that's what he is, if you ask me. I'm sorry

416

for his kids, of course. But I can't help thinking that maybe his wife being killed is divine retribution for him.'

Vanessa wasn't sure what to make of Robbie. On the one hand, she despised him for leaving Janie after the accident. But on the other, she knew all too well that people made stupid decisions when they were scared, especially when they were young. And, of course, no one deserved to lose their wife that way.

'Hello, Vanessa,' sang Janie, looking up from her computer.

She really did have a beautiful voice. It was like an angel's. Then she took in the Labrador sitting next to her. So Derek had taken her up on the idea she'd suggested during the trial!

'Hello, Janie. Have I interrupted you?'

'It's all right,' sang Janie.

'What a gorgeous dog!'

As Janie reached down to stroke him, the animal gazed up lovingly. The affection between the two proved Vanessa been right. An assistance dog was exactly what Janie needed!

'I've only just found out that she's writing a diary on the computer,' said her father, in a low voice. 'I'm afraid I took a peep. Of course, we don't know how reliable it is, given her memory.'

A diary? That could be interesting.

'May I look at what you're writing?' asked Vanessa, a little shocked that Derek had 'taken a peep'. She fully expected to be turned down, so she was surprised by Janie's reply.

'Yes,' she sang. 'I've been trying to piece everything together. I think I'm ready for people to read it now. You have to start at the beginning, though. It begins when I was run over. Of course, I couldn't write it then but I've tried to go back to what I remember.'

She pressed her specially adapted mouse, taking them back to page one.

As Vanessa began reading, she felt a shiver go down her spine.

Was it possible, after all this, that Janie herself had been responsible for the accident?

107

Judge

PLEASE RING

Judge was playing online chess when the text popped up. His bishop was in a rather delicate situation but he could sense Vanessa's panic in her capital letters, so he called her immediately.

'Is something wrong?'

Vanessa's voice was unusually breathless. 'Janie has been writing a diary. She describes how she cycled in the wrong direction down a one-way street and got hit by a van going the *right* way. Do we know whether that street was one-way in those days?'

'I don't.' Judge could kick himself. How had no one checked that? Surely the police would have known at the time.

'Can we find out?'

'We could,' he said, 'but what use would it be? Jacob is in prison.'

Privately, Judge was mightily relieved about this.

'But what if he doesn't deserve to be?' persisted Vanessa.

'He still left Janie for dead. Still tried to pervert the course of justice.'

'Even so . . .' insisted Vanessa.

'You know,' said Judge slowly, 'a prison governor once told me that there was usually one man inside his jail who didn't deserve to be there for the crime he'd been convicted of. But that prisoner might well have committed another crime that he hadn't been caught for. So in a way, justice had still been done.'

Vanessa was silent for a moment.

'I think we should do the right thing,' she said eventually.

Judge was beginning to feel uneasy. 'Would it be the "right thing" to put Janie through a trial again? Besides, I think it's highly unlikely that the Crown Prosecution Service would allow an appeal for that reason alone.'

'Do you think she deliberately lied about the one-way street?' she persisted.

'She was never asked about it. No one was. If anything, it was more of an omission than a fib.'

Vanessa's voice was firm. 'I'm not sure that makes a difference.'

'I wish more people thought like you. The world would be a better place.'

'So what are we going to do?'

'Do you really want to add any more problems to Janie's life?'

'No,' she said.

'Then let's just leave it at that, shall we?'

'OK,' she said.

He sensed her uneasiness. It didn't make him feel great. Who was he to play God? But surely Janie White had suffered enough.

108

Extract from Janie's diary

I knew I shouldn't have cycled the wrong way down that road but I was hungry for breakfast and, anyway, it was early, so there was no traffic about. Then I came to the bend. The blind one. The bit you couldn't see round.

My bike began to wobble, like there was something wrong with it again.

That's when I saw it – a white van hurtling towards me out of nowhere, so fast that I couldn't brake in time. The chrome bits at the front looked like it was grinning at me. And then it happened.

I had meant to tell them that bit about the one-way system in court but I forgot. My mind does that – it remembers things and forgets them again at random. They often come back again if I start writing but, even then, I don't know if they're true.

When you think about it, who knows what is true in life? We can choose to make up whatever we want. Can't we?

109

Vanessa

She was baking scones for Molly and Thomas's tea – they were actually going to come to her house that afternoon! – when the doorbell went.

It was Judge.

'May I come in?' he asked.

Vanessa was taken aback by the impromptu visit. Their conversation about Janie and the one-way street had continued to niggle away at her. Maybe he'd come round to say he was wrong and that, yes, they should tell the police about the diary entry.

'Of course you can,' she said. He didn't look well. 'Your face is rather grey, if you don't mind me saying. Are you ill?'

'No,' he said, 'although I have got something difficult to tell you.'

'Is it about Janie's diary?'

'No. It's just that . . . well . . . despite being retired, I still hear things through the grapevine. It appears that Jacob has told his lawyer about a "bent cop" who was being bribed by his father . . . Apparently, he helped to hush everything up after the accident.'

Vanessa's mouth suddenly went very dry. 'Hush what up?'

'The policeman in charge of the area appeared to . . . Well, let's just say that he turned a blind eye to some of the clues that might have been picked up.'

'And why are you telling me this?'

'I think you might have guessed, I'm afraid,' he replied quietly.

Vanessa swallowed hard.

'No,' she said. 'Please, no.'

'I'm sorry.' He came towards her, as if to give her a hug, but she stepped back.

'Why would Jack have done that?' she asked.

'He got paid handsomely, I gather.'

Vanessa thought of Jack's 'pay rise' shortly after the accident, and of the new conservatory they'd built.

'But my husband made it his mission to find the driver.'

'Maybe he was protesting a bit too much . . . I'm sorry, Vanessa.' Judge reached out and held her hand. For a second, she allowed herself the comfort of staying in his grasp but then moved away.

'Thank you,' she said. 'I think I need to be alone for a while now.'

'Of course.'

She saw him out and shut the door before going to Jack's wardrobe. She found his police uniform and then she took the large shearing scissors from her mending basket and spent the next hour snipping it – tough as it was – into bits.

After that, she went into the garden, took an ornamental rock from the side of the pond and hurled it at the conservatory windows, until the panes cracked into several, satisfying pieces.

'Fuck you, Jack!' she screamed. 'Fuck you!'

The neighbours would hear. But who cared?

Vanessa waited for Jack to make his usual 'it's not my fault' argument.

But nothing came.

110

Judge

Judge was standing at Ian's grave, updating him on the case, as he always did. Ian had been very good at listening. Even more so now he was dead. But he'd left one detail to mull over in his head since the case and now he was ready to share it.

'So you see,' Judge said, 'they got it wrong. All of them. And I didn't point it out.'

'*Go over it again, will you?*' says Ian.

'It was when Janie said in court that she'd died on a Tuesday. The date – September the 15th – always struck me because it is our anniversary.'

'*Glad you still remember,*' said Ian.

'Of course I do. So I went onto Google and checked which day it fell on in the year the accident happened. And I found it was a Wednesday. Neither side – not the prosecution nor the defence – seemed to notice that. They just went on. I could have questioned it but something inside me didn't.'

'*You could argue that she didn't die at all,*' Ian pointed out. '*Not like I did.*'

Pancreatic cancer was wicked. It gave you so little time to prepare.

Judge carefully traced the *dearest friend* lettering on Ian's headstone before replying. 'She was medically dead for an unknown length of time.'

'Yes, but she wasn't dead for ever, like me.'

True.

There was a short silence.

'I miss you,' said Judge.

'I miss you too. But I don't get it. Why didn't you call both barristers into chambers to point out the Tuesday mistake?'

'Because I feared they'd then discredit the rest of Janie's statement and even throw out the case. It was an understandable error – she could have got the days muddled up. And now Vanessa has told me that Janie might have gone down a one-way street and caused the accident herself. But we can't be certain because, like I said, the victim is muddled at times and not at others.'

'In other words, she's an unreliable witness.'

'We always knew that, but then she'd say something that was verifiably true, so we believed her.'

'Well, we won't ever know for certain, will we?'

Judge liked the *'we'* bit. It made him feel like Ian was still there.

'No, we won't.'

'Does that matter, love?'

Judge also liked it when Ian called him *'love'*. It gave him a warm feeling.

'Heard any more from the investigator?' asked Ian.

'Not yet, but I'm waiting.'

'Still, Jacob Senior deserved to go down, in my opinion.'

'True.'

'The other one, Robbie, got his dues too, didn't he?'

'Dreadful. It's the kids I feel sorry for.'

Ian's voice was softer now. '*I'd have liked children.*'

Judge nodded. 'Me too.'

'*We could have had them if I'd lived longer.*' Ian's voice turned wistful. '*It's more common nowadays.*'

Judge's eyes smarted with tears. 'That would have been nice.'

'*But now you've got Vanessa to keep you company.*'

'It's not the same as having you,' said Judge quietly.

'*I know, but she's a good person. Does she know about your stepmother?*'

Judge shuddered. In two weeks' time, she'd have been dead for exactly forty-five years. The date was imprinted on his mind. 'No. You're the only one I've ever told.'

'*I don't mind if you want to confide in Vanessa. She sounds like the kind of person who might understand.*'

'Thank you.'

'*See you next time, then.*'

'See you next time,' Judge repeated. Gently, he kissed the cold marble stone before rearranging the spray of freesias he'd brought for the urn. Then he walked away.

It always helped, talking to Ian. Their conversations meant he could keep going. But still, something was missing from the Janie puzzle. Something else. Something that had nothing to do with the one-way system (which had indeed been in place at the time) or the Tuesday/Wednesday mix-up.

If only he could put his finger on it.

Vanessa

Vanessa had been so upset by Judge's revelations about Jack that she'd cancelled Molly and Thomas's visit, pleading a migraine. She lay awake all night thinking about what Judge had told her about her husband.

When morning came, she decided there was only one person she wanted to confide in. But first she phoned to check it was convenient.

'Sure,' said Molly. 'I'm glad you're feeling better. I'll get the kettle on. It's a good day to come over. Thomas is here.'

Despite her heavy heart, Vanessa felt excited. She'd bought him some of those stickle brick things she'd seen in the toy-shop window the other day. 'They're for my great-grandson,' she'd told the assistant.

'That's nice. I'm a grandad myself. Wonderful, isn't it?'

Finally, Vanessa felt part of the club she'd always longed to be in!

'Thank you,' said Thomas when she gave them to him. But Molly was giving her a knowing look. 'Something's up, isn't it? I can see it in your face.'

Funny how her daughter could sense that after such a short acquaintance. Or was it? There was something about blood ties that really bonded you to someone, wasn't there?

'Jack was a bent copper?' Molly gasped when she told her.

She gave Vanessa a brief hug. It was the first time she'd done so and Vanessa felt a lovely thrill.

'You must feel really shitty,' Molly continued.

Vanessa rather admired the way her daughter spoke her mind.

'Yes, I do.'

'I felt like that when I discovered Lewis's dad was stealing.' She gave a short laugh. 'Looks like crime runs in the family. I hope it doesn't pass on to Thomas.'

'It won't,' said Vanessa firmly. 'You're doing a great job bringing him up.'

'Well, you know, there are three of us.'

Vanessa's heart warmed. It was so lovely to be included!

'That reminds me. Thomas's mum said she'd like to meet you. Her name's Michelle.'

Of course. When she'd said 'the three of us', Molly had been referring to herself, Thomas's mum and his other grandmother, Grace – not her at all. Vanessa couldn't help feeling a little pang but then again, she couldn't expect to waltz in and instantly become family.

'In fact, I'm due to take Thomas back to their place now,' continued Molly. 'Michelle's just finished her shift. She's a nurse, you know. Want to come with us?'

She began putting Thomas in his pushchair. 'He's almost outgrown this but it's easier when there's a bit of a walk, especially as I get breathless sometimes. I've been like that since birth.'

'Do you have any other medical problems?' asked Vanessa, feeling horribly guilty even though it was Jack who had given her away.

'No, I was lucky.'

Do you hear that, Jack? she wanted to say. *You and the midwife were wrong.*

Together they walked down the road towards the high street. 'Bat!' called out Thomas when they passed a sports shop.

'He's dead keen on sport,' laughed Molly.

Vanessa made a mental note to buy him a toy cricket bat. She'd seen a bright blue plastic one in a shop window only the other day.

'You can push if you want,' said Molly when they reached the shopping precinct.

'Really?' What an honour! 'That would be wonderful.'

'That there is the brake and this is the lever that you slide if you want it to go into the recline position.'

Molly spoke as if Vanessa was going to do this again. Oh, she did hope so! It felt wonderful to walk along with a little one, after all these years. She thought she'd got some healing when Lewis had come into her life until he'd betrayed her.

But now she had her great-grandson and . . .

'LOOK OUT!'

Vanessa heard the shout seconds before everything went black.

112

Judge

Judge had just finished the final chapter of *The Advanced Guide to Chess* when the phone rang.

He'd thought he might be bored in retirement but there was so much to do that, at times, he wondered how he'd ever had time to work.

Prompted by a piece in the local paper, he'd signed up to help with the local homeless project. His jobs included raising money through persuading friends to donate and advising the committee on certain legal matters.

He also started going to the Thursday morning Silver Screen showings at the cinema. Maybe, he told himself, he'd ask Vanessa to the next one.

In fact, he'd been trying to get hold of her all afternoon to suggest it but there had been no reply.

Not recognizing the number, he almost didn't pick up the phone when it rang.

'*What?*' he said, his legs turning to jelly. 'I don't believe it.'

Judge had always despised that phrase as a cliché but it was exactly how he felt. He grabbed his jacket. 'I'll be there as soon as I can.'

113

Vanessa

The first thing she saw were the grey squares on the ceiling above her. Her neck felt stiff; it seemed to be in a brace. And she couldn't move her left leg.

'Vanessa,' said a man's voice. 'My name's Adam. I'm the nurse in charge. You're in hospital. How are you feeling?'

Then it came back to her. Pushing her great-grandson down the shopping precinct. Someone shouting. And then blackness.

'Thomas!' she cried out. 'Is he all right?'

'He's fine,' said a tearful voice.

Was that Molly?

'You saved him, Vanessa! You pushed our boy away just in time, but the cyclist ploughed straight into you. He shouldn't even have been there at all, let alone going at such a speed.'

The pain in her legs and neck was excruciating but she needed complete reassurance. Vanessa turned to look worriedly at her daughter. Thomas was clinging to his grandmother's neck, eyes wide and face pale.

'You're sure he wasn't hurt?'

'Not a scratch. We've been worried about *you*.'

The Adam voice chipped in. 'You've broken your collarbone and right leg. But they will both heal in time.'

Thomas was now stretching out his arms to her. 'Nessa,' he said.

Vanessa felt her heart melt.

'Is this the right room for Vanessa Grossmith?' asked a familiar voice.

It was Judge.

'My dear! Are you all right?'

'Yes,' she said, clutching his warm hand. 'Nothing that can't be fixed.'

She saw him taking in this crowd of strangers.

'Judge, this is my family. Everyone, this is Judge. He's . . . He's my special friend.'

Then Vanessa couldn't help it. She burst into floods of tears. Not sad ones this time. Tears of relief and joy.

114

Judge

It had been three months since Vanessa's accident. Thank God, she was on the mend. Ironically, he'd been going to tell her the full story about his stepmother just before the bike accident but he was glad he hadn't now. She was so happy with her extended family that he didn't want to puncture her new peace of mind.

Meanwhile, Lewis was still in prison – a different one from Jacob Senior's. Everything had gone very quiet: journalists appeared to have grown bored of what they called the story of the year. No one seemed to know where Robbie and his children were hiding out, which was a good thing. Judge couldn't bear the idea of more deaths.

Yet, every day, Judge woke up with the feeling that something threatening still hung in the air.

So when the call came and a voice at the other end asked if he would kindly come as fast as possible to a care home on the outskirts of London, Judge knew that the day of reckoning had come.

'*Hold firm*,' Ian had said.

That was all very well but Ian wasn't with him. This was something he had to do on his own.

115

Judge

The old woman looked like the figure from Munch's *The Scream*. Her yellow skin was wafer-thin and, even when the nurse tried to straighten her head, it would flop back to the same position on the left of the pillow.

'It's her liver,' the nurse said, as if he already knew, which he didn't.

'Sometimes,' she added, 'she's quite sleepy, but you've caught her at an alert time. Mrs Brooks was very insistent when she told me to ring you.'

Judge didn't know what to say, so he said nothing. To be honest, that wasn't difficult – the last time he'd walked through those heavy oak doors was the final day he'd seen his stepmother. This place made him feel physically sick.

He'd thought he would never be back. So why was he here? Because this woman was dying, and you couldn't refuse a dying person's wish, could you?

Or maybe, because he was curious about what she wanted to say.

As soon as the nurse left, those beady eyes focused on him.

'You didn't do what I said, Mr Baker.'

'What do you mean?'

'You got my note during the trial and –'

435

'*Your* note?' broke in Judge. So this was the answer to the puzzle which even Gary, his investigator, hadn't been able to find out! 'I thought it was from your husband until Robbie Manning gave evidence and said he was dead.'

'Thought you might. Everyone assumed he wore the pants in our marriage. He had a real temper on him – roughed up Robbie's mother pretty bad to make the boy do what he wanted. My old man was ambitious, see? He liked the idea of having rock-star sons but I was the one with brains. I sent notes to Robbie in prison, warning him too, but the silly fool took no notice.'

She paused to gasp the next breath.

'Then Jacob told me that the girl Janie could sing. Some stupid woman who worked at the court had let it slip to a mate of his. So then I had to keep an eye on her too. I couldn't have her implicating my boy in her evidence, could I? I got someone to tail the woman every now and then – you never know what useful things might arise.'

Judge stiffened. She must mean Vanessa. 'Why are you telling me this?'

'Because I'm dying. And because, despite what you might think of me, I do have a conscience.'

'I'm glad of that,' he said quietly.

'Having said that, it's your fault that Robbie Manning's wife is dead. If you hadn't sent my son Jacob to prison, it would have been all right. Robbie would have gone down instead and that prisoner wouldn't have shot his wife – something I had nothing to do with, by the way.'

'*I* didn't send him down,' said Judge. 'The jury did.'

She snorted as if she didn't believe him.

Judge was still taking in the fact that it had been Old Man Senior's wife who had been blackmailing him all along. Of course. How stupid had he been?

Mrs Brooks. The wife of the man who had bribed half the town. The man who owned the nursing home where his stepmother had died. What was it they said? Behind every successful man stands a great woman. Or a she-devil.

Then she stared at him. It was a look that froze his bones with fear. 'What I want to know,' she rasped, 'is how a judge can get away with murder for so long and yet send down others who have done the same.'

Judge felt a wave of unease. 'I don't know what you're talking about.'

'I think you do. You smashed your stepmother's head against the bars. Don't lie to me.'

The room started to swim.

'Why would I do that?'

'Because she didn't care for you one bit. My old man heard the things she said to you and then he told me.'

'That doesn't mean I would kill her.'

'Oh yes you did. I admit we had our doubts at the time, but there's been a development.'

Judge was well aware of this line of questioning. He'd seen it hundreds of times in court. Suggestive comments designed to make the accused think that there was some proof.

'Why are you bringing this up after all these years? Your eldest son is in prison. Nothing I say is going to get him out. I've retired. I have no judiciary power anymore.'

'But you have a conscience, don't you?' she wheedled.

'Come on, tell me the truth. Don't deny a woman on her deathbed.'

Judge looked up at the ceiling.

'The room isn't bugged, if that's what you're thinking,' she said.

It was *exactly* what he was thinking.

'I did not kill her.'

'So you say,' she snorted. 'But I've got new evidence. One of the women who worked for me at the time saw everything. She's only just told us.'

'If that's true, why didn't she report it back then?'

'Money. We were paying her cash in hand, and, unknown to us, she was an illegal immigrant.'

'Come on. Of course you knew. It meant you could pay her less.'

Ignoring the comment, Mrs Senior carried on. 'If she'd reported the crime to us at the time, there would have been a formal investigation and the authorities would have found out she shouldn't have been here at all.'

'So why has she told you now?'

'Because she's just retired and it's been weighing on her conscience. She's also got British nationality so can't be deported.'

Judge gave her his cold stare. 'You're lying.'

'She's prepared to give evidence.'

'How much are you paying her to perjure herself?'

'I might be able to keep her quiet if you can get my Jacob out of prison.'

'That's not up to me. The only legal way is to appeal, but he'd need good grounds to do so.'

'Don't give me all that. You might have retired but you can make it happen.'

Sometimes Judge was horrified by the number of people who thought that judges could just wave a wand and get justice overturned.

'Actually, I can't. And even if I could, I wouldn't.'

'Then be prepared to go to jail. I tell you – this woman will say anything I ask her to. There's something else too. Something you don't know about . . . about Janie White's case.'

She seemed to be gasping for breath as she said the last bit.

'What?' asked Judge.

'You'll need to look in your own house to find out,' she rasped. 'I could have revealed it during the case. It might even have led to a retrial. But it would have put my old man in an even worse light. And I didn't want to do that.'

'What do you mean?'

But the old woman was pressing her bed alarm. 'The nurse will come now. You can go.'

'Don't worry,' he said. 'I will. Frankly, I feel sorry for your kids. Jacob is better off in prison than out. Do you know why? Because he's safely away from an evil, manipulative mother.'

Then he left. But as Judge walked to the station, the memories of his stepmother's last night on earth insisted on flooding back. Suddenly, he wasn't Judge anymore. He was Richard.

116

Judge

She was trying to grab him. Grasping him with her long fingernails, ripping his skin the way she used to when he was a child.

All because he'd told her that his father had never loved her the way that he'd loved his first wife. Richard's mother.

So the young man had grabbed her back in return. By her neck.

'You're hurting me,' she'd wailed. She'd tried to pull away but in his fury, he'd smashed her head against the bed bars. There was a sharp snap.

Her eyes rolled and then set as if she was staring right at him, unblinking. Instinctively, he knew she was dead. He had killed her.

Then he'd run. No one was around – all the staff were busy with other patients down the corridor.

He was free at last! That woman would never hurt him again. But what if he got caught? The young Richard began to panic. How could he have been so wicked? What had come over him? Yes – his stepmother had been cruel. But that didn't warrant murder. How many times had he heard criminals describe how they'd just 'flipped'? And he had done exactly the same.

Now what? He began to shake. Should he go straight home? Yes. No. 'Make up your mind,' he told himself. Maybe just run away and hide? No. Too suspicious. But how about going back? He could pretend he'd found her dead after going outside for a break.

So he did just that. As he opened her door, his heart was in his mouth. Maybe she'd be sitting up. Maybe she'd scream at him for trying to kill her.

But no.

Her head was bleeding as it slumped against the bars. Her eyes were open, still facing him with that glassy death stare. There could be no doubt.

As if in slow motion, Richard rang the alarm.

'It must have been an accident,' he told the police. The crocodile tears came surprisingly easily. 'Perhaps she was trying to get out of bed. I should never have gone outside for a breath of fresh air.'

'Don't upset yourself,' one of the policewomen had said. 'My mum's in a home too. When I visit, I need to go out for a break as well.'

Was it possible to murder someone and then convince yourself you didn't do it?

Yes. It was the ultimate crime.

117

Judge

'What an evil bitch,' declared Vanessa when Judge told her about his recent visit to Mrs Brooks. He hadn't intended to but he felt so shaken that he had to talk to someone. Someone who was still alive. Purposely, he'd left out the crucial bit.

'Sorry,' she continued, blushing at her use of the word 'bitch'. 'But she is. And what did she mean about you looking in your own house?'

'I have no idea. It's not as though I live with anyone. I don't even have a cat.'

The last part was meant to be a joke, but Judge was aware that this wasn't the time or place. Besides, he was too old to kid himself that he could be funny.

Especially not when murder was involved.

'Maybe she didn't actually mean your house,' suggested Molly who'd been at Vanessa's bungalow with little Thomas when he'd called round. 'You were a judge, weren't you? So how about a court or the House of Commons?'

'Nessa,' interrupted Thomas from the dining-room table, where he was colouring in. (The blue cricket bat that Vanessa had bought her great-grandson after getting out of hospital stood by his side, leaning against the chair, waiting for the rain outside to stop. It went everywhere with him!) 'I can't find the green pen.'

'Maybe you've dropped it, love. There it is!'

Then she eased herself up from her chair – that leg still troubled her from the accident – and passed it to the little boy.

'I could have done that,' said Molly. 'Be careful, love.'

Since Vanessa had saved Thomas's life, Judge observed, the relationship between the two women seemed to have become much warmer.

'You might have something there,' he said now, in reply to Molly's suggestion. 'Think! Who works in the court who might have been related to Janie's case?'

They brainstormed for a bit but gave up. 'It could be anyone,' said Vanessa. 'Anyone of a certain age, obviously. I mean, we're all connected in life, aren't we? Six hand-shakes away, don't they say?'

'Four now, apparently,' said Judge.

'I thought it was three,' said Molly.

They agreed to leave it there. And so it might have stayed, if Judge hadn't been invited as an honorary guest to the Christmas legal quiz a few months later.

He was on a team with some youngish barristers (for that, read middle-aged) and a stuffy judge who, in his opinion, should have retired years ago.

They were doing quite well, actually, although they needed to do better if they were going to win.

Then came the round on 'modern music', which one of the barristers was particularly good at.

'I used to be in a band,' he explained.

'Really?' asked Judge. 'What was it called?'

'Nothing special. I wasn't in it for long. My parents thought I ought to concentrate on my studies. And then we moved away.'

The subject turned to the next round on fallen politicians. But Judge noticed the man's unease and the flush on his face and then something dawned on him. 'Weren't you involved in the prosecution of Jacob Senior?'

'It wasn't my case – I just covered one of the early hearings,' the man said quickly. *Too* quickly.

When he got home, Judge looked him up. His suspicions were correct. So *that's* what had been niggling away in his mind all through the case. He went back to the pictures of the band on Google. And there he was. Matt Watson. The kind of name that wouldn't necessarily have stood out. A fresh-faced youth who had been one of the original three before dropping out. Both the prosecution and defence barristers had missed something there. So had the police.

The man's phone number was in the legal directory. No point beating about the bush. Best to come straight to the point. So he did. 'Why didn't you declare an interest?' asked Judge.

Rather to his surprise, he didn't try to worm his way out of it.

'Because I wanted to face that bastard Jacob fair and square.'

'He didn't recognize you.'

'I'm twenty years older than I was when he last saw me. And the wig helps.'

'He would have known your name.'

'There are a lot of Matthew Watsons around, sir.'

'You could be in trouble for this. You helped to send him down.'

'I don't care if I am. I'm glad to have played a part. I've been feeling guilty every day since the accident. I told my parents about it and they were so scared I'd get arrested that we moved that night to the other end of the country, as far away from that evil Senior family as possible. Of course, they found us. Old Man Senior tried to buy my parents' silence but they told him where he could put his money. Dad also said that he'd left a sealed letter with his own lawyers, describing what had happened, so that if any of us were hurt in an "accident", the police would know. My parents told me to never talk about it again but I couldn't get it out of my head. I felt so guilty for not standing up to the others. I should have called the police.'

His voice sounded shaky. 'Are you going to report me now?'

'No,' said Judge. 'I want you to carry on trying to put the world to rights. Sometimes, it takes someone who has done wrong to be able to do that.'

Weren't they the words that Ian had used to him?

'Thank you,' Matt said.

'No thanks needed,' said Judge. 'Good luck. By the way, Mrs Brooks – Old Man Senior's wife – seems to know where you are.'

'I'm aware of that. After Robbie was arrested, she got in touch. I expect they secretly continued to keep tabs on us after Dad refused to give in. She wanted to pay me to give evidence against Robbie but I said I'd report her to the police. "Threatening a barrister would be seen as a very serious crime," I told her. It seemed to work because she left me alone. Besides, that family doesn't have as much power as they used to.'

'She might still try to make trouble for you.'

'Not anymore.'

Judge felt a cold prickle going down his back. 'What do you mean?'

'She died. I'd been keeping tabs on her.'

So she'd passed away shortly after his visit. Was it wrong, Judge wondered, to feel an enormous relief?

'There's something else I want to tell you,' said the barrister. 'When Mrs Brooks tried to blackmail me, she said I needed to take my share of the blame for the crash. She was right. Like I said before, I ought to have called 999 at the time. And that's exactly why I took up law as a career. To make up for my past. To put things right.'

'I get that,' nodded Judge.

But what was it that Ian used to say? *A lawyer doesn't always know when he's lying. Instead, he learns to convince everyone of his own views.*

Including himself.

118

Vanessa

'Are you sure?' asked Carol when Vanessa explained that she was giving up her witness support work.

'I am,' said Vanessa. 'I just feel it's time to take life a bit more easily at my age.'

Carol made an 'I'm sorry to hear it' face. 'You're one of our best, Vanessa.'

But she wasn't. She'd got too involved with her cases. She'd allowed herself to become closer than she should have done – a good witness service volunteer didn't do that. Perhaps it was because she'd been so lonely.

'What will you do?' Carol asked gently.

Vanessa could have given some vague reply about going on holiday more or seeing friends. But instead, she found herself coming out with the truth. 'I'm going to spend time with my daughter and my great-grandson,' she said proudly.

'Your daughter? I thought you didn't have children?'

'I didn't think I did either, until last year,' said Vanessa. 'It's a bit of a long story.'

Her supervisor clearly wanted her to elaborate, but Vanessa stopped there. Some things were too private and too complicated to explain. She wasn't even sure she understood herself.

All she knew was that she loved being with Molly and

Thomas. She also enjoyed the company of Granny Grace and Thomas's mum, Michelle.

Sometimes, Judge came with her to visit Thomas. 'Want to learn chess?' he'd asked.

'He's only five!'

'You could give it a go,' said Molly. 'He's very bright. You're always hearing about these chess prodigies who started really young.'

Vanessa was more of a snakes-and-ladders person herself.

'I've won!' Thomas would always say after a game, leaping up in excitement.

'You let him, Vanessa!' Molly teased her.

'Shhh,' she giggled.

Part of Vanessa would have loved it if Molly called her 'Mum' but she wouldn't have suggested it in a month of Sundays. Her daughter still referred to her departed parents as 'Mum' and 'Dad'. And Vanessa could see why.

She would also have liked to have seen her daughter and great-grandson more but they had their own lives. She didn't ask if Molly visited Lewis in prison and Molly didn't mention it. Sometimes Vanessa tried to have those mother/daughter conversations that others seemed to have, such as had Molly ever thought of finding someone else again? Her daughter had laughed. 'Where am I going to find someone who'd accept my past?'

'But you were coerced into shoplifting.'

'It was still a crime, wasn't it? Even if I got away with it, unlike our Lewis who fleeced you.'

Vanessa felt very silly and hurt that her own grandson had deceived her. Her lawyer was still trying to get the money back.

She'd waited for Jack to give her a piece of his mind like he usually did, but he had gone very quiet since the trial. Vanessa was glad of that. 'You don't have a place in my life anymore,' she'd told him. Clearly, he had listened.

Or maybe, if she was honest with herself, the truth was that she had gone a bit mad after his death and had imagined his replies to make her feel comfortable. Until she'd discovered what he'd done with their daughter.

She was also worried about Judge. Something wasn't right about him, she could tell. Maybe he was bored with retirement. 'Do you miss the law?' she'd asked him.

'Not at all,' he'd answered firmly, but Vanessa's instinct told her there was more to it than that.

Then, one day, a phone call came out of the blue.

It was Janie's father.

'I hope you don't mind me asking,' he said, 'but I wondered if you might be interested in a small part-time job. Janie enjoyed your company so much that she's been asking for you. I explained we wouldn't be seeing you again and she got rather upset, especially when she heard about your accident. So I thought that maybe I could pay you to come and visit her every now and then –'

Vanessa couldn't help but cut in before he could finish. 'Certainly not! I mean not to being paid. And yes to coming over. I'd love to!'

'Thank you,' Derek said, with a lightness in his voice. 'That's absolutely wonderful. It will help her so much.'

'It will help me too,' said Vanessa, feeling an excited

flutter inside her. She was at her best when helping others – providing she didn't mess it up . . .

'Are you by any chance free tomorrow?'

'How about now?' she said.

'If you're sure?'

'I'm on my way.'

'Thank you. Actually . . .' Then he stopped.

'Is there something else?' asked Vanessa.

'No, no. I was only going to say we're looking forward to seeing you.'

But she had a distinct feeling that Janie's father was holding something back.

119

Judge

Judge had to hand it to Vanessa. She should have been a lawyer, or maybe a detective. She had a way of reading people; a sixth sense that could well have told her not to believe him when he said that nothing was wrong.

Part of him wanted to tell her, but then she might not care for him anymore and Judge wasn't sure he could cope with that. He loved her too much. Not in the way that most people might view love but in a special, non-sexual, comforting way.

So he'd cancelled his appointment with Vanessa, pleading a cold.

The truth was that there was only one person on earth who would understand. So Judge made his way to the cemetery, bracing himself for the conversation.

'*I know what you're going to say,*' Ian began, before he even got to the headstone.

'How?' asked Judge, kneeling down to replace last week's anemones with a bunch of his favourite freesias.

'*Because I feel it too. It's time, isn't it?*'

'Yes,' said Judge, getting to his feet and stumbling a little.

'*I'm surprised you've lasted so long,*' said Ian.

'Me too,' said Judge, polishing the headstone marble

with the cloth he always brought. (Who would do this when he'd gone?)

'*Gets to you after a while*,' added Ian.

'It does indeed.'

'*I expect you're scared.*'

Judge shivered. 'I am.'

Ian's voice was warm and comforting. '*When you've told them, you will feel lighter.*'

'Perhaps.'

'*So when are you going to do it?*'

Judge kissed the headstone one last time. 'As soon as I've said goodbye to you.'

'*I won't leave you*,' said Ian. '*I'm not just here, you know. I'm in your head and your heart. I'm with you wherever you go.*'

'Really?' said Judge.

'*You'd better believe it.*'

'I do.'

'*Is that a wedding vow?*'

Judge smiled. 'Why not?'

Then he forced himself to turn away. It didn't take long to make his way back into the city. How often had he been to the police station as a lawyer before he'd become a judge? Countless times. But this was different.

'Good afternoon,' he said politely to the uniformed officer at the desk. 'I've come to confess to a crime.'

As he spoke, he saw his stepmother's head slumped against the bed bars and a scared young man standing next to her.

'Forty-five years ago, I committed a murder.'

I2O

Earlier, Just After Robbie's Trial

There they are, thinks the blonde woman, who had watched the case from the public gallery and was now waiting by the court's rear entrance.

She leans into the doorway as they go past, shielding her face from the cameras snapping away. Then she peeps out from under her scarf to watch a man with silver hair steering a woman in a wheelchair.

Janie. Her daughter.

How could she have left them?

Miranda Rogers, as she now calls herself, sometimes looks back with a mixture of disgust and relief.

At the time, it had seemed the right thing to do. She couldn't go on living a half-life. Oh how she'd hated being married to Derek. She'd never felt she'd been a very good mother either. To be honest, all she'd wanted was to follow her dream of being a singer.

Was that so awful? There must be thousands of parents who wanted to pursue their calling instead of constantly putting themselves last. And yes, that sounded selfish, but that's how it was. She'd known that if she'd said she was leaving, it would have broken her daughter's heart. Death was surely better than rejection.

So she'd simply walked into the sea, swam round the bay and come out on the other side, hidden by the rocks.

Then she'd reinvented herself in London.

Of course, there were times when she missed Janie so much that her heart physically hurt. Sometimes she wondered if she'd had a mental breakdown. On the nights when the pain became too much, she took out her most precious possession – the little shell – from her bedside drawer and went to sleep, sobbing. Holding it in the palm of her hand. Janie's heart.

Occasionally she'd returned to Devon so she could watch her beautiful daughter from a distance.

But then one day, Janie had turned round and locked eyes with her. Miranda raced to lose herself in the crowds of shoppers but she was too slow. Derek soon caught up with her and told her to stay away for Janie's sake. 'Haven't you hurt her enough already?' he'd demanded.

He was right. She'd made her decision and now she had to live with it.

So she'd stayed away for years, singing in Paris and Berlin and Madrid. But in between, she always came back to London because it was closer to Janie. If people asked whether she had children, she said no.

And then, like everyone else, she read about the accident.

At first, she'd thought the name 'Janie White' was simply a cruel coincidence. It was only when she saw the 'before' and 'after' pictures that she realized 'The Girl Who Came Back from the Dead' was actually her own daughter. Miranda's insides felt as though they were going to drop out of her with shock.

Why hadn't Derek told her? But he didn't know where she lived. Didn't have her new phone number. She'd cut as many ties as possible.

So she'd made her way straight to the hospital.

'What are you doing here?' Derek had asked furiously, catching her just as she was heading for Intensive Care. 'Janie's in a coma, and when she comes out, I don't want you upsetting her. You left us. You have to live with it. Go, and don't come back again.'

She'd fled in tears. Her husband was right. She had to put Janie's interests first. So instead, she had followed every scrap of news.

She knew when Janie had turned the corner. She knew when she went into an assisted home.

And when someone was finally accused of the accident – of all people, Robbie Manning – she went along to the hearing, wearing sunglasses and a headscarf.

It was such a shock to hear her child sing. To see, in the flesh, the grey middle-aged woman who had once been her beautiful daughter. It took every ounce of strength not to run down to the witness box and fling her arms around her.

How could a mother leave her child?

All too easily. Some people just weren't born to be mothers.

Yet the strange thing is that Miranda feels more maternal towards Janie now than she had ever done before.

And she still wonders – is it too late to make amends for the grief she's caused?

Maybe. But at least her daughter has justice now.

Miranda walks towards the car that's waiting for her. It's

455

time to go back to work. She enjoys her job. High-class escort work isn't what she'd originally hoped for but she'd found it impossible to make it big in the singing world, so she'd had to find another calling. Society might look down on it but it pays extremely well and she's built up quite a client list of men who prefer a more mature woman. Some might call it exploitation, but there are always different ways of seeing things. Always will be.

'Back to London now?' asks her driver.

'Yes, please.'

They drive past the woman in the wheelchair. As they do, Janie seems to look Miranda straight in the eye.

Miranda can't stop herself. 'Can you slow down for a minute?' she asks.

She blows a kiss.

Janie stares. She clearly hasn't recognized her. What else had she expected? She'd made her choice when she'd left her daughter. Now she has to live with it. Derek had made that quite clear in the public gallery. Then she touches the shell, which she wears round her neck every day.

'Please drive on,' she says.

Vanessa

It was after one of Vanessa's weekly visits to Judge in prison that Derek asked if he could have a 'quiet word'.

Vanessa's head was still full of the visit. Judge seemed to have settled in pretty well, all things considered, although she wished he'd just confided in her in the first place.

'I feel more at peace with myself now I'm paying my dues,' he'd told her in the noisy visitors' room.

'Are they treating you all right?' she'd asked, worried that people would target a former pillar of the institution.

'I'm fine, thank you,' he'd replied, skirting round her question in his typical fashion.

Of course, she'd heard most of the details when he'd been sentenced but there was still something that troubled her.

'There's only one thing I don't understand.'

Judge raised his eyebrows, which had now gone quite grey. 'How can I be so evil?'

'No. Because you're not. At least I don't think so. I want to know why you threatened to sue the home after your stepmother died. Surely you wouldn't want to draw any more attention to yourself?'

He nodded, almost approvingly. 'Good question. It's because attack is the best form of defence. I wanted to

457

threaten Old Man Senior so he wouldn't come after me. He would have been scared of the publicity if I'd bad-mouthed his home. And it worked. I dropped the case and he didn't go to the police with his suspicions about me.'

'And why did you agree to visit his wife towards the end?'

'Call me superstitious, but one should never ignore a dying person's request. I was also curious.' His face grew thoughtful. 'It wasn't a pleasant meeting. But I'm glad I went. It helped me see life in perspective. That's why I handed myself in.'

All this gave Vanessa a lot to think about when she left the prison. So when Derek had suggested a walk along the seafront while Janie was having physio, she found it hard to concentrate, especially as the seagulls were screeching overhead.

At first, he opened with small talk about how much he and Janie appreciated her company and how excited his daughter was about her album coming out.

'I still don't like the fact that Robbie Manning put the record company in touch with her, but it's given her a new lease of life.'

'I can see that,' said Vanessa. She herself couldn't wait to hear it.

Then he said something that made her stiffen.

'There's something I have to tell you, Vanessa. I've tried to summon up the courage time and time again but chick-ened out. But it's no good; I can't carry it anymore. It's why I'm so angry with Robbie Manning. It's my way of dodging the truth.'

'What is?' she asked. Yet even as she said it, Vanessa

knew that, finally, she was going to hear the full story. Hadn't it always felt as if there was a piece missing?

Derek's anguished voice came out like a cry. 'If it hadn't been for me, Janie's accident might not have happened.'

A cold shock went through her. This she *hadn't* been expecting. 'What do you mean?'

He stopped, gripping the railings of the promenade so tightly that his knuckles were white.

'The day before the accident, Janie had asked me to check her bike. The chain had been slipping off. I'd been in a rush. My boss had been on my back. It wasn't easy being a single dad in those days. I'm not saying it is now but then, it wasn't so common.'

Vanessa held her breath. *Don't say anything*, she told herself, *or he might stop*.

'So I did a bit of a rushed job. I mean, I thought I'd fixed the chain and that it was secure but I should have spent more time on it. It's why I didn't want Janie to give evidence in court. I was terrified in case they brought in a technical expert to show the chain was at fault.'

He was looking at her in a strange way. Vanessa had had enough experience from her store-detective days and from her time as a witness support to read Derek's face. He was beginning to wish he hadn't confided in her. Part of her felt the same.

'I'm telling you because I feel you'll understand,' he said, as if reading her mind. 'You've got to know us well over the months. I need to be level. I'm going to go mad if I don't tell someone.'

'You don't know for certain that the chain caused the accident,' she managed to say.

'It was off when they found the bike in the road,' he groaned. 'I saw it when they took me to the scene.'

'That might have been the impact of the van.'

'Or it might have caused her to lose her balance and swerve into it.'

Derek began to cry. Some people thought it was a sign of weakness when a man did this. Vanessa had always seen it as a sign of strength. Jack had never cried.

'I can't help it,' he sobbed. 'It's haunted me all these years.'

'None of those boys should have been driving,' said Vanessa quietly. 'That's the nub of it. But the thing is that it happened. We can't do anything to turn back the clock.'

'I know,' Derek sniffed.

Vanessa couldn't help it. She put her arms around him. 'Sometimes, we make decisions we regret. But it's all part of life's learning curve.'

'Have you made decisions you regret?' he wept.

'Yes,' she said as she moved away. 'But you have to let go of them. Otherwise, it's like living in mental darkness, isn't it?'

'That's what I'm doing,' he cried out again. 'It's the not knowing that makes it so hard. What if it *was* my fault?'

'Then there's nothing you can do about it,' says Vanessa bluntly. 'It will just continue to eat away at you. And it isn't good for your relationship with Janie. She's only got one parent. She needs you.'

Derek shook his head. 'Actually, she *hasn't* only got one parent.'

Vanessa froze. 'What do you mean?'

'My wife . . . She was mentally unstable. Once, she tried to hit Janie with a gin bottle when Janie had tried to stop

460

her drinking. I'm afraid I got very angry and said things I didn't mean.'

'We all do that last bit,' said Vanessa.

'She was always threatening to do things to herself, which she then didn't do. She didn't drown. I mean, at first I thought she had, but then I saw her watching us from across the road.'

Vanessa gasped. 'What did you do?'

'I told Janie to carry on walking and that I'd catch her up. Then I ran over and asked my wife what the hell she was doing. She gave me some stuff about not being able to live with us but not being able to live without us either. I told her that Janie was better off with just me.'

Derek sighed heavily. 'Then Janie said she'd found a receipt for a train ticket to London in her mum's bag. It was dated for the day she "disappeared". I told Janie she'd obviously changed her mind and that the police suspicions were right . . . she had killed herself instead.'

'Did you tell your wife about Janie's accident?'

He hangs his head. 'No.'

'Why not?'

'I didn't have an address for her. Even if I had, it would have made it more complicated. Janie was in such a state. She had brain damage. What was it going to do to her if she knew her mother was still alive?'

Vanessa swallowed. She would have given anything to know that Molly was still alive before she'd finally found out.

Derek continued. 'But then she read about it in the papers and came to the hospital to see Janie. I turned her away. I wouldn't let her see her own daughter.'

His eyes were wet with tears. 'I told her she'd already put us through hell and I wasn't allowing her to do the same again. For years after that, she went quiet. Then she turned up in the public gallery, heavily disguised, during Robbie's court hearing. I was furious. She said she had every right to be there. I told her that she was to get out of our lives.'

'Did you mean that?'

'I did,' he said in a quiet voice. 'But now I'm wondering.'

'Maybe,' said Vanessa, 'you should hear my story.'

She paused. She hadn't meant to tell anyone else. But it might help this poor man who needed someone to give him peace.

'There's someone I want you and Janie to meet. Her existence was kept secret from me until recently. She's my daughter and she's called Molly. She's been through a lot in life too. I've got a funny feeling that you might enjoy each other's company . . .'

Epilogue

From the *Daily Mail*:

Janie White, the girl who came back from the dead, reaches number one with her song 'I Died on a Tuesday'. Janie has dedicated her album, *RIP*, to her mother, who drowned when Janie was a teenager. Janie's record company has given us permission to print the lyrics.

> What a beautiful Tuesday
> Down by the sea!
> I cycled along
> With my life before me.
>
> But all the time,
> I thought of you.
> Drowned in the waves,
> Reborn anew.
>
> I did not know
> That in seconds or two
> I would be with you
> In heaven so true.

But then came the van –
I *had* to be dead.
'It's all right,' you whispered.
Or was this in my head?

My mind played such games
What was right then seemed wrong.
And then wrong became right
Until I found song.

This allowed me to sing
To the world about me:
The girl on the bike –
Who died by the sea.

For a while – so they told me –
My heart was a ghost.
They thought they'd lost me.
They thought I was toast.

But that's when I glimpsed you.
Shrouded in light.
I will never forget
That celestial sight.

Your death gave me hope.
For then I saw
You had not left.
To life, there's more.

You are still there,
Right by the door.

So when it's my turn to be dead
I will not fear what lies ahead.

I'll just drift out into the sea
Where you, Mum, I know, will be waiting for me.

Acknowledgements

Many people are involved in making a book happen. Thank you so much to everyone, including:

My amazing agent Kate Hordern, who keeps me calm.

The talented team at Penguin:

Harriet Bourton (Editorial)

Rosa Schierenberg (Editorial)

Ellie Hudson (Marketing)

Natalie Wall (Editorial)

Sara Granger (Production)

Annie Underwood (Production)

Amelia Evans (Rights)

Monique Corless (Rights)

Catherine Turner (Rights)

Samantha Fanaken (Sales)

Ruth Johnstone (Sales)

Kyla Dean (Sales)

Eleanor Rhodes-Davies (Sales)

Laura Ricchetti (Sales)

Rebecca Gray (Publicity)

Jane Gentle (Publicity)

Dan Mogford, Richard Bravery and Alice Chandler (Cover Design) and Bhavna Chauhan (my brilliant Doubleday editor in Canada).

Trevor Horwood, my copy editor.

Proofreaders Sarah Barlow and Sally Sargeant

Steven, who helped me with research.

Richard Atkinson from Tucker Solicitors, who advised me with great kindness and patience on certain legal points (I may still have used some artistic licence at times).

The joy of cycling safely.

The sea, which is always inspiring, grounding and invigorating.

My loyal bloggers, readers and kind souls whom I've been fortunate to meet as a result of my writing.

My supportive and understanding friends and family, including our dog, who sits behind me while I write.

Betty Schwartz, who gave me hope in the early days.

You – the reader. Thank you.

All characters are fictitious. Any resemblance to real people, events or places is entirely coincidental.

You can follow me on:
X @janecorryauthor
Instagram @janecorryauthor
Facebook janecorryauthor
TikTok @janecorryauthor

blood sisters

THREE LITTLE GIRLS. ONE GOOD. ONE BAD. ONE DEAD.

Kitty lives in a care home. She can't speak properly and she has no memory of the accident that put her here.

At least that's the story she's sticking to.

Art teacher Alison looks fine on the surface. But the surface is a lie. When a job in a prison comes up she decides to take it – this is her chance to finally make things right.

But someone is watching Kitty and Alison.

Someone who wants revenge for what happened that sunny morning in May.

And only another life will do . . .

Praise for Jane Corry

'A fearsomely good thriller'
Nicci French

'I raced through this'
Teresa Driscoll

'So many brilliant twists'
Claire Douglas

I Looked Away

YOU MADE A MISTAKE.
BUT THEY'RE SAYING IT'S MURDER.

Every Monday, 49-year-old Ellie looks after her grandson
Josh. She loves him more than anyone else in the world.
The only thing that can mar her happiness is her husband's
affair. But he swears it's over now and Ellie has decided
to be thankful for what she's got.

Then one day, while she's looking after Josh, her husband
gets a call from *that woman*. And – just for a moment – Ellie
takes her eyes off her grandson. What happens next will
change her life forever.

Because Ellie is hiding something in her past.

**And what looks like an accident could start to
look like murder . . .**

Praise for Jane Corry

'Sensitive and thought-provoking'
Adele Parks

'Thrilling, emotional and pacy'
Claire Douglas

'Dark, sinister, compelling'
Nicci French

The Lies We Tell

**YOU DID WHAT ANY MOTHER WOULD DO . . .
AND NOW SOMEONE ELSE'S SON IS DEAD.**

Sarah always thought of herself and her husband, Tom,
as good people. But that was before their son Freddy
came home saying he'd done something terrible.
Begging them not to tell the police.

Soon Sarah and Tom must find out just how far they are
willing to push themselves, and their marriage, to protect
their only child . . .

As the lies build up and Sarah is presented with the
perfect opportunity to get Freddy off the hook, she is
faced with a terrifying decision . . .

Save her son . . . or save herself?

Praise for Jane Corry

'Everything I love in a book'
Lisa Jewell

'Jane Corry's best yet'
B. A. Paris

'Brims with suspense'
Louise Candlish

my
husband's
wife

**FIRST COMES LOVE . . . THEN COMES MARRIAGE . . .
THEN COMES MURDER.**

When lawyer Lily marries Ed, she's determined to make
a fresh start. To leave the secrets of the past behind.

But when she takes on her first criminal case, she starts to
find herself strangely drawn to her client. A man who's accused
of murder. A man she will soon be willing to risk everything for.

But is he really innocent?

And who is she to judge?

Praise for Jane Corry

**'Jane Corry is the new queen of the
psychological thriller'**
Kate Furnivall

'Chilling and suspenseful'
Elizabeth Haynes

'Twisty, feverish and utterly gripping'
Eva Dolan

We All Have Our Secrets

YOU KNOW SHE'S LYING . . . BUT SO ARE YOU.

Two women are staying in Willowmead House.

One of them is running.
One of them is hiding.
Both of them are lying.

Emily made one bad decision and now her career
could be over. Her family home on the Cornish coast is
the only place where she feels safe. But when she arrives,
there's a stranger living with her father.

Emily doesn't trust the beautiful young woman,
convinced that she's telling one lie after another.
Soon, Emily becomes obsessed with finding out the truth . . .

But should some secrets stay buried forever?

Praise for Jane Corry

'Clever, gripping, nuanced'
Phoebe Morgan

'An unputdownable read'
Emma Curtis

'The twists just keep on coming'
Celia Walden

Coming to Find You

**YOU CAN RUN AWAY FROM YOUR LIFE
BUT YOU CAN'T RUN AWAY FROM MURDER**

When her family tragedy is splashed across the newspapers,
Nancy decides to disappear. Her grandmother's beautiful
Regency house in a quiet seaside village seems like the
safest place to hide. But the old house has its own secrets
and a chilling wartime legacy . . .

Now someone knows the truth about the night Nancy's
mother and stepfather were murdered. Someone knows
where to find her. And they have nothing to lose . . .

**So what really happened that night?
And how far will she go to keep it hidden?**

Praise for Jane Corry

'A compelling read'
Shari Lapena

'Deliciously dark'
Claire Douglas

'I couldn't put it down'
Heidi Perks